DEATH BE
NOT
PROUD

"An ominous sense of developing tension …
a most fluent writer" – *COLIN DEXTER,*
creator of *Inspector Morse*

MORTAL FIRE

C. F. Dunn

THE SECRET OF
the Journal

DEATH BE NOT PROUD

C. F. Dunn

LION FICTION

Published by Lion Fiction
an imprint of
Lion Hudson plc
Wilkinson House, Jordan Hill Road,
Oxford OX2 8DR, England
www.lionhudson.com/fiction

ISBN 978 1 78264 034 9
e-ISBN 978 1 78264 054 7

First edition 2013

Background image acknowledgments
iStockphoto: pp. 10–11 Alexey Popov; pp. 12–13 JVT; p. 79 Kim Sohee

Cover image acknowledgments
Corbis: Patrick Strattner/fstop;
iStock: peter zelei, Diane Diederich

A catalogue record for this book is available from the British Library.

Printed and bound in the UK, March 2013, LH26

Contents

For my mother and father,
who made all things possible.

Acknowledgments

My gratitude, as ever, to Tony Collins and a great team at Lion Fiction – especially Kirsten, Jude, Jessica, and Simon – who have guided me with infinite patience through the labyrinthine process of publishing, and to Noelle Pederson, in the USA, and her team at Kregel Publishing for their fantastic support. To authors Fay Sampson and Colin Dexter I owe thanks for their generous endorsement.

Thank you to Wendy Rowden, whose power of persuasion is second to none. My mother, Mary, whose unstinting encouragement is matched only by my father, Bill Turnill, whose sterling work makes him a one-man promotion team to be reckoned with.

To Dee Prewer, who once again cast her velvet eye over the manuscript, and to Lisa Lewin, who had the fortitude to read the first draft.

To Mark Nardi-Dei, whose knowledge of the aircraft industry helped to join up the dots, and Kate Nardi-Dei, who understood the flight plan. Thanks for the lift to Bridgton, Maine, and the chowder, guys. Oh, and Mark… told you so.

My thanks to the staff at Stamford Museum (alas a victim of the cuts), and for the enthusiastic advice given to me by staff at the Rutland County Museum (Oakham); also to the gentleman at Gunthorpe, for giving me access to Martinsthorpe, where I could step back in time.

My enduring love to Richard, Kate, and Sophie, who keep my feet on the ground, and our corgi – Stig – for the walks that keep me moving.

Last and foremost, my thanks to the many readers, whose feedback and support make writing worthwhile: this book is for you.

Characters

ACADEMIC & RESEARCH STAFF AT HOWARD'S LAKE COLLEGE, MAINE

Emma D'Eresby, Department of History (Medieval and Early Modern)

Elena Smalova, Department of History (Post-Revolutionary Soviet Society)

Matias Lidström, Faculty of Bio-medicine (Genetics)

Matthew Lynes, surgeon, Faculty of Bio-medicine (Mutagenesis)

Sam Wiesner, Department of Mathematics (Metamathematics)

Kort Staahl, Department of English (Early Modern Literature)

MA STUDENTS

Holly Stanhope; Josh Feitel; Hannah Graham; Aydin Yilmaz; Leo Hamell

IN CAMBRIDGE

Guy Hilliard, Emma's former tutor

EMMA'S FAMILY

Hugh D'Eresby, her father
Penny D'Eresby, her mother
Beth Marshall, her sister
Rob Marshall, her brother-in-law
Alex & Flora, her twin nephew and niece
Nanna, her grandmother

Mike Taylor, friend of the family
Joan Seaton, friend of the family

MATTHEW'S FAMILY

Ellen

Henry
Pat (Henry's wife)

Margaret (Maggie – Henry's daughter)

Daniel (Dan – Henry's son)
Jeannette (Jeannie – Daniel's wife)
Harry
Ellie
Joel

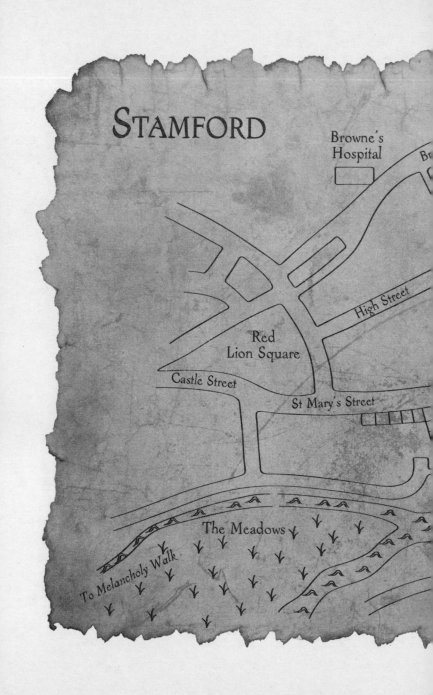

RUTLAND

LEICESTERSHIRE

Oakham

Rutland
Water

Gunthorpe
River Guash

Martinsthorpe

Manton

River Chater

Losecoat Field

;ham

LINCOLNSHIRE

Stamford

River Welland

CAMBRIDGESHIRE

N

STAMFORD TO OAKHAM
APPROX 11 MILES
EXTRACT OF RUTLAND,
PRESENT DAY

The Story So Far

Mortal Fire introduced the 29-year-old, independent, and self-assured Cambridge history lecturer Emma D'Eresby, who has one obsession in life: the curious journal of a seventeenth-century Englishman, a portion of which was left to her by her late grandfather.

Leaving her Cambridge college for a professorship in an exclusive university in Maine, USA, where the complete journal is housed, Emma meets the enigmatic 33-year-old surgeon Matthew Lynes, a quiet and thoughtful widower. Haunted by an illicit relationship with a senior tutor at Cambridge, she is confused by her feelings for Matthew; but she senses that he is not all he appears, and the ghost of his dead wife seems ever present. Encouraged by her vivacious Russian friend and colleague Elena Smalova, Emma begins to contemplate a possible future with Matthew, despite the unwanted but persistent attentions of the seductive Sam Wiesner. Meanwhile, a series of attacks on women leaves Emma fearful that the sinister Professor Kort Staahl is somehow involved, and she begins to suspect he is stalking her.

Driven to learn more about the elusive Matthew, Emma takes the unique journal, in which she believes there are clues to his family's past, from the college library. Although she means to return the journal, fate intervenes as Staahl mounts a vicious psychotic attack on her. Matthew's intervention saves her, but in the days that follow, as he nurses Emma back to health, his unusual attributes raise questions that he is unwilling to answer, and the possibility of a darker side becomes apparent.

Emma's parents fly to Maine and it becomes clear that she has a strained relationship with her domineering father. Although they pressurize her to return to England, she defies them, but on a day out in the mountains, Matthew's ability to survive a bear attack and his refusal to disclose the truth ends in an emotionally charged encounter. Emma decides that things cannot remain as they are. Bewildered, and still suffering from the effects of the attack, she flees back to England with her parents, taking the journal with her in the hope that, given time to think, she will discover what Matthew conceals.

Abyss

*Death waits for us all; it is only a matter of time
and the when and the where and the how
are the only variations to the song we must all sing.*

I had good days and I had bad days.

It wasn't as if I could blame anyone else for the condition I found myself in, so I didn't look for any sympathy. I knew that my near-vegetative state caused my parents hours of anxiety, but I couldn't face the questions that queued in my own mind, let alone answer any of theirs.

I stayed in my room. Where I lay at an angle on my bed, I could watch the winter sun cast canyons of light as it moved across the eaved ceiling. Sometimes the light was the barest remnant from a clouded sky; at others, so bright that the laths were ribs under the aged plaster, regular undulations under the chalk-white skin.

I hadn't spent so long at home for many years. Here at the top of the house, the cars droned tunelessly as they laboured up the hill beyond the sheltering walls of St Mary's Church. Below, the voices of the street were mere echoes as they rose up the stone walls, entering illicitly through the thin frame of the window. I listened to the random sounds of life; I watched it in the arc of the day. And the sounds and the light were immaterial – the days irrelevant – time did not touch me.

Sometime – days after fleeing Maine – my mother knocked softly on my door, her disembodied head appearing round it when I did not answer.

"Emma, you have twenty minutes to get yourself ready for your hospital appointment; your father's getting the car now."

Her voice hovered in the air above my bed, and I heard every word she said, but they didn't register. I didn't move. She came into the room and stood at the end of my bed, her hands on her hips, her no-nonsense look in place. The lines creasing her forehead were deeper than I remembered, or maybe it was the way the light from the window fell across her brow.

"I know you heard me; I want you to get up and get dressed *now*. I won't keep the hospital waiting."

She hadn't used that tone with me for nearly twenty years and I found it comforting in its severity.

"*Emma!*"

My eyes focused and saw her shaking, her hands clutching white-knuckled at the old iron-and-brass bedstead.

"Emma, I am asking you, *please…*"

My poor mother; with my Nanna in hospital and her youngest daughter tottering towards the edge of reality, she was strung out just as far as she could go, eking out her emotional reserves like food in a famine. I blinked once as I surfaced from the dark pool of my refuge, my mouth dry; I half-rolled, half-sat up. Wordlessly, I climbed off the bed and went stiffly to the bathroom down the landing, my mother a few steps behind me. I shut the door quietly on her, and turned to look in the mirror above the basin. Sunken eyes stared back from my skull-like head, skin brittle over high cheekbones. Even my freckles seemed pale under the dim, grim light from the east window. Mechanically I brushed my teeth and washed, not caring as the cast on my arm became sodden. The bruises above my breasts and below my throat stood out against my fair skin. I pressed my fingertips into them, hands spanning the space between each smoky mark. I closed my eyes at the subdued pain and remembered why they were there.

Mum waited for me outside the door, and I aimlessly wondered if she thought I might try and escape – or something worse. I understood the effect of my behaviour on my family; I understood and cared with a remorse that should have torn the very heart from me, had I one. But my head and my heart were divorced, and I witnessed my distress in their pinched, tight faces and harried, exchanged looks as no more than a disinterested observer.

I also realized that, from a clinical point of view, I probably suffered from delayed shock – the result of two near-fatal attacks in a very short period of time with which I struggled to come to terms. But neither Staahl nor the bear seemed even remotely important when compared with what had passed between Matthew and me that precipitated my leaving the only man I had ever really loved.

I dressed in what Mum put out for me, substituting the cardigan for my sage jacket, and all the while I ached, but I couldn't tell whether the pain came from my broken body or from my heart.

The hospital wasn't far from where we lived and my father parked in a lined disabled bay, ignoring the disapproving stares of the people sitting on a nearby bench. They stopped staring and averted their heads when he helped me out of the car, all the justification he needed in my fragile frame as I leaned against him for support. The strapping still loose, my ribcage felt as if the semi-knitted bones grated with every step I took, but I welcomed the pain as relief from the indescribable emptiness that filled every waking moment.

The double doors to the reception hissed back into their recesses, releasing a gust of warm, sanitized air. Feeling suddenly sick as it hit my face, I retched pointlessly, my hollow stomach reacting to the acrid smell of disinfectant, each spasm pulling at my chest, and I felt my legs give way beneath me. A flurry of activity and hands and voices alerted me to the fact that, although I was drifting, blissful unconsciousness eluded me.

"When did she last eat?" a pleasant-voiced man asked from beside my head. He lifted my eyelid and a beam of directed light hit me; I twisted my head to escape it. He lifted the skin in the crease of my elbow and it sagged back into place like broken elastic.

"She's dehydrated as well; how long's this been going on?"

Mum sounded tense. "Five days. She refuses to eat, she barely drinks a thing and she was already too thin. We don't know what to do with her; she just won't talk to us."

Five days? Had it been so long? I counted only three. Five whole days without him.

"I'll have to admit her – get her rehydrated. These injuries need seeing to and I'll contact someone in the mental health team at the same time."

My eyes flicked open.

"No," I muttered weakly.

Humorous hazel eyes met mine. "Ah, she speaks; you're back with us, are you? Did you have something to say?"

"No – I won't be admitted," I said, strength returning along with my stubborn streak.

"Well, you haven't left yourself with much of a say in the matter – you're a right mess. However..." he continued, "if you promise to eat and drink starting from now, I could be persuaded to reconsider."

"If I must."

I wasn't far off being churlish but he didn't seem to mind, and I wondered why everyone was being so kind to me because I didn't deserve it, not after the way I treated them, not after what I had done.

The dry biscuit scraped my throat and the tea from the little cafe next to reception tasted stewed by the time I drank it, but it helped.

"Sorry about the biscuit." The young doctor eyed it, pulling a face. "The nurses ate all the decent ones; there's not a Jammy Dodger left in sight. Hey ho – at least that's better than nothing, and I suppose we must be grateful for the little we are given." He smiled cheerfully, his harmless chatter scattering brightly into the bland room. I stared at the ceiling, impassive and beyond caring.

I finished the tea under his watchful eye, his excuse being that business was a bit slow and he had nothing better to do than to sit there and watch me. He took the empty cup, chucked it in a bin and rolled up the wide sleeves of my jacket, revealing both arms.

"So, what happened here, then?"

He started to unwind the bandage on my left arm. My throat clenched uncomfortably, remembering the last time it had been dressed by Matthew as he stood so close to me – his hand on my arm, my skin running with the connectivity between us.

He misunderstood my reaction. "That hurt?"

"No."

"OK, so what did you do here... *heck*, whew!" he whistled. "That's quite something; not a case of self-harm, I'm guessing. Accident?"

The long scar had lost its livid appearance, and the edges of the bruising were beginning to fade.

"No."

"This is healing well; nice job – very impressive stitching, almost a shame when they have to come out." He admired the fine stitches, turning my arm to catch a better look under the glare of the overhead lamp.

"Our daughter was *attacked*." Dad sounded none too impressed by the young man's obvious enthusiasm about my injury. The doctor's tone moderated.

"Ah, I didn't know – not good. This as well?" He indicated the cast on my arm, looking only at me for an answer.

"Yes."

"And two of her ribs," my mother interjected. "I think Emma's in a lot of pain but she won't tell me."

He stood up straight, pulling at one earlobe as he contemplated his course of action, his hand barely visible beneath thick, brown hair that curled up a little over his collar.

He checked his watch. "This cast is sopping wet – you're not supposed to swim the Channel in it – it needs changing. I could send you to the main hospital in Peterborough, or you could let me have a bash at it – your choice."

"Whichever, I don't mind."

He came to a decision.

"Right then, we'd better get on with it – I need the practice anyway. Footie's on tonight and I want to get home for the kick-off." He winked at me. "Off you go, I'll manage without you," he said, ushering my surprised parents out and

beckoning to a nurse at the same time. "So this happened…
when? Three, four weeks ago?"

"No."

He waited and I realized that he wanted an answer with
more information than that.

"Two weeks – just over two weeks."

"You're sure? This is healing well – looks nearer four weeks
old, and you wouldn't believe the number of lacerations I've
seen over the last few years, 'specially on a Saturday night in
A and E, though none as clinical as this, I grant you. Just over
two weeks; hmm, well, if you say so…"

For all his cavalier chatter, he was surprisingly gentle as
he re-dressed my arm, and then started to remove the cast
Matthew had so carefully applied all those dark nights ago.
I felt a pang of regret as it fell to the floor, as if he were slipping
away from me along with the cast. A stifled sob came out of
nowhere, catching me off-guard.

The young doctor didn't look up. "Want to tell me about
it?" He must have thought I remembered the attack.

"No."

"Can sometimes help to talk," he encouraged, still focusing
on the messy process in front of him, a fixed grimace on his
face as he tried to get the gauze under the cast on straight.

I wiped my eyes on the back of my sleeve. "No, thanks."

He made a pretty good job of it, although the new cast felt
heavier than the last one, and my arm objected to carrying
the additional weight.

"Two down, one to go," he said, nodding in the direction
of my chest. The nurse started to unbutton my jacket and,
instinctively, I drew my arms in front of me to stop her.
She looked to the doctor for back-up, and he smiled
apologetically.

"The top has to come off, sorry."

Reluctantly, I let my arms drop and she continued. I felt exposed under the harsh light as he interrogated my body, and I kept my eyes fixed on the shadows of people moving across the floor, just visible in the crack at the bottom of the door where light peered under. He became suddenly businesslike and professional as he unwound the strapping and probed my ribs. I caught my breath and craned my head to look. "That sore?"

"Yes."

I tried not to react but, from what I could see, at least the intense bruising from my collision with the edge of the shelves in the porters' lodge was definitely fading and, although my ribs ached, I could tell they were on the mend.

"They're OK – just need strapping again."

He completed the task and thanked the nurse and she left. The doctor stood with one hand on his hip.

"Like to tell me how you got those?" he said, looking at the small, regular-shaped bruises across my breastbone and around my neck. "And don't tell me they were done at the same time as the rest of the damage – these are more recent."

"They don't bother me."

"That wasn't what I asked; has someone been hurting you?"

I laughed hoarsely, the irony not lost on me. "Not in the way you think; this is *entirely* self-inflicted."

He lifted an eyebrow, obviously not happy with my reply. I dragged my soft jacket back on and, although my hands were more free, my stiff fingers struggled to do up the buttons again. He leaned forward to help.

"So, there's nothing more you want to say; I can't contact anyone for you?"

His brown-green eyes were kind and concerned; he had a sweet face.

"No – thanks."

"OK, you've got your reasons, no doubt, but if you were a dog, I'd be calling the RSPCA right now. You're all done. I'll call your parents, but remember, I don't want to see you in here again in your emaciated state. Drink plenty, eat lots and I won't report you."

He chucked the remains of my old cast in the pedal-bin, the lid clanging shut long before I took my eyes off it.

"Report me? For what?" I asked dully.

"Oh, I don't know, causing unnecessary suffering to the NHS budget, or some such; doctors like me don't come cheap, you know."

No, I knew that.

He left the room, taking my notes with him, and took longer than I expected to return. Minutes later, when I joined my parents in the seating area, the expressions on their faces were ambiguous. He must have said something. I sighed internally, dreading what conclusions they might have drawn between them, and deciding I needed to make a bigger effort to appear more normal to prevent a repeat of the earlier farce. When we reached the reception area I did something I had longed to do for the last month or so.

My grandmother resided in a side ward in a part of the hospital to which I had never been. Single-storey and purpose-built, its windows overlooked a paved courtyard with raised stone beds filled with semi-naked plants, now shivering under the overcast sky. Although made as pleasant as possible, even the brightly coloured curtains and cheerful prints that decorated the windows and walls of the assessment unit could not disguise the sense of imminent death that accompanied the living corpses inhabiting the beds.

Mum went over to talk to the nurses, and I was left to gaze at my grandmother from where I stood. Better than expected, she looked well, her face full and her skin still softly coloured, not sallow and drawn. She lay with her eyes closed. I went over to her and tentatively reached out to touch her hand as it rested on the peach-coloured cotton cover, to find it warm.

"Nanna?"

She did not respond. I pulled the high-backed chair close to her bed. The card I sent from Maine weeks ago sat on the bedside cabinet along with the regulated clutter of my family's gifts, a few personal items and a photo of my grandfather in its over-polished frame.

"How are you, Nanna?" I asked softly. "I'm so sorry I haven't been to see you; I've been away but… but I'm back now."

Her breathing came as a rhythmic pattern of in and out. I held her small hand between my newly liberated fingers, stiffly stroking it in time to her breaths.

"I've been working. I went to America, do you remember? I went to where the journal came from – as I said I would – and I've found it, Nanna; I've found Grandpa's journal."

Perhaps I hoped that she could hear me or would somehow respond. I laid my head on the bed, the movement of her chest so slight that it barely lifted the bedclothes. I watched as it rose and fell.

"I haven't read it yet, but I will; we've waited so long, haven't we? Will you wait a little longer – until I've read it – then you can tell Grandpa for me, because he'll want to know, won't he? He'll want to know all about it, like the last chapter of a book." Her breathing halted for a second, and I lifted my head to look at her anxiously, but she seemed peaceful and the pattern of her breaths returned to their slow, shallow beat. I laid my head down on my arm by her hand and closed my eyes.

"I met someone when I was out there. I think you would like him – he reminded me of Grandpa; his hair is the *exact* same colour – the colour of ripe corn." I smiled to myself despite the wretched ache somewhere in the middle of my chest.

"But I left him there, I had to. He's different… I can't explain it, there's so much about him that I don't understand and, until I do – until I've worked it out – I can't be with him, I can't go back…"

A soundless tear heralded an unlooked-for stream and I let them flow, glad that Nanna remained unaware of my sorrow.

"Sorry, Nanna," I managed after a few minutes, the top layers of bandage on my wrist already soaked. "That wasn't supposed to happen. You're stuck in here and I'm blubbing all over the place; what would Grandpa make of the pair of us?"

The faintest touch on the crown of my head startled me and I lifted my face. My grandmother's eyes were open, their faded blue alert. The corner of one side of her mouth lifted in a weak but discernible smile.

"Nanna? *Nanna!* You can hear me? Oh – you heard me," I said as I realized that she might have heard my ramblings. "I'm sorry," I said again. "I didn't mean you to hear *all* of that. I'll get Mum for you." I turned my head and saw my mother still talking to one of the nurses. I felt a slight touch against my fingers and looked down. My grandmother had moved her hand towards mine.

"What is it? Don't you want me to get her?"

Her fingers lifted and tapped against mine again, a slight question in her eyes.

"Oh this – it's nothing; I had an accident, that's all."

I looked away from her, hating lying. She tapped again, a persistent glare in her eyes. "All right, I was attacked, but I'm fine now; I had someone to look after me."

I couldn't hide the shake in my voice. Nanna made a guttural sound in her throat made of frustration that she could not speak.

"I bet if Matthew were here he could help you – he's like that – full of surprises."

Raw pain twisted inside me, but it was worth it just to be able to speak his name. Her fingers fluttered again, accompanied by the smile, and I smiled back. I heard a noise behind me.

"Hello, Mummy, you're looking *much* better," my mother said over my shoulder.

"You didn't tell me Nanna's awake, Mum!"

"I did tell you she is much better, but you weren't listening, darling."

She leaned over from the other side of the bed and kissed her mother tenderly on her forehead. Nanna smiled her half-smile in response, then swivelled her eyes to look at me, then back to her daughter again, questioning.

"Emma's fine; nothing time won't heal." She looked at me. "Darling, I need to talk to Nanna for a minute…"

I nodded and kissed my grandmother's warm, soft cheek. "Thank you," I whispered in her ear; "I will come and see you again soon." She grunted in her throat, her blue eyes watching my face.

That evening, I sat in the dining room and ate for the first time in days. It felt cold by the great floor-to-ceiling windows that let in a steady stream of air through the insubstantial frames, and I remembered that I needed layers of jumpers to survive the raw winter here. I moved around to the other side of the table, closer to the electric fire that did its best to make inroads on the chill. Dad pushed the kitchen door open with his foot, carrying several plates and bringing with him a waft of cooking-scented air. He laid a plate of hot food in front of me, spirals of steam rising.

"Your mother said not to wait, and tuck in while it's hot. It'll do you good – put some colour in your cheeks," he said in an attempt at being positive. I regarded the food with a singular lack of enthusiasm. "Come along now," he chivvied, "step to it. Chop, chop. Remember what the doctor said. We don't want you ending up in hospital now, do we? And it'll take a load off your mother's mind," he added, as the door began to open and she came in.

The increased mobility of my hands made eating much easier, although my right arm ached with the effort and my left hand could barely grasp a fork. My parents said nothing but the questions were not far away. I sensed they were waiting for me to eat something before they started. I was right.

"What a very pleasant young doctor you saw today," my mother ventured. I put my fork down and waited. Dad had almost finished his food and he eyed my near-full plate.

"Eat up, Emma; don't let it go to waste." Mum shot him a glance and he shut up; she continued.

"He said that you're healing very well and your stitches can come out in a week's time; that's good, isn't it?"

I loathed being humoured.

"The thing is, darling, he is a little concerned…"

Here it comes, I thought.

"He mentioned that you have some bruises that weren't caused by… well, by the attack, and that you said that they were self-inflicted. He thinks that you might benefit from a little help."

My dearest mother – always trying to be diplomatic – but she might as well have just come straight out with it and said: "The doctor thinks you're off your rocker, darling, and you should be committed."

I had to laugh. Dad looked shocked.

"It's not a laughing matter, Emma. What your mother is trying to say…"

"I know what's being implied, Dad," I cut in, "but they weren't self-inflicted, not in the way he means, so I don't need any *help* – of any kind."

I moved my plate away from the edge of the table, ready to rise, the silver fork sliding to one side, the remnants of my fragile hunger gone.

Dad frowned at the food on my plate. "And that's another thing – you're not eating; it can be a sign of emotional difficulties. It's nothing to be ashamed of; it can happen to anyone."

I stared at him and then at Mum in disbelief.

"I don't need any help because there's nothing emotionally wrong with me. I've told you, I need time to get my head straight about… things… but I don't need anyone to do it for me. I just want to be left alone to get on with it."

I pushed my chair back, the legs scraping painfully across the stone floor as they left the quietening pile of the rug, and picked up my plate to take it through to the scullery.

"So if *you* didn't make those bruises, darling, who did?"

The subtle approach, direct but always when I'd dropped my guard; Mum knew me well. She saw me falter and stood up, taking the plate from me and putting her arm around my shoulders. I looked straight into the depths of her eyes, inflicting as much sincerity as I could pile into a few words.

"*Nobody* has hurt me, Mum." I ducked out from under her arm, reclaiming the plate, and into the steamy kitchen. I washed my plate under a stream of hot water, the steam condensing almost immediately on the uneven stone walls. There were sounds of subdued whispers, then the door opened behind me and I heard the heavier tread of my father's footsteps, but I didn't turn around.

"Emma, did that *man* do this to you?"

For a moment I didn't know to whom he referred, then anger flashed through me, blood rushing to my face.

"Matthew has *never* hurt me. How can you accuse him, after all he's done?"

Disgusted, I flung down the tea-towel I had just picked up to dry my plate; it missed the draining board and sank below the bubbles left in the washing-up bowl. I went to push past my parents as they stood blocking the doorway.

"Don't be angry, darling, but you did leave the States in a hurry – what else were we to think? That broken table in your room… and you had been out with him all day; I mean, what else…"

"Not *that*, Mum."

Guilt twisted my voice. I was angry all right – angry at them for even suggesting that Matthew would have purposefully hurt me – but furious with myself for all the doubt and fear I had put them through – and tormented by what Matthew himself might be feeling right now. They let me pass and I slammed out of the kitchen, through the panelled sitting room and up the stairs. In the fading light, the watchful eyes of my ancestors followed me, the only points of light in portraits blackened with age.

I reached the sanctuary of my room. I seemed to make a habit of wrecking people's lives. Guy had deserved it and I felt little guilt in that respect. But my parents? If I were in their place and I saw my child behave in the way I acted, and witnessed the damage I bore, would I not also have come to the conclusion they had logically reached? And Matthew? I turned and buried my face in my pillow.

Matthew — what have I done to you? Would you ever believe me if I said that I loved you beyond boundaries, and that the only limits to that love were those defined within the mess in my head?

I made certain to be seen eating and drinking regularly, and my parents watched me, never leaving me in the house alone. Despite the size of the building, I felt confined and couldn't clear my head enough to think. Flashes of thoughts and images lingered on the edge of dreams I wasn't sure I had, words and faces tugging at my memory but always just out of reach.

I woke early several mornings later and lay under the thick duvet listening as the first birds began to stretch their voices; but the world sounded remote. Climbing out of bed, I drew the curtains to one side, letting in the feeble dawn. A dense fog shrouded the windows. I washed and pulled on my clothes, and found my quilted coat that I hadn't worn since the fight with the bear. From under my bed I dragged the bag that had lain there since my return home. Through the soft wool of his scarf, the hard edges of the two books – one the transcription of the little Italian treatise Matthew had made for me, the other the journal I had stolen – made their presence known. I dared not look at them, placing them instead on my desk and, doubling the long scarf around my neck, I went quietly downstairs.

My parents still slept as I let myself out of the house and made my way past the Town Hall, crossing the road to the Norman arch where the entrance to the ancient passage made a black mouth in the golden stone. I entered it as I had always done as a child – with a sense of crossing a threshold into the past.

Beyond the passage, the Meadows were silent except for the soft rush of the river running through them and away under the bridge. Shaggy tufts of grass, decorated with beads of glass, left my shoes saturated within minutes of wading through them. Out here I found a sense of freedom I hadn't felt for days. Out here, in my solitude, thoughts and ideas began to coalesce, and from the disorder in my mind, take shape.

By the time I returned to the house, traffic piled up the hill, filling the air with heavy fumes and protesting engines. The front door opened before I could turn my key in the lock, Dad's face instantly relieved when he saw me.

"I just went out for a walk," I explained a bit defensively as I went into the hall. Mum came out of the sitting room, cup in hand. Her brow cleared when she saw me and I started to unzip my coat.

"We have a visitor, darling," she said brightly. I bristled, because what she meant was, "*You* have a visitor", but I didn't let it show. She went back into the sitting room where I heard her say something, and a man's voice answered. My father helped me out of my coat.

"Do this for your mother, Em," he said quietly; "she's

finding all this a little tough." I looked at him with a degree of surprise at his uncustomary sensitivity, but he didn't elaborate and instead indicated the open door.

The wiry, white-haired man stood up when I entered.

"Hello, Emma – it's been a long time."

He held out his hand and I shook it automatically; he was careful not to squeeze too hard. I remembered him as a friend of my parents.

"Mr… Taylor."

"Mike, please – it must be at least eighteen years since I last saw you."

"At least," Dad said, balancing on the edge of the sofa arm, adjusting his position as it creaked under him. "Emma had just won the inter-house tennis tournament at school and developed sunstroke."

I was surprised he remembered that; I'd been forced to spend the rest of the blazing summer day in bed with the curtains drawn and a cold flannel on my head. I knew Mike Taylor as a doctor of some kind, and he had ruffled my hair and tugged my thick rope of a plait when last we met, congratulating me on my win before I succumbed to the effects of the sun. He had been easy going with an open, approachable manner, and nothing seemed to have changed. I sat in one of the old armchairs, the high sides and padded wings supporting my back and arms which ached from the unaccustomed exercise. He sat on the sofa, stretching his arms across the back and crossing his legs, revealing lively red socks. I eyed him guardedly. My mother called from the dining room, and my father went to help with the tea. He had lit a fire and curious flames tentatively explored the kindling; I watched them.

"You've been busy since I last saw you," Mike said cheerfully.

Ah, so this wasn't a social call; I thought as much. "You've been in the States, Hugh said. What did you make of it?"

I cut straight to the point. "What did they tell you?"

He cocked his head on one side and eyed me speculatively beneath thick eyebrows, their colour long gone.

"They're worried about your emotional state."

I blinked at his bluntness.

"Oh – yes."

"Do they have any reason to be worried?"

"No."

"You've had a bit of a rough time out there, I believe – the attack nearly killed you; is that right?"

I kept my tone quite even.

"Yes."

"And then something else happened, your mother said?" He stroked his top lip, waiting, but I said nothing; he didn't need to know about the bear, or anything else that followed. "Not bad going for one term, all things considered. How are you feeling about that, then?"

"Oh *please!*" I rolled my eyes.

"That's too obvious a tack, is it? I'm out of practice," he said ruefully, running his hands through his shock of white hair, his scalp bright pink where the dense thatch thinned. "Well, I said to your parents I'd give it a try." He grinned. He must be in his sixties, his good looks grizzled by time.

"You must have had a good doctor to get you back on your feet so quickly," he went on. I viewed him suspiciously.

"Did my parents say that?"

"Well, no," he admitted, "but they did describe your injuries in some detail, so it doesn't take a brain surgeon to work it out – which is a good thing, because that's not my line; stands to reason. A *Dr Lynes*, I think Penny said."

I recoiled at the mention of his name.

"Yes."

I looked away. The new-lit fire snapped and hissed greedily as the damp wood began to catch. The vigour of the flames made me feel tired.

"He must be good. Does he work at the university?"

I knew what he was trying to do in engaging me in conversation, drawing me out until he could delve deeper, penetrating the darker recesses of my mind; but it took less effort to go along with the pretence than to oppose it.

"Yes, Matthew heads up the medical faculty there." I felt a swell of pride for him but I tried not to let it show in my voice in case it spilled onto my face, and then goodness only knows where it would end, and I didn't want to cry – not in front of this near-stranger.

"Matthew... *Matthew* Lynes?" he said sharply. "Matthew Lynes treated your injuries?"

I sat up, alert to the changed tone.

"Yes. Why, have you heard of him?"

"It can't be, it was *years* ago, but... the name," he said, almost to himself. He looked at me. "What is he like – describe him."

I struggled to find words to capture him. "He's quite tall, slim, blond, reserved and quietly spoken... he has very blue eyes..."

"Very good-looking? Or, he was," he interrupted.

"Yes, he still is – very." I blushed, wondering why he shouldn't be.

He stared at me curiously. "How old is he, roughly?"

I frowned, "Early thirties, I think."

He dismissed the notion with a wave of his hand. "Hah, well, obviously not the same person, then. That would've been quite a coincidence, though," he mused.

"So you knew someone by the same name?" I probed.

He sat forward on the sofa, the old feather seat squishing under the pressure.

"Yes, some thirty years ago, it must be. I had a difficult op to perform – still the early days of some forms of cardiothoracic surgery, you see. We'd run into difficulty, and the only person who'd performed this particular procedure – pioneered it, actually – was in the States. Well, I had the patient on the slab – chest open – you're not squeamish are you?" I shook my head. "Heart failing as we watched, and we had nowhere else to turn. So we called this young chap up on a sort of improvised video link – very grainy picture, but it worked. It was the middle of the night there and he talked us through it – didn't bat an eyelid, very self-possessed, very calm for his age. Remarkable man. Only in his late twenties, early thirties, I'd say, but years ahead of the rest of us. Wonder what's happened to him?"

My heart leapt erratically and I stared at the man sitting in front of me. Even with my dodgy maths I could work out that Matthew would have been a young child at the time Mike referred to, yet I had never believed in coincidence.

"Remarkable chap," he said again, shaking his head. "What a coincidence – that name. Still…"

I made an attempt to appear politely indifferent, but really my mind was in turmoil. It made no sense whatsoever, yet that made it all the more plausible. Matthew never added up, and here – in this chance meeting – I had the first indication other than my own observations, that my growing suspicions might be right after all.

My face cracked into a smile. "Yes – *what* a coincidence," I said brightly. "Gosh, I'm hungry – it must be breakfast time; would you like a cup of tea?" I stood up. "So, what are you going to report to my parents?" I asked, blithely, showing him the way.

He beamed. "Oh, that you're a basket case quite definitely, young lady; no doubt about it," he replied, genially. *He had no idea...*

I smiled at his joke. "And that's the medical term for it, is it?"

"From a cardiothoracic surgeon's point of view? Quite probably!"

I couldn't wait to leave them all drinking tea and chatting. I knew that as soon as I left my parents would press him for a medical diagnosis, and I felt confident now that he would give them what I wanted. I made my excuses, grabbing toast and a mug of tea for appearances' sake and retreated to the sanity of my own room where I could filter out the information I had gleaned.

How many blond, unusually attractive and highly skilled American surgeons with his particular name could there be? And thirty years apart? That would make him in his sixties now and that would hardly describe the man *I* knew – not by a long stretch of the imagination. I thrummed my fingers on my desk as I thought, pleased that at last I had the flexibility in my hand to do so. Matthew's translation of the Italian medical treatise lay on top of the journal, and I opened it halfway through. His beautiful script – so unlike a typical doctor's scrawl – antique in style, and quite different to anything I had seen outside historic manuscripts. I closed the book, tapping its front cover, and thinking while my tea cooled enough to drink.

A thought struck me and I seized my handbag, emptying it of trivia onto my bed. I found my bank card and stuffed it in my back pocket. I gulped the hot tea, sending it scalding down my throat, before hurrying downstairs and through the front door without stopping to say goodbye.

The fog had partially lifted by the time I tracked down a computer shop, but the day remained grey and lowering, the damp sky clinging stubbornly to the rooftops. It didn't take long – I knew what I wanted – my eyes glazing as the salesman started to point out all the irrelevant details of the laptop in front of me. Exasperated, I pushed the bank card towards the dazed man, thanking him and leaving the shop before he could tell me about its superior memory. As long as it was better than mine, I really didn't care.

I took it straight back upstairs to my room, grinding my teeth in frustration every second it took to load, drawing Matthew's scarf around my neck and feeling him closer to me now than I had dared for the last week. Only a vague idea presented itself but, in terms of regaining my sanity, whatever I did must be better than the indeterminate state in which I remained suspended.

Using my mobile to connect the laptop to the internet, a search of his surname brought an overwhelming number of results, none of which looked promising. I thought for a second and then typed in his first name as well. There were innumerable references to "Matthew" and various ones to "Lynes" – some in other languages – but the two names did not occur meaningfully together until the mention of his appointment to the college in Maine issued by the Dean some six years ago. I continued to scroll down until – on the eleventh page – I stopped. On impulse, I clicked a link to a site specializing in archival material – sports memorabilia and its ilk – mostly from the USA. I typed in a search and watched as a photograph of a yellowed newspaper sheet appeared, the foggy picture inserted in the tight type of a previous century. The headline seemed clear enough – "Triumph for Top Team". I smiled at the use of the well-worn alliterative title, then peered at the article more closely, wondering how on earth anybody could be expected to read it. I tapped the "Magnify" icon in one corner, and the page enlarged. I read the caption under the photograph:

Squad celebrate athletic title in record time.

I pulled the cursor over the photograph and right-clicked "Magnify" again… and choked. Behind four other young men and looking as if he didn't want to be there – stood Matthew. A little taller by perhaps an inch or two, his fair hair and distinctive good looks set him apart. Even the sepia photograph aged by time and corroded in quality, could not disguise the attraction that exuded from him, nor extinguish the fire that he set ablaze within me.

"*What on earth…!*" I exclaimed out loud, then breathed deeply to calm my scratchy nerves, and searched for a date on the paper: 1932.

I began to laugh and then found I couldn't stop, hysterical tears blurring the image in front of me. Confused by intermittent sobs and barks of renewed laughter, I wiped my eyes and blew my nose, carefully checking the article, the date and the photograph once more, noting in the text that he had been given an age of twenty-four, and the accolade: "an outstanding sprinter and athlete of our time".

"And the rest," I thought – and *all* the rest. If this was indeed Matthew – and I saw no reason to disbelieve it other than the date – he must be around a hundred years old now.

"Yeah, *right*." I started to describe the boundary of my

room in short steps, shaking my head periodically to clear it, like a dog with ear mites. "This is so weird," I said to the mice in the walls to whom I had habitually talked as a child. "Oh come *on*; he's an anomaly, sure, but a *hundred-year-old* anomaly? Is that rational? Is it *reasonable*?" As usual, the mice remained passive. "Fat lot of good you lot are." A thought struck me. "He's not a ghost, is he? No – no, he can't be; he's too *alive*. Who are you, Matthew? *What* are you? Come on – talk to me, for goodness' sake – this will drive me insane!"

A rattling on the door made me jump.

"Emma, who are you talking to? Can I come in?" The door-handle turned impotently in my father's impatient hand. "Emma – let me in; *now*."

I minimized the page on the screen, at the same time calling out to him, "I'm fine – hold on a mo, I'm just changing."

I grabbed the big auburn knitted jacket and pulled it over my top, hoping he wouldn't notice the minimal change in attire, and turned the key in the lock. He pushed the door open, and looked around the room as if expecting to find someone else sitting there, then at my face, which burned. He peered suspiciously at me.

"Who were you talking to?"

Picking up my hairbrush, I ran it through my hair, hoping the action would lend a semblance of normality.

"Only the mice, Dad – you know – they're great listeners."

He grunted; I had spent many hours in angst-ridden solitary conversation with the mice before leaving home for university, and it was something of a family joke.

"As long as you are all right. Your mother wanted you to know that lunch is ready; we'll expect you in five minutes."

"Great – I'll be down in a moment."

Taken aback by my enthusiasm, he paused before leaving

the room, checking it out once more, his thick eyebrows drawn together. My heart galloping, I saved the link as a bookmark and shut the screen of my laptop, before joining him on the stairs.

I ate lunch with them around the family table with more gusto than I had shown for a long time. My mother couldn't disguise her relief.

"Darling, you're looking much better. Did your chat with Mike help at all?"

I thought about our exchange and answered with absolute honesty.

"It was a revelation – thank you so much for inviting him over." I felt a smile come from nowhere, and she smiled back.

"Are you *sure* you're all right? You seem a little flustered, and Mike did say that the effects of shock can last for some time; *acute stress*, I think he called it." She exchanged glances with my father at the other end of the table.

"Quite sure," I said firmly. "I'm starting work again – you know how it gets under my skin."

"Oh, Emma, that's wonderful." She rose from the table and came over and kissed me on the forehead, her hands around my glowing face. I felt the slow creep of guilt but pushed it away before it could get a hold; she didn't need to know anything that would destroy her happiness at this moment.

"But I might spend an awful lot of time on research; you won't worry, will you?"

"Darling, no, of course not." She seemed genuinely pleased and I hugged her.

Dad still regarded my sudden zeal with caution; he hadn't yet told my mother about my conversation with the mice, and I hoped that he wouldn't feel the need to any time soon. "What are you researching?" he asked.

"The journal."

"Ah, that." He looked both relieved and gloomy at the same time. The journal had been a constant in our family since long before my birth, and he viewed it almost as a rival. I picked up my empty plate and glass.

"Leave that, darling; we'll clear up. You go and get on with your work." Mum took them from me as I began to argue, and pushed me gently towards the door of the room. "Just don't overdo it; you know what you're like. And Mike said you need to rest," she called after me as I disappeared around the curve of the staircase. "He said you're not as strong as you think…"

But her words were lost as I passed beyond earshot, already travelling back in time and into another life.

2

Revelation

I raked the internet for any more information I could find on the athletics team, but they seemed to have disappeared from view. I sat back in my desk chair and rocked onto the back legs, chewing the end of my pen.

Stalemate.

I went through what I knew and realized that it amounted to very little. I contemplated the ceiling and the fine web of cracks that ran all over it, noting that it was in need of redecoration. At times like these, when seemingly faced with a dead-end, I made lists.

I opened up a blank page on the screen and began randomly, letting my ideas begin to flow before attempting to arrange them in something resembling order. After a page, I stopped again, rising abruptly from my chair and stomping around my room with my hands on my head, trying not to verbalize my thoughts above a whisper. I returned to the desk and reviewed what I had written: disparate facts without a pattern, which all added up to a bunch of nothing.

I looked at the disjointed, jumbled mess on the screen and it mirrored the inside of my head. I wanted to go out and walk it through, but dark smothered day, and the fog had been replaced by a steady rain.

I unplugged the laptop and carried it over to my bed, sitting cross-legged in the middle of it, and tried again. Wrapping my blue blanket around my shoulders, smelling the faint scent of my apartment in its wool, picturing us together again, brought spasms of loneliness, and I hurriedly readjusted the image in my mind and focused on the ragged thoughts, trying to pin them down like random butterflies. After what I had done to him, I couldn't be sure that Matthew would still feel the same way about me and, even if he did, whether he would – could – ever trust me again. Could I trust myself?

Mike Taylor had a point; in the States events had piled up one on top of the other in such rapid succession that I had no time to stop and think things through. In a few short weeks I experienced a tangle of emotions: doubt, fear, love – all equally intense, and underpinned by raw pain, so I could no longer tell where one ended and the other began. I fled from Maine because I had nowhere else to go: emotionally it became a fight-or-flight situation, or perhaps, more accurately, a case of retreat, retrench and regroup. Now that I was able to sit back and contemplate and process all the information without distractions, what had appeared peculiar in the States now seemed downright bizarre.

Looking back on it, the confrontation with Sam was wholly predictable, and I could almost understand Staahl's attack if I accepted it as insanity. But Matthew was another matter. Perhaps because he seemed so normal, his anomalies stood out, as if he were playing a role all the time, a charade. If he was as old as the photograph suggested, then what? If Mike really had spoken to him thirty years ago, what did that lead me to conclude? It made nonsense of everything I thought I had begun to understand. Did it make a mockery of me as well? Did he laugh at me behind my back, call me a fool for not seeing the blindingly obvious, if only I scratched the surface and peered beneath it a little harder?

Who was he? *What* was he? If human – good grief! – that was an avenue I fought shy of exploring – *if* human, he must have been born somewhere and at some time, and he would have had parents, possibly siblings. A sudden rattle followed by scratching noises from behind my head brought me back to reality with the night antics of the resident mice. I thumped on the wall half-heartedly and the scuttling stopped just long enough for me to imagine them cocking their heads before they ignored me as usual, and continued their game of running up and down inside the framework of the old wall.

What did I have at the moment? His name and three dates – consistent in the 1930s, 1970s and 2000s. And possibly – just possibly – a country. He sounded too English not to be, despite the slight American accent that all but disappeared when we were alone together. His reaction to being asked about his name, the mention of his colouring although little in themselves – when put together added up to a big heap of… what? If I took another, say, twenty to thirty years off 1932 – it would give a birth date of around 1900 to 1910. So, that was where I would start; I needed to look for references in the UK or the US about a hundred years ago. If I treated this as any other research project, applied the same methods, the same rules, I might be able to get closer to the "*Who?*"

That would only leave me with the "*What?*" – and that was too big to contemplate, too scary to consider. And without the *who* and the *what*, I had nowhere to go with this relationship. Matthew might as well be a figment of my imagination, as solid as grasping at air.

I pressed my fingers against the bruises his lips had made on my skin, and felt with relief – with gladness – the welcome twinge of pain it brought, because it made him *real*. I laughed out loud at the thought: a relationship? I could no more contemplate a relationship with a man about whom I knew nothing except that he shouldn't exist, than I could with a phantom.

A ghost, yet as substantial as me? No. An alien? A Time Lord? Something from another world or a freak of nature? For an instant I considered whether he might be dredged up from the underworld, a demon disguised, but instantly knew it not to be the case with a certainty beyond understanding. I pressed my cross to my lips and strained to hear the guiding voice again, but my own thoughts drowned it out. Matthew had said it was something I should be scared of, or something that he thought would scare me. Would his age be enough to frighten me? Not really; I lived so thoroughly in the past that at times I found it a wrench to leave it and come back to the present. If anything, what worried me most was not who or what he was, but that I didn't care about it as much as I should. I should be running scared. I should – were I sane – reject him and save my own skin and sanity. I shouldn't be sitting here in the twenty-first century thinking how long it would be before I would see my anomaly again. That posed another question – and one which I found potentially far more frightening: had I lost my mind?

The possibility alarmed my parents. It lay behind the young doctor's eyes in the hospital, and framed Mike Taylor's questions earlier today. Could they see something I missed in myself? Had I spent so much time in the company of the dead that I could no longer relate to the living? Had so much happened to me in the past weeks that I sought refuge in the solitary confinement of my mind? And would I know if that were the case? Would I care?

Of some facts I could be certain: that Matthew Lynes existed in the present seemed evident enough. That he practised medicine – without doubt. I knew he had been married and I had met his niece and nephew, but what else? Could I be confident that the photograph in the newspaper was indeed Matthew? Could it be coincidence that several years before my birth, Mike had seen a man – a doctor – who looked like Matthew and shared his name? Had I imagined his strength, his speed, or the moving lights like flames in his eyes? Did he eat and sleep as I did, and mere chance prevented me from seeing him do so? Had the bear rent his jacket and a miracle saved Matthew's skin from being torn from his back, and his life with it? Where, on this sweet earth, did the boundary lie between reality, certainty, sanity and what I had found in this strange man? And where, on that frontier, did I sit?

I raised my head at the sound of footsteps outside my door and covered my face with as near normal a smile as I could muster as my mother came in bearing a tray.

"Darling, I can't see a thing – put the light on, *please!*"

I hadn't noticed I had been sitting in the dark, the light from the laptop casting a lurid glow against the walls. I switched on the bedside light and its muted terracotta shade warmed the room instantly. The fork rattled against the glass on the tray as my mother set it down on the bed in front of my crossed legs. I steadied the glass as it slid precariously to the edge of the tray, and put it on the bedside table.

"Mum, you didn't have to bring this up – I'd have come down for supper."

"I called and called but you didn't answer, so it was much easier to bring this to you and save my voice. I need the exercise anyway. Are you engrossed?"

"I must have been. I didn't hear you, sorry." I listened to myself, and wondered if what I said could be interpreted as a sign of madness.

She squeezed my arm. "Not to worry, darling; I'll never know how you can expect to hear anything, let alone think when you're plugged into your music machine."

She twanged the long cord of my earphones hanging around my neck; I had forgotten it was there.

"It helps me concentrate. Thanks for bringing my supper up – it looks good."

I picked up the fork with what I hoped looked like eager anticipation, but my mother continued to sit on the edge of my bed, her hand still resting on my arm.

"What is it, Mum?"

She played with the edge of my sleeve, tidying the cuff so that it sat neatly against my bandaged wrist.

"Guy phoned today; your father spoke to him."

She pulled a stray hair out of the weave. I put my fork back down on the plate abruptly, the noise cold.

"And?"

"He'd heard you'd had problems in America, and he wanted to know how you are."

"I hope Dad told him everything's just *fine*," I said, with an undercurrent of a threat.

"Yes, but he still wants to see you. He wants to come over."

I shoved the tray angrily to one side. "Not a chance. No way. Get Dad to phone him back; I don't want him anywhere near me. I've got enough to deal with at the moment."

"That's what your father told him," she said quietly.

"He did?"

"Don't underestimate your father, Emma. I know he gets it wrong sometimes – well, quite often – but he's on your side, don't forget that. He didn't get to know you like I did; we grew up together, didn't we? He never had that, so you're still a bit of a mystery to him. But he's making a real effort at the moment, and he knows that he was wrong about Guy and wrong about how he handled the situation with you, too."

My shoulders slumped, my anger deflated like a pot going off the boil.

"Oh."

"Another thing…" she said, seeing my defences down, "Beth's been asking how you are and she's been over a few times; now you're feeling a bit more like yourself, perhaps you can get together? You haven't seen Archie for months and he's gorgeous – all red hair and dimples."

"Poor child…" I began, and she looked at me reprovingly. "Yes, all right, I'll see them. I know all this has made me… oh, I don't know… too self-obsessed, I suppose. You must think I'm barking."

I glanced swiftly at my mother and, catching the hint of a frown, suspected I was right.

"She'll be at the coffee shop tomorrow, if that's any help," she suggested.

Game, set and match to my mother – as proficient off the court as on it. She had accomplished exactly what she wished to achieve without so much as a murmur from me.

"OK, I'll see how I get on here," I acquiesced without making any promises, and she smiled her golden smile, where her face lit up and the tired years fell from it, softening the lines. I put my arms around her, trying not to thump her with my cast. "I don't know how you put up with me, but thank you, anyway."

"You have your grandfather's passion and your father's determination – how could I not put up with you? All I ask for, darling, is that you allow yourself to be happy; just for once, let happiness find you."

I unfolded myself from around her.

"And there's no need to look at me like that, Emma; you have a knack of pushing people away and keeping them at a distance – and you know you do."

"Circumstances and complications," I muttered.

"Well, perhaps, but you have a part to play too. Sometimes you have to make things happen."

She regarded me with her deep, wise eyes, but I couldn't tell her what I wanted more than anything at this moment, because it registered off the scale of absurdity and I was trying to be normal – if such a thing existed.

"Now eat, before your food get cold. I don't want your father fussing any more about you not eating enough."

Sharp shafts of sunlight drove across the steeple of St Mary's, irradiating the stone in shades of pale gold that lit the dark canyons of the ancient streets below. Arrows of light glanced off the soft greyed stone roofs where – wet from last night's rain – the sun caught the surface. I had been awake when the rain stopped sometime in the middle of the night, and still tossed fitfully as I listened to the first calling of the morning birds as the sun rose.

I took a bath, one limb at a time, when I thought that the sound of my clumsy splashing would alert no suspicion from my parents because of the early hour.

By the time the great church bell struck seven, I decided that the only way forward would be to approach the whole subject of Matthew Lynes as one of historical research and to do what I did best – methodically, thoroughly and dispassionately. I would begin with what little I had –

his name – and the few dates and, like a tapestry, weave the multicoloured strands into a picture I could understand. And then? And then I would see where those strands led me.

Scooping the last of his special porridge made with raisins and ginger into his spoon, Dad broke through my reverie.

"Are you seeing Beth today?"

Bother, I'd forgotten. "I'll pop down to the coffee shop after breakfast," I said, a tad too brightly to be real; he raised a heavy eyebrow.

"While you're there, pick up a couple of croissants, will you, please?"

Reaching into his pocket, he retrieved his wallet, handing over a pristine five-pound note and ensuring I went. Much more subtle than usual, he must have been taking lessons from my mother.

The air stung straight from the east, the light breeze cold and sharp. I wrapped Matthew's scarf around my face and drew the collar of my coat up to my ears, the zip holding the combination together like the bevor on a suit of armour. I found the narrow passage that led to the old High Street and regarded the tide of humanity in front of me before stepping into the current. Apart from the brief encounter in the computer shop and the hospital, it had been weeks since I'd been among people outside the confines of the college, and the assault on my senses left me unprepared. I felt a stranger, although the blood of my ancestors stained the streets, and their money had built the walls of the old stone houses around me. I knew each cobble, every stone, the smell of the market stalls in Red Lion Square, the familiar voices – teeth gritted against the biting wind – yet I found no comfort in them, cast adrift on an ocean of faces. Out of sorts; out of place; out of time.

My sister's coffee shop lay off the High Street, its Georgian windows at odds with its medieval origins. I pushed open the heavy glazed door with a mixture of anticipation and relief as the crowds gave way to the coffee-scented sobriety of the interior. The hour still being early, only a handful of caffeine addicts decorated the warm, mocha-coloured room. Embedded in deep leather sofas set in alcoves, they spread wide their newspapers in defiance of the morning. A few faces looked up as the frigid air made me an unwelcome visitor, stirring the static pages and diluting the heady aroma of freshly made coffee. I walked quietly across the stripped-wood floor which bore the accumulated scars of several centuries of life, to where weak sunlight, the colour of winter, bleached the tones of the oak counter curving seductively towards the back of the shop. Behind it, the back of a tall, skinny man in his early forties, dark floppy hair greying at the edges, stooped as he wrestled with the filter mechanism of the shiny Italian coffee machine. He yanked at the black handle and the filter jerked free, scattering dark coffee grounds across the floor. He swore under his breath.

I unwound my scarf and drew the zip of my coat down far enough to reveal my face. "Hi, Rob, how's things?"

He jumped, spinning round, grinding a circle in the damp coffee under his shoe.

"Emma! Good grief! Where did you come from?"

His soft Scottish accent seeped through his precise articulation, as it always did when he was surprised. He came round the end of the counter, wiping his hands on the cream apron around his waist, and enveloped me in a cautious embrace.

"Beth's feeding Archie – she'll be out in a moment. Now, what've you been up to?" He held me at arms' length, inspecting me as he did so, taking in the cast on my arm and the hollow wanness of my face.

"So what's happened to the vermin who did this to you?"

I shrugged, not wanting to go into details of the attack again.

"They've got him banged up somewhere."

He took the hint. "They should've fed him to your dad; let him sort the scum out, like he did Guy."

"Oh, you heard about that, did you?"

I wondered what exactly he had been told about my father's confrontation with Guy – not the full story, I bet. He grinned, his smile lifting high cheekbones, and his face looked no longer severe.

"I heard enough to know I wouldn't want to be on the wrong side of his temper – or yours. There's laws against terrorizing university staff in the States, you know, Emma. They won't let you back in the country if you persist in molesting academics."

An image of Staahl's face, screwed in terror moments before Matthew released his grip on him, intervened briefly. I recovered, punching my brother-in-law on the arm as hard as I dared. He was the only person I knew who could get away with making a comment that cut so close to my quick. He gave me another brotherly bear hug, reminding me of a leaner version of Matias Lidström. "Yes, well, I'm glad to see you're in one piece; Beth's been worried sick about you."

A flurry of feet from the back of the room and the high-pitched clamour of children's voices broke through the muted tones of the adult conversations around us, as my nephew and niece sprang out of nowhere, launching an attack of hugs around my waist. Heads – one curly haired and bright gold, the other straight and dark – looked up at me expectantly.

I kissed the tops of their heads, returning their embraces as best I could amid the wriggling.

"Hello, you two – my, how you've grown! Shouldn't you be at school? Christmas is coming, and I hope you've been *good* little children. Are you eating your greens?"

My fingers ruffled their hair stiffly and the twins creased up with giggles at the familiar greeting. Flora's pretend pout lasted for all of two seconds.

"It's *Saturday*, Emma, and there's no school at the weekend, but Daddy says we should be in school *every* day and Christmas Day, and he says he's going to talk to Mrs Abbot about it 'cos *she's* the head teacher and she can tell the teachers they've got to teach us and Amy's mum says we don't because it's the law we have holidays and Daddy says he'll get the law changed and have you brought us any presents?"

"Slow down, slow down, my little river of words, one thing at a time!"

I laughed at my irrepressible niece, her eyes sparkling and her curls bouncing as she jumped up and down in front of me. "And no, I'm very sorry, but this time I didn't bring any presents. Do you forgive me or shall I leave and never come back?"

She flung her arms around my waist again, managing to nudge a rib in the process.

"Don't go, we forgive you. But you have to do better *next* time," she smiled impishly.

I felt a tentative hand on my arm and looked down at my nephew, pale and shy with the dark, soft hair of his father – the opposite of his twin.

"Does your arm hurt, Emma?"

I bent down as far as I could, and brushed his hair out of his thoughtful eyes, gentling my voice.

"No, Alex, it doesn't hurt any more, but thank you for asking.

How's the coin collection going? Any new acquisitions?"

The little boy's face lit up. "I've seen a Hadrian sesterce on eBay, but it's too much money already, but Daddy says he'll take us to Bloody Oaks at Losecoat Field if the farmer'll let us. James' dad found a groat there last summer."

I smiled at the light in his eyes and made a mental note for a Christmas present.

"Your great-grandfather used to take us to the battlefield when I was your age; that's where my arrowhead came from; do you remember it?"

Alex nodded eagerly, making his hair flop back into his eyes. "Will you come too, Emma, please?"

"Yes, please, Emma, please, please, *pleeeease*," Flora chanted.

There was almost nothing I would have liked to do more. Almost.

"Perhaps, babes – I'll have to see."

Flora started to pogo up and down in front of me again, winding herself up for a full-on begging session, but her father intercepted just in time.

"All right, you two, the DVD's set up, if you want to watch it; give your aunt room to breathe."

I relieved my muscles of their awkward posture while he shooshed his offspring towards the back of the shop, where they disappeared in a cloud of exuberance through the staff door, passing my sister as she came out. Beth saw me and pulled her dark-blue jumper down over her bottom with her free hand, hiding her white T-shirt in the process. She balanced eleven-month-old Archie on one broad hip, his chubby legs swinging; he was full of milk and good humour.

A deep crease formed between her eyes as she took me in, reminding me of our mother, and I bridged the gap between us in a few steps, kissing her on one cheek.

"Beth – how are you? Mum said you've been over; I'm sorry I didn't see you."

"Dad said you couldn't see anybody, not even me; he said you were too… ill."

She transferred Archie onto her other hip and put her arm tentatively around my back, wordlessly holding me close. I breathed in her warm, familiar scent of motherhood and soap. She stood back, wiping the back of her hand across her eyes.

"I'd never have forgiven you if you'd got yourself killed," she whispered. The baby kicked his legs against us, then thrust his curled fist into my thick plait and tugged it like a bell-pull. I gently disengaged his hand and kissed his dimpled fingers.

"Hello, Archie."

He regarded me soberly with huge blue eyes, broke into a half-smile, frowned, then his face crumpled and a thin, siren-like wail filled the coffee shop. I cringed apologetically as the patrons stared as one.

"Sorry, I'm not good with babies," I said helplessly, backing away.

"How would you know until you've had one? Babies cry, Em; it's what they do."

Beth shot me a glance as she swept Archie up and around to face her. He stopped crying immediately, tears drying on his red cheeks, and he chuckled as his mother rubbed noses with him, the overhead lights giving him a halo through his wispy, red-gold baby hair. The customers retreated into their newspapers and cups.

Archie's head swivelled as the door shouldered open and a woman in a bright red jacket edged through it, dumping bags bulging with vegetables from the market on the floor, and looking expectantly at Rob.

"Go into the back and I'll bring you both coffee in a minute," he said to us, indicating the rear of the shop with his elbow, and moving towards the woman in red, pad and pen poised.

I followed Beth through to the family's private area at the back of the shop where a large, saggy, carroty-coloured sofa faced a TV with a cacophony of brightly coloured plastic toys scattered in front of it. The twins were already ensconced, lounging at various angles off the sofa with their eyes fixed on the screen. A limb occasionally waved abstractly as they gave their total concentration to the garish moving images. Expertly clearing a path through the toys with her foot, Beth eased herself down on the sofa with Archie still firmly attached, grasping his mother's jumper with determined fists and revealing her creamy skin. She pushed a twin off the other end so that I could sit down, and tucked her leg under her, shuffling until comfortable.

I removed a well-chewed teddy bear before I sat on it; it grinned lopsidedly up at me, one of its ears coming unstitched at the corner. I recognized it as one of Beth's from a lifetime ago, and clasped it to me as I sat down gingerly, feeling the springs of the old sofa protesting. The noise from the film was overwhelming in the small room.

"Here."

Beth unceremoniously deposited Archie on my lap as she retrieved the TV remote control from under a pile of colouring books and turned the volume down. The baby considered me cautiously, then reached out a little hand and scrabbled his fingers against the rough surface of the cast on my arm, his mouth the shape of an "o". I smiled at him hopefully, but his head pivoted away from me as he heard his mother sit down beside us, and a beam crossed his face.

"Babies are a complete mystery to me; how do you communicate with them if they can't talk?" I said, probably sounding more spinsterly than I intended. Beth rearranged her jumper, the knit baggy after years of being washed and dried contrary to the care label.

"You're not born knowing what to do, Em, and you can't get it all from books; you've just got to get on with it and learn on the job. It helps if you get pregnant first, of course."

"There's not much chance of that," I said, answering her unspoken question. She leaned forward and picked a crumpled square of muslin off the floor, draping it over my shoulder.

"You might need this; he's just had a feed and he's a bit possety at the moment."

She made no attempt to take Archie off me and I couldn't lift him to give him back, so I resigned myself to ensuring that my writhing nephew didn't throw himself backwards unexpectedly – or throw up all over me. In the light from the window behind us, his hair shone. I touched the fine wisps.

"He has the same colour hair as Grandpa, Beth." My heart lurched unexpectedly and she looked at me curiously. Archie stuffed his hand in his mouth and gummed it, dribbling.

"Well, you knew him better than I did, Em – I don't remember him that well, but I recall Nanna saying something like that."

There was an awkward silence between us, filled with a gabble of raucous cartoon voices. Flora rolled onto her back, oblivious.

"You look well, Beth; is Archie sleeping through the night now?"

It sounded like the sort of thing my mother would ask.

"He's been doing that for months, except for the odd night, but thanks for asking anyway. I'd look better if I had your frame and I could shift a few stone, though."

She wrinkled her nose at Archie who rumbled a laugh back. "You look like crap, by the way."

"Gee, thanks Sis," I moaned.

"At least you have an excuse; I don't." Archie bounced on my lap, and I put a protective arm out to prevent him from launching at his mother. "You're skinny, like Mum and Grandpa – you lucky wench. This is what three kids and two mortgages does for you." She thwacked her thighs, bound tight by her jeans like over-stuffed sausages. Beth had always been comfortably stocky, like our father, and there had been an undercurrent of resentment for the genes she had inherited.

"Yeah? Well, who ended up with the ginger hair and freckles, then?" I reminded her, trying to make light of it and regarding her perfectly even, milk-white skin and glossy, dark-brown hair that did what it was told.

She pursed her lips. "You did; what I wouldn't have done to have *your* hair!"

"Since when?"

"Since forever. You had all the attention, Em; boys only ever talked to me because they wanted to get to know *you*. Remember Jack?"

I frowned, flipping back to my childhood and a lanky, unprepossessing youth in his early twenties. "Yes – sort of; he was your first boyfriend, wasn't he?"

"He was – until I brought him home that Easter."

I looked blankly at her.

"You haven't a clue, have you?"

I shook my head.

"All he could talk about was you, Em – you and your long, perfect hair. Pre-Raphaelite red, he called it."

I vaguely recollected he had been an art student who

hadn't stayed around for long, which explained why he hadn't made a lasting impression on me.

"But I was only about... twelve-ish, wasn't I?"

"*Pre*-cisely."

I opened my mouth to say something, then closed it again, stumped. Alex rolled into Flora on purpose, making her squeal, before using her legs in their candy-striped tights as a runway for his model aeroplane. It soared over her head and she walloped him with her Barbie, its flimsy skirts flying as they broke into a tussle. I watched them, anxious to be sidetracked, waiting for the simmering tension that had sprung up between us to cool.

"I didn't know, Beth – I'm sorry. But you've forgotten what it was like at school. I had years and *years* of the pointing and the whispering and '*ginger* nut' or '*ginger* pixie' and '*parkin*', and forever trying not to stand out as being different."

"At least you weren't *inconspicuous*," she twisted the word. "At least you were noticed. Not packed off to boarding school like me because I wasn't the clever one – the *scholar*."

Beth's normally gentle expression had been replaced by a mask of sourness in no more than a moment. I stared at her, open-mouthed.

"*What?*"

"Well, you *were* a scholar, weren't you?" she scowled defiantly. Archie grizzled, rubbing his eyes.

"Yes, but so what? You went to boarding school because Dad was always being posted and you had to keep changing schools. They wanted some stability for you."

"Yes? You think? And how come you got to stay at home with Mum?"

"But... but that was years later, and I never saw Dad because of it. It had nothing to do with being a scholar, or anything."

"Emma, you were *always* Dad's little star. He didn't bother about what *I* wanted to do. I could've made a living on my back and he wouldn't have cared. But you – *you* had to be the best – nothing was too good for you. He wouldn't have had you working in a shop. And now you've got them running around after you again, just like the old days. All I've heard about for the last month is '*Emma this, Emma that.*'"

Her mouth screwed. Stunned by her attack, I went on the offensive, my face flaring in anger and hurt. "That's not true, Beth. You were always closer to him; he understood you, and at least you had a father when you were growing up. I only saw him when he came home on leave, and even then he was always tired and grumpy. All he wanted to know was what my end-of-term reports were like and what my predicted grades were. I don't ever remember him asking if I was *happy*." I fumed, years of bottled-up resentment spilling from me. "By the time he retired and he came home for good, all I had from him was pressure and flak. Do you have any idea of what it was like at home after you left? I dreaded coming downstairs in the morning because of the questions, the criticism, the constant barrage of... of *rubbish*."

More hurt lurked behind my words than I would have thought possible, and it ambushed me as it poured out, my voice rising. Archie jumped, startled, and gazed at me, his round head wobbling uncertainly. Beth snatched him from me, and he wrapped his pudgy arms around her neck. She glared at me over his head. The twins stopped fighting and untangled their arms and legs, sitting up and staring open-mouthed at us, Barbie suspended in mid-attack.

"Oh yeah, you poor thing, and look at you *now*," she spat, sarcastically.

"Mummy..." Alex pulled at her arm anxiously.

"What's that supposed to mean?" I demanded, half off the sofa, nails biting into the palms of my hands. Flora's mouth hung open, her eyes wide.

"Who's a Cambridge professor...?"

"Doctor," I muttered, seething.

"*Doctor*," she ground the word with her teeth. "And who has the career; who gets to travel – who lives in *America*, for God's sake?"

"Don't blaspheme," I snapped automatically.

She ignored me. "And who has a *life* outside all of... *this*..." and she flung her arm out, taking in her entire world with one sweep of her hand.

I looked at the shocked faces of her children, at the plethora of normality in the furnishings, the toys – the wonderful, sublime, utter ordinariness of it all – and I knew what I was missing.

"And who's holding her baby?" I pointed out, my voice suddenly quiet. "And has a husband, and a home and... and *amazing* children? What do I have? What can I honestly say I've given to this world, other than a lot of grief, from what you've said? Where has all this come from, Beth? What happened to you?"

Beth calmed down. "*You* happened. It's not your fault, Em, but I never felt I could compete with you."

I looked at her swiftly as she echoed my own thoughts.

"So – you're jealous of me because of... what? You want some of this?" I held my damaged arms out to her. "You want to have been stalked and mauled by a psychopath, or pursued by a self-pitying drunk? Or perhaps you'd like to swap places and have a relationship that probably isn't happening and, even if it is, *shouldn't*. I mean, with which one would you like to spice up your life a bit, because I sure as hell would like a little bit of what *you've* got."

I shoved a strand of hair out of my eyes, scowling at my big sister, as she returned the look.

"Don't be such a flippin' drama queen, Em."

I would have retaliated but the door flung open, the handle hitting the wall with a *thud* as Rob came in, his face furious.

"I can hear you in the shop, for pity's sake. What do you think you're doing?" He took in his wife's flushed face and my blazing eyes. "I don't know what your problem is, the pair of you, but *get over it*," he hissed. "Kids…" He held out a hand to the twins and they went to him without a word. He scooped Archie into his free arm and turned his back on us, following the two older children out of the room.

"Golly," Beth said.

"*Heck*," I echoed.

We looked at each other, and I saw for the first time in years the similarities between us, not the differences.

"Do you think he'll forgive me for that?" I ventured.

"I'm the one who has to live with him," Beth said and looked at me out of the corner of her eye. I burst out laughing, pent-up tension and relief flowing as one unstoppable tide, and she honked back a laugh, another then another rising from her until she too became engulfed, and we fell against each other sobbing intense, wrenching laughter that was an amalgam of joy and grief.

"He has a point, though," I said, catching my breath.

"He's useful for something, then," Beth heaved out. "Does that mean we have to have therapy or something?"

"Oh, definitely *something*. I know a simply fantastic doctor."

The irony of it set me off again. This time Beth didn't join in, but sat back and looked at me with the same curious expression she had employed earlier. I sobered, swallowing the convulsions until I was in control once more.

"What?"

"Would that be the same doctor Mum mentioned – the one in the States?"

Instantly on my guard, I said, "Might be; depends what she said about him."

"She said there's something between you – or there was. Did something happen? Did he hurt you? Dad said…"

My short, guttural laugh had her blenching from me. I unfolded myself from the sofa as I stood up. Beth put a hand on my arm, looking up at me.

"Emma, Rob's right, we've got to sort ourselves out. We were good friends once, weren't we – before I left home? If there's something I can do – *anything* – please let me help. If this man did something…"

I put my hand on hers and patted it in just the same way our mother would.

"Thanks, and you're right – Rob's right – we've things to sort out, but *he's* not one of them. He's all mine to deal with." *One way, or another,* I thought. "We'll get together, won't we, over the next few weeks?" I offered.

She stood up and put her arms right around me, and there was real warmth in her gesture, which I returned with more feeling than I thought possible, given the years of unspoken acrimony between us. It was at this juncture that Rob returned, and he surveyed us with his hands on his hips.

"I didn't know what I would find, but a cessation of hostilities wasn't expected. But it's good; I'm not complaining. Would you now like to reassure your progeny, Beth – and your niece and nephews, Emma – that all is well? All *is* well, I take it?"

"Very well," we chimed.

He managed a smile. "Emma, stay for lunch, will you? Don't abandon me to suffer Beth's résumé of what just went on between the two of you for the next couple of hours."

"I would love to, but I have things to do."

Beth put her arm around my waist. "Won't they wait?"

I shook my head regretfully. "No – not any longer. Let me say goodbye to the children; I don't want them remembering me for the wrong reasons."

It didn't take long for the twins to lose their caution, and I extricated myself before I was hugged to death. Archie was another matter; he swung his head around and buried it in his father's chest, fingers firmly in his mouth. Rob put a reassuring hand on his back.

"He's tired and he's at that age where all strangers are anathema; don't worry about it, Em."

I kissed the back of the baby's head through the tousled soft fluff. He had a warm, clean baby smell – utterly enticing, totally memorable – and it stayed with me long after I left the shop and made my way towards the museum and my search for some answers.

The Museum

The air felt degrees less cold as I walked down Broad Street, a cardboard cup of milky coffee in one hand, an almond croissant in the other. I caught sight of my reflection in the windows of the shops on the sunless side of the street where the shadows made a mirror of the glass. Hollow-cheeked and hollow-eyed, I looked half-alive, except for the dark purpose burning in the black depths of my eyes.

The crowds of early morning shoppers had eased. Now was the best time to search the museum records, before parents and children descended on it with an idle hour to spare before tea, and bath, and bed.

I stuffed the last of the pastry into my mouth, and drained the cup, caffeine tearing through my bloodstream, sending my heart thumping erratically as it tried to keep up with the excessive amounts of unaccustomed stimulant. Within moments, the world became sharper, brighter and, as the door to the museum opened, expelling an occupant, for the briefest second, Staahl's dead, grey eyes looked at me from another man's body. But it wasn't Staahl, it couldn't be, and the man walked by – a stranger passing a stranger in the street – and no more. I blamed my jittery state squarely on the coffee and pushed through the door.

The hushed and darkened galleries of the tiny museum were devoid of life bar a subdued rustle from around the corner. A woman – not much older than I – struggled with a catch on a display case, clenching a sheaf of papers beneath her arm. She yelped as she nicked her finger, the papers slipping haphazardly towards the floor, and I rescued them as they fell. She succeeded in securing the lock on the glass case before turning to retrieve them from me.

"Thanks – I should've put them down first, but you know..."

She shrugged, surveying her finger. She was from somewhere in Wales – perhaps Cardiff – the soft lilt in her voice not yet diluted by the local accent. She exuded colour from the inside out, her rotund body encased in layers of brightly coloured clothes that clung to every curve. She smiled engagingly, deep dimples on her apple-blossom cheeks. I returned her smile and the papers.

"Yup, I know; we've all done it. My pleasure, anyway."

As I handed them back to her, shuffling them in order, the top page caught my eye: a numbered printout in a mind-boggling small font.

"Is that an archival list?"

The young woman glanced down at the wad of paper. "Uh, yes – are you looking for something?"

It was just a chance. "I'm looking for anything on the Lynes family."

"Lynes, Lynes." She juggled with the name for a moment, then shook her head, her shoulder-length hair catching on the collar of purple-sequined embroidery; she pulled it free, the light glinting off the tiny metallic circles. She swam in a sea of colour, and not just her clothes, but her whole personality sparkled with it.

"It's not one I've heard of, love. Have you any more information – a date, first name, location, occupation – something I can cross-reference?"

I felt like an idiot, and I should have known better after all the research I had done.

"Matthew Lynes, possibly around 1900. Location – I'm not too sure, perhaps South Lincolnshire – Cambridge." I waved my hands vaguely and the curator's eyes followed the path my cast made in the air. I hid it behind my back and she refocused on my face. Instead of looking impatient – which is what I think I would have done – she looked faintly bemused.

"I'll do a search and see what'll come up on that. *Lynes*, mmm…" she mused. "It might take some time; have you got a mo?"

"Ye-es, I have, but I didn't expect you to do this immediately…"

"No problem, love; I'm done here and it's better than filing this lot…" she brandished the papers, wafting warm air towards me, "… or fiddling about with the Neolithic case; those burins and scrapers are so tricky. Follow me, I'll just get a plaster first, if you don't mind." She cheerily led me past an image of Daniel Lambert looking smugly replete on the wall.

"Researching your family?" she enquired over her shoulder.

"No – this is work," I said, evasively.

"Historian? Genealogist? We get a lot of those here."

"Uh huh – historian."

She led me down the stairs and along a corridor where one of the ceiling lights flickered intermittently like a moth's wings against a bare bulb.

"I wouldn't normally bring the public here – staff only, you see – but since you're professional, I reckon it's OK. Where do you come from?"

She shoved a door with her foot and held it open for me with her elbow.

"I'm from Stamford."

"Are you? You don't sound it. Here… sit down; if we can't find anything, it's not on the web. We've got complete access to all the records available, you see. You're lucky to find anyone here now. I'm only on loan from Lincoln doing an audit of the collection before it's mothballed. The museum's on the hit-list, see; might get the axe."

Neither of us commented; we didn't need to, the very thought of closing the museum abhorrent to both of us for different reasons. I remembered coming here with my grandfather countless times. Summer, winter, rain or snow – all those visits were warm in my memory.

She dumped the papers on a desk next to a computer monitor, and pulled the keyboard out from underneath a glossy museum periodical. "*Lynes*, did you say? L-i-n-e-s?"

"L-*y*-n-e-s," I corrected.

Her fingers sped over the keyboard as I sat down next to her, searching the database. She sucked at her cut finger, regarding the monitor through narrowed eyes.

"Nothing for Stamford for that date. I'll widen the search. Hey, can you do this while I grab that plaster?"

She was out of her chair and across the room, hoicking a green First Aid box out of an overhead cupboard. I dragged the keyboard around in front of me and tapped in the next search parameter.

"No, nothing for South Kesteven either. I'll try Cambridgeshire next."

It was a long shot and it, too, drew a blank.

"Fancy a tea, love?"

The sound of a plastic kettle being filled from a tap in

a tiny adjacent room the size of a cupboard, crammed the space for an instant, almost too loud in the small area.

"Thanks…" My eyes remained fixed on the screen. The curator gathered a couple of mugs from beside me, the remains of the last drinks clinging languidly to their interiors, the liquid slopping as she picked them up.

"Biscuit?" she asked.

"I have chocolate in my bag," I offered.

I fished out a couple of Kit Kats without looking, tapping in another set of data with one finger. Water sloshed in the mugs in the sink and a faint scent of washing-up liquid drifted. The young woman returned and leaned over my shoulder while drying a mug.

"Try Northampton – they've just digitized their collection," she suggested.

The screen hesitated, then coughed up a snazzy home page with interactive links. I scanned through them, opening page after page of irrelevant information.

"Nope, nothing there either. This is going to be a waste of time without any more information to go on."

I scrabbled my hands through my hair, feeling my plait begin to unfurl, and becoming conscious for the first time of a slight numbness in my fingers. I disregarded it and pouted at the machine. It wouldn't have been so bad if I were working on my own, but I was all too aware of eating into someone else's time.

"Naw, love, there's plenty more where that came from." She put a mug of steaming tea down next to me. "You're not supposed to drink in here, but we don't take any notice. No original documents to worry about, and if they're closing it down, what does it matter? Do you have an occupation to go on?"

"Thanks for the tea. Doctor – no, surgeon, but I don't know when he qualified – or where, for that matter."

"Try the National Database for the Royal College of Surgeons – that's the most comprehensive."

This was straying from my own territory; I wasn't as familiar with the sources for later archive material. She sat on the wheeled office chair, her ample frame spilling comfortably over the edges of the seat, and picked up the remaining Kit Kat, unwrapping it and slicing cleanly through the foil with a fingernail. Mine had already begun to melt in my fingers; I nibbled the chocolate, feeling it dissolve further in the warmth of my mouth.

"Mmm... not a bean," I mumbled stickily. "Perhaps I should be widening the time frame. I'll try another thirty years."

"Worth a try."

The door opened behind us.

"Judy, there's someone at the front desk for you – said you were expecting them?"

"Yes, right love, I'd forgotten. You OK here?" she said to me, already standing. "Be back in two ticks. Biscuits in the tin by the kettle."

I found no record of Matthew in any of the Surgeons' databases I searched; his name drew a blank wherever I looked. I found "Lynes" all right, some with an "i", one or two with a "y", but no one with his first name in Britain, and I began to think my hunch that he originated in England had been wrong all along. Which meant looking through the US databases. I groaned, but before I resigned myself to that inevitable route, I took one last long shot at the English records.

I went back in fifty-year chunks, typing in key words and scouring the records for each period from 1850 backwards for 200 years, covering the region from Cambridge through Rutland to Stamford. Again, nothing.

I pushed away from the desk abruptly, and leaned back in

the chair, rocking on the back legs, my cross between my lips as I wrestled with the problem facing me.

I knew that a Lynes family had lived in the region in the early seventeenth century – that had been confirmed by the reference to the name in the journal, and had jogged my memory when I first met Matthew. I knew that they held land there, and that one of them had been Nathaniel Richardson's master. But as Matthew had pointed out so evasively when I mentioned it to him, Lynes was not such an unusual name, and the chance that it might be the same family was remote beyond the realms of reasonableness. But then, there was nothing reasonable about my suppositions, so why let a little thing such as being reasonable stop me now?

I racked my memory for the name of the parish Richardson had come from. My grandfather had completed a great deal of background research on him, so it would have to be somewhere in the paperwork he left me all those years ago. This was the right time frame and the right region and the possibilities were narrowing all the time, but the parish eluded me. I would have to start from the only other reference point I had and work forwards.

"Blast this," I muttered crossly, rolling the chair forward onto its front legs so it thumped on the thin commercial carpet, and whacked in: "Parish records, Cambridge, Rutland, Stamford, Lynes, 1550 to 1650."

And there it was – the first reference to the Lynes lay in a series of names and dates in an obscure county record for Rutland.

"Of course! Twit!" I admonished myself out loud. Rutland was a small county, and the parish of Martinsthorpe had few occupants even then – no wonder it hadn't loomed large in my memory. I read down the list, looking for clues:

Marg't Lynes b 1584 d 1611 formerly *Fielding*
Name unreadable possibly *Lynes b 1609*
Infant d 1611
Henry Lynes b 1577 d 1646?
William Lynes b 1586 d 1643

The records were incomplete – a footnote stated that information had been purposefully expunged, or damaged through flood or age.

I started with presuming that either Henry or William had been married to Margaret – and that represented a guess at this stage – and that the infant was their child and probably a victim of the very high mortality rates among newborns. Given the contemporaneous date of death, I thought it reasonable to suppose that the mother's death related to birth complications, possibly puerperal fever.

It was a start.

The expunged name posed more of a problem. The interesting question for me as a historian was *why*? The footnotes didn't amplify. If this was also a Lynes child, it might have been the older sibling by two years. Or someone completely unrelated. Whoever had researched the records, obviously believed there to be a relationship by the very proximity of the names they had transcribed. No date of death had been recorded, so presumably this person died in another parish, or was a suicide.

William Lynes died in the 1640s, so that wouldn't be so much of a problem to trace; perhaps William and Henry were related – brothers? Uncle and nephew? Cousins?

I homed in on the scanty parish records for Martinsthorpe, but came up with the same list of names. Margaret seemed to be related to the Fieldings who held a nearby manor at that time, although her relationship to them wasn't clear; that might be another line to follow, but not now, not yet.

I heard voices in the corridor outside and checked my watch: 4.55 – the museum would be packing up for the night. I clicked on the "Print" button and hoped for the best. From somewhere beneath a mountain of unfiled papers, came the familiar *whirr* of a printer starting up. I zeroed in on the noise, retrieving the single sheet from the machine as Judy entered the room in a multicoloured wave of cloth, beaded tassels at the edge of her skirt jiggling as she swayed through the door.

"Sorry to have been so long. Any luck?"

I folded the page and put it in my bag.

"I have a lead of some sort; I don't know where it's going but it's more than I had when I came here. Thanks so much for your help and for giving me access to the database." I kissed her on the cheek and she blushed.

"Not at all, love; it's what I'm here for, and glad I could help. I'll see you out and then I'm off to meet my husband; he's a historian as well. Funny lot you all are." And she laughed happily.

The sun had just set, the roofs of the buildings silhouetted against the pale salmon sky to the west. It threatened to be cold again and I made my way home as the shops began to shut. Christmas lights hung in abeyance across the street, waiting like a widow to shed the garb of mourning and be clothed once more in light. I had a lead on the name and the place; now all I could do was follow its thread, and hope that where it led, I wanted to follow.

4

The Box

Man is no starr, but a quick coal
Of mortall fire.
GEORGE HERBERT (1593–1633)

I needed to concentrate fully if I hoped to make any inroads on the negligible information I had tracked down. As I entered the broad hallway, the signature tune of the early evening news blasted from the television in the sitting room, the house otherwise quiet and at peace with itself. I started for the stairs, then changed my mind, doubling back to make my presence known to my parents and to forestall any questions.

They looked up as I came in, my mother's hands still twitching the wool around the fine knitting needles as she smiled at me, working all the time, the air around her strangely bright as if she were back-lit like an exhibit in a gallery. I made a mental note to have my eyes checked. Our fat tabby cat waddled over to greet me, head-butting my leg in the eternal quest for food and attention. I had barely seen him since coming home; I bent down to stroke him.

"Hello, Tiberius – how's things?" I scratched behind his ear just the way he liked. "Hi, Mum, Dad."

Click, clickity-click, Mum's needles went without pausing.

"Hello, darling, how did that go?"

"Yep, Beth's fine, so are the children, and Rob said to say 'Hello'. Oh, and I forgot the croissants – sorry, Dad. I've left the money in the hall."

I didn't wait for an answer, and I heard him grunt behind my back; I imagined a dark cloud with incipient rain hanging over him. Mum's voice followed me into the dining room through the door.

"Have you eaten? Your father's made a wonderful casserole for this evening."

"I've had coffee, thanks, and I'm going to grab something to eat now, so don't worry about supper for me – I've too much work to do."

"You don't drink coffee, darling, and there's tea in the pot," Mum called after me.

I raided the stone-lined pantry set into the thickness of the wall, the temperature only a degree or two above the cold night air outside. A slab of Lincolnshire pork pie, an orange, and a handful of grapes balanced on a tea plate would have to do for now, as neither hand would support any more weight. I grabbed a half-mug of tea and collected my bag on the way back through the hall. Tiberius followed, trotting upstairs beside me.

The old tailor's box had once held a man's dress shirt, back when gentlemen still expected to wear stiff wing collars and to never venture forth without gloves and a hat. Now the shabby box I retrieved from the top of the cupboard squeezed in beside the fireplace contained the tatty remains of the papers my grandfather had specifically left to me in his will.

I sat cross-legged on my bed and removed the lid, the tired cardboard smelling faintly of his cigar smoke and mothballs.

Tiberius jumped up beside me, his long tail flicking in my face; I tickled his ears and he settled in a heap, half hanging off my lap, and began to purr. In lifting off the translucent layer of tissue paper that protected the contents, my heart suddenly scuttled unevenly. I breathed slowly, easing out the anxious niggle, and it settled once again to its regular beat. Here, in this old box, had lain the portion of Ebenezer Howard's unfinished transcriptions of the journal, along with the other papers Grandpa had picked up in the auction, and his notebook containing his research. I remembered him writing in the fat, foolscap book, its red cloth spine and marbled covers stained with ink. I had an image of him sitting at his desk in his bedroom by the window in the sun, a silver bowl with large, foil-covered penny toffees by his elbow, and a copper ashtray the colour of my hair. An inevitable cigar smouldered, the acrid fragrance spiralling into the rays of morning light. The toffees were his way of cutting back on the last of his vices. When very young and not too heavy, I crawled onto his knees and he would unwrap the gold discs for me which, crammed into my mouth, would keep me quiet as he told me the stories of our past, his bristly chin grazing the top of my head, my ear against the slow beat of his dying heart. When I became sleepy and had stopped listening, my grandfather would continue writing in his book, the movements his arm made as it crossed the page a soothing rocking that lulled me to sleep.

Tiberius stretched out a paw and padded my arm. I looked down at him and he gazed back with his enormous green eyes as I stroked his warm head. The central heating struggled to heat the top floor and, tonight, frost would line the roof tiles and attempt to seep through the fragile frames of the windows. I tried to remember where I had last seen a fan-heater in the house.

Nanna and Grandpa shared the room opposite mine in the years before he died. It faced east over the many pitched gables and slates of the old roofs behind our tall house, and the early morning sun would ripen the colours of the faded wallpaper in the summer. It smelled of my grandmother – the clean talc-and-medicine smell that seems to accompany old age. The room was as she had left it when she had been taken ill; I felt at once comforted by her presence but also an intruder in what had been her world. I retrieved the fan-heater from under her bed and retreated to my room, wrapping my blue rug around my shoulders, as much for the memory it brought me as for the warmth it would offer, and started to organize my thoughts.

Grandpa's familiar thin, spidery writing in dark-blue ink scored each page in meticulous formations, dates in red and place names in capital letters underscored once for a parish and twice for a town. It was a system I still used. As part of my own research I had read Grandpa's notes, of course, but they represented nothing more than background information and a short-cut into the world of the seventeenth century. Now that I added purpose to my labours, each word held the potential to transform the mundane into a revelation.

My grandfather concentrated his research on the Richardson family rather than the Lynes, whom they had served as stewards, so I expected that much of the information he gathered would be largely irrelevant for my purposes. Apparently, Nathaniel Richardson had been the third generation of his family to act as steward. His grandfather – also Nathaniel – had been employed by the Lynes estate after his own land to the east of Martinsthorpe had been enclosed during Elizabeth's reign. He brought his son – John – and his young family with him. Nathaniel junior had been born sometime in the first decade of the century, and became steward on the death of his father in 1632. None of this was new to me, but now I needed to focus on any information that would cast light on the Lynes family itself.

I leafed through the notebook, looking for significant references, my eyes already tired from deciphering my grandfather's space-saving script. He had made brief notes on what he discovered about them, followed by a sketchy family tree with bits missing. I squinted at it, his abbreviations not making the tiny print any easier to read.

Henry Lynes Knt d. 1485
m
Alice Seyton

Henry b. 1472 d. 1475 — Alice b. 1473 m Hugh Lane — infant — Henry b. 1481 m Emma Cope — infant

Henry b. 1514 d. 1573 m Eliz'beth Seyton — Frances d. 1549 m W'llm Chapman — Edward b. 1521 d. 1592 m Marg'rt Cope

Eliz'beth d. m J'n Fielding — Henry b. 1539 d. 1603 m Emma D'Eresby — infant — William m Susan Digby

Eliz'beth b. 1575 m M'tthw Monfort — Henry b. 1577 d? m Marg'rt Fielding — W'llm b. 1586 d. 1643

name expunged b. 1609 d? — infant d. 1611

It read like a social history. In footnotes, my grandfather had described how Henry Lynes had been knighted by Edward IV after the battle of Losecoat Field in 1470, which explained the advantageous marriages over the next generations to the progeny of local notable families, including – it would appear – our own. I idly wondered if that was why Grandpa had spent so much time researching them, then decided probably not. As much as I didn't believe in coincidence, our family name cropped up in the most peculiar places throughout the region and down the centuries, so that being linked to the Lynes at some point wasn't so surprising.

As interesting as the family tree was, it didn't take me any further than the parish records had done, except that it appeared that the Lynes family died out on the male side with the death of Henry Lynes in the 1640s. At least the relationship between Henry and Margaret was now clear, as was that between the two brothers, Henry and William – Henry being the elder by a number of years. But that was the sum of it.

I wriggled my toes in front of the fan-heater as they began to cook, and stretched my legs out either side of it, nudging the cat in the process, and elongating my arms as far as they would go without my ribs twingeing. I found myself able to stretch further each day, and each day I was reminded that Matthew should have removed the strapping for me, not some stranger in the local hospital. The thought of his closeness now all but a frail memory, my heart wrenched in loneliness. I tried not to think about what he might be doing, might be feeling. To endure the emptiness that swallowed all sensation, as it did for me, I found bad enough, but the thought that he might feel nothing at all was much, much worse. "Don't you *dare*," I snarled out loud in an attempt to forestall the temptation to wallow. "Stick to the script and get *on* with it – it won't solve itself."

Tiberius blinked sleepily and stretched, his fuzzy tummy golden-olive; I stroked his soft fur and nibbled a bit of pork pie. I wasn't tired; the coffee still raced around my body like chipmunks in a cage, and there would be little point in trying to sleep.

I flipped over to the next page and stopped – hunger forgotten. Bingo! Grandpa had sketched six shields – family shields: five belonging to the landed families mentioned in the tree, and then the sixth – the Lynes shield. I recognized it at once: it had decorated the worn gold ring Matthew wore on his little finger, the one he had played with when deep in thought, the one he reluctantly let me see. I found what I had been looking for – a definitive link between Matthew Lynes of Maine, USA, and the Lynes of Rutland, England.

A blue shield: "Argent a tesse azure with three mullets d'or thereon." And rearing above the silver inverted "V", a gold lion, rampant.

Grandpa had used yellow ink to colour the three gold stars or mullets, one either side of the silver band, the third within, and it had faded a little over time, but the pattern remained quite clear. So why had Matthew claimed that his family originated in Scotland? Did he not know his family came from England – did he not question the emblem on the signet ring he wore? Did he not know, or didn't he want me to ask? And if not, why not?

OK, so I could think of three possibilities: first, that he didn't know his family's origins. Second, he knew where they came from but for some reason as yet unknown to me, felt ashamed of them. Third, he knew, but wanted to keep it secret.

The first was a possibility spoiled by the fact that he so

obviously lied. The second – perhaps he descended from an illegitimate branch of the family, and if so, so what? Who cared nowadays? It happened in the best families and I could name a dozen without thinking. The third – well, I already knew that he was hiding something from me and, given that he seemed to be a hundred years old or so, the last seemed the most likely explanation. How ridiculous! How totally fantastical. I paused in my soliloquy and waited for the impact of my supposition, but none came, and I wondered again if my sanity might be in doubt. I sucked my teeth, shrugged and continued my analysis.

Next question: If Matthew descended from the Rutland Lynes, from which branch did he spring? In the family tree Grandpa had traced, only two children were born to Henry and Margaret Lynes; of those, the youngest child had died – probably shortly after birth, since it had no recorded name. The older child's name had been expunged from the record – usually a sign of disfavour from the ruling regime, or possibly suicide, in which case there might not be records of the death. If the child had been male and had gone on to marry and have children of his own, his line would have carried his name, no matter what the ignominy of the father. The only other possibility might be that one of the Lynes daughters had carried the name with her, just as less-elevated families sometimes adopted a prestigious wife's name on marriage, either to continue it where there was no male heir, or for the sheer social advantage it would give the match. It was possible – but not likely. The Lynes were newly titled compared with the families they married into, and their name would not have carried the same kudos. No other children were recorded from male issue, although that didn't discount the possibility that the records were simply wrong or incomplete.

My grandfather must have found the information on the family from somewhere. He must have seen the original parish records. I had to see them for myself. I wanted to see what had been erased four centuries ago.

5

Martinsthorpe

Death be not proud, though some have called thee
Mighty and dreadful, for, thou art not soe,
For, those, whom thou think'st, thou doth overthrow,
Die not, poore death, nor yet canst thou kill mee.
JOHN DONNE (1572–1631)

The warm scent of plants, green and growing, I found comforting in the bleak depths of early winter.

"Dad...?" I began. He looked up from the wooden greenhouse staging of his tiny potting-shed tacked onto the outside wall of the scullery, his brow knitted in concentration. "I need your help."

He barely concealed his astonishment. It had been a long time since I had asked him for anything, and I didn't find it easy to ask now; but this rated as more important than my stubborn pride or hurt sensibilities.

"Oh? And what might that be?"

From somewhere in the scullery, my mother tortured the washing machine, its worn bearing grating against the dividing wall.

"I need to get to Oakham, and there's no bus there today..."

He made it easier for me. "And you would like me to take you?"

"Yes, please. I would drive, but…" and I waved my arms to illustrate my predicament.

"When do you want to go?"

"Now – this morning – if you're free, that is. There's some research I need to do there – some records I want to see first-hand. It shouldn't take long."

He finished bedding-in the tiny cineraria seedling into its own pot, tenderly tamping down the loose compost around its fragile, translucent stem, before fixing me with one of his probing looks.

"Is this all part of what you've been working on for college?"

I nodded emphatically so that I wouldn't have to lie out loud. He adjusted the setting on the heater in the corner, and squeezed a fine mist of distilled water from the spray bottle, watching it settle over the series of pots ranged across the bench. He sighed, content.

"Well, I'll be ready when you are."

I suppressed the urge to throw my arms around him and more sedately leaned forward to kiss his jowly cheek instead. He grunted, looking awkward.

"I'll tell your mother; she might want to come too. She hasn't been out in a long while and she deserves a break." He didn't say it, but from the way he wouldn't look at me as he secured the flimsy door, I took him to mean she needed the break because of me.

Late last night, I had managed to trace the original records back to Oakham, the county town of Rutland, where I happened to know an archivist. I emailed him at a ridiculous time of night, but he replied almost immediately and with an alarming degree of familiarity.

It hadn't been easy. The tiny parish of Martinsthorpe had drizzled into the footnotes of history along with the family of Lynes many years ago, and the meagre documentary evidence of its inhabitants was to be found scattered within the pages of the parish records for the larger community of nearby Manton. The records had been preserved in a broken series of bound volumes that had somehow survived the near extinction of the village. The old church had been absorbed into the body of the manor that now existed fragmentarily as a farm, becoming no more than the private chapel for the family of occupation. As far as I was aware, the Lynes never lived in the old house. Their lands had bordered the River Chater, and their manor had long since crumbled into the rich soil. But the Manton records were where their lives and deaths had been recorded, and this was where I must begin.

Mum opted to stay at home and finish knitting Archie's jersey, and we left her in the warmth as Dad and I slid across the ice-coated cobbles outside our house to the car parked beneath the Church of St Mary. I had heard the call of the Sunday bells as I dressed and ignored them, fearful of confronting the gaping hole where my heart had been. Yet now, as we nosed out of Stamford, following the gentle undulations of the frozen land, with each vale deepened by the low morning sun and their crests illuminated by the subtle light, for the first time since returning home, I felt hope where all before had been coloured by grey despair.

The small county town of Oakham competed with Stamford by virtue of the sheer allure of its honey-coloured buildings, all higgledy-piggledy old and new and, at its heart, the marketplace and Buttercross stocks. This morning, the market was all but empty and the only people in sight were on their way to church or to buy a pint of milk and a paper.

My archivist friend looked as if he would rather be in bed. Greg owed me a favour, and he greeted me at the door to the squat stone building where the archives were kept, key dangling from his finger, his chin roughened by several days' growth. He scratched it as he eyed me, before giving me a hug and kissing me clumsily on both cheeks. He grinned ruefully.

"You could have given me a bit more warning; I'd have made myself more respectable."

I thought that unlikely; I detected a shade of hangover in the bleary way he glowered at the sun.

"You always liked to live dangerously, from what I remember," I reminded him with a smile. I had covered for him after one of his all-night raves at university when we were undergrads. It would have been his last chance had he been caught, and he would have been sent down.

"I suppose I owe you that one," he agreed, "but you look as if you've been up to no good yourself. I take it you didn't get *that* climbing over a college wall after lights out." He indicated my broken arm and I made a gesture of non-committal. "Serious?"

"Nothing as exciting as something I'd get sent down for."

"Yeah, well… So you want to have a look at the Martinsthorpe records, do you? Any particular reason, or just general interest?"

I let my focus drift off into the distance and look vacant.

"Something like that."

Nonplussed, he opened his mouth to reply, then thought better of it.

"Follow me. Can't promise we have anything. You've tried the main archival repositories, have you?" I nodded. "Nothing there?" I shook my head. "Well, we'll give this a bash, then."

Most of Rutland's records were kept in Leicester or on microfiche in the county museum in Oakham. Just a few, though, were kept here. The metal racks held the odds and ends of records and artefacts no one else wanted to give shelf-space to in the tiny county. The cardboard boxes reminded me uncomfortably that I still had the journal in my possession and I wondered guiltily if it had been missed yet.

Greg ran a finger along the alphabetically organized shelves, stopping at "M", and looked at me enquiringly. "Date?"

"1550 to 1650, or thereabouts."

He selected several volumes and lifted them carefully from the shelf, supporting the fragile books with both hands. He carried them to a table set at one side, where a single light burned brightly in the otherwise muted light of the room. My heart beat a little faster and I felt as if life stirred in my veins – on the hunt, my quarry in sight.

"Anything else you need?" he said, laying the first book down reverently, aligning the foam book supports either side of the spine. I shook my head.

"No thanks, I don't think I'll be too long."

He indicated behind him with his thumb.

"I've got stuff to do while I'm here. Give me a yell if you want anything."

He retreated to the depths of the room, his shambling figure barely visible behind the shelving.

I traced the ridges of the brown leather book, noting the worn edges, the blunted corner where it had been dropped, the water stains on the hand-cut paper inside. It smelt musty like the interior of an old church, an unmistakable smell, resonant with age. I leafed through, scanning each page briefly. The hand in which names had been inscribed changed – sometimes in a matter of months, sometimes after many years – as the incumbents came and went. The records were clearly incomplete, some indecipherable. A form of secretary script seemed to have been used in most instances, occasionally Latin, and the spelling of surnames depended on the level of literacy of the writer, or fashion, or the education of the family itself, but most were identifiable and some familiar. I found Seyton and Seaton, Harrington and Fielding and, by 1577, Henry Lynes. I even found Nathaniel Richardson senior, his death being the first of his family registered in the parishes of Manton and Martinsthorpe. This is what my grandfather had come to find long before my birth.

In the sixteenth century, the village had been more populous than now, but it still ranked as no more than a hamlet by today's standards, and it took me only minutes to find Margaret Lynes and the dead infant, their short lives all but obscured by water stains. I had missed the expunged name. The ink was scratchy, parts blurred where the lettering had worn; I concentrated hard, focusing on each line, not wanting to miss anything.

1607, 1608. I skipped a bit. 1609... nothing for January. A rash of deaths in February. March. A marriage in April, two in May. I ran my finger down the list without touching the page. Three births in June; two babies dying within weeks of each other. July – nothing. August. September – a flurry of activity as the Christmas conceptions were born and at last – on the thirtieth day of September 1609, a child born whose name had been obliterated by a single, thick line drawn deliberately and categorically through it. I sat back and adjusted my eyes and tried again. The riser on one of the letters of the Christian name was barely visible – an "l" or "t", perhaps. Only the very tips of other letters could be made out, but nothing that could be identified. The surname was a little better – the riser on the initial letter clear enough to be made out as an "L" and the line just stopping short of the final letter, which looked like an "s". The descender of the second letter could be the tail of a "y", so it was possible – probable, even – that this was a Lynes child, as had already been proposed in the past. I scrunched up my eyes and peered at the Christian name again, trying to count the number of letters behind the line. I found it virtually impossible to decipher. I thumped the table with my cast, making a harsh sound in the silent room. Greg appeared around the edge of a unit, looking even more dishevelled than he had done half an hour before.

"Problem?"

"I can't read this *blasted* name." I scowled at it.

"Still impatient, I see," he smirked, coming over to the table and bending close to the page, squinting at the name I pointed to. He stood up, fingering his chin, his thin, fair hair flopping untidily into his eyes. "It's been expunged."

"*Ye-es,*" I said slowly.

"That's unusual."

When I didn't respond because my pulse thudded incoherently as I restrained my frustration, he went on.

"Oh *ri*-ght, and I suppose you want to know the identity of the person, do you?"

"Uh huh. Please."

He pursed his thin lips and looked at his watch.

"What's it worth to you? Fancy a pint at the White Lion?"

"Your degree, perhaps?" I reminded him again. I liked

Greg, but his pint would turn into three or more, and I wanted to get on.

"Worth a try. OK – follow me."

He lifted the book from the table, carrying it over to a large flat-bed machine nearby. He slipped a stiff, thin sheet of what looked like plastic underneath the page and flicked a switch, illuminating it from beneath. He then picked up a small block which emitted an ultraviolet light, and drew it across the erased name. Greg peered at the computer screen above the table, angling the block to get a better view. I tried to make out the blur of lines, then suddenly, out of the indistinct shapes, identifiable letters emerged. I craned forward, my fingers tracing each letter on the screen, then fell back, stunned.

"*Matthew*," I whispered. "It says *Matthew*."

"Looks like it," Greg said cheerfully. "Is that all you want?"

"Want?" I looked at him, dazed.

"Yes. Is that all you wanted to look at?"

"Oh. Yes; that was all I wanted to know. Thanks."

My mind whirred, going around and around in circles like a hamster in its wheel frantically going nowhere. Matthew. Lynes. *Matthew* Lynes, born 1609, here in Rutland. What a coincidence. Greg switched off the machine.

"If it's the Lynes you're interested in, have you been to Old Manor Farm?"

I snapped back into focus. "No – why, what's there?"

"Not much, but there's a few bits from the period in the remains of the church. You'll need permission to see it, of course, but the old lady's quite accommodating. Why don't you give it a go? Turn right when you leave here and take Brooke Road south out of Oakham for a couple of miles, through Brooke, then left for about a mile and a half along the track to the old house – bit narrow – gets boggy. Not much of it left now, but you can't miss it. Simple."

I frowned.

"Right. Brooke Road. Through Brooke. Turn right, then left. To the end and you're there," he simplified the directions for me.

"Right…" I said.

"That's right," he grinned. "Time for a pint?" he added hopefully.

"I'd love to, but I've things I need to do. Here…" I stuffed a ten-pound note in his hand. "Have one for me – for old times' sake."

He looked at it ruefully.

"That wasn't what I had in mind, Emma."

I looked at him, puzzled, then twigged what he meant and reddened.

"Sorry, but thanks all the same for giving up your morning for me. I couldn't have done this without you."

I stood on tiptoes and kissed his rough cheek. It was his turn to look bashful.

"Any time."

I made good my escape with Greg trailing limply behind me to the door. My father waited in the car, his fingers tapping on the steering wheel. Greg leaned against the stone jamb, sagging to one side as if standing straight constituted too much effort. He raised his voice, calling after me, "I don't suppose you know what's happened to Dr Hilliard, do you?" I stopped with my hand on the passenger door, suddenly wary, and turned to look at him.

"Why – have you heard something?"

"No, just wondered if you'd kept in contact. Seeing you reminded me of him. Difficult to forget, really – his sort always is." He gave a half-hearted shrug and scratched under his arm. "Well, I'd better be going; keep in touch though, won't you? Who would've believed it's been nearly ten years?" And he waved in farewell and went back inside.

The car was warm and smelled of mint humbugs.

"Successful?"

I thought about that for a moment, then decided it had been.

"Yes, in a way. But I'm not sure how yet."

He looked quizzical but didn't push for details. "Where to now?"

"Martinsthorpe, please – via Brooke. Old Manor Farm?"

He nodded. "I know it – not far from the Guash – I used to go fishing down there with your grandad."

"Did you? Have you been to the farm, then?"

He turned the car around in the road so that it faced south, and checked over his shoulder before pulling out.

"Before your mother and I were married, my mother and Nanna used to go for tea there before the war."

"That's extraordinary!" I exclaimed.

"It's a small world where we come from, Emma, and our family has been here a long time."

"I suppose…" I mused, thinking back to the Lynes family tree, wondering where the D'Eresbys fitted in. It occurred to me that, if Matthew proved to be a descendant of the Rutland Lynes after all, which seemed to be a fair possibility now, then he and I could be very distantly related. It would be an uncanny coincidence perhaps, but not as outlandish as what I proposed.

As we left Oakham's suburbs and ran through the countryside once more, I pondered why I wasn't finding that so hard to believe as I should have done; it didn't make sense

– *I* didn't make sense. Perhaps all that had happened over the past months had addled my wits after all, and I just didn't realize it yet.

The frost had lifted from the southern slopes of the rises but still clung in the hollows and on the north-facing dips, reminding me that the air temperature had hardly risen above zero. I nuzzled the scarf around my neck.

"That's his, isn't it?" Dad looked accusingly at the scarf; I noted he didn't use Matthew's name.

"It's Matthew's, yes," I said.

"You wear it a lot," he observed.

"Yes," I said quietly.

We didn't speak again until we reached the tiny village of Brooke and branched right. My father knew where to turn off the road onto the rough track, relieving me of the responsibility of finding our way. He slowed right down, allowing the wheels to negotiate the frozen ruts. Grass sprouted down the centre of the track like green tufts of hair from an old man's ears, long enough to brush the underside of the car as it wobbled and rattled at no more than walking pace. My father frowned hard, concentrating.

I broke the silence. "What do you remember of the farm?"

"There's not much of it left as a working farm, but what there is, is pretty old. It belongs to – or *belonged* to – a distant cousin on my father's side. Nanna was a friend of the family and Grandpa met her there during the war."

"Was he researching, then?"

My father paused whilst he negotiated a particularly deep rut.

"No, he was recuperating. You know he was injured in the war, don't you?"

I nodded.

"Well, he came here to recover – psychologically as well as physically. He had a job as their pig man to help him through it."

"A swineherd! No, really?"

The image of my gentle, learned and erudite grandfather mucking out the pigs tickled my sense of humour, before I remembered why he had needed to do it.

"Did it help him?"

"He met Nanna, so it must have done."

"Small world," I murmured, thinking about someone else; "and getting smaller."

"It is," he agreed.

We came to an opening in the low hedge that indicated an entrance, and he turned into a driveway of sorts that ran along a ridge of land east–west with far views over the gentle hills towards the expanse of Rutland Water in the distance. Tall, sand-yellow stone pillars flanked the entrance, each capped with a swan made of the same material, the carving worn with time. A large, ornate metal gate lay drunkenly to one side, entangled in a decade of broken brambles, their brown stems forming a twisted stranglehold on the rusting metal. A startled hare darted out in front of the car. Dad peered out of the window, his mouth turned down at the corners.

"It's changed – it wasn't always this ramshackle. I take it you have phoned to let them know we're coming?" he asked as we pulled to a stop outside the remains of a small gatehouse.

"No, not really," but I had already climbed out of the car, shutting the door as he began to remonstrate. Leaning on the warm bonnet, I shaded my eyes and surveyed the building some fifty yards away. Trees had grown up around the old house, shrouding the aged stone walls with bare branches, camouflaging the outline that gave away its age. The drive – or what was left of it – led anyone approaching the house over a deep moat and through the high stone arch of the gatehouse. Originally, this was an expensive and well-defended building, but not any more. Now, the moat was filled with the twisted cousins of the brambles that decorated the gate, the visible floor matted with the long stems of seasonal grasses, brown and decaying. It was anybody's guess whether it held water in its day. Much of the simple gatehouse had collapsed, the stone robbed for the building of a later range of barns, partially visible beyond a line of trees to the east. All that remained intact seemed held together by the tendrils of ivy that covered most of it. I glanced over my shoulder at my father, still sitting in the car as if ready to make a quick escape, and walked purposefully towards the entrance.

Sunlight dissolved into darkness beneath the arch, cushions of emerald moss, dew-dripped where the frost had lately melted, no longer catching the low winter sun. Although it was only just past midday, deep shadows clung to the walls of the stone-flagged courtyard into which I passed, and here the air felt perceptibly colder. The only signs of habitation were a thin curl of smoke from the tall chimney close to the east wing, and a bedraggled pelargonium – stem split brown by the frost – sitting by the side of the broad stone step in a lopsided pot. My heart thumping loudly in the still air, I raised a hand to the ancient door. Oak – bleached silver with age and studded with nail-heads the size of my thumb – it echoed hollowly to my enquiring knock. I didn't have a moment to prepare my introduction, as the door swung silently open, and an elderly woman – eyes wide at the sight of me – halted abruptly on the step. Her hand had shot up to her mouth and she now brought it down to clasp the other in front of her, automatically compiling her face into a mask of serene composure almost as soon as it had registered her surprise.

"Goodness, you gave me such a fright," she said, her enunciation precise and clipped, instantly making me want to stand up straight and behave myself. She stood with the confidence and poise of someone who knew where she belonged, and I felt awkward and clumsy in the presence of this elegant stranger whose privacy I had invaded.

"I am so sorry, I do apologize. I… this was a mistake. I'm sorry to have bothered you," I flustered, my mind blank, already beginning to turn and flee. A small, bird-like hand shot out and clamped firmly on my arm.

"My dear, do you have any notion of how utterly tedious it is here by myself? I only wish that I were *bothered* more often. Now, what did you come for? I hardly think you are selling anything, unless…" she eyed me sharply, "you are a purveyor of religion, in which case, I'm not interested, thank you."

She removed her hand and stood waiting expectantly, and I faced her, realizing how rude I must appear. Her small, wiry frame and quick, black eyes reminded me of a wood mouse, but she had the stillness and composure of a hawk. The two sat more comfortably beside each other than I would have expected.

"My name is Emma D'Eresby," I began, "and I'm looking for information on the Lynes family. I understand that there is some connection with the family here?"

"Are you, indeed?" She didn't say which of the two statements she referred to. "Those are two names I haven't heard in a long while. You had better come in…" Her eyes flicked away from me to focus behind my back. "There's a man lurking near my gatehouse; does he belong to you?"

I twisted sharply, and guiltily saw my father hovering uncertainly by a mounting block.

"He's my father," I confirmed.

"Well, bring him with you – he makes the place look untidy."

I caught the flash of humour in her dark eyes and beckoned to my father. The old woman had already disappeared, and I followed, pulling my reluctant father behind me, my eyes adjusting to the gloom. We entered a musty, dark hall where curtains hung across the great stair window, partially blocking the light struggling to find its way in. "Close the door behind you," her voice called from a room leading off the hall. Dad shut the wide door, making the frame shake as the iron lock found its home with a satisfyingly reverberant *chunk*. The hall wasn't big, but it had once been very fine with linen-fold panelling on all sides, now dull with age and damp. Beneath the tall window, the stairs dog-legged around a massive baluster that gave it strength. Light from the window fell across an Italian inlaid table in the middle of the hall, on which stood a bowl of last summer's hydrangea heads – faded blue and spun with the gossamer threads of a spider. The woman reappeared, her white hair an insubstantial aura framing her face.

"This way – don't trip over the cat," she added, as my foot stumbled over a large, soft, immovable object lying in front of an old Gurney radiator that looked as if it had come out of the Ark. The radiator belted out heat, and the huge ball of dark-brown fluff stretched and rolled onto its back languorously at the touch of my foot, wantonly inviting me to tickle its exposed, softly striped stomach. I stepped around it carefully and entered the room.

We stood in the remains of the great hall: not the cosy familiarity of the first-floor solar that would have served the family in terms of privacy, but the high-ceilinged public domain, with windows running down one side. Houses like this inspired Ebenezer Howard to build his concoction of the college in Maine. At least he had the luxury to include central heating, but here a fire burned in the coal-black grate of the large stone fireplace without making much of an impression on the overall temperature of the room. Our hostess, already seated on one of the two large faded chintz sofas huddling close for warmth either side of the fire, sat bolt upright with her legs crossed at the ankles. The stronger light from the range of windows showed that she must have been in her late eighties, but her eyes made her look much younger. They scrutinized us as we crossed the room towards her.

"May I introduce my father, Colonel D'Eresby," I said formally. Her mouth twitched as he held out his hand to her; she shook it lightly.

"Well, well, Hugh, it has been a long time." Recognition spilled across his face, and it lit in the broadest smile I had seen from him in many years. "Didn't recognize me at first, did you? Must be something to do with these," and she pulled at the wrinkled skin that lined her face.

"Joan… I had no idea you were still living here," he stammered.

"Still living, don't you mean? And I haven't seen you for… now, let me see… an outrageously long time. Your mother was still alive then, and you had only been married for a few years. Is this your eldest?" she asked, peering at me.

"No, Emma is my youngest daughter."

"Well, well. I can see both your parents in you, my dear, but you look more like your grandmother. How is she, by the way?"

I was thoroughly confused, but my father seemed to be following the thread.

"She's had a stroke, but she's holding her own. Penny will want to be remembered to you." He saw the query on my face. "I'm sorry, Joan; Emma – this is Mrs Seaton. This is Mr and Mrs Seaton's farm, where your grandfather came to recover. It was Mrs Seaton who was your grandmother's friend, if you remember."

"*Both* of them, my dear; all the families knew each other back then. We had such fun, but that was an age ago." Her eyes misted fleetingly, then her tone became brisk. "Now, you said you wanted some information on the Lynes family…"

"Emma! You said this was about your research," my father interjected, his face clouding with displeasure.

"It is…" I began, already on the defensive, but Mrs Seaton patted the sofa for me to sit beside her while giving my father a stern look.

"Be quiet, Hugh; the girl's old enough to know what she wants to ask."

My father puffed but kept quiet, eyeing the pair of us as if we had just won his favourite marble.

She neatened her tweed skirt over her knees. "The Lynes – yes. The family's died out now, of course, and they never lived in this house, but there are still remnants of them in the church – what's left of it. Is that what you are referring to?"

"I think it must be; I'm afraid I have very little to go on."

"Well, my dear, my husband was most interested in the history of the area; that's why he got on so well with your grandfather, of course. My husband was twenty years older than I am – if you are trying to work out the numbers."

I smiled sheepishly and tucked my fingers away in my sleeves where they had been secretly adding them up.

"Now, my husband did a great deal of research into the notable families of the area – including the Lynes – who, being a *new* family as such, proved somewhat elusive to trace. However…" she said as she saw my face fall, "there is a window – and a tomb – commemorating them, if you would like to have a look. Oh, and then, of course, there are the *stories*."

Stories. She could see she had my full attention.

"Just local tittle-tattle, embellished over the years, no doubt, but quite intriguing, nonetheless."

Dad's eyebrows were drawn so close together, barely a millimetre existed between them.

"Joan, I have to tell you – and I'm sorry to have to say this in front of you, Emma – but my daughter has been quite unwell lately. We have been very worried about her."

"Dad – *no*," I moaned.

Mrs Seaton smiled. "Well, I can see you have obviously been going the rounds with a pugilist, but you're on the mend now, aren't you, my dear? Now, where were we…"

"Joan, that is not the whole problem. Emma has been quite… low… recently, and Penny and I don't want her indulging in anything that might be *unhealthy*."

"*No*, Dad," I hissed, my face scarlet.

Mrs Seaton looked first at my father, then fixed me with an interested but hard stare.

"Surely there can be no harm in a little genealogical investigation, Hugh?" she said to him while still looking at me.

"The young man in question is a Lynes," my father continued, disregarding my glare.

"Leave him out of it," I warned, my temper only just under control.

"A Lynes?" It was Mrs Seaton's turn to be intrigued. "But not from around here, surely? The family died out centuries ago."

I couldn't help myself. I swivelled where I sat and faced

her, engaging her full attention to the exclusion of my father, who glowered at us from where he sat.

"But he is – he *must* be. Matthew Lynes; his family did come from this region, I'd stake my life on it. I know the family was supposed to have died out, but…"

She didn't let me finish. "Doesn't he know where he comes from?"

"He either doesn't know or doesn't want to say."

Her eyes sparkled. "Well – a mystery *and* a man's involved – how splendid. I'm *so* glad you dropped by. Hugh, I have a little job for you. You remember where the kitchens are?" He nodded, subdued. "Good, I'm parched, and I'm sure we could all do with a pot of tea. Do be a dear, will you?"

He started to say something, but she raised a bird-like hand to stop him.

"Don't worry about Emma. I'll make sure we don't discuss anything… unhealthy. Come along, my dear, I'll show you the chapel."

Joan Seaton led me through a series of dark corridors, each looking more dilapidated than the last, until we reached the highly decorated arch of what had once been a fine perpendicular church. The arch and doorway had been absorbed into the body of the house when the manor had been extended. She patted the gently eroded figure of a saint.

"This is what remains of St Martin's; it fell into disrepair several centuries ago when the village all but disappeared. My husband's family adopted it and it was still consecrated up until the outbreak of the war."

She turned the wrought-iron handle, and together we heaved the huge door open. She hopped down the raised stone step, more spry in her advanced years than I felt at nearly sixty years her junior. She tweaked a Bakelite dolly switch, and a number of dim bulbs soaked the interior in a wash of yellow light. The church smelled of damp stone and decaying plaster, white flakes of distemper hanging like patches of peeling skin from the walls. Above our heads, wooden angels, borne on dainty columns of stone, smiled benignly from the hammer-beam roof, and beneath my feet were worn images of knights on horseback and fleur de lys in alternate red and cream squares. All of one aisle had been lost to time, the pillars now blindly embedded in a featureless wall. But the other aisle remained intact, and Mrs Seaton drew me towards the far end beneath a sun-bright window. I let my eyes adjust. The figures of a man and a woman slept on a raised marble tomb set against the wall. Darkened through years of neglect, but still clearly discernible, their mode of dress defined their religious ideology and the era in which they died. I knew – even before I deciphered the basic Latin inscription set in the plaque on the side of the tomb – who they were. Buried decades apart, Henry and Margaret Lynes lay together in devout repose. Either side of the plaque, two other figures knelt in supplication: one a young child, the other clearly older but defaced, so that only the kneeling body remained. I ran my fingers over the mutilated form, feeling the score marks where a metal blade had been taken to the cold marble: this had been no random act of vandalism but a calculated violation of someone's memory.

"Quite strange, isn't it?" Mrs Seaton was saying. "We always wondered why this one was targeted so deliberately."

To suffer such condemnation in an age where belonging – whether to your family, your village or your God – was everything, must have been like being consigned to a living death. My heart went out to this stranger across the centuries.

"His name was Matthew Lynes," I said, quietly. "He was their eldest child and his name has been expunged from the parish records as well. He must have done something heinous to have deserved this."

"*Matthew* Lynes – yes, of course."

His name seemed to strike a distant chord, and she became suddenly and vibrantly alive.

"But he wasn't removed from *this*, my dear."

She took me by my shoulders, shuffling me back until I could see the window above the tomb through which the sun streamed, throwing rainbow colours across the tiled floor.

A memorial window, the sort you see in parish churches everywhere, celebrating the good fortune of the family, and recording its endowment of the church at which they worshipped. It must have been made sometime before the outbreak of the Civil War, perhaps in the 1630s, although I found it difficult to pin a date to, as the style of the image looked at least a decade earlier. I scanned the window, the finely painted detail bearing witness to the wealth of the three generations of family it depicted.

The family had been divided into age groups either side of the window – men on one side, women on the other, facing each other. The oldest generation wore high Elizabethan clothes, heavily decorated and rich in colour; this must be Henry Lynes the grandfather and his wife – who, I remembered, carried the same name as I did. Next, Henry and Margaret opposite each other in simpler, dark attire with less extravagant collars, the fabric of their clothes still expensive, the cut of the doublet and the full dress, ample. Margaret must have been dead for some years when the window was commissioned, her face fresh and youthful, her blue eyes bright, but it was the figures opposite her that kept me transfixed. Below the image of her husband, a baby bound in shrouds, eyes closed in death, and the other – a young man of about twenty, handsome even in glass, his hair radiant gold – unmistakably a Lynes – unmistakably *Matthew*.

A sudden, violent thrumming filled my ears and the room rotated horrendously, light fading fast as I sank towards the ground and it swallowed me whole.

"My dear, are you all right?"

Mrs Seaton's thin, knot-veined legs in flesh-coloured tights stood over me, her face a mixture of curiosity and concern. Her long necklace of jade beads swung as she bent towards me. The ground felt hard, the cold tiles rigid beneath my back. I blinked, feeling stupid. I managed to sit upright without the aisle cavorting around me, then clambered to my feet, leaning against the Lynes tomb for support.

"Don't tell my father," I said queasily.

"You took me by surprise; that was quite a spectacular faint. What could have caused that now, I wonder?"

She looked up at the window so familiar to her, trying to see it through my eyes.

"I expect it's nothing more exciting than low blood sugar." My head pounded – a mass of conflicting information at once vying for attention. I checked the window again, expecting it to have somehow changed, but Matthew still regarded heaven as calmly as if he were standing next to me, his hands together in prayer, a tiny painted line across his little finger indicating a ring.

Matthew. *My* Matthew?

What madness was this? Blood burned my veins, pushing prickled sweat to the surface of my skin. I felt overwhelmed as much by the visual imagery as by the significance it held.

I blinked, and blinked again, but the image remained the same.

"Are you quite sure you are all right?" Mrs Seaton was asking. "I can fetch your father if you wish, my dear?"

That shook me out of myself.

"No – thank you. Really, I'm fine." Yet I couldn't take it all in, trying to imprint the window as best I could. "Would you mind terribly if I take some photos while I'm here? It'll save me so much time trying to describe things in words."

Mrs Seaton seemed relieved at the normality of the request.

"No, of course not, take your time. I'm going to see if your father has managed to locate the kettle. Please don't faint again when I'm gone; it does quite give me palpitations and I don't think my old heart can take it." She turned to leave the church.

"Mrs Seaton – please, don't say anything to him…"

"I won't," she assured me. "As you say, there is nothing to tell." She glanced at the window once more, then hopped up the step like a sparrow.

I went and sat down with my back against a column and stared up at the window, and at the painted cross around which the little family worshipped.

"I don't understand," I implored. "Please help me to *understand*."

Black branches of an old yew, grown vast with age, waved against the glass, throwing figures into sudden darkness through which sharp shafts of sun struck. Random shafts, shifting then stilling as the wind dropped, leaving his face radiant and alive. I breathed out slowly. One thing appeared certain: if that was Matthew, then whoever he lived with in Maine could not possibly be his father and mother, because his *parents* lay stone dead and buried in front of me.

I took a series of photographs from every conceivable angle using the little mobile phone Matthew had given me and which I carried close as a reminder of him. It seemed somehow fitting that I captured his past using something of his so ostentatiously from the present. I tried to persuade myself that the image in front of me must be an ancestor of his, his striking looks no more than a genetic throwback to an earlier age. It would have made sense – would have taken a far lesser leap of the imagination. But that Matthew's image looked serenely out of the past I believed to be beyond debate. *Complications* – he had once told me came between us. Complications.

I took one final look around the church before closing the door behind me, reluctant to leave, not knowing when – or if – I would see him again. I made my way back the way we had come and heard my father's deep bass and Mrs Seaton's clear peal; they were laughing.

"Tell me about the stories," I urged, once I had my hands wrapped around a delicate bone china cup filled with strong, fragrant tea. I almost sat in the fireplace trying to keep warm. Mrs Seaton – cheeks glowing with the unaccustomed company and the thrill of an unsolved mystery – began to talk.

"Henry Lynes the elder had two surviving sons – Henry and William." I nodded, remembering the family tree. "Henry was the elder by quite some years and he had been betrothed from a young age to Margaret Fielding, who was the heiress to one of the minor noble families in the area. Well…" she inched forward like a schoolgirl eager to share some fresh piece of gossip, "the younger son – William – was quite taken by Margaret and tried to persuade her to break off her betrothal to his brother. Of course, that would mean that the Fielding fortune would be his, putting him in a much stronger position politically as well as financially. Their father got wind of the situation and told William in no uncertain terms what would happen if he tried any tricks like that again." She placed the palms of both hands together. "Now, all was well for the time being; Henry married Margaret and it seemed like a happy union and she gave him an heir – Matthew – wasn't it?" I nodded again. "What a *coincidence*..." she mused, her eyes suddenly on me. I didn't react and she shook her head a little before continuing. "Anyway, tragedy struck when, a few years later, she gave birth to a baby who died shortly after, and Margaret died days later." So, my supposition had been correct on that point. "Henry was heartbroken and he never married again."

"Where did the gossip enter into the equation, then?" I asked, puzzled, as so far the story seemed straightforward.

"Wait – I haven't reached the good bit yet."

Even my father leaned forward, eager to catch every word. The old woman's face became animated, her normally still hands circumscribing the air.

"Henry went about his daily life with one eye on his estates and the other eye on Heaven. He had a reputation as a plain-speaking, pious man with Protestant leanings, so it came as no surprise when he backed the Parliamentary cause at the outbreak of the Civil War. William, however, had developed a reputation of quite another kind. He had never forgiven his brother for marrying Margaret and seemingly held a grudge. He never married but had a string of liaisons with some notorious women. Old Grandfather Lynes died fearing the reputation of the family would be lost, and he charged Henry with the task of sorting William out. Well, of course that was *nonsense*, my dear; William was having far too much fun to allow his older brother to do anything of the sort. William took up with a group of Royalist supporters just to spite his brother." She broke off to catch her breath as her voice became increasingly thin, and patted her flat chest, making the jade beads vibrate with the motion.

"Henry had brought up his surviving son and heir to be a dutiful and God-fearing young man who believed it his Christian duty to serve God, his father and his country, using the gifts he had been given. After graduating from Cambridge, he came back to help run the estate but, when things were looking sticky – politically, I mean – he joined one of the military bands in the area, much to his father's dismay. He became a formidable swordsman and had the respect of officers and men alike. Well, in 1642 tensions grew between the king and Parliament – I'm sure you know all this – but trouble was also brewing between the brothers. William used his allegiances as an excuse to threaten the family seat by the River Chater. The house has long since gone, you know – there was only a pile of rubble when I was a girl, and that must be almost a century ago." She sighed and I nearly bounced in my seat in an agony of anticipation. "William drew together a band of hotheads and their men – they gave the Royalist cause a terrible name – such a shame…" I groaned out loud. "Yes, yes, I'm getting to it, my dear. William and about forty men marched on the house one night; the flames from their torches could be seen from here, you know; they quite lit up the sky. Henry was too ill to do much more than stand, but his son…"

"Matthew," I whispered, seeing him there.

"Yes, Matthew – met them at the gatehouse with as many men as he could muster in the short space of time. He had little warning – the gatekeeper had fallen asleep; he was an old man and Henry had kept him on out of pity. Anyway, William liked his nephew and had no quarrel with him and invited him to join him as his heir. Matthew, of course, declined and made a counter-offer that, if William withdrew immediately and sought terms of peace with Henry, then the matter would be forgotten. William had been drinking as usual and he was full of bravado and, in any case, he didn't wish to lose face in front of his comrades, who were happily cheering him on since it wasn't *their* fight to lose. William jeered at Matthew and threatened to give him a thrashing, but Matthew stood his ground, although the household staff were outnumbered. William grew more and more angry with his nephew, who still refused to give way; it seemed that he would defend his home with his life, if that was what it would take – how dashing! The scene became increasingly hostile, when Henry at last rose from his sickbed to plead with his brother, fearing for his son's life. He promised William half his estate if he would withdraw, but William saw Henry's weakened state and pushed the advantage. There was a harsh exchange between the brothers, with Matthew trying to make peace, but then a trigger-happy bandit let loose his pistol and the bullet struck the wooden bridge, just missing Henry. Well, my dear, all hell broke loose, so to speak. Matthew drew his sword and would have killed the man there and then if he had been given free rein, but his father stopped him. William lunged forward to attack his unarmed brother, but Matthew leapt between them, although he'd only had time to don a leather coat and neckpiece – oh, what's it called, the bit that protects the neck?"

"Do you mean the gorgette?" I offered.

Mrs Seaton nodded and her whole body shook with her

vehemence. "I do so hate getting old – it quite turns one's head to porridge. Anyway, as Matthew turned away to protect his father, his uncle struck him from behind, like the coward he was… are you all right my dear?"

I could feel my eyes staring in abject horror, my hands covering my mouth to prevent a moan of alarm from escaping. My voice strained where I had been holding my breath.

"Yes – carry on."

"If it hadn't been for the leather… oh, what *do* you call it… the jerkin thing they wore beneath their armour…?"

"Buff coat."

"Ah, yes, well, if it hadn't been for the buff coat and William's inebriated state, Matthew would have been killed outright. As it was, the weight of the blow knocked him to the ground, but he managed to turn just in time to raise his sword to ward off the next strike. By now, the whole bridge swarmed with William's men. But Matthew had trained the household staff well over the previous months, and they took defensive lines, protecting Henry on Matthew's orders and taking him back behind the walls. Gradually, with a few guns on the defensive wall, William's men were driven off the bridge – they didn't have the guts for a protracted fight. But William was as stubborn as his nephew and at last they faced each other. Now, William had been drinking, it's true, but he wasn't so far gone as to not be able to put his years of brawling to good use. Matthew was younger and well trained, but not as heavily built as his uncle, and he had a damaged shoulder from the first blow – he couldn't use it properly. He was quick on his feet though, and he dodged the sword as his uncle brought it down on his head. William tried to wear Matthew down by raining blows on him in quick succession, but Matthew was too quick and too skilled for him and, as his uncle raised his arm to strike again, he thrust his rapier up into his unguarded shoulder, and down William went."

I breathed a sigh of relief but Mrs Seaton hadn't finished. She adjusted her posture and pulled the sleeves of her worn cardigan down over her bony wrists.

"Everyone thought the fight over and William's men retreated – even his so-called friends – disappearing without waiting to see what happened to their leader. Matthew hadn't intended to kill his uncle, just stop him, and he went to help him get up, but at that moment, William struck, piercing Matthew through the lacing of his leather coat, stabbing straight into his heart with his long knife – it had a special name, my husband said – main... *main gauche*. Matthew collapsed and his uncle actually laughed at him as he lay dying in front of him. Can you believe it, my dears? *Laughed* at him."

The blood drained from my face as I watched Matthew bleed to death in front of me, and my heart faltered; it wasn't Matthew – at least not *my* Matthew – after all. If this man died in the seventeenth century, as it seemed he did, what wild goose had I been chasing, and what sort of insane fool did that make me? I drew my hand across my eyes, willing my mouth to work.

"But... but then, why wasn't his death recorded in the parish records, since everything else had been so well documented?"

"But that's just it!" Mrs Seaton exclaimed, clapping her hands in delight. "He *didn't* die. His men carried him into the house with the knife still in his chest, expecting him to take his last breath at any moment. His father sat by him all night and the following day. And the next. And the next. Matthew remained unconscious but alive for weeks and weeks, and then, one day, over a month later, he woke up and spoke.

People thought it a miracle, my dear, and he even had a visit from the bishop and a special service of thanksgiving."

The goose wasn't looking quite so wild after all.

"He *survived*?"

"Yes, against all odds, and gradually – as he grew stronger – people began to forget the miracle. But then the rumours began."

She paused to take a sip of her now cold tea, taking a lace-edged linen hankie from her sleeve and dabbing at the tide-mark around her lips. "That's better!" she exclaimed.

"Rumours?" I prompted, never for one moment taking my eyes from her face, as if doing so would break the spell she cast over us.

"Ah yes, the rumours, my dear. Matthew grew stronger and stronger and he began to take risks..." She hiccupped delicately. "Oh, I do beg your pardon." She waited for it to settle, then continued. "It was almost as if he were testing himself to his limits – testing God, some said. It was the height of the witch trials and ugly rumours began to circulate, some saying that it hadn't been a miracle at all but that he had made a pact with the devil. Well, you can imagine – in a climate of fear like the one that prevailed at the time..."

Imagine? I didn't need to – it had formed the basis of my research for years. I shivered involuntarily. "What happened?"

She sank back against the upholstery. "Nothing."

"Nothing at all?"

"Nothing. Matthew disappeared, and all the fuss died down. His father died sometime afterwards – in despair, it was said."

Silence hung like a shroud, the gentle decay of the old building around us mirroring the decline of a once proud house.

She shook her head. "No wonder the tomb was desecrated and his name obliterated; his poor father."

"Poor Matthew," I murmured.

My father broke through our reflection for the first time since Mrs Seaton had begun her tale. We both looked up at him in surprise, forgetting he sat there. His thick-set shoulders hunched forward with a challenge in them.

"Who recorded it? How is all this known in such detail?"

That was a very good question and one I might have thought of myself if I hadn't been so preoccupied.

"There *were* lots of witnesses, of course, but the estate manager – the steward – oh, what was his name? – your grandfather did tell me…" She flapped an insubstantial hand, trying to conjure the name from the air.

"Richardson," I supplied.

"That's the chappie – well, he was the main witness at the trial and he recorded everything."

"Whose trial?" my father and I both asked simultaneously. Mrs Seaton plainly thought it obvious.

"William's, of course. He *was* the ringleader and the attack *was* unprovoked and the local Royalist families didn't want their cause tainted by his renegade actions. Even if Henry Lynes was a Parliamentarian, his reputation and standing in the area meant that William's behaviour caused outrage among Royalist and Parliamentarian factions alike. And as for the way he attacked his nephew – well, my dears, nobody tolerated cowardice on *that* scale. Richardson had William taken into house arrest, patched up and handed over to the local militia or magistrate or something, and held for trial."

"You said that Richardson was the main witness and that he made a record of the event; where is it now?" I asked, thinking of the journal.

"Did I say *he* recorded it? Oh dear, how very imprecise of me. No, it was his *evidence* that they recorded, along with the other witnesses. I think it must be in the county archives, or it might not have survived the war – I'm not sure. Your dear grandfather would have known, of course. But it is part of our local history, as well as the family's, and it's what my husband remembered being told by his granny when he was a little boy, and she by hers. It was just considered a small skirmish at the time – outrageous, of course – but not important in the grand scheme of things."

No, I could see that it would have faded into obscurity along with the family, both a footnote to the much more significant events of the time.

"So they executed William?" I said.

"Yes, and the male line died out, or at least it supposedly did. But you say you know a descendant? Where – is he local? I don't believe I've heard of anybody of that name around here."

I felt my father fix his gaze on me, watching for signs that I might be cracking up, no doubt. Perhaps I was.

"No, the Matthew Lynes I know is an American doctor; I must have been mistaken. His name is just a coincidence."

I saw, out of the corner of my eye, my father look askance at my lack of consistency.

Mrs Seaton's face took on the aspect of a disappointed child. "What a shame! Wouldn't it have been thrilling if he had been a descendant of *our* Matthew Lynes after all."

"Or William Lynes," I pointed out. Whatever my thinking, no way would I share those thoughts with anyone else, especially since my sanity was one white coat away from having me committed. "There might have been an illegitimate line through William." A thought struck me. "Matthew would have been what – thirty-two, thirty-three at the time of the attack; wasn't he married?"

"No, not married. He had been at Cambridge, you see, studying divinity – or was it medicine? – before he took up arms. Anyway, he hadn't married…" I drew a silent sigh of relief, "… but he was engaged. To a Harrington heiress, I believe."

My relief was instantly replaced by a warm flood of unprovoked, indefensible jealousy that rose to burn in my cheeks. I looked down and pretended to fiddle with my shoe. Mrs Seaton went on, oblivious.

"By the time Matthew – I am *so* glad you've reminded me of his name after all these years – by the time he recovered, the girl's family had broken off the engagement and she married someone else."

I couldn't help the trickle of satisfaction I felt, and silently admonished myself for my selfishness.

"If no male heir survived, what happened to the lands?" asked my father, ever practical in these matters, since he found himself in the same position. Last of the D'Eresby male line, our family name would die with him unless I married a man willing to adopt my name. I chewed my lip, thinking the likelihood of that looked distinctly remote.

"… And the lands were bestowed on the older sister and her heirs, but not the Lynes *name*, of course," Mrs Seaton was saying. "But the house wasn't lived in again, and it fell into disrepair, with much of the stone robbed. I believe this building has a fair amount in the new wing. I like to think it lives on in this old pile, although for how much longer I really couldn't say. Once I'm dead, I doubt that my son will want the bother of the old place."

She appeared quite matter-of-fact about the matter but, as she sat there all vital and sprightly, I couldn't imagine her not being part of the building, a living embodiment of its history and nearly a sixth of its age. Perhaps she would imbue it with some of her spirit, as some of my forebears resonated in the walls of my own home.

"Well, well, so there you are, my dear. I do love a good story."

Dad stood up, pulling his still-buttoned tweed jacket down at the back, ready to go. Mrs Seaton seemed reluctant to let us leave. She put her bird-like hand on my arm and leaned conspiratorially close to me while looking sideways up at my father.

"My dear, did I mention that your father was a bit of a rascal in his day?"

I shook my head automatically, still embroiled in the story just recounted.

My father blustered. "I really don't think Emma needs to hear about that…" but Mrs Seaton cheeped on.

"Don't be taken in by his veneer of respectability," she twinkled at me. "He cut quite a dashing figure, you know, quite the ladies' man. Before he met your mother at one of our tennis parties – did you know we had the most *splendid* grass courts back then? Tennis and Pimms… I swear the summers were longer then… Anyway, before he met your mother, there was Susan Forde…"

"*Aunt* Susan?" I turned to stare at him. It was one of those strange facts that comes as a shock when you realize that your parents had a life – a sex life – before you were born. "You said that Grandma and Nanna used to come here, Dad; you didn't say *you* did."

"Good heavens, your father was a frequent visitor and Susan was definitely not your *aunt*, my dear. She thought – and we all had the same impression – that there would be an engagement before the year was out, but then we had that fabulous tennis party – you remember, Hugh, don't you? The one where Teddy broke his elbow…"

"… And Penny had to take his place in the doubles. Yes, of course I remember; how could I forget? She had a magnificent backhand." His face softened.

"You jilted Aunt Susan? How could you, Dad? That was a rotten thing to do!"

He missed the intended jibe and grumped, but Mrs Seaton caught it and we both burst out laughing at the look on his face.

"I think it's probably time we were making a move, Joan; we've imposed on you quite long enough." He tried to maintain his dignity but failed miserably, succeeding in looking awkward instead.

"Never mind, Hugh," Mrs Seaton said, chortling at his discomfort. "Your secret's safe with me. Don't take yourself so seriously. Ah, but I haven't had a good laugh like that for a long while; you've been quite a tonic – the pair of you. And as for you…" she said, taking me by the arm and looking directly at me, "… there's nothing wrong with *you* that a good doctor can't fix."

It was my turn to colour horribly, and I didn't know where to look – certainly not at my father, who made his displeasure perfectly clear.

She walked us slowly, reluctantly, to the gnarled front door, which had seen so much history that I wanted to absorb it through my living skin; instead, I let my fingers trail along its surface as the cold air greeted us.

"I do hope that we will meet again, but at my age, my dear, that might be asking too much. Life is always too short for all the things we hoped to do but never quite got around to doing.

Well, there you are; do remember me to your grandmother and mother, won't you?"

I assured her that I would, and we left her looking suddenly frail and shrunken on the doorstep of her world.

6

Ghosts

The tension in the car on the way back home became palpable as my father sank into a brooding, tight-lipped silence. I ignored it for as long as I could, but my hopes were futile, and the simmering suspense boiled into a familiar rant, starting with an accusation.

"I thought you said you were researching for your college work – not anything to do with that… doctor."

I stared out of the windscreen, watching the white lines in the centre of the road whip before me, waiting for the rest of it.

"You lied to me, Emma. Don't think that I'm taken in by what you told Joan Seaton. I know you think there's some connection between *him* and this Lynes family Joan spoke about. What I want to know is why you find it necessary to lie about it – why you have to deceive us."

That hurt and I bit my lip, fighting the urge to snap back. He was right, of course; I had lied about why I wanted to go to Oakham and Martinsthorpe, but the obfuscation went far further than that, far back into my childhood, and I didn't want to get drawn into a fight with him. He continued talking, using that "I'm being the responsible parent" tone he always adopted when he lectured me.

"There's a lack of trust here, Emma – a fundamental lack of trust. If your mother and I can't believe you over something as simple as this…"

I tried not to let my voice wobble. "Don't bring Mum into it; this is between you and me."

"Trust," he continued regardless. "A question of duty and trust. You were not completely honest about this boy, were you?"

Anger, uncontrollable and hot, welled up in me and I clutched at the edge of the car seat, on the brink of combustion. My broken arm ached from the pressure.

"Matthew – his name's Matthew – not *him*, not *that doctor*, not *boy*. Matthew – use his name."

He grunted. "*Matthew* – if you insist." He twisted his name into something ugly. That did it.

"Yes, I bloody well *do* insist!"

"There's no need to swear…" He swerved to miss a rabbit at the edge of the road. I ground my teeth together, feeling the edges grate painfully.

"This Matthew – you lied to us about him."

"No – I didn't tell you the whole truth – there's a difference."

"Not in my books…"

"Always *your* books, *your* rules. Have you never asked yourself why I find it necessary not to tell you everything that goes on in my life? Have you? I'll tell you, shall I? Do you remember what happened when I was stupid enough to tell you about Guy? I thought that I could trust you when I needed your help. I came to you and you let me down. You went behind my back and…"

"It was my duty as your father to protect you; the man took advantage of you."

"But you didn't have to *hit* him – what century are you living in, for goodness' sake!"

"Being a father means making some difficult decisions on your behalf."

"How could you make any decisions for me when you don't even know me? How *dare* you make assumptions about me based on… based on your antiquated notion of duty."

My voice had risen until it filled the claustrophobic interior of the car.

"I'm driving, Emma."

"Well, bloody well stop driving and *listen*."

He didn't correct me this time and instead glared ahead at the road, taking a sharp right turn, crossing the trickle of oncoming traffic. He drew into a parking area above the reservoir, where a few other cars slumbered with their windows misted with condensation. He switched off the engine and released the catch on his seatbelt, pivoting cumbersomely in his seat.

"Now, what is all this about?"

I saw his closed expression, his mind made up before I could explain mine.

"Haven't you heard a word I've said? Or don't you *want* to listen? I don't tell you about my life because you have *never – been – part – of – it*."

I emphasized each word, driving it home with all the venom of years of hurt that I could muster. His heavy face blanched, then flushed, then lost all colour again. I had hit home and I was merciless.

"When were you ever there for me when I needed you? When… when were you there to help me with my homework or to watch the Christmas play at school? I don't ever remember you just *being* there at all. My friends had fathers who were at least visible. But you – the only times I saw you were when you had my school report in your hand. 'Why did you only get a B, Emma?' 'I expected you to do better than that, Emma.' 'History isn't a proper career, Emma.' I was never good enough, Dad; I was always a *disappointment*."

He didn't say anything, but I could tell that at last he was taking in everything I could fling at him.

"Do you know what Beth said to me the other day? She said she's jealous of me because she thinks you love me more than her because you paid me more attention; and all the while I was jealous of her, because at least she got to see you when she was young. Hah!" I spat. "We've wasted years being jealous of each other, and for *what*? The only time I felt truly loved – other than by Mum and Nanna – was by Grandpa…"

I remembered what Matthew had said about my father's perception of my grandfather's role in my life, but I strode roughshod and callous on ground brittle with years of battle, beyond caring.

"He loved me for who I am, not for what he could make me. He spent time with me, he taught me things – he *talked* to me. And he listened. Even when it must have been as boring as hell for him, he still listened. And he didn't judge me, or criticize me. He let me *breathe*, he let me *grow*. Do you understand?"

My father's voice came rough and low.

"I had to be a father to you; your grandfather didn't have that responsibility – he didn't have to discipline you. I didn't like it, but that's what a father has to do."

I shook my head in disbelief. "Dad, listen to yourself – while you pontificate about the duties of fatherhood, did you not think that one of them might be *loving* your children?"

Hurt flashed in his eyes. "I do love you, Emma – and your sister – of course I do…"

"When did you last tell us that you love us?" I challenged, not wanting to soften the attack, but sensing creeping compassion for a wounded animal nonetheless. I steeled myself, but he made it easy to resist giving in.

"Tell you? I shouldn't have to tell you, you should know."

"How? By telepathy?" I shot at him. "When did you – *do* you – ever show us you love us? You haven't and you don't. I'll tell you why I don't tell you everything about my life – it's because I can't trust you to support me in the decisions I make, and part of loving me as a father is to *trust* me."

"I don't want to see you get hurt."

"You see? That's just my point; you don't trust me even to make my own mistakes. You smother me, Dad, you always have. You smother me with your expectations and your criticism and you just won't *let me go*."

"But you can trust this… Matthew – is that it, Emma? You can trust this stranger whom you've known for a matter of weeks, more than your own family – than your own father."

"With my *life*… I already have."

He became angry now, all pretence of maintaining dignity lost beneath a welter of gall, his mouth distorted. I looked at him, suddenly aware; I saw him and I understood.

"You're *jealous*!" I said, stunned.

"Ridiculous," he barked back.

I gave a short, mirthless laugh. "Matthew said you were jealous of my relationship with Grandpa, but it's not just that, is it? You're jealous of Matthew. You were jealous of Guy. Of course. Of course, of *course*…"

My father slumped back in his car seat like a deflated balloon, all fight gone. It all began to make sense. All the years spent arguing, and neither of us had even begun to understand where the other was coming from.

When he spoke, it was almost to himself, and his voice shook.

"I should never have let the family be separated – it was a mistake – we should have stayed together, or I should have left the Army earlier. But we wanted you to have more stability than we had given Beth, and I was too driven to give up my career. My *career*." His face skewed.

I had just heard him admit for the first time in my entire life that a decision he had made had been wrong.

"I didn't want you growing up thinking I didn't care. And you were always such a bright little girl. I tried to show an interest in what you were doing…" His voice broke, and he held his clenched fist to his mouth, biting on the knuckle. "I always found it difficult to be close to you, Emma – to show you how much I loved – love you. I still do."

He sounded like a little boy – lost, alone, affectionless. The hurt that had driven my anger turned to pity.

"I know, Dad. I think I understand."

We sat together as the car steamed up, both staring blindly as the sharp blue of the wind-rippled water below us disappeared behind the misting windscreen, lost in our own parallel worlds. I wondered when they had ever touched. It was well past teatime, and the setting sun ripened the western sky apricot.

"Dad, let's go home."

He nodded mutely and turned the key in the ignition, letting the air from the engine warm and clear the windscreen before reversing the car across the rough surface of the car park. Now our wounds had been laid bare, what salve could we apply that wouldn't irritate them further? And would time in itself prove to be the healer, or merely provide a scab that could be picked at whenever our tempers itched? I knew from my past that some wounds can only be healed from within, but only once all infection has been excised. I had cut Guy out of my life and allowed God into it, but if healing were to begin, first I had to remove my defences. The problem with that was that they had been built for a purpose. Sometimes, though – as Matthew had found to his cost – the enemy lies within.

CHAPTER

7

The Horse's Mouth

My father went straight to the potting shed when we arrived home. My mother watched his broad back from the dining room window as he retreated down the narrow courtyard. I explained what had happened between us, abbreviating some of it, leaving out the bits about which I felt ashamed – but basically keeping to the gist of the truth. Mum didn't seem very surprised, her careworn face neither critical nor judging – just accepting this crisis as inevitable.

"Your father gets very low; he always has done. It's why he's been so concerned for your... well, your mental health; he thinks you might have inherited the same problem."

We sat on the side of the rosewood dining table closest to the electric fire, a large mug of tea and a pile of toast with last year's wineberry jam in front of me.

"I didn't know."

"No, of course not. Why should you, darling? He's always tried to hide it from you. He's ashamed and he doesn't want you or your sister to be burdened by it."

"So Beth doesn't know?"

"Of course she does. She's seen much more of him than you have recently, and she remembers Grandad's black-dog days – which I expect you don't?"

"No – not really."

Tiberius emerged from the cupboard by the fire and jumped onto my knee, wobbled, then settled into an ungainly heap as heavy and immovable as a doorstop. I tickled his paw until he retracted his claws.

"You know that both of your grandfathers served in the Royal Engineers, and that Grandad rose to the rank of general, don't you? He was always very ambitious, and he expected your father to equal his rank. And he could have done, you know; he had a very promising career ahead of him. It came as a terrible disappointment when he wasn't promoted. I didn't care, of course; he did well enough for me, but then, I was part of the problem…"

"Why?"

"I didn't fulfil the role of the dutiful Army wife, did I? By the time we'd managed to nearly ruin Beth's education, I'd had enough of coffee mornings and jamborees and the endless, *endless* parties – oh, you have no idea of the tedium! Well, I decided I wasn't going to put you through all that, and came back to England when you were a tot. It was the best thing for your education, but perhaps not for you." She considered me sadly. "Do you know, it broke your father's heart not having you with him, but he let me have my way – even if he didn't agree with it."

The cat's tail flicked towards my uneaten toast; I pushed the plate further away.

"He said it was because of his career… that it was his choice."

Mum laughed quietly. "Ever the gentleman." I looked surprised. "Oh no, that's more like him than you think, darling. The decision to return to England was entirely mine, and it ruined his chances of promotion; he was passed over from then on. It mattered then, you see – the wife not being there to support her husband's career. But do you know, not once in all these years has he brought it up, and he's never held it against me…" her face softened, "… and definitely not against you. But he didn't want you to make the same mistakes; he wanted you to achieve everything he hadn't."

I ruminated, chewing the toast without tasting it.

"I said some pretty horrible things. He didn't deserve everything I said – some of it – but not all. I think I might have really hurt him."

Mum looked down at her hands folded in her lap and started to twist her wedding ring around and around before replying. When she did, she spoke with understated wisdom.

"I think it needed to be said – whatever it was – for both your sakes. You have been at each other's throats for so long, you've both lost sight of where it all started and now… well, now perhaps it is time. You are as stubborn as each other and more alike than either of you would wish to admit. Let's just hope that it will help you both in the long run." She stood up stiffly and eased her shoulders. "I've finished Archie's sweater at last; I just have to sew up the seams. I do hope he behaves himself and doesn't grow too much before Christmas; I've almost run out of wool." She looked down at me. "I'm going to take your father a cup of tea and a slice of Dundee cake, and see if that'll do the trick."

I leapt up, startling the cat, who slid onto the floor with a *thud* and a loss of dignity.

"Let me do that, Mum."

She smiled tiredly. "That's very sweet of you, darling; he'll appreciate it."

I didn't try to initiate a conversation when I took him his tea and my father didn't say anything to me. It felt earthily warm in the potting shed, and I found him perched forlornly on the upturned milk crate he used sometimes as a makeshift seat. I put the small tray down carefully in a free space on the potting bench, next to some sturdy cuttings, and kissed him on his weathered cheek with more affection than I had shown him for a very long time.

The old house resounded with the great bells of St Mary's as they called worshippers to the evening service. I climbed the broad stairs with a Thermos of tea in one hand, a plate of Dundee cake and pork pie in the other, and the strap of my document case over my shoulder. I didn't intend leaving my room until I had accomplished the one task I had put off for far too long.

I had avoided thinking about what I had seen and heard in Martinsthorpe because a part of me didn't want to believe it. It complicated matters and could make no sense in a rational world, and the fact that I even contemplated it placed me beyond wisdom. The little phone sat sleekly in the palm of my hand, silent as ever but now containing the photographs – the evidence – that had turned my life inside out. If I felt this way, how would Matthew react when I told him what I knew? For that matter, what did I know?

I knew his identity now. I knew where he came from, who his family were – no, who his family *had* been – where he was born and where he should have died. I knew *how* he should have died and I knew the name of the man who tried to kill him. But what I didn't know and couldn't understand was why he wasn't dead and why, *why* this knowledge didn't frighten me. I flipped the mobile in my hand and summoned it to life. I could call him – I ached to hear his voice – and tell him... what? Would he deny it? Laugh at me? Become angry? Where would that leave me? Did I risk more in telling him what I knew than in keeping silent and playing dumb? It wouldn't work; his was a secret that broke the bounds of everything I thought I understood, putting him in the sphere of the unknown. Yes, I knew who he was – but I still hadn't a clue as to *what* he was.

I allowed the mobile to slumber once again, nestling dormant in my hand. I would summon the pictures from the phone as ghosts from his past, when – and if – I had the evidence to confront him.

I undid my tight knot of hair and let it fall in a relaxed wave to one side. Light from my bedside lamp emphasized the pink hues that made it so distinctive – as distinctive as Matthew's own. I recalled the image in the window; there could be no doubting what I had seen. The figures hadn't been representations, but portraits – clearly identifiable as individuals – his parents, his grandparents, even his infant brother. So who were the people he claimed were his *current* family? Henry couldn't be his father and, come to think of it, I never remembered Matthew saying that he was. Could he be Matthew's father-in-law? Daniel wasn't his brother – perhaps his brother-in-law? I vaguely remembered, in an almost forgotten conversation, Matias saying something about Matthew's dead wife's family – Ellen's family. But Ellie and Harry looked so like Matthew that they must be related by blood to him – so similar... oh, so *obvious*! Of course, they weren't his niece and nephew – they were his children! That explained the physical similarities, the close bond between them; and Matthew couldn't have told me before, because he would have had to explain the discrepancy in ages that would have made a nonsense of his lie, there being only ten years or so between them. Which meant that he must have fathered them about twenty years ago, which presupposed their mother – Ellen – had been older than I always imagined, perhaps in her early forties when she died in the car crash that made him a widower. Well, why not? I wondered whether she knew who Matthew was, if he had told her; but then, something like that could hardly have been concealed from his wife.

"Why is this so *difficult*?" I said out loud. But I already knew the answer. When I went to America, it had been with the express purpose of locating and studying the Richardson journal. I meant it to be not only the culmination of my own research, but also the fulfilment of my grandfather's dream. It would mark not the end of my career, but the turning point around which I could begin the rest of my life. I had known this, understood it, and accepted it as inevitable. But the intervening months brought with them changes that I had not predicted and were beyond my control. I didn't like being out of control.

The journal had become a means to an end rather than an end in itself. It now lay beneath the newspaper I had placed on top of it – not so much to conceal it from my parents, but to hide its accusing face from me. I shifted the insubstantial paper and picked up the book, feeling its corners through the soft leather pouch that protected it, and removed it. Its black, scuffed cover represented not only my past but also my future, and that of another whose life lay bound within its pages. I sat in the middle of my bed, and started to read.

It was not like reading somebody's diary today; writing material had been scarce and every millimetre had been covered in the tight, compact script that Nathaniel Richardson used to record the everyday happenings of his family. The journal was not only physically difficult to read, but Richardson had also adopted abbreviations which he used throughout to represent words familiar to him. Without the benefit of a key, these were a mystery to me. Added to which, the variations in spellings plus his use of colloquialisms made deciphering the journal a maze of language which had to be negotiated before it could be understood. But I'd had a decade of practice and a lifetime of patience. I started by making a list of every abbreviation he used, one by one decoding them as they occurred until I worked out their meaning through association within the text. Gradually, I became accustomed to his handwriting and to the style of language he used. Names became familiar – people, places – as those aspects that concerned him most cropped up again and again.

I already knew he had become steward to the Lynes family on the premature death of his father, having served as his apprentice since he completed his education at Oakham. But I didn't know that he and Matthew had grown up together, nor that they were friends.

Richardson started his journal in the 1630s, when he seemed particularly concerned to record a series of crop failures and murrain in cattle following a number of poor summers. Most of his early entries recorded items to do with the estate, his family's affairs and very occasionally, the increasingly unstable national political situation, as it affected the prices that the crops fetched at the local market, or the ability to export fleeces to the continental weavers. He grumbled about the increase in taxes and excise duties and the burden it placed on the family. Once or twice he mentioned religion as it touched his conscience or that of his master. But on the whole his comments were mundane and sparse, sometimes months passing between entries.

Normally, I would have disregarded information that did

not have a direct bearing on what I researched at the time. Now, however, I absorbed every detail, as they filled in the background to Matthew's life – like a painting-by-numbers – and gradually the outlines provided by history were enriched by a man who knew him well.

As the years passed in pages, Richardson recorded his increasing concerns with the governance of the realm as it intruded on the daily lives of the family. On the rare occasion he referred directly to Henry Lynes or his son, it was to do with the gradual polarization, both politically and religiously, of the family, as the rift grew between Henry and William. In between his own marriage and the birth of his first child, Nathaniel mentioned Matthew training to bear arms to protect their lands, his betrothal to an heiress of a family of worth, and Henry's increased dependency on his son to help him run the estate as his years and the weight of the discord between the brothers bore heavily upon him.

My eyes strained dryly to read the congested script. The room had grown cold again when the central heating switched off around midnight, and the clock in the church tower no longer struck the quarters as the town slept. A strengthening wind rattled the window, and I uncurled my stiff legs and stretched my arms until they felt loose again. Tea from the vacuum flask warmed me, and the thin stream of air from the fan heater riffled the pages of the journal. Outside, the wind whined like an old dog, and I began to read once more.

In 1643, between a local minor outbreak of plague and a particularly good return on a shipment of wool, tension rose within the family as the nation descended into full-blown civil war. Richardson's entries became punctuated by snippets of news reflecting his preoccupation with the safeguarding of the estate and the welfare of his growing family. He also worried for his friend. In July, Richardson recorded just one entry, the hastily scratched words setting my stomach jangling:

> *Upon said day the Heavens burned with a mortal*
> *fire as William came forth with a company of divers*
> *men and made war upon this house and did cut*
> *from him by grievous means the young masters life.*

The impact of the words was not lessened, although I had heard the story from Mrs Seaton. The entry contained nothing more than what she had already told me, and I scanned the next couple of pages looking for further references that would tell me more, conscious of my straining pulse. On the third day after the attack, Richardson wrote:

> *The master makes prayerful vigil both night and*
> *day and he is sustaineth in his hope.*

Ten days later, he recorded:

> *The fever is broke yet he wakes not from sleep, yet*
> *praise be to God his wound be healed. Small blood*
> *brought forth.*

That was interesting. It told me four things: that Matthew had a fever, that he lay in some kind of coma and that, thirteen days after he had been severely injured, his wound had healed. The final piece of information puzzled me, though; it sounded as if bloodletting had been resorted to as the standard medical practice of the time, but the reference to "small blood"? I deduced that meant only a *little* blood had been drained, which seemed a good thing too, given the weakened state of his body. But I questioned my interpretation when almost three weeks later, Nathaniel wrote:

> *Master Matthew breathes but his blood floweth*
> *not on letting. The Master called for the surgeon*
> *who tended Lord Harrington at Michlemas, but*
> *yet he cut him many times, no blood was had. The*
> *surgeon saith he had not seen the like of it and the*
> *Master sent him forth and will not permit the*
> *cutting of his son henceforth.*

This put a different slant on things. "Small blood" might have indeed meant that little was taken, but from this later entry, it sounded as if it wasn't for the want of trying. Matthew had not bled when cut and his father would not let anyone attempt to bleed him again. Why?

But a day later, a single entry:

> *At eventide did he wake and spake with his father,*
> *all Hev'n be praised beyond reason for there be none.*

So, five or so weeks after being stabbed through the heart, Matthew Lynes woke up and spoke to his father. Miracles happen and Richardson obviously thought this was Divine intervention, yet I detected an element in the words he used to record Matthew's recovery that made me wonder if he thought otherwise. I sat back against the hard vertical ribs of the iron bedstead and assessed the information gleaned so far.

OK, so I had almost come to terms with the fact that the Matthew Lynes I met in the States was the same Matthew Lynes recorded as cheating death almost 400 years earlier. I found it a bit of a struggle to get my head around it, but there you go, so be it. Whatever had happened to allow this freak of nature to occur, I couldn't begin to pretend this was normal – although I shied away from using the term "freak" in relation to the man I loved. It would appear that what happened must have been the result of the life-threatening injury he received at the hands of his uncle. The question being, *what*? I mean, what had happened – physically – to have altered his state? At this point it would have been to my advantage to have been a scientist rather than a historian. Then again, that was exactly what Matthew was, and that – patently – was no coincidence.

I yelped as cramp shot through my right leg and I leapt up, tipping my plate over on the bed, strewing cake and crumbs with it. I took it as a sign that my body required some exercise to pump oxygen into my blood, so I took to striding around the confines of my bedroom. The heart circulates blood around the body. Cut the body and it will bleed. It has to bleed, or the heart has stopped and it is no longer living. Matthew didn't bleed, but nor was he dead. What did that make him then – alive?

I did a few star jumps, trying not to shake the floor too much – although, as my watch read a quarter to three in the morning, I hoped my parents wouldn't be awake to hear the floorboards squeak under the pressure of my pounding feet. I stopped as my ribs protested, and took to flexing each leg in turn instead. A sudden creak from behind had me spinning around in horror. I stifled a scream as the door opened, already beginning to cower as Staahl's grey form stood in the doorway of my mind's eye. But nothing appeared except the cat, sublimely oblivious to the rank terror he had momentarily caused. He jumped onto my bed, making directly for the upturned plate.

"No you don't, Tibs, you piglet," I said affectionately,

distracting him by stroking his long back while I rescued the plate. I nibbled the tart Dundee cake. I never understood why Dad favoured it; it must be something to do with growing old – an acquired taste, as Nanna would say. I pictured my father sitting alone in the potting shed in his own dark world, drifting, and ached for him – for the unrecognized sacrifice he had made for his daughter, and for her rejection of him. Tiberius rolled onto his back in a portly streak of contentment, catching the warm air from the fan-heater. I pulled myself back from reality and faced the past again for fear the present would engulf me.

I turned the next few pages. A gap in the entries covered a number of months, then there were a few concerning a minor dispute over a field boundary in late October, and finally there was one in November, which intrigued me:

> *The south barn did burst afire when the lad did*
> *up set the flame he carried thence to affix the doors*
> *agin the great wind. And though the fire would*
> *have taken his life, yet Master Matthew did save*
> *the boy by throwing him hence from the roof to*
> *the men below. And yet his flesh be burned, he is*
> *marked not and is whole.*

I read the entry again, slowly this time, but there could be no mistaking what Richardson had written. I remembered seeing Matthew pick up the ember in his bare hand when he thought I slept. What reason did he give the watching men when he emerged, unscathed, from the burning barn? Mrs Seaton said the stories told of how Matthew increasingly put himself in danger. But it had also been said that he challenged God, and that his survival was more to do with being the servant of the devil than the child of the Almighty. I read on, nervously.

The following spring, Nathaniel recounted a series of events:

> *In Lenten time did the river rise up and flood the*
> *land taking many ewes… but the Master with the*
> *Grace of God, pulled all but one from the spate and*
> *did save them thereof and though he is but one man*
> *he had the strength of many.*

So here I found a reference to Matthew's strength. Richardson used the term "Master" rather than "young Master". I wondered whether that reflected a change in the way he regarded Matthew, or whether Matthew had indeed taken on a more prominent role in the running of the estate, or whether perhaps – more simply – Nathaniel made a mistake. Next:

> *Widow Harries yet she has not the use of her legs,*
> *was seen to cast berries of the yew upon Browne's*
> *field whereupon his cattle grew lesions of pox upon*
> *their feet and their tongues did swell to the delight*
> *of Satan. And it is of his work she stands accused*
> *though the young Master will not have it thus and*
> *would look to the sickness of the soil for answer. Yet is*
> *she taken by the magistrate and stands trial thereof,*
> *though my Master pleadeth for her life and his father*
> *beg'd him cease for fear that he be acus'd with her.*

I shuddered, the pattern of persecution so familiar that I could have written it myself. I wondered what happened to the poor woman, what happened to Matthew himself? I didn't need to read much further to find out. After a gap of a few weeks, an entry brought me to the brink of tears:

> *When Matthew did enter the church upon Easter*
> *tide, the old gossips did cross themselves thrice like*
> *Papists in Queen Mary's time. E'en the young*
> *maids who oft before would look upon his fair*
> *countenance and sigh turn'd their backs on him.*
> *The old Master spake full fierce to them that would*
> *treat his son thus, who was ever their good and*
> *dutiful lord, but Matthew would not have them*
> *chid and left the church with sorrow heavy upon*
> *him. Daily doth he prey God for deliverance.*

The final mention of Matthew came one full year after William had betrayed the family so irrevocably:

> *This day the young Master fell from life, 'though he*
> *liveth yet and I know not where he be but that his*
> *father seeks him daily and will not have him lost.*
> *In him had I the truest friend.*

Gut instinct – it worked every time.

The answer was so blindingly obvious as to be untrue. That it might be true, inconceivable. The evidence lay before me in the pages of the journal I had searched for, and my grandfather had sought before me. Two unrelated matters: one of the head, one of the heart, drawn together in time and space by an anomaly – by a freak of nature – the very existence of whom ran contrary to all known laws of science. At what point would I wake from this protracted dream?

When would I wake up to reality? When would I reject the reality presented to me? When would I *run*?

I put the journal down and hung my head, slow tears seeping through my closed eyes as I felt the burden of loss in the relentless beating of my heart. I bent my legs, cradling them in my arms. I did not know what Richardson meant by "fell from life" – whether he spoke metaphorically or physically – but I definitely knew how I would react if someone I loved as much as I did Matthew had been lost to me.

I stared blankly towards the side of the room where the plain ceiling met the palely sprigged wallpaper at the edge of the eaves. My desk sat under the eaves, and under my desk, a printer.

The first photograph that fed through the printer showed the monument to the Lynes family; the second, the memorial window. Thrumming my fingers on the desk, I surveyed them critically, then selected the second one. Barely hesitating, I dragged my chair over to the corner cupboard, feeling around the top shelf with a blind hand and stitches pulling, until I found the shoebox in which I kept my odds and ends. Among the Mickey Mouse key ring my best friend had given me when we were seven, and the school report I kept hidden from my father and told him was lost, I found a partly used pack of greetings cards in their flimsy plastic film. The front of each card bore an identical picture of St Mary's Church, its towering spire piercing an intensely blue sky. I checked the back of the card: "St Mary's Church, Stamford, Lincolnshire." Plenty enough information. The photograph of the Lynes window just fitted inside and I carefully glued it in place, but I didn't know what to write; I didn't know how I could put into words what I knew. Whatever I wanted to say sounded vapid.

"I need some help here," I said to the ether. From where he lay on the bed like an elongated sausage, Tiberius purred, a deep affirming noise that made his whole body vibrate. I arranged Matthew's scarf as a narrow shawl around my shoulders. My hand slipped to the familiar shape of the cross on its gold chain and I pulled it free of my jumper, mumbling it between my lips, the metal warm and comforting.

"Thank you," I whispered, as the wind found a way into my room and with it, the words I would use.

From the list of quotes I had extracted from the journal, I copied part of one onto the blank side of the card, hoping my cold, stiff fingers wouldn't render it illegible:

> *This day the young Master fell from life, 'though he liveth yet…*
> **Nathaniel Richardson, July 1644**

Primary evidence. Were anyone else to read the card, it would be meaningless; only Matthew would understand the reference. I waited for the ink to dry before closing it, kissing it once and placing it in its envelope. On the front I wrote:

Dr Matthew Lynes,

Hesitating, I realized that I didn't know how to address him properly. In Britain, as a surgeon, he would have been plain "Mr"; then I thought that, given what I had written inside, in all likelihood he wouldn't care.

I finished addressing the envelope and fished in my bag for some stamps, sticking on a half-dozen to make sure it would get there and not get stuck in some forsaken corner of a post office for lack of postage. I flipped the card against the back of my hand before deciding that I couldn't risk waiting to post it in case – in the cold light of day – I changed my mind.

At 5.40 in the morning, the streets of Stamford were just beginning to hum with the first commuters. The freshening wind blew away the fumes of the few vehicles, lifting the clean, green scent of the Meadows from the riverbank. I took a deep breath as I stood in front of the narrow mouth of the red metal post box, touching my lips to his name on the envelope before quickly posting it and hearing its hollow echo as it hit the base of the empty box.

The house was as quiet on my return as when I left it, bar the rhythmic resonance of the clock marking time by the stairs. I reached the broad landing of the first floor when I noticed my father. He stood in the doorway to their bedroom, his thick, dark-red dressing-gown a zone of colour against the white-painted door.

"I'm sorry, did I wake you?" I whispered.

He shook his head. "I was already awake and I..." he stopped, his hesitancy uncharacteristic, "... and I didn't want you coming home to a dark house."

I expected him to ask me where I'd been, but he just turned and went back into his room. He shut the door quietly before I had time to thank him for turning on the light.

My mother woke me with a cup of tea at eight. I had managed to kick off my shoes as I crawled into bed, and I slept in my coat with my blue rug pulled around me. I felt revolting and probably looked worse.

"I'm not going to ask you why you're sleeping in your clothes, as I'm sure you have a perfectly logical explanation;

however, I don't want you to miss your appointment at the hospital, which I know you haven't forgotten."

I managed a bleary, blank look and she tutted.

"It's 'C' day, Emma, remember?"

"Umm…"

"Your cast, darling, it's being removed. And your stitches. Your appointment's at ten."

I wasn't sure how I felt about that. I moved my hand protectively over my stitched arm; whatever the reason for them, it had been Matthew who put them there, a tangible link to him sewn into me – a part of him I felt suddenly reluctant to let go. My mother squeezed my hand.

"I'm sure it won't hurt, darling; it's routine to them – you'll be fine."

I played along with her misconception. "I know I will." I smiled as brightly as my face would allow. "I'll get ready."

Whatever my misgivings, it would be a blessed relief to be rid of the trappings of my injuries once and for all, and have the luxury of a long, hot, wallowing bath. Or shower – I would settle for a shower as long as I could soak every pore of my skin and shake off the ravages that the sleepless night had wreaked upon my hapless brain.

The hospital seemed quieter than the last time I'd been there, and the doctor looked even younger. He slid off the counter in reception where he had been reading the sports pages of the local rag.

"Hello there, again; come back to keep me busy or couldn't keep away from the place? Must be my magnetic personality, or something." He grinned, dropping another five years or so; they were taking them young at med school these days.

I smiled back. "Oh, definitely something," I agreed.

I followed him to one of the cubicles and sat on the edge of the bed. A nurse, who looked no older than he did, poked her head around the door and waved a thin brown file at him. "These what you're after?"

He took them from her proffered hand, checking the details on the cover. "Cheers, I owe you one."

"Six-thirty at the Red Lion?" she suggested.

"Sorry, busy tonight." Still reading my notes, he didn't see her pout at him before she left rather abruptly. I wondered if Megan had redoubled her efforts in Matthew's direction if she sensed me off the scene. Megan – with her long blue hair and blonde eyes… I shook my head to get rid of the unholy image. "Christmas, I must be tired," I thought.

"What's it to be first: cast, strapping or stitches?"

I answered without needing to think. "Strapping definitely, then the cast, please."

"Righty-ho, I'll get a nurse…"

"Don't bother," I said. "Can't we just get on with it?" Then seeing the look on his face, I couldn't resist adding, "Your virtue is perfectly safe where I'm concerned; I won't lay a finger on you."

He stood with his hands on his hips.

"Blimey, you're feeling better, aren't you? I wish more of my patients were like you. Most would no sooner look at me than try to sue the pants off me." I smiled at his use of the American term, but he thought I reacted to his legal reference. "Not that any of my patients have had grounds to sue me, you understand – not yet, anyway."

"I'm glad to hear it," I asserted.

He removed the strapping without further ado, and I felt my lungs expand without constraint for the first time in weeks.

"Better?"

"Much."

"Cast next?"

"Yup."

He picked up a lethal-looking implement and switched it on, wielding it with the air of a man with a brand-new hand tool. I flinched back, eyeing it suspiciously.

"Do you need training to use one of those things?"

"It would probably help." He cut through the cast with a degree of care that belied his nonchalant appearance. "I must say that I was surprised when I had a look at your most recent X-ray. Either you heal quickly or you've lost a couple of weeks somewhere. You say this happened at the end of October? Could you be wrong about that?"

It was hardly a date I could forget. I shook my head.

"Oh, well, just goes to show the limitations of scientific knowledge and all that..."

"Mmm," I agreed. The cast fell off with a satisfying *thunk*. I flexed my hand weakly.

"Two down, one to go. Ready?" The young doctor washed his hands and pulled on a pair of surgical gloves. He took the dressing off my arm, exposing the stitches, and examined the long scar carefully.

"Yeah, this has healed really well too, but these'll have to come out. Pity, though – they're a work of art." I shared his sense of regret. "Tell me if it hurts – it might sting a bit."

It did, but I didn't say so. The young man lacked Matthew's finesse but he did his best to be gentle, and I used the discomfort to distract myself from what he was taking away.

The rattling clang of the surgical tweezers hitting the metal dish told me he had finished before he asked – somewhat anxiously – whether it had hurt.

"I hardly noticed a thing," I reassured him.

He seemed pleased. "You're going to need to be careful with the new scar tissue for a few weeks, and you can have some physio for your other arm if you want, but they'll both mend fine if you give them time. Last time I saw you, your dad asked about possible nerve damage to your left hand. That's not my field, but I can refer you to a neurosurgeon if you like?"

"No, it's OK, thanks – I'll get it checked out if it bothers me; otherwise…" I shrugged.

"OK, but I did tell him I'd find out, so…"

"I'll let him know, thanks."

I should have been elated, or at least relieved, but instead I felt bleak. I inched off the bed and stood up, decidedly sombre. The doctor stripped off the surgical gloves, looking at me sideways.

"Feels a bit strange now, does it? Now that it's all off."

I nodded. "Just a bit."

He opened the door, revealing the corridor beyond, pausing.

"You know," he said wistfully, "I'd really like to meet the man who did that stitch job for you."

I had to laugh at that. "So would I," I said.

Propped up on pillows and with the back of the bed raised, Nanna looked so much more alert. The corner of her mouth lifted when she saw me. I told her some of what I had been up to, touching on my visit to Beth – mostly the positive bits, about Archie and the twins and how we were going to meet up; and then at length on my visit to Martinsthorpe and her old friend Mrs Seaton. I described the house and the tennis party where my parents had met. Nanna had been there, of course – I could see it in the way her eyes became exuberant and she chortled in the back of her throat. She closed her eyes then, and I thought that she needed to rest. I gazed out at the courtyard garden, prettier now that the sun shone, and I remembered the sunlight through the window in the church, making Matthew's hair glow impossibly gold. I sighed. A slight touch on my hand brought me back to the present; Nanna observed me keenly, and I smiled self-consciously.

"I've written to him, Nanna, but I don't know how he'll respond." The hope in my voice came tinged with sadness, and she made a noise in her throat that sounded like a question. I bent close to her and she tried again, the effort obviously taxing her meagre reserves of strength.

"You want to meet him? I don't know if that's possible, Nanna. I don't know if I'll ever see him again. There's so much I don't understand."

She grunted fiercely and I leaned down again.

"All right – yes – I love him, I know that much; don't bully me."

She smiled her half-smile and rubbed my hand in a short, stiff movement of reassurance and I hugged her gently back, the years dissolving in the familiar comfort of our embrace.

"Mum says you're making such a nuisance of yourself that the hospital's expelling you for good behaviour. She showed me the brochure of the new place; it looks lovely and you can have all your own things there. Home from home, really."

I looked away, neither of us wanting to read the other's expression. Nanna would never be coming home; moving her to the care home merely represented a more comfortable interlude before time or another stroke took her. I touched her hand and tried to make light of it. "At least there aren't any stairs to climb and you'll have lots of nurses to torment.

And I'll come and see you, so you can boss me around as well." I was relieved to see her eyes sparkle at that. "Is there anything in particular you would like me to bring you?"

Her eyes fluttered over my face and her lips moved almost noiselessly. I bent close.

"But I can't, Nanna, I told you – I left him... he's in America." A stubborn look came over Nanna's face. Her lips moved again. I strained forward to catch the outline of her words, and then slowly straightened as I stared at her, her eyes sharp and bright. "You want to see the journal? But... but how do you know I have it? I've told no one. No one knows I took it."

The Call

The wings of a black beetle were beating against the sides of a jar.

I knew at once something must be wrong. The mobile whirred tunelessly next to me, and I woke with a jolt, my heart vibrating in time to the pulse of the phone as I reached out to answer it.

"Matthew?"

A short silence followed, filled only with the faint sound of breathing from the phone.

"Matthew?" I repeated, alarm creeping.

A woman's voice, barely audible at the other end, did nothing to calm me.

"Emma it's me – Elena. Did I wake you?"

I recognized her then. I glanced at my clock, my eyes straining to focus; 5.20 in the morning, so it must be night there.

"Elena! What's wrong? Is it Matthew? What's happened? How did you get this number? Is he all right?"

My questions poured out incoherently as I rubbed sleep from my eyes and struggled to sit upright. She sounded louder now; she must have adjusted the position of the phone.

"Emma, you gave me your number before you left. Are *you* OK? I hadn't heard from you and I was worried…"

Alert and tense, I broke in through her anxious, animated chatter.

"What's happened, Elena? It's twenty past five in the morning here; why are you calling? What's the matter?"

"*Da*, I'm sorry. Listen, I do not wish to worry you, but I thought you might want to know…" She paused, my heart rate increasing proportionately to the lengthening gap. "It's Matthew. Matias says he hasn't seen him for a few days and he has missed a meeting, and he never does that. Emma, Matthew has – how do you say? – not been himself since you left. He has been…" I could hear her asking a question, her hand covering the mouth of the phone, muffling her voice. I heard a murmured reply and recognized Matias's deep tenor in the background. Her voice became clear and loud again. "Yes, Matias says that he has been *morose*, withdrawn – he thinks he is changed, more… angry?" I could hear her asking him again. "Yes, angry. He has never seen him like this before, Em. Emma? Did you hear me?"

I heard her, but my stomach had become a mass of black, faceless creatures scratching and clawing at each other to escape. "Emma?" She sounded concerned.

"Yes, I heard you," I forced a reply. "Has anyone tried to contact him at home?"

"Matias has, but there was no answer. He wanted you to know, in case… well, you know, in case something happens…"

She trailed off, not sure how to finish, but she didn't need to; I had already silently completed the thought for her. Guy's ashen face, lying against the hospital pillow, gazed reproachfully at me, hovering unbidden from a long-suppressed memory. "Emma? Matias thought you should know," she repeated, uncertain now.

"Yes, thanks, Elena, and thank Matias for me. I... I don't know what to do. I didn't think he would react... not like this."

I felt helpless, thousands of miles away across an ocean of pain. I had spent so much time hurting for myself – for my own loss – that I didn't imagine he might respond the same way. If truth be told, I never thought anyone could feel that strongly about me. I always believed Guy's attempted suicide had been a sign of his weakness rather than an indication of his feelings for me. I tried to think rationally, pushing the unwelcome fears into the background for now.

"Elena, have you spoken to Matthew? Did you tell him what I said?"

"No, I haven't seen him since you left; but Matias saw him. Do you want to speak to Matias, Emma?"

"Please."

There was a fumbling and a flurry of Russian as Elena handed the phone to Matias. It seemed to take forever and I found I gripped the little mobile so tightly that my fingers were going numb.

"Hi, Emma, it's Matias."

He didn't ask me how I fared – he didn't need to; it was clear from the tortured pitch of my voice as I fired a succession of questions at him.

"Matias, have you spoken with Matthew? What did he say? How was he?"

"I've seen him a couple of times; the first time was the day after you left. I was clearing up that broken table before anyone else saw it – you remember? He came to find you. I said that you had gone back to England with your parents."

"How was he – I mean, how did he react?"

He paused before answering.

"Difficult to say; he didn't at first. He went very quiet, very still, then he asked if you were hurt and I said that I didn't think so. He asked if I knew whether you were coming back and I told him that I thought you were, but..."

I interrupted again, malignant dread growing in the heart of me.

"Did you tell him what I'd said, Matias, what I'd asked Elena to tell him?"

His silence confirmed my fear.

"I'm... not sure what that was, Emma. Is there a message she was supposed to pass on?"

The writhing creatures inside me died, leaving only a cold, hollow void. Elena hadn't seen Matthew; he didn't know that I wouldn't – couldn't – leave him. Matthew must think that I wasn't coming back – that I didn't love him.

"Emma. Emma? Are you still there?" Matias asked.

My voice became a coarse whisper. "How... how did he seem?"

Matias took on a paternal tone. "Now look, Emma, don't overreact; he can probably cope better than you can..."

"Matias," I broke in insistently, "*how did he seem?*"

The gap which followed spoke ominously. "He was... he seemed... distressed."

"*No...* why didn't you tell me?" I moaned, barely audible.

He sounded faintly aggrieved.

"We did try, but we couldn't get through. Elena even thought that she must have the wrong number. Was your cell fully charged?"

How long had it been like that? Had Matthew been trying to get hold of me? Did he think I was ignoring him? An agony of uncertainty joined the mass of broiling emotions.

"You... you said that you've seen him a couple of times.

When did you see him last? Was he all right then?"

"Yes, I saw him…" he stopped to calculate, "… three – no – four days ago now." Something in his tone told me he held back.

"What, Matias? Please – *tell me*."

He sighed. "I saw him in the lab, last Friday evening, I think it must have been. He's been working all hours lately. Heck, Emma, he's been driving us *all* hard lately. We've been working on some pretty… well… cutting-edge stuff, I suppose you'd call it. I've never seen him like this before, not this *driven*. I had some results – took them to him in the lab. He was just standing there in the dark, staring out of the window – I only saw him because of the moonlight. Anyway, I went in and he didn't turn around, so I thought that he hadn't heard me, though goodness only knows I make enough noise. So I called his name and then he turned, but… sweet heaven, Emma…"

Matias's harsh, hushed voice jangled unnervingly down the phone. "His face, his eyes… I swear they *burned*. There was so much anger, no – more than anger – deeper than that, he looked… tormented – yes, that's it – he looked as if he were in *hell*."

I might as well have been there myself. The void inside me imploded, taking with it every ounce of the hope I had been holding on to.

"I'm sorry, Emma – you wanted to know. I haven't seen him since. I went to his house, but there was no one there."

"His family?" I asked, all emotion drained.

"It was dark – the house, I mean. No one answered – I think it was empty. I'll go back again if you like, but…" It was obvious he thought it a pointless exercise. "I don't know what else I can do, Emma – for either of you."

"I don't think there is anything you can do – it's over, it's finished," I said with finality.

"Emma…" he sounded a warning. "Don't do anything impulsive, will you?"

I didn't answer him and let my hand, still clutching the mobile, fall beside me. In the distance I heard him say something rapidly to Elena and her gasped response. Shuffled noises came down the phone.

"Emma…" Elena's voice, high pitched and alarmed. "Please, Emma – don't be stupid." My hand felt like a dead weight as I brought it back towards my ear.

"No, I've already been stupid, Elena – so, *so* stupid."

"Are you coming back? You've got to come back! *Nyet…*" she hissed to Matias, and then said something else I neither understood nor cared about.

"Bye, Elena. Thanks."

I terminated the call as if we had been having an ordinary conversation about everyday things, such as the weather and clothes and work, and switched the mobile off – once and for all.

I guessed – no, I didn't need to guess because I knew – what had happened. I had sent the card last Monday morning and he would have opened it and seen… what? He hadn't received the message I gave Elena before I left the States. Matias hadn't known about it so he couldn't pass it on, so as far as Matthew was concerned, I had left America – and him – for good. And then he received a cryptic message from me. Blast it – not a message – an *accusation*. He would read it as a revelation, a threat to his identity, something being flung in his face like a sordid scandal dragged up by the gutter press, but much, much worse. Scandals come and go like squalls upon the water and, as long as you don't drown in them, they pass. But what I had uncovered – what I represented – was akin to a tornado because it came out of nowhere and threatened to tear his life apart. He would feel betrayed; I might as well have stabbed him in the heart.

Matthew – what have I done to you?

I thought the depths of wretchedness I experienced when I left America had been as much as I could bear, but this was beyond anything I had ever felt before, the anguish both physical and emotional. Amplified, extended, intensified, it racked both my body and mind without remorse. Images, words, emotions – all scrambled and incoherent – fought to gain precedence, but all I could feel through the morass was glacial sorrow seeping relentlessly, and all the time the words, "I have betrayed you", over and over and over again.

The last little blue-and-yellow capsule he had given me gave my mind the numbing rest it craved, but it did not take away the remorseless pain on waking. When my father came to see me when I hadn't appeared for lunch, I pleaded a touch of flu to buy more time, and he left me alone.

I curled up in a ball on my side, conscious that I had been here before. It wasn't feasible that I should put my parents through it all over again, and I knew that I wasn't going to be able to hide it under the cloak of illness for long. Where I went from here would be anybody's guess, because I hadn't a clue. For the first time since childhood, I felt rudderless. Up until my teenage years, my parents and grandparents had always been there to steer me in the right direction – clothes, homework, school, dentist – all more or less dictated by caring adults whether I liked their choice or not. By the time I reached adolescence and a degree of independence, my obsession with history and the journal determined my course and, later, my new-found faith had given me all the rest – until now. It all seemed so pointless, so utterly futile, and I had nowhere left to go. I wrapped my arms around my head, blotting out the world, and tried to pray, but my words slipped through my thoughts and vaporized before I could give them form, and they meant nothing more than the sum of my fear.

I gave up and tried to think practically; if I couldn't help myself, perhaps I could help him. Despite what he might think, I would never reveal Matthew's secret to anyone else, but he didn't know that, so my priority would be to make sure he felt secure. He might not be able to forgive me, but I would not have him live in fear of exposure. I needed to get a message to him – and quickly – either before he disappeared, or before he did anything I would regret for the rest of my life.

But *how*? If he wasn't at home, he wouldn't be at the college, so I saw no point in sending anything there, and I doubted if he left a forwarding address. I ran my liberated hands through my hair, tugging at it as if to pull some semblance of sense out of it. Email. He must have some way of being contacted – a website for his department perhaps, something he could access from anywhere, as long as he chose to look. The creaky board halfway along the landing alerted me to an imminent arrival, and gave me enough time to huddle under the duvet. I didn't need to act forlorn.

Mum entered, carrying a small tray with a jug of squash and some digestive biscuits. A packet of paracetamol sat next to the glass. Invalid rations. She set it down on the bedside table.

"Your father said you're not feeling well; you do look a bit… rough." Her eyes constricted as she scanned my face and felt my forehead. "There's a nasty cold doing the rounds; see how you feel later on," but the look on her face suggested she had another theory. I gave her an approximation of a smile and pulled the duvet up to my chin.

"It's nothing. I'll stay up here until I feel better; there's no point in spreading my germs."

Or anything else; despair is contagious.

I waited until I could hear her footsteps no longer before going to my laptop. I found the website easily and clicked the "Contact" tab before I realized that I didn't know what I should write. I knew what I wanted to say. I wanted to say something along the lines of:

> *Matthew, I love you, and I'd rather have my heart torn from me and burned on a bed of coals than let anyone know your secret.*

But somehow that would defeat the object in such a public forum as the department website, so in the end I simply wrote:

> *Dr Lynes – My apologies for the delay in contacting you. I regret to report that I have found nothing in my research that will ever be of any interest or relevance to anyone other than myself.*
> *ED*

It sounded impersonal and terse. If he read it at all, it should at least achieve its purpose. I checked it before clicking "Send". That done, I would have to decide what to do for the rest of my life, now that he could no longer be the focus of it.

I tilted my chair onto its back legs and swung back and forth, chewing at my cross, the chain strung across my chin as tight as the nerves holding me together. Just about anything would do other than stay here, dragging everyone else down with me. I had my work obligations, of course – especially to my students. I did feel bad about letting them down, but I could resign from the university without too much difficulty, even given such short notice. It wouldn't take much to persuade a doctor – or even better, a psychiatrist – that I bordered on the edge of sanity. The college wouldn't oppose it; the dean would be too scared I'd sue for compensation. And I would have to go a long, long way away. I'd always fancied a trip to New Zealand – kiwi farming, perhaps.

I thwacked the chair back onto all four feet and shoved my hand out to tap a search into the laptop, knocking a small stack of books off the back of my desk as I did so. *Blasted things!* I bent sideways and rifled under my desk, trying to retrieve them. My fingers found the edge of a book; I didn't need to look to know what I picked up. *Wretched, cursed book, haunting me.* I suddenly remembered that I had effectively stolen the journal and that it had to go back where it belonged, and guilt released in me a tide of invective I screamed into the book's blank, black face, while I rocked rhythmically on the chair. "Why can't you let me go? Let me *go*," I whimpered, clutching it to my chest, my heart beating erratically against it, feeding it my life. The clock in the church tower opposite began to strike and I swayed back and forth with it. Who was I kidding? I wasn't going anywhere – not like *this*. I dragged myself to my feet and, ripping his scarf from around my neck, let it fall to the floor without a second glance.

Years had passed since I last set foot inside St Mary's Church, but the smell of old stone and recently extinguished candles and incense remained the same. I didn't know why I came here, but this was where my legs had taken me when, blinded by misery, I left the house. As I sat numbly watching the strengthening glow of the lurid streetlamps force their way through the church windows, I couldn't be sure that Staahl hadn't been right all along. I searched, but couldn't locate the well of faith that had been my guide ever since I knew it was there to steer me. Where was God now when the roots of that faith lay exposed and shattered by my betrayal? I had left Matthew when he needed me most, when he needed someone who could accept him for who he was. No wonder he lied – he had been protecting me from a bigger truth – one nobody in their right mind could accept.

At the far end of the nave, the cross rose from the altar as the timeless guardian of my faith, and I cried out into the body of the church, seeking comfort. But I heard nothing, saw nothing, felt *absence*. Staahl must have been right – I was alone.

After a while I became aware of the strange, thin, keening sound filling the high columned space, and a moment more passed before I realized that it must be I who made it – an empty sound, devoid of hope, lost.

Out of Time

A sigh – like the sough of wind through tall grasses.

I looked up. I sat alone but for the constant hum of traffic outside – and something else – something as indiscernible as the movement of air. Stock still, I followed the sound, and there above the altar, where the single candle burned as token of Christ's living flame, soft wings beat against the glass.

Out of place, out of time.

But in the frail spectre of the butterfly lay the promise I had all but forgotten: *I have carved you upon the palms of my hand,* and I no longer felt alone. I had never been alone and, while I searched blindly in the dark for my faith, I failed to look at the eternal light inside me.

By the time the elderly sexton came to secure the church for the night, I had drawn two conclusions: first, I would return the journal to its rightful owner even if it meant going back to the college to do so and, second, I needed professional help to prevent my inexorable slide into a nervous breakdown. As my mental state crumbled in stages, I decided that time was probably of the essence and, before my determination dissolved along with my ability to make decisions, I would go back to the hospital in the morning. The journal would have to wait.

The following morning, after a sleepless night, I lay in the bath letting the deep, hot water cover me as it inched up the iron sides, steaming water pouring from the antiquated chrome tap in strangled bursts. First my stomach, then my breasts, then shoulders, the water finally making its way up my neck and over my lips and nose, my hair spreading out around me. It would be so easy just to stay there, submerged and warm where the world couldn't touch me and I wouldn't have to face tomorrow, or the next day, or the next.

So easy.

To let go.

Painless.

Quick.

My lungs began to strain and ache as they searched for oxygen, but it was my scar – stung by the hot water – that had me sliding back upright. I ran a finger down the thin, pale slash of the new, baby-pink skin, but it wasn't the man who put it there whose voice I heard inside my head, but Matthew, and the sound of it was *agony*.

More than I could bear.

Yes, today, I thought, is a good day to get help.

I dressed slowly and abstractedly. My hand did not hesitate as I chose the tailored tweed coat, leaving the beautiful quilted one Matthew bought me hanging next to the sage jacket. I took a look around the room which I had tidied earlier. The blue blanket had been folded and put away in the bottom of my chest of drawers, leaving only the scarf as a reminder of him. I picked it up from where I had let it fall the day before and ran it through my fingers, seeing it around his neck, feeling it around mine, and I hung it over the back of my chair before leaving the room.

The morning ran cold; the sky, heavily overcast, threatening rain or worse. I loved the promise of snow as a child, but it rarely came, and now it didn't matter.

I frowned as familiar heads bobbed past the window by the front door, followed by the homely figure of my sister, tucking the baby under one arm as she wrestled to find a key in her handbag. She looked up and saw me watching and waved, frantically cheerful. My reactions were painfully slow and my face immobile as I opened the front door for her. She breezed in with a flurry of cold air and children.

"Hi! Oh… were you on your way out?"

I remembered to bend my face in a smile. "Yes, I was."

"Oh, we won't be long, then. Are Mum and Dad in? Brrr, it's bitter out there. All the kids have talked about this morning is whether it's going to snow. Honestly, it's more nuisance than it's worth; I can't see what all the fuss is about. How are you, anyway?"

She stopped talking just long enough to take off her coat, struggling to free one arm of its sleeve while holding the baby with the other. I stood watching stupidly. She noticed my arms.

"You're out of the cast – great; here, take Archie for me, will you?"

The baby was thrust into my arms and I automatically held onto him. The twins had disappeared in search of their grandparents and chocolate biscuits.

"School holidays – they're already bored. Rob's minding the shop but he'll take them out rubble-cruising to the battlefield later. You remember doing that with Grandpa, don't you, Em?" Beth took out the hangers from the hall cupboard, hanging up the children's coats from where they draped abandoned on the banister. "You're quiet; everything all right?"

Archie did a rolling burp and I patted his straight back. He smiled, his little cheeks rosy from the cold.

I answered mechanically with someone else's voice. "I'm fine. It is cold, isn't it?"

"Yeah – it is." Beth eyed me suspiciously. "But you don't need this on, young man, do you?" She took Archie from me and unzipped his all-in-one suit with the rabbit-eared hood. He rubbed his fist in his eyes and yawned, showing the edge of a tooth in a pink gum. Beth nuzzled his ear and he gurgled happily. "I'm gasping – join me for a cuppa?"

"Well…"

"Aw, c'mon, it won't take long. You can tell me what you've been up to, and I'll tell you all about Archie's teeth and the twins' school reports – just like old times, huh? Bet you can't wait!"

She was in such a good mood that I hadn't the heart to rush away. The hospital would wait for another hour.

I followed her into the sitting room. When we were little, Beth and I would sit, legs bunched and giggling, on the two deep window sills squirrelled behind the long velvet curtains. Nanna and Mum would pretend they couldn't find us until they eventually lured us out with talk of buns and chocolate milk in theatrical whispers. Now we sat on the old sofa like the adults we were supposed to be while Alex and Flora each sat on a window sill cross-legged, dunking biscuits into their milk.

"Aren't you going to say hello to Mum and Dad?" I ventured, wanting to move the process on as quickly as possible. "I thought you wanted a cup of tea."

Beth adjusted her bottom comfortably and plumped Archie down between us, his legs sticking out stiffly in front of him. He gazed at me with his saucer-like eyes but he hadn't begun to cry yet, which was probably a good thing since I would have joined in.

"I'll see them in a mo. What've you been up to, then? I like your get-up – very elegant; where were you off to in such a hurry?"

I frowned. Elegant – was it? Did it matter? Outside, an elderly couple walked slowly past the first of the windows, partially obscured by Flora's dancing curls. By the time they reached the second window I could see a plastic shopping bag with long rolls of wrapping paper; it must be nearly Christmas. I struggled for something to say, something approaching normality.

"Shopping – I haven't done much for Christmas, Beth. How about you? Done all your shopping yet?"

I tried to inject some enthusiasm into my voice, but it still sounded flat to my ears. Beth noticed. "I've told Rob he's doing it this year, but I expect I'll end up doing it as usual. Are you sure you're OK? You do sound a bit… off."

"Absolutely fine. I'll go and see Nanna too, while I'm at it."

"So you're going to the care home? That's a long walk; still, she'll like to see you." She flattened Archie's scrolled hair with the palm of her hand. "Em, Mum said Guy's been in touch." When I didn't react, she went on. "She says he wants to see you. Will you?"

What was Guy to me now? Another life. Irrelevant.

"Dad's dealt with him."

She glanced over the back of the sofa at the twins but they were happily engaged in playing a sort of hide-and-seek with the curtains, the only visible evidence of the biscuits and milk a smudge of chocolate and cream around their mouths. They weren't listening.

"It looks to me as if you could do with getting away from here for a bit – get some sun."

"Perhaps."

She stretched, her plum-coloured jumper riding up above her waist, showing her pale skin with shiny silver stretch-marks. Archie lunged forward and I caught him as he began to topple.

"Well caught," she commented. "Golly, what I wouldn't do for a bit of winter sun. Sun or snow – don't care, it all sounds good to me."

I admired her capacity for life; even with three young children and her own business, she still found the energy to be interested in it.

She pulled her jumper back down. "Still, you haven't said what you're doing for Christmas. What are you going to do?"

I thought of the shopping and the decorations, the carols and the food, and felt crushed by the expectation of joy it placed on me.

"I don't know. I'll stay here probably, and then…" I trailed off, indifferent to the options open to me.

The children had evolved their game, which now included the occasional passer-by who used St Mary's Place as a short cut. It involved a lot of giggling and a fair degree of bouncing up and down on the window seats, waving wildly.

"That lady's going shopping and she's going to buy a newspaper… a turkey, er… and a Intergalactic Battle Cruiser."

"*An* Intergalactic Battle Cruiser, Alex," Beth said without looking at him.

"*An, an, an*…" sang Flora, waving at the woman. "She's waving, look, look, see… she waved to me first!"

Beth turned around on the sofa to watch them for a second.

"You're not making nuisances of yourselves, are you?" she said with that low, almost threatening tone mothers use with their offspring, in much the same way as dogs growl at their pups when they're stepping out of line.

"Naw, she's *smiling*, Mummy."

Archie found the big buttons of my coat and tugged at them curiously. I looked down at him and he stuffed his hand in his mouth and grizzled before resuming the investigation with a wet fist.

Beth persisted. "So when are you going back to the States? I take it you *are* going back, aren't you?"

Flora's voice rose above our own. "They're going to the shops to buy…"

"Shh, Flora, not so loud," her mother said.

"I have to go back – there's something I need to get done, and then…"

"… Christmas decorations, three French hens and…"

"A Barbie up a gum treeeee," sang Alex. "Beat ya, beat ya, wouldn't want to eat ya! They're waving to *me*. Nah, nah!"

A couple were unlocking their car in one of the residents' parking spaces opposite the house. I recognized them as neighbours from two doors up. They waved at the children before climbing in.

"The neighbours won't be talking to us if you two carry on like this," Beth warned.

"They like us, don't they, Emma? Go on, say they do, *please*," Flora begged.

I spoke over my shoulder, keeping an eye on Archie, who began to tug hard at a button. "Yes, they do, Flora."

"Can't think why," Beth muttered. "And then?"

"And then… what?" I'd lost the train of thought.

"You were saying you're going back to the uni, and then…"

"Oh, right, then – I'm not sure – but I'm thinking of taking a sabbatical." Why hadn't I thought of that sooner? It seemed a perfect solution. "Six months, maybe a year. To New Zealand." I could hide in New Zealand. I could be nothing – not a sister, or a daughter, not a lover, nor a friend. Not a disappointment.

Beth pouted. "All right for some. Can you do that – I mean, will they keep your job open for you?"

Excited squeaks came from the windows. "It's snowing, look, look! Emma, Mummy, *look*!" We both looked; outside the sky had darkened to a solid slate above the roofs, and big, soft, mushy flakes fell lumpenly until a gust of wind herded them together before scattering them randomly once more. Without reason, my pulse quickened. Alex pressed his nose against the glass, his breath misting the space in front of him instantly. "It's settling on the cars."

"Aw – no it's not, it's melting," Flora mourned.

I remembered where we were in the conversation. "They should do; I haven't had a sabbatical since starting work, so…" I looked up again as the wind picked up, now driving sleet against the thin glass, and I rubbed a hand across my chest where my heart thudded noticeably. Beth wiped dribble off Archie's chin and the baby fought her hand.

"You OK?" she asked me.

I didn't mean to sound impatient. "Fine, you don't need to keep asking."

Behind us, the twins were chanting, "Snow, snow, snow… ally, ally aster, snow fall fa-ster…" as if invoking a weather spirit.

"Sorry, it's just that you look strange, a bit…"

The children stopped chanting and resumed their game.

"*He's* going to the shops and he's going to buy…" Flora shouted.

"*Flora!*" Beth half-turned to rebuke her overexcited daughter. "No, Em, it's just you've gone a funny colour."

My pulse raced, my collar itching where the wool began to stick to my damp skin. I felt trapped, suffocating. "I'm too hot." I started to unbutton my coat and Archie set up a wail of frustration, trying to grab at the buttons. I slid my coat off, and he began to bellow, his red face clashing with his sand-gold hair.

Flora was jumping up and down. "An elephant, an emu and... nine lords a leaping... and..."

My mother came in from the next room, summoned by the noise.

"Golly, it's gone dark... goodness, Flora, what *are* you doing?"

"No he's not," Alex interrupted. "*That* man – he's just standing there and he's getting all wet."

My head swivelled. "Who is, Alex?" My nephew turned towards me, pointing out of the window. "That man is – he's just standing by the church looking at us."

I followed where he pointed and the hammering in my chest stopped. I went cold.

I leapt to my feet, thrusting Archie into his startled mother's arms as the room went suddenly quiet and everyone stared. And then I flew out of the room running, running across the stone-flagged floor to the front door, flinging it wide, sleet stinging my face, driving into my eyes. Down the broad steps, then stopping dead, frozen onto the pavement, yards away from him. He hadn't moved, his arms stiff by his sides with knuckles white-clenched, oblivious to the freezing water running down his face, soaking him as he watched me watching him.

Waiting.

I dragged the back of my hand across my eyes, clearing them of ice and tears.

"You'll catch your death out here, Matthew..."

He moved then, across the cobbles, and he held me, his face pressed in my hair, and I cried and laughed, feeling his strength against me, not letting him go. And I felt warm again although the water drenched every inch of our bodies.

"I thought I would never see you again," I whispered into his neck, when I could trust myself to speak without my heart breaking.

"Emma, my Emma," he said, and he didn't need to say anything else because the contentment in his voice said it all.

"I thought you were angry with me, f... for what I found out. I thought I would never see you again."

He unwrapped his arms from around me long enough to take my face between his hands, and his eyes echoed my agony. Very gently, he kissed each of mine in turn. His voice became low, and saturated with the emotion he fought to govern.

"There is *nothing* you could do to make me angry with you, Emma. I could no more stay away from you than..." He shook his head and my heart thudded unsteadily as I reached up with my fingers to touch his face, to smooth away the furrow from his brow. Ice clung to his dark lashes, and formed drops like tears on his high cheeks.

"Matthew," I murmured, "I understand now why you couldn't tell me; I'm so sorry for what I've put you through."

He opened his eyes and looked down at me.

"What *you* put *me* through? Emma..." He seemed at a loss for words and he raised his face to the sky as if the freezing water would help clarify his thoughts. "After all you have been through... and now that you know... now that you know who I am... I don't understand how you can still be standing here with me, like this, knowing what you do."

"I love you – whoever you are."

"But is that enough? It isn't fair on you; none of this is fair on you. None of it."

I heard an ominous undertone to his words, and began to shiver uncontrollably. He smiled, but it spoke of regret. "Come, your family are watching and you need to get warm."

He took me by the hand and started to walk towards the open front door, but I hung back, reluctant to share this moment with anyone else. Understanding my hesitancy, he stopped, draping his coat – already dark-patched and heavy with frozen rain – around my shoulders. I had to know before we went inside.

"Do you forgive me?"

He shook his head. "No, my love, you've done nothing wrong – nothing I didn't deserve. It's more of a question of will you be able to forgive me?"

In answer, I laid my head against his chest, my arms around his waist, pulling myself close to him. "Will you forgive me, Emma?" he said, almost to himself. Above us, the street lamp had been fooled into thinking it was dusk as low cloud compacted and the wind redoubled its efforts, sleet thickening into snow. A car drove past slowly, its headlights on, dancing flakes in the yellow beams of light. Matthew glanced towards the house.

"Let's get you inside before you freeze. Will your family let me in, do you think, or am I *persona non grata*?" And he smiled again – a tired, restrained smile.

The light had been switched on but the hall stood empty and quiet once we shut the door on the wind, and I breathed a sigh of relief for the brief respite before we faced the family.

"Before we're interrupted…" Drawing me towards him, he kissed me again. He took my hands in his – warm as mine were cold – and where a smile had touched his eyes, now I saw worry. "You look so pale, my love; how are you?"

I remembered my silent prayer for him in the church and the peace that followed, and understood that now I knew he was all right, I would be too.

"I'm better now."

"I'm glad…" he started to say, but then his head snapped around as the brass handle of the sitting room door turned and, whatever he had been about to say, he kept to himself. My father appeared in the doorway, his expression giving nothing away. Behind him, sitting on the sofa, the twins sat remarkably still. Beth stood behind them, watchfully, jigging a fractious Archie up and down in her arms.

Dad spoke. "Emma, your mother wants to know if she needs to lay another place at the table."

I tried to keep my tone even, as if Matthew had been expected all along and just dropped by for a chat.

"Yes please, Dad; Matthew will be staying."

I took Matthew's hand in mine possessively, and he squeezed it reassuringly. I waited for the challenge, the bullish response, but there was none. My father unexpectedly smiled.

"Right, I'll tell Penny; it'll be good to have another male to talk to." He addressed Matthew directly. "I don't know if anything I have will fit you, but you are welcome to have a look. Emma, you know where my things are; would you show Dr Lynes, please? Lunch won't be long."

The door closed behind him. Matthew put a finger under my chin and tipped my open mouth shut.

"There, that wasn't so bad, was it?" he chuckled.

"What did you do to him? That wasn't my father – that

was an… an *alien*," I stammered, still staring where my father had been a moment before. "Alien," I repeated, taking in Matthew's features, so familiar to me now, so beloved, that I found it hard to question his existence. "Matthew, what happened? Why are you…?" But my questions were cut short as the door opened again and the blonde curls of my niece appeared. She squealed in surprise as she saw us, and bobbed back behind it, accompanied by a burst of laughter.

"Perhaps now is not the time to discuss your mortality," I muttered, taking him by the hand and leading him towards the stairs.

Few of my father's clothes fitted Matthew's athletic frame, but since he didn't feel the cold and would hardly suffer from hypothermia, he opted to borrow a thick jumper that made it look as if he had made the effort to change. I placed him in front of the fan-heater in my room to dry the rest of him while I changed. He turned his back as I took off my wet clothes, giving me a degree of modesty, and examined my room.

"So this is where you grew up," he stated.

"Uh huh." I slid the zip up the auburn panelled skirt and wriggled the waistband around until it sat at the back.

"How long have your family lived here – in this house?"

"I'm decent," I announced, dragging a boot out from under the bed. He faced me, catching me around my waist; I giggled.

"Decent? Ah well, never mind," he said with a note of disappointment. "So, how long?"

"Um, about since… 1780-something, I think. It was a much grander house then but they divided it just over a hundred years ago. We have the bigger half but next door has a lovely garden. Shame, really; Mum would have liked the tennis courts and Dad would have killed to have a proper garden to poddle in. And you won't dry if you don't stand in front of that thing, you know." I pushed him back until he stood obediently in front of the fan-heater again, and he pulled me with him so the warm stream of air flowed around us both.

"Did you know Stamford – you know… back then, before… well, before…?" Since I was not sure how to continue my line of thought, my question petered out. He rested his chin on the top of my head as I leaned against his chest and breathed in the smell of him – a mix of his fresh, mountainy scent and the wet wool of his clothes.

"Yes, it's changed quite a bit, except for the churches. And the inns. And the river; it was always flooding then."

"It still does." Moments passed in which he began rocking me gently. "Matthew?"

"Mmm?"

"I've been to Martinsthorpe, you know. Yes, of course you do – the photo – but what I mean is, I've been there and your house – your home – it's gone. I don't know whether you want to, but I can take you there, if that's… if you would like to see where it was." He stopped rocking and I looked anxiously up at him.

"Thank you, but it was a very long time ago; I didn't expect it to be there still. I haven't thought about it in a long time." He resumed the rocking.

I chewed my lip, wondering how far I could go. "Do you remember much about your life then or… or about what happened?"

He stopped again and leaned back a little so that he could see my face clearly.

"You arc quite remarkable, Emma D'Eresby. Any woman

– any*body* – in their right mind would have turned tail and run, given what you know of me. But here you are, worried about hurting my *feelings* about something that happened nearly four hundred years ago." He rubbed his forehead with the knuckle of his thumb. "Emma – I should be dead. You should be worried about *why* I'm not dead. You should be worried about *you* – not me."

I nodded. "Oh, yes, I know I should and all that, but time is only the passing of moments, Matthew, and that doesn't alter your past or the nature of… of what happened. And it's bound to leave its scars on you, in the same way it has – to a lesser extent, perhaps – on me. Just because it was a long time ago doesn't mean it doesn't matter."

He took my left hand and extended my arm, pushing the sleeve up a little to reveal the scar. He checked it with a professional eye, kissed it, then rested his cheek on my warm skin.

"I didn't mean *that* sort of scar," I said, watching the play of light through his hair.

"I know you didn't," he said, his voice reflective. I stroked his hair and, for a moment, he remained quiet and still under my touch. Then he straightened.

"I should have known better than to take up with a historian. First she discovers who I am and then she has to analyse the data. I suppose you have lots of questions for me?"

"Yes, lots. But if it makes you feel any better, you are still a man of mystery. I said that I know *who* you are, Matthew, but I still don't have a clue about *what* you are."

"That makes two of us." He shook his head incredulously. "And yet here you stand."

"Yes, here I stand," I agreed.

On the way down the stairs, hand in hand, I remembered what had been bothering me since my father asked if Matthew would stay for lunch.

"But you don't eat anything, do you? It's going to look very obvious."

He didn't appear to be troubled by the prospect.

"I can eat a little, even if I don't need to; it won't kill me. And besides, I've had plenty of time to perfect avoidance tactics." He glanced out of the corner of his eye. "A bit like you, somewhat." I nudged him in the ribs before I remembered how hard his body was. He rubbed my elbow better for me.

"It's a good thing that wasn't the other arm; that really *would* have hurt." He grinned, kissing my frown.

We went into the sitting room, the heavy door's squeaking hinge announcing our arrival. The twins had long since given up being good and were rolling around on the floor between the furniture, seeing how far they could go before they crashed into one another. Mum and Beth had heard us approach through the children's raucous play, and were already sitting in receiving mode, bolt upright and correct. Archie swayed and rocked on Beth's lap. My sister smiled anxiously when she saw us and stood up, pulling her jumper down over her hips in the nervous way she had. Our mother was sitting quite still on her chair, her hands clasped in front of her, her mouth thin like a straw.

"Mum...?" I started to say, but Matthew let go of my hand, stepping forwards and inclining his head as he neared her.

"Ma'am."

Beth's jaw dropped but Mum assessed him unsmiling, and then me, before smoothing her hands over her tweed skirt as she rose to greet him. The children stopped rolling, and lay still on the floor on their backs, heads bent backwards as they watched the adults upside down. In the hall, the long-case clock *donged* ominously.

"Dr Lynes, this is quite a surprise. I don't think we expected to see you, but you are… welcome."

Matthew looked at her steadily. "Thank you, ma'am, I'm glad to be here. I'm grateful for your hospitality."

There was a pause in which Beth and I exchanged glances, then Mum let her shoulders drop and put out her hand to him, and they declared an unspoken truce. "Now, if you will excuse me, I must help Hugh get the vegetables finished if we are to eat this side of Christmas."

The conspicuous tension went with her. I exhaled quietly and turned to my sister as I introduced her, and she swung the baby onto a hip, extricating a hand. "And this is Archie," I added. Archie held a strip of peeled cucumber in one fist which he attempted to fit into his mouth, eyes wide as he stared at Matthew. As she held out her hand, Archie chose that moment to lunge forward. Quicker than a whip, Matthew caught the baby in mid-air as he plummeted towards the floor.

"Here you go, young man," he said, handing him back to his shaken mother, who clasped his squirming, protesting body close to hers. She gazed at Matthew with undisguised awe.

"Thanks."

"Not at all," he said and broke into one of his melting smiles. Beth hadn't been exposed to him before, and she flushed a deep red. I would have been outrageously jealous had it been any other woman but my sister. My married sister. My happily married sister who was eight years older than me.

"Thanks so *much*," she said again, weakly, finding it necessary to concentrate on wiping Archie's chin free of dribble. Matthew turned to the twins. Alex viewed him warily from around the edge of the sofa. Flora still lay on her back, a dark-brown plastic horse with a black mane forgotten in one hand.

"Hello, you must be Flora," he addressed her. The only time I could remember telling him about the twins was weeks ago, and in passing. Perhaps with long life came a good memory. He tilted his head on one side so he could see her better.

The little girl frowned at him. "Are you from the television?" she asked, rolling onto her stomach. Matthew looked at her, puzzled by the context.

"No, he's from America, bubblehead," her brother observed from his vantage point. I had forgotten Matthew would sound American to everyone else; I could hear only the English undertones.

"Quite so. And you must be Alex." Matthew curved around and matched my nephew's rather serious expression. Alex nodded cautiously, backing away.

"I understand you are a collector of coins." He crouched down so as to be almost level with the boy's dark head. Alex stopped retreating and raised his chin, his initial shyness waning.

"And military mem'rabilia – especially arrowheads. I've found arrowheads *and* a piece of armour. Daddy took me to Losecoat Field; there was a battle there in 1470."

"That's very impressive," Matthew commented.

"And he took me," Flora butted in, now on her knees and wriggling until close to Matthew's elbow. "And *I* found a piece of horse harness – it was from a warhorse, you know, the piece that goes here." And she illustrated by clamping her pink finger crosswise in her mouth.

"The bit?" Matthew asked. Flora nodded earnestly.

"Daddy's taking us again this holiday – he said he would – and Grandpa says there was a de Eresby there and he got his head chopped off by the king. King... king..." Alex turned to me for help, looking vexed as the name evaded him.

"Edward the Fourth," I whispered.

"Edward the Fourth," he repeated gravely, as if he had remembered it himself. "And Emma said she's going to go too, didn't you, Emma?" Alex challenged me to deny it.

"Did you indeed?" Matthew looked at me, trying not to laugh.

"I might have said that I would think about it."

Flora fixed me firmly with her most teacherly expression – the one she normally reserved for Alex when she thought he was getting beyond himself.

"Yes, you did, Emma, I r'member. But you can come too," she said, beaming up at Matthew. "I can show you where I found the bit, if you like."

Beth gave her a hushing look. "I'm sure Dr Lynes has better things to do than walk around that pile of mud, Flora."

Flora's face fell and Beth flustered as she realized she had overstepped the mark.

"There's nothing I would have liked better," Matthew said, chucking the little girl under the chin so she smiled again.

"So you will come? And Emma too?" Alex said eagerly, his thin little face animated as he looked between us both.

Matthew shook his head slowly. "I'm sorry, I can't this time. I'm flying back to the States tomorrow and I'm taking your aunt with me. Maybe next time."

I barely disguised an involuntary gasp with a cough. The twins started to plead, their joint wheedling rising in a familiar drone. Matthew dropped his voice so the children stopped moaning and had to lean forward to hear him.

"I used to beg my father to take me to a battlefield when I was about your age, and do you know what I found?" The twins shook their heads in unison, eyes round. "A long sword, about…" he narrowed his eyes as he looked at the twins, "… as long as you are, Alex."

My nephew jumped to his feet. "This big!" he put his hand on top of his head.

"Indeed – just as big as you, with a broad cross hilt about here…" he drew a bar across Alex's collarbone, "… and a well-weighted pommel. Do you know what that is?" The children shook their heads again. "That's the handle. And this was a fine hand-and-a-half sword, so whoever it belonged to would have been very sorry to lose it."

I realized with a start that he must be referring to the same battlefield, only he would have walked it nearly 400 years before the children were born.

"Whose was it? Whose was it?" Flora bounced up and down on her knees, making the Imari bowl on the fragile side table shake worryingly.

"Well, my father thought that it must have belonged to at least a knight, if not a lord, and he dropped it during the battle."

Alex grabbed Matthew's arm. "Did he try to escape?"

"I think he must have done. He wouldn't have thrown his sword away casually, so he either dropped it, or…" He let the question hang between them.

"Or he was *killed*!" Alex whispered, fascinated.

Beth inched forward to listen, despite herself. "Do you still have this sword?"

Matthew untangled himself from the children and stood up, ruffling Flora's hair as she tried to hang on to him.

"I do – it's at home." He looked fleetingly at me, before being distracted by Flora riding the toy horse up his back. He caught her under the arms and swung her up as easily as he had held Archie, and she squealed with delight.

"That is a *mi*-ghty fine steed you have there, young lady," he drawled in a perfect Midwest accent. "What's his name?"

Flora started telling him and Beth took the opportunity to pull me to one side by my sleeve.

"Where on earth did you find *him*?" she hissed. "He's downright gorgeous and he's great with kids. No," she corrected herself, "he's not so much gorgeous – though he is, mind you – he's *compelling*."

"Yes, and he's mine," I retorted, pulling a face at her, but liking her description of him all the same.

"Doesn't have an older brother by any chance, does he?" she said, peering around me. The three of them were engaged in discussing the finer points of the plastic horse and possibly horse armour at the other side of the room.

"No, he's unique," I said wryly.

She shook her head in mock wonder. "What's wrong with him, then?"

"There's nothing wrong with him," I said abruptly, and she picked up on it immediately, raising her eyebrows in questioning surprise.

"I didn't say there was, Em. That's the point – he seems almost too perfect." I opened my mouth to reply but she went on rapidly before I had a chance. "So you're going back with him tomorrow? You'll miss Christmas. Golly, what will Mum and Dad say to that?"

"So it seems."

Her eyes widened. "You didn't know, did you? You mean you didn't discuss it first? He *assumed* you would go? And you *agree*? That's a first!" She guffawed and Archie put a wet fist of fingers to her mouth. "Bleagh, thanks Arch." She blew a raspberry at him and he laughed. "I can't say I blame you, though; I can quite see what all the fuss was about."

"What fuss?"

"Ah," she grimaced, "I forgot, I shouldn't say anything."

"Well, it's a bit late now; spit it out, Beth, and keep your voice down, because he also has excellent hearing."

On the other side of the room, Matthew raised an eyebrow. Beth missed it as she observed her children trying to use him as a climbing frame.

"Mum said he has Grandpa's hair colour," she reflected, seemingly oblivious to my growing impatience. I plucked her sleeve to recapture her attention.

"Beth!"

"What? Oh, yes. It's nothing really, it's just that when you came back and you were… well, you know… down in the dumps."

"That's one way of putting it, I suppose. Yes, I know, they asked Mike Taylor to have a little chat with me to see if I could be considered a basket case." I watched Matthew carefully and saw the slight frown cross his brow, confirming he could hear every word we said. I raised my voice to make doubly sure he could hear me.

"And you know he concluded I was nothing of the sort, don't you?"

Alex was demonstrating something that involved tying Flora's Barbie up in a part-used ball of knitting wool.

"Ye-es," Beth hesitated.

"But?"

"But…" she glanced first at me, then at the little group by the window, and lowered her voice. "He did think you might need *watching*." I must have been particularly vacant. "Oh, c'mon, Em, do I have to spell it out? That's why Mum asked me to come over this morning. She's been worried about you; you've been all over the place lately. Mike Taylor thought you might be suicidal."

"Shh!" I hissed, but too late; Matthew's head whipped round and he looked directly at me.

Blow, that's opened a can of worms!

"Beth, that's nonsense! I'm obviously nothing of the sort. Shows he should stick to his own branch of medicine."

I tried to sound derisive, but Matthew disengaged himself from the children and started to walk towards us purposefully.

"Thanks, Beth," I muttered.

"Oops," she said as she saw Matthew's expression, but he stopped short as Dad appeared at the door from the dining room, looking incongruous in one of Nanna's frilly aprons, tied tightly and straining around his middle.

"Lunch is ready, if you would like to come through. I forgot to put the carrots on – sorry it's a bit later than scheduled."

He was trying extra hard to be convivial and Beth saw her opportunity to escape, taking him by the arm and calling to the children.

"Let's see if Mum needs anything doing. Come on, you two, wash hands, it's lunch time." She glanced over her shoulder at me as the children scrambled past to get to the door first. I made to follow.

"Suicidal?" Matthew held me back with an iron grip, his eyes as dark as the sky. I craned up and kissed him lightly on his tight lips.

"Don't be daft; parental over-reaction. Of course I was miserable – what do you think I'd be if I wasn't with you? But suicidal? Don't go thinking you're that great."

He loosened his grip slightly, but concern still channelled his forehead. "Anyway, you're here now, so none of it matters any more – does it, Matthew?"

He searched my face for clues. "And you haven't asked me whether I want to go back with you tomorrow; I might not, you know."

At that his face relaxed, and he tucked his arm around my waist, kissing my neck.

"'Compelling' and 'gorgeous'," he reminded me, his breath tickling my ear as his mouth found the sensitive skin below it, sending little shivers of pleasure down my arms.

"All right, you win. You're not bad-looking for your age, I suppose, but don't let it go to your head. And behave yourself."

With a quick final kiss, he sketched an apologetic look that might have been more effective had he meant it.

"I'll try to, but I might need frequent reminding – I'm a very slow learner."

"But I'm an excellent teacher," I pointed out, to which he responded with an impious grin.

Outside, the wind rattled the windows, driving snow against the fragile glass. Archie fussed in his high chair, squirming against the reins holding him in place. Flora offered him another tree of broccoli and he grabbed it, squishing it on his tray as if it were a personal affront, and rubbed his eyes. I sat as close to Matthew as decently possible. He kept up an even flow of conversation with my father who had already consumed two glasses of Burgundy while regaling him with tales of his early days building Bailey Bridges with the Royal Engineers. I sneaked peeks whenever I could, in between snatches of conversation with Beth and Mum about Archie's teeth and Alex's latest obsession.

Flora stayed unusually quiet throughout most of lunch. Her horse grazed on the vegetables at the side of her plate, riderless for the moment, while she dabbed small pieces of chicken in her gravy, chewing absent-mindedly. Archie made a grab for Flora's horse but she held it safely out of reach of his sticky fingers. He picked up his beaker instead and, leaning sideways, held it out and watched it drop to the floor. His mouth turned down at the corners.

"Archie, you did that on purpose!" Flora scolded. He turned his big eyes on her and his chin began to wobble. Beth sighed; she had barely eaten in between interruptions from the baby, who became increasingly fractious. She undid the straps on his high chair and began to lift him out at an awkward angle. I held out my arms.

"Let me take him, Beth – you finish your lunch. Come on, Archie; give your mother a break, huh?" He scowled at me but didn't complain. I walked over to the French window with him in my arms, and listened to the conversations as we watched the spiralling snow fall onto the grey flags of the courtyard.

"Emma?"

I had been watching Matthew's reflection in the glass surreptitiously; I dragged myself away from his face.

"Yes, Flora?"

Her clear child's voice sailed across the room.

"If you are going away tomorrow, does that mean you won't be here for Christmas?" Conversation around the table came to an abrupt halt. I counted to five before answering.

"Yes, that's right, Flora, I'll be in America."

I waited for Dad to react, for the huffing and the puffing and the remonstration; but instead, he kept his eyes on his half-filled glass, and it was my mother whose tone went from wounded to pleading. I felt the snake-head of childhood guilt rise up, ready to strike. She must have anticipated this moment Matthew arrived.

"Oh, Emma! You didn't say you are going back! This is rather sudden, darling; couldn't you wait a few more days? Surely it'll take that long to get your ticket – it's such a busy time of year. Or Emma could join you after Christmas perhaps, Matthew?"

This wasn't going to be easy. I could see them behind me reflected in the window – Mum's face unnaturally pinched by a warp in the glass; Matthew still, except for his right hand stroking the stem of his untouched wine glass.

"If we're going to travel soon, Mrs D'Eresby, we'll have to do so in the next twenty-four hours. There's a big area of low pressure developing over the States, and prolonged snow is forecast, so the airfields will shut. It could be a couple of weeks until they're clear – especially at this time of year, and I don't want it to stop us travelling."

I loved the way he said "we" – not "I" or "me", but "we" and "us", and I warmed at his words. Archie thumped the window with his fist, trying to squash snowflakes, and the thin glass shivered. My father attempted to work out the logic of it.

"So the big airfields shut down for snow for that long? Surely they can't operate commercially on that basis?"

Matthew concurred. "Quite so. The big airports stay open most of the year, but we're not flying to a commercial airfield."

"But what about Emma's ticket?" Mum interrupted. "She can't travel without one and it'll take days. It did for us, didn't it, Hugh?"

Matthew addressed her. "She doesn't need one."

I spun around, surprised. "Don't I?" Archie strained to get closer to the window, starting to fret.

"No, you're flying with me."

Crump. The baby managed to thump the window again and

Dad winced. I enclosed his hot fist in my hand. He struggled and whimpered but I had just cottoned on to what Matthew said and wasn't taking that much notice of my nephew.

"Oh – *you're* flying. Oh!" I came and sat down, beaming idiotically up at him. Archie began to wail, his arms flailing over my shoulder at the window. The unaccustomed weight of the fidgeting child made my newly healed arm ache and I began to feel the familiar sensation of failure where anything to do with babies was concerned. I made a last attempt at trying to soothe him.

"What's up, grizzle-chops?" He arched his back and opened his mouth in a big "O", ready to roar. My arm yelled in sympathy. Matthew put his hands out.

"Emma, let me take him, he's too heavy for you." He scooped him from me and held him against his chest. Archie stopped crying and they surveyed each other.

"Teething are you, Archie?" The baby put his fingers on Matthew's chin and he rubbed Archie's back. "Never mind, you'll feel better when you've had a sleep."

"So will I," said Beth with feeling.

"You have a pilot's licence, do you?" said Dad, still mulling it over. "What do you fly?"

"A Global Express XRS twin jet; it's very reliable."

"And very fast?" I said, remembering his car.

"Quite possibly," he said, grinning at me over the baby's head and moving his leg until it touched mine beneath the table.

"You have your own plane?" Mum removed Flora's plate as the horse trotted around it. "Surely if it's snowing here it's far too dangerous to fly anyway."

I collected Matthew's plate from in front of him as Archie's foot came dangerously close to the cold gravy, and stacked my father's empty plate on top of it.

"These are only snow showers; they won't amount to much. I wouldn't take Emma if it were dangerous, but we need to reach Maine before the heavy weather sets in. Also, I have my family to consider, and I need to get back." Archie gave a little sleepy burp and Matthew patted his back gently. Mum's head shot around to give him one of her glares, which would have Beth and me quaking when we were children.

"Emma has *her* family *here*, and it's such short notice."

I didn't want him pressurized into agreeing with her, and I knew just how persuasive my mother could be, but Matthew regarded her steadily, watching the short, sharp movements that betrayed her anxiety. I felt it echoed in the ball of my stomach.

"Mum, you know I planned on spending Christmas with Matthew."

"But that was before you were…" She was going to say, "Before you were on the verge of a breakdown", but she saw the expression on my face and modified the sentence. "… Before you came back home, darling. You're still not fully recovered and we can look after you. Hugh, please…" She looked desperately at my father for support and missed the imperceptible tightening along Matthew's jaw.

"I understand that this is sudden, Mrs D'Eresby, and were circumstances different, there would be no need for urgency; but unless she wishes it otherwise, Emma is coming back to Maine with me, and we are leaving tomorrow. We will spend Christmas there together with my family, as originally planned." He looked at me and I nodded. The tone in his voice hadn't altered; he had neither raised nor lowered it, but there was no mistaking that he was resolute.

Mum stared at him, and then at Dad, her mouth marking an angry line. She didn't argue, but her silence spoke volumes.

She stalked out, taking a pile of plates, with Dad following. The murmur of voices rose over the clattering of plates and forks. I reached for Matthew's glass and gulped half the contents in an attempt to drown my guilt, avoiding my sister's eyes.

"Gosh," Beth reflected in hushed awe. "Em and I wouldn't have *dared*; Mum would've had our guts for garters."

Archie twitched in his sleep and Matthew stroked the baby's back.

"It must be difficult for her, with her mother ill, and her daughter barely recovered. Change is rarely simple, whether for good or ill, and sometimes decisions are easier to accept when someone makes them for us. Sometimes." The slow movement of his hand hesitated. So much lay behind the statement – so much history, so much life; but there was something else – an uncertainty, regret. He met my eyes. "However, Emma has her own life to lead, and her own decisions to make." He smiled briefly, then referring to the sleeping Archie, said, "I think he has the right idea; where's the best place to stay around here now?"

I didn't miss the "now" he dropped in casually at the end of the sentence. I arched an eyebrow at him when Beth wasn't looking, and his eyes widened innocently.

"You're staying here," I said. "Or I'm staying where you do; either way, I'm not letting you out of my sight."

Matthew shook his head. "I don't think it will go down well with your parents if you suggest I stay here."

I scrumpled the paper napkins Mum used for day-to-day meals into a ball. The wine made me gung-ho and not likely to take *no* for an answer.

"Here, there – whatever – I don't mind; you know my conditions."

"Of course, you can always stay with us," Beth suggested.

"We need someone who can tame the Archie-monster."

Matthew twisted his head to check the baby.

"He's not so bad. Once that tooth is fully through he'll settle again." Archie snored softly against Matthew's shoulder, cherubic when asleep. "Would you like me to put him down somewhere so he can sleep properly?"

Beth looked less than enthusiastic. "He has a cot upstairs for when we visit, but he'll probably wake up if you put him down, and then he'll scream blue murder." She eyed her son. "And you won't think he's adorable then, I can tell you. He can bellow for England; I swear he's got his eye on being the town cryer. Ask Em, she'll tell you. He *will* wake up; it's guaranteed."

Archie whimpered as if in acknowledgment, thrusting an arm sideways and exposing a roll of soft, pink baby tummy to the chilly air. Matthew pulled his jersey down.

"No, I don't think so; he's out for a while, he'll be fine. Show me where to put him. You need to watch your lower back; how long has it been hurting?"

And he followed her from the dining room, leaving me wondering how he knew my sister had a back problem.

"You could have backed me up, Hugh."

In the silence that followed Beth and Matthew's convivial conversation, I could hear my parents in the kitchen. I moved nearer to the door and their voices became clearer. They stopped whatever they had been doing and I could hear Mum's fraught tones.

"You know Emma's not been herself and I'm not convinced she's fully well. Only this morning she was acting very peculiarly and, just because Dr... Matthew's turned up... well, let's just say that I think that he's the root of all her problems.

And now she's spending Christmas with him! What happens if they break up again and we're not there to bring her back? We don't know much about him and certainly nothing about his family. I can't help remembering what happened after she broke up with Guy. That was such a *mess*, Hugh; I don't want her going through that again."

There was a rattle followed by a subdued thump as the front of the dishwasher closed, then a hiss as water from the spray began the cycle. Dad's base tone boomed in the enclosed space.

"But as I remember it, it was Guy who ended up in hospital, not Emma. I think she's probably stronger than we have given her credit for, Penny, and, let's face it, we're not doing her any good at the moment. I've spent too long protecting her from my gaffes, and one of the things she said to me was that I don't let her make her own mistakes, and I think she has a point. So, if she goes back with him now it might work or it might not – but at least it will be her decision and she won't be able to blame it on us if it does go wrong."

"Hugh, really!"

He chuckled – a deep, rolling laugh I hadn't heard in ages, accompanied by a tinny slopping as he washed a saucepan, then the tap running briefly as he rinsed it.

"You know I wouldn't wish that on her, Penny, but we have to let her go sometime and…"

Thinner, and drawn so tight that it severed the conversation like a cheese-wire, Mum's voice cut through his.

"But he lives in America – when would we see her? It's such a long way."

"Only a flight away, Penny, and he *does* fly. Fancy owning his own jet," and he chortled again.

Maybe the wine had ameliorated his mood, or maybe what

I had said to him on the return journey from Martinsthorpe had finally made some sense. I saw a side of my father I hadn't seen since my early childhood – the man he had been before the depression had set in, which, I now realized, had dogged him for most of my adult life, colouring my perception of the man beneath. It had always been my mother who had stood up for me, who had argued my cause and now, it appeared, the roles were reversed. Perhaps only now did she feel me slipping away, whereas before my father had represented the immovable block that prevented me from going very far.

I didn't hear Matthew come in and only when the air caressed my neck did I realize he had returned.

"Interesting conversation?"

"How much did you hear?"

"Enough. Who's Guy?"

"A previous life. He's not important and now's not the time." I indicated to where the sound of my parents' voices drifted towards us from beyond the kitchen door.

"A complication?" he said, keeping one eye on the door, while pulling me closer, making my insides flutter delightfully. I cuddled against him.

"No, not any more, and nothing – *nothing* – compared with you."

The door started to creak open and he let me go. By the time they appeared, Matthew was examining an article on the front page of *The Times* while I was trying my best to look neither guilty nor too innocent, as both would have given me away.

"We were just discussing sleeping arrangements," I announced. Mum looked askance and Dad began to bluster like the good old days. "And I wondered if Matthew could have Nanna's room for the night. What do you think?"

Goodness only knows what my parents thought I got up to with Guy; they never asked and I never said although, given the thumping my father bestowed on him, it seemed likely that he guessed. But my attitude to sex as well as life had changed since then, and I wanted to make it quite clear that there were certain boundaries I would not cross. Matthew and I had not yet discussed our attitudes to sex – when, for that matter, had we had the opportunity? But despite our physical proximity at times, he never assumed we would consummate our relationship. Perhaps, given his upbringing, I understood why, but in the light of modern sentiments, our restraint might appear archaic. I didn't care what other people thought, but I did wonder just how long I could hold out against the desire simmering below the surface. And if one of us pushed a little too far, how resilient would the other need to be to resist temptation? I felt myself warm at the thought.

I wasn't insensitive to how my parents – and Mum in particular – might feel about Matthew using Nanna's room but, although cavernous, the house still had only three bedrooms. The fourth had been converted into an additional bathroom; I bet my parents were regretting *that* decision at this moment.

"The east bedroom it is, then. Which reminds me..." I swivelled to look at him. "Matthew, I would like to visit Nanna this evening. If we are going tomorrow, it might be..." I hesitated, then decided not to finish the sentence. I didn't need to – all three understood what I had been going to say.

10

Saying Goodbye

We made our way down the High Street between the Georgian shop façades. Windows glowed with Christmas lights and street decorations danced in the light wind that still blew the occasional flurry of snow between the varicoloured strands, briefly illuminating the flakes in a glow of red or blue or green before they passed once more into darkness. The streets were gritty with slush that clung in clumps to my boots.

I wore the coat Matthew had given me in Maine, but not gloves, as I wanted nothing between his hand and mine except our skin. Before leaving the house, I wrapped his scarf around his neck, tucking it under the collar of his coat, which was still wet and heavy from the morning's sleet. Now I shivered without it and he stopped, uncoiling the scarf and muffling my protests in its soft folds.

"You need this more than I do," he said, drawing the scarf up and cocooning my ears. "There, that's better." He stroked away a snowflake from my cheek. "That was very brave and forthright of you – with your parents and the sleeping arrangements, I mean – although I'm not sure if it will endear me to them."

"I can be brave, especially if I've been plied with your wine beforehand; it can make me outrageously outspoken and reckless. That is all right with you, isn't it? I mean, I didn't ask you, I just assumed." I paused when I saw the look on his face. "Now what have I said?"

"*You* assumed, Emma?" he mocked me gently and I clapped my hands over my mouth. He drew me away from the side of the road as a car passed, spraying slushy ice in an arc from its tyres.

"I did, didn't I? I'm so sorry – I broke my cardinal rule. Would you prefer to stay somewhere else, or… er… or to be alone? I didn't mean to assume that you would want me to… oh, *blow*, you know perfectly well what I'm trying to say."

I tied myself in knots as I realized I had made more than one assumption. The door to the shop closed behind the last customer, releasing a drift of chocolate-scented air into the street. Matthew tipped my chin with a finger, but I avoided looking at him in my embarrassment.

"If there is one thing you are safe to assume, Emma…" he began, and I dared to look at him again, and he held me in a steady gaze, "… that is that wherever you are, I want to be." My heart lurched, caught off guard. "Now," he said, "tell me about your grandmother."

I led us down a quieter side road, and told him about Nanna and how her effervescent personality had brought sunshine into my childhood home. I described how she and Grandpa met, and their connection to Martinsthorpe. Finally, I spoke again of how my grandfather's obsession had dominated my life. Matthew grew quiet, his brow drawn together in concentrated thought. The hushed streets were lit by an occasional lamp, but many occupants had not yet drawn their curtains, displaying their intimate worlds with flagrant disregard for privacy. I loved to look in on other people's lives, not because I knew them or wanted to know about them, but because they offered a source of stability and continuity which I found comforting. It was the same reason why I liked antiques or why I had become addicted to history. Matthew questioned why I hadn't fled in horror when I found out about his past. The wonder of it for me was why I hadn't taken flight *before* I knew his identity. The fact that he was a walking, talking, loving piece of living history was as much a magnet for me as his intellect, or thoughtfulness, or good looks. I wasn't sure how aware of that he might be, or whether it could be considered relevant now anyway. There were so many questions I wanted to ask him, so much that I needed to know but, as we walked along side by side, the plain fact that he shouldn't exist didn't matter to me at all. Not yet, anyway. I squeezed his hand and his frown cleared, dissolving into the night.

Awake and alert, Nanna sat up in a high-backed chair by the window in her new room. She smiled with the good side of her face when she saw me, and I bent down to kiss her soft cheek. Although the sun had long since set, the garden onto which her window looked gleamed prettily in the remains of the snow lit by pools of light from nearby rooms. I had asked Matthew if I could see her for a few minutes alone before I introduced him, and I could see him now through the open door as he waited in the communal entrance hall, studying a reproduction eighteenth-century map of the area.

My grandmother put her hand over mine and looked surprised.

"It's cold outside, Nanna. I know, I know, I should have worn gloves. Beth brought the children over this morning. The twins love the snow; they haven't seen much of it in their short lives, have they?" I held her hand in mine as we looked out of the window together.

"Do you remember when we had snow on Boxing Day when I must have been about…" I wrinkled my nose, trying to think, "… about five, and Beth nearly fourteen – when Dad was stationed in Germany again. And we were in the car because I think we had been to see someone for a second Christmas Day – I can't remember who – and we saw all those moths in the headlights – hundreds and hundreds of them, and I couldn't understand why there were so many moths in winter. And everyone laughed at me except you, and you said, 'These are no ordinary moths; these are the ghosts of the moths that fly under the summer moon, and they come back as snowflakes to fly again beneath a winter sun.' And when we arrived home and I opened the car door, my feet sank into the snow and I cried for all the lives of the moths that lay there, but you said, 'Don't cry, Emma; the moths never really die, and next winter they will fly as snow again.'"

I sighed. "There aren't so many moths now, are there, Nanna?" When I looked at her again, a single tear had fallen down the hollow of her cheek. "Nanna?" She crooked her head towards me and the corner of her mouth twitched as she patted my hand. I checked over my shoulder and, seeing Matthew still absorbed, from inside my coat I drew the leather bag containing the journal, removed the book, and placed it carefully on the rug covering her knees.

"You wanted to see the journal, Nanna; this is it. This is what Grandpa and I wanted. This is what it is all about."

My grandmother made a strange noise in her throat, almost an excited gasp, followed by a grunt of frustration as she tried to open the diary. I raised it to her eye level and opened the first page, then slowly turned the pages for her to see.

"Nanna, how did you know I had the journal? Nobody else knows except you, not even…" and unintentionally, my gaze slipped towards Matthew. "Nobody," I repeated, and when I looked at her again, she studied my face, then directed her focus towards my heart. "Ah, I understand. You knew because you know me, yes? And because it's what Grandpa would have done. But, Nanna, Grandpa wasn't a *thief*…"

She let out a fierce growl, cutting me short. Alarmed, I interjected, "OK, I know I meant only to borrow it; still…"

Again the sharp retort, and this time I acquiesced before she strained herself.

"No, all right, I didn't steal it and yes, I mean to return it just as soon as I can. In fact…" I had prepared what I wanted to tell her, but now that it came to it, the words stuck. When I spoke again, my vocal cords vibrated uncomfortably against the obstruction. "I… have something to tell you, Nanna; I'm going back to America tomorrow, so I won't be here for Christmas. Also… I've brought somebody to meet you." I glanced over to where two nurses were trying to engage Matthew in conversation. He wore his polite-but-distant expression as he kept one eye on me, waiting for my signal to join us. Nanna grunted a question.

"He's the doctor I told you about; he came back for me. I don't know what's going to happen next, but I wanted you to know – before I leave – I wanted you to know that this is what I want, what I've waited for. Mum and Dad aren't too sure, but I am, and I want you to be as well."

She whispered something I leaned forward to catch.

"Yes, I am happy," I said. "Very." I might have added "confused", but she didn't need to know that. "Will you meet him? Please?" She brushed my hand with hers in assent and I tucked the journal away out of sight and motioned to

Matthew. He seemed unaware of the impact of his departure on the thwarted nurses as they watched him move with muscular grace down the corridor towards us. He closed the door behind him, cutting off their view. I moved to one side so that he could greet her.

"Nanna, this is Matthew Lynes."

My grandmother responded immediately; the old woman's eyes opened wide with the shock of recognition, her thin, bony fingers clasping the bright knitted rug over her knees. She stared at him, her mouth moving without uttering a sound. Matthew looked perplexed as I sat down next to her, holding her clenched hands in mine.

"What is it? What's the matter?" I followed the direction of her gaze and then realized. "Oh, how stupid of me! I should have reminded you, I'm sorry." I laughed nervously, "Matthew, it's your hair, I forgot; it's just like Grandpa's, isn't it, Nanna? It confused me too, when I first met him." She moved her hands beneath mine and grunted. "I'll be staying with Matthew and his family over Christmas and I don't know when I'll be back next."

She whispered something I didn't catch and Matthew drew another chair towards mine and sat next to her. She fixed him with her inquisitional look and he returned it steadily, as if a conversation without words flowed between them. She whispered to me again, the effort strenuous as she tried to vocalize her thoughts. Matthew touched her arm lightly.

"Ask me directly; I can hear everything you say. I live in Maine but I originally came from this region; is that what you wanted to know?"

I disguised my astonishment at his casual revelation by pulling the sagging rug over her lap and tucking it in. Nanna narrowed her eyes, searching for something hidden in the back of her memory. Slowly, hesitantly at first, she raised her hand and touched his face, and my breath came short and shallow as I waited for her to remember where she had seen his image before – from her childhood, from her youth – when the sun shone through the window of the old church. He didn't flinch, and she rested her hand for the briefest moment on his cheek before sighing and letting it drop. The moment passed, the memory gone, but her lips moved although I didn't hear her speak. Matthew looked up at me.

"Emma, your grandmother would like some tea. Is it possible you could ask one of the nurses?" He saw my eyes flick to the half-finished beaker standing on her bedside table before I rose to do as she asked.

Instead of bothering the nurses, I went in search of the kitchenette at the other end of the care home, which would give Nanna and Matthew more time to discuss whatever it was they didn't want me to hear. I found the kettle, and sat on the seating next to the utility area, waiting for it to boil. I leaned my head back and contemplated the strip lighting, feeling suddenly very tired. This wasn't going exactly as planned, although I don't know what I thought would happen. I wanted my grandmother's blessing, I suppose – her approval. I always sought it when things weren't going my way or when I doubted a decision I had made. But it was more than that, and she would understand. I reached out to my grandfather through her, as my last tenuous link to that part of my childhood which made me the person I had become, because he always believed that I could do whatever I set out to do, and do it well. What would he have made of this turn of events that linked our past and present to an unknown future? What indeed?

As I put the tea on the locker, Matthew stood up and put his arm around my shoulders. He seemed quite serious and, whatever they had discussed must have taxed her, because Nanna rested her head against the dark green back of her chair, her eyes closed. Wisps of flimsy white hair contrasted with the material, and her skin – tight and thin – stretched like vellum over her cheekbones. Her pulse beat visibly in her neck and she looked very frail.

Before he could answer my questioning look, my grandmother opened her eyes and one side of her face lifted as she saw me – saw *us* – confirming her approval in a way no words could. Then she looked at Matthew and he nodded once, and stopped me before I could sit down, holding on to my hand, his voice quiet.

"Emma, your grandmother is very tired; you need to say goodbye."

"Of course, we'll go in a minute, but…"

"Emma." Looking evenly into mine, the changing colour of his eyes conveyed an unspoken message: *It's time to say goodbye.*

Crushing realization drained blood from my face, a gathering weight in my chest drowning my heart.

"No, Matthew – not yet! She can't, not now!" I gasped, trying to get around him to Nanna, struggling to free my hand from his grip. Instead he drew me to him, holding me until I stopped fighting. His heart beat evenly against the stuttering pulse of my own. "But Nanna…" I tried, but found my throat closed up.

"She knows, Emma, she's ready. She doesn't want to stay any longer." His voice mellowed, flowing in calming rivulets. "Your grandmother is content now; she's waited this long and that's long enough. It's time for her to go."

Resisting the effects of his voice, I pulled away from him, and this time he let me go. "Enough? Nanna, what's enough?" I slid onto my knees next to my grandmother, taking her hand. "Nanna, what's enough? I don't understand. How do you *know*?" I fired the question over my shoulder at him. As I looked desperately at her, she smiled sadly at me, and with a great effort lifted her good hand to touch my face. She looked at Matthew and he held out his hand so that she could take it shakily in her own, placing his palm against my cheek in a gesture of union.

"Emma, this is what she wants, this is what she has been waiting for; let her go." I clasped their hands to my face – the one thin and dry and faded, the other strong and vital. I closed my eyes and breathed consciously until the overwhelming need to cry receded, mitigated by the stronger desire to maintain control for her sake. I wanted our parting not to be stained with my tears. Finally I spoke again.

"I don't want you to go, Nanna, but I understand; you want to see Grandpa again, don't you?"

She made a gruff noise from the base of her throat and smiled her crooked smile, a remnant of what she used to be, but sad no longer, and I laid her hand gently back down. I took Matthew's hand in mine and kissed it, and my grandmother's eyes sparkled.

"Tell Grandpa – when you see him – tell him about Matthew and about the journal. And tell him…" I paused, "… and please tell him that I've found what he was looking for."

Nanna's eyes darted to Matthew and then back to me, and deep in her chest she laughed – a happy, contented sound that lit her face from within.

I couldn't face going home immediately, and we wandered the back streets of the now silent town until I could cope with what had passed without sliding towards grief once more. The slush began to freeze in the gutters and in patches on the paths. The slow drip of melting snow from the branches of the occasional tree now ceased, the illuminated drops tiny stars of light in the street lamps.

We found ourselves in Broad Street beneath Browne's Hospital, the ancient almshouses solidly reassuring in their great age. My legs tired, I sat on a bench by the memorial and stared back up at the buildings. Matthew sat close. Minutes passed.

"How did you know about Nanna?"

"She told me."

"But she couldn't have told you when she is going to… go."

"No, Emma, nobody knows the hour of their death."

"Then how did she – do you – know that she is dying?"

His tranquillity wound itself around the turbulence raging within me, taming it despite myself, making it easier to accept the inevitable end that Nanna – and I – faced.

"She said she is ready, and her body told me. She's worn out by life and by waiting. There's nothing left for her here, not living the way she is."

I considered what he said, pulling my legs under me as the wind bit through my skirt and tights. Matthew adjusted the scarf around my neck, covering part of my head. "You're freezing; do you want to go back home?"

Home represented warmth and comfort, solidity and continuity. Home was Nanna pouring tea from her dented silver pot into old Minton teacups with worn gilt edges, laughing with Mum and Grandpa over shared history as I sat listening on the floor nearby and made patterns out of bamboo mah-jong pieces.

"No, not yet."

He took off his coat, mirroring his action of that morning, and spread it over me.

"Emma, your grandmother doesn't want your mother to know."

"I won't say anything." Another minute passed. "What about Dad – can I tell him?"

"That's up to your judgment, I think; she didn't say not to."

"Will she…" I couldn't bring myself to say "die" without the choking sensation in my throat building again. "Will it be soon, do you think?"

"Yes, I think so – in the next three or four months – but not before Christmas and, before you ask, she doesn't want you to stay until she does; she wants you to get on with your life."

"But how do you *know* that, Matthew? She couldn't tell you." I twisted around to look up at him, but he contemplated the old stonework of the range of buildings behind us, with an expression I couldn't fathom.

"No."

"Well, how then?"

He looked at me, coming back from far away.

"In the same way that I know that your father's left knee hurts with arthritis and your arm ached holding Archie, or that Beth has a bad back where she's bruised a lower vertebra."

"And Archie's tooth?"

"No, that was obvious."

"You're being obtuse again. I thought we were beyond all that. *How* do you know these things?"

He breathed deeply, his chest rising against my shoulder.

"It's something I can do. I can tell when, and where, and how much someone is hurting. It's very helpful in my job, as you can imagine."

I remembered the searing agony of the knife wound, the constant pain from my arm and ribs, and I thought that I couldn't endure him suffering for everyone else.

"But surely that means that you can feel *everyone's* pain; how can you bear it?"

"I've learned to be selective. I can shut off most of it so that it's just a background... noise... for want of a better word, except where it proves useful as a diagnostic tool. Otherwise I would be overwhelmed by people's suffering and I wouldn't be able to focus on the person I'm helping at the time. I was always sensitive to other people's pain before I altered – you might call it having physical empathy – but it seemed enhanced afterwards and has become more acute over the years. I don't know why – perhaps I'm more attuned." He drifted to a meditative close, unaware of me staring at him, horrified by this strange new dilemma.

"Why didn't you tell me before? Whatever this is, it's a curse."

He looked at me directly. "No, Emma, no it isn't; it allows me to help people. I'm glad I can feel their pain. It reminds me to... well... believe that I'm here for a reason; that I'm not just some incongruity with no right to exist. You once told me that what you liked most about one of your posters was that it depicted hope, and that hope is not futile – that there is redemption for those who believe."

I nodded mutely, miserably.

"I have hope, Emma, that one day I will be redeemed – that I will be released from this life. If I can help people – just one person – I have justified my continuing existence and, if helping them means that I feel their pain, then so be it."

Emotion – already so close to the surface – began to break as I realized all the years of suffering he had been through.

My voice cracked.

"This… this is all the result of what happened when you were stabbed, isn't it? That night when you were betrayed…"

He put his fingers against my lips, hushing me. A small group of lads appeared from around the corner, sliding on patches of ice, whooping and noisily exuberant, cans of lager sloshing in their hands. They jeered when they saw us and Matthew's back stiffened.

"Not now, Emma, please; there is so much we need to talk about – that you need to understand. Wait until we have time to ourselves without distractions."

His eyes followed the group until they were out of sight, leaving the fag end of their cigarette smoke as a token presence. "Please?" He looked at me again.

"When, Matthew? We *never* seem to have the time."

He rested his forehead on mine. "Then we will make time. Do you remember I promised you a trip into the mountains?"

"Hmm," I hummed doubtfully, remembering only too well what had happened last time we were in sight of them. He remembered too.

"No – I mean *right* into them – not just in the foothills. I will take you into the heart of the mountains when we get back. I know someone who has a cabin there and I'll take you – just you and me."

"And no bears?"

"And definitely no bears," he promised, kissing my forehead, letting his lips linger for a moment longer than he needed to. "Agreed?"

"You, me and the mountains? And no bears? And you'll tell me everything?"

"Yes," he said eventually, but heavily, as if a weighty

decision had been made. I looked up at Browne's Hospital without replying, wondering what lay behind the tenor of his answer, what more there was to know, and reckoned that, as much as I had to come to terms with his past, he possibly needed to do so as well, sitting here as we were.

"Matthew, did you ever see these almshouses when you were… younger?"

He glanced up at them, then back at me, puzzled. "Yes, they haven't changed much."

"Doesn't it make you want to at least see the land you came from?"

"As I said this morning, it was a very long time ago."

"A long time ago yesterday?"

He smiled. "Indeed."

We returned to the house as the air began to snap with frost. I felt cold through to my core despite being wrapped in Matthew's big coat, the hems of which dragged the ground as I walked beside him, although I lifted them like petticoats. He had refused to take it back, saying that the cold didn't touch him, and at last I began to understand the extent of the differences between us. Although I saw, through my own film of grief, that Nanna had come to terms with her mortality, nonetheless her imminent death and the effect it would have on my family still bore heavily upon me, and that was the sort of cold that no number of coats could dispel.

My parents were watching the news when we entered the sitting room. Beth and the children had gone home after lunch, but Flora's Barbie had forgotten a pink shoe, and it now sat forlornly on the mantelpiece. Mum began to get up when we went in.

"Stay there, Mum, we're going to get something to eat. Can I get you anything?"

"No thank you, darling. I was just going to ask how Nanna is."

I suspected that really she wanted to know what Nanna thought of Matthew and he thought so too, because he apologized for not joining us, sitting down next to Dad with the excuse that he wanted to see the weather forecast for the morning.

"How was she?" she asked as I made tea in the largest mug I could find.

"Do you know, Mum, I think Nanna is probably happier than I've seen her for a long time," I answered truthfully, the toaster popping and the inviting smell of fresh toast filling the kitchen. She looked relieved; her mother's death would hit her hard, but it would be easier if she could look back and know that Nanna had been happy in the last months of her life.

"And what about Matthew; did she like him?"

I retrieved the hot toast, juggling it between my fingers until cool enough to handle.

"I think you will have to ask her yourself, but yes, she liked him; she likes him a lot." I smiled to myself, letting her see it as confirmation that what I said was true.

"And Mum, I'm sorry if I seemed insensitive earlier – about Nanna's room, I mean. I don't think Nanna will mind, but if it upsets you…"

"No, I'm sure it's fine, darling; I think that it was just a bit of a shock with you returning to Maine so soon. I hadn't expected that the two of you would get back together, but if it's what you want, I'm happy for you."

Dad must have stuck to his guns and refused to budge, his stubbornness for once acting in my favour. She smiled bravely and I put my arms around her, my heart breaking just a little, knowing how hard it must be for her, and how hard it would get.

11

Revolution

"Warmer?"

I sat propped up on my pillows, the duvet pulled to my chin and the blue rug doubled around my shoulders. The fanheater whirred at the end of my bed where I stuck my feet out in the flow of warm air. Despite wearing a dressing-gown and pyjamas, I couldn't shake the cold that clung like a ghost. Even the tea and toast had made little impact.

"Not really."

Matthew sat next to me, his long legs almost reaching the iron-and-brass footrest, and I snuggled into him. "But you could help," I said with longing but without intent.

"I think sleep would be more efficacious in your case," he murmured into my hair. The skin of his neck felt cool, his scent of clean air untainted by sweat, and it occurred to me that I had never seen him flush with heat or shiver with cold. His skin always remained the same temperature, whatever he was doing, wherever he had been. Beneath my ear, his heart beat as constantly as a metronome – neither faster nor slower – as his chest rose and fell with the same regularity.

"Tell me how you found out where I came from."

He didn't say "come from", which is what I think I would have said, but "*came* from", distancing himself in space as well as time. I thought back to when I first met him and the impact he made on me then, before I knew what I knew now.

"It was lots of little things," I said ambiguously, "But mainly your colouring and then, of course, your name – although I couldn't place it at first. I told you about my grandfather and his corn-coloured hair; do you remember?"

"Yes, I do."

He had almost lost his temper. Now I understood he had done so because I had stumbled across a grave that he thought lay safely undisturbed.

"And there were other things, such as your use of language – it can be quite archaic at times. And you still have an English accent, you know, even if it is tinged with American."

"Is it so obvious?"

I knew what concerned him. If I had traced him back, then so could somebody else. "No, don't worry. I think that it's only because I'm tuned in, so to speak, and looking. I expect, to most people, you sound transatlantic. Flora and Alex both think you're American, don't they? And as for your use of language, you just sound old-fashioned, and that's very…" I kissed the base of his throat and he laughed, "… attractive. But if you hadn't been so touchy and secretive, perhaps I wouldn't have kept digging. I knew something wasn't quite right about you, of course – with your strength and speed and being able to pick up burning embers…"

"Ah, yes – you saw that, didn't you?"

"Yes, I did. And then, of course, there was the bear…"

"I should have killed it," he muttered.

"What – with your hands? Now that *would* have given the game away!"

He shrugged sheepishly.

"Anyway, there were all those minor incidents that added

up to one big question. And you wouldn't tell me what was going on, and that became just too much for me to cope with. One minute we were together, and the next you were gone. But I didn't know why."

"And then you left," he stated without any hint of blame.

"Yes. I asked Elena to tell you when she saw you that I hadn't left you – that I would come back, but…"

"I didn't see her," he finished.

"No, and Matias didn't know to tell you either. When they phoned the other night and said you'd gone and that you'd been upset, I didn't know what to think. I thought that you must have been so angry when I sent you the card that you…" My voice – which had been a whisper – now faltered.

"I'm sorry, Emma. I wasn't angry with you. I felt so relieved to get your message – I understood immediately. It came as a shock, of course, but the fact that you had contacted me at all, despite knowing the truth about my past – it meant everything to me. No, it wasn't you who made me react when I saw Matias."

I waited for him to explain, but he didn't. I raised my head to look at him, but again he had that distant look in the darkness of his eyes that I recognized.

"Matthew?"

He smiled, but it did nothing to lessen the distinct impression that he was holding out on me. "Just one of those complications. I will explain – when we get back. Emma, please tell me one thing that's been worrying me."

"What?"

"When we were together that last time, did I hurt you – physically?"

My hand went involuntarily to my chest.

He recoiled from me, aghast. "I did, didn't I?"

"No, no, you didn't really. It was nothing."

Mortified, he asked, "What was nothing? Good grief, Emma! What did I do?"

I had never heard him so shocked before.

"No, Matthew – really," I twisted onto my knees to face him. "It's just that you kissed me quite hard – but it didn't hurt," I said hurriedly, before he said anything. "You didn't hurt me; there were just a few little – *tiny* – bruises, here." I held my hand to my chest, fingers spread across my breast-bone. "And I was glad you did, because it was something of you I could carry with me, to remind me of you."

He no longer looked shocked but disgusted, and for a moment I thought he considered me depraved. He stared at where my hand lay spreadeagled, as if the bruises were still visible, then swivelled to the edge of the bed and turned his back, appalled. When he spoke, self-loathing filled his voice.

"How could I have hurt you! How could I have been so intent on my own desire that I could have done *that* to you?"

His dismay hurt more than any bruise he had inflicted. Leaning against the curve of his spine, I put my arms around his waist and my face against his lean, muscular back. His shoulders were taut under his shirt and shook slightly with tension.

"It was my desire, too," I whispered.

He shuddered, "*You* didn't hurt me."

"I know, but they're all gone now – look – and you didn't mean to, did you, Matthew?"

I put my hand around the side of his face and tried to turn his head, feeling the rigid muscles in his jaw as he resisted my attempts to comfort him. I persisted and he looked at where my skin lay exposed in the "v" of my pyjama jacket. He touched the tips of his fingers to my breastbone as gently as a butterfly wing.

"There, you see? Nothing – they're all gone; there's nothing to reproach yourself for."

"I forget..." he said so softly that I could only just hear him, "... how vulnerable you are, and how strong I am – how *durable*." He sounded so dejected that I wanted to wrap him up and tell him everything would be all right.

"If you weren't, would you still be here?" I asked. "And then where would I be without you? Alone," I answered my own question, "safe in my own little world with nobody touching my life, and I not touching theirs. And where's the challenge in that? I can't just drift through life. Mum said I must let happiness find me. Well, it has," I said, looking at the source of it. "And anyway," I added, "I like to live dangerously."

He scanned my face, before he chuckled, and the tension dissipated, the corners of his mouth tipping up again in just the way I liked and very close now, his lips just inches from mine.

"There is something very appealing about you when you're in one of your philosophical moods and you become quite adamant," he mused. "I think it must be something to do with how your eyes light up..." He brushed my eyelids with his lips, "... or when you flush right down to the base of your throat..." and I quivered as he pressed his mouth into the hollow of my neck, "... or how your mouth turns down at the corners, just so..." and he kissed each corner very carefully. "I've missed this closeness," he said. "I can't begin to tell you how I've missed you. There's so much we have to talk about – things we need to discuss."

"Such as our future?" I queried softly, hopefully – almost forgetting the immense length of his past that made a nonsense of my short life. Pulling away, he stood abruptly, scrubbing his hands through his hair and making it stand up at all angles. "Yes. Our future. But not now; not here; not yet, Emma. Not yet."

I squeaked with frustration and flumped back against the pillows, burying my face in my arms and knocking the fan-heater sideways in the process. Matthew switched it off before it could set fire to the bedding, and I peeked out at him. Folding his arms on the iron frame at the foot of the bed, he gazed at me, a half-smile on his face.

"A little patience will stand you in good stead; it's something I've had to develop over the years and it doesn't come naturally to me, I assure you. I promised you we will talk about everything, when we are alone – truly alone – and undisturbed: my past, your past, our future."

I scowled at him half-heartedly. "I can't wait that long."

"Yes, you can, and you know it, even though you would like to pretend otherwise. And anyway," he came around to the side of the bed and ran a long finger from a point on my forehead, down my nose to my lips, until he made a full stop on my chin; "you haven't finished telling me about how you tracked me down."

"And what makes you think I'm going to tell you now, when I don't get anything in return?"

He grinned cheerfully. "Because you want to tell me. Now, the question is, do I lie next to you, or do I sit in this chair over here?" He motioned to my grandfather's campaign chair by the fireplace. I made a show of considering the two options before patting the empty space beside me and he obediently sat down.

"Warmer?" he asked, as he put his arm back around me. "So, where were we?"

"I came back to England to sort myself out; that was the idea anyway, not that I could have been described as thinking straight at the time – I was quite a mess." Matthew shifted uncomfortably. "And that's not all down to you; there were other factors involved, if you remember – such as Staahl, and the bear. Anyway, when talking to a friend of the family, Mike Taylor…"

"The 'basket case' man?"

"Do you always listen in on other people's conversations?"

"It's a bit hard not to – especially when it's relevant."

"It turns out that he knows you – had spoken to you – sometime in the late seventies, I think. You helped him out with a tricky heart operation via a video link – a procedure which you pioneered, apparently. He was very complimentary and, at that point, he decided that anyone who had been treated by the wonderful Doctor Lynes couldn't possibly be off her rocker."

I looked up to see what effect this information had on him, to find him looking doubtful.

"What?"

"Well, apart from the fact that your parents regarded it as necessary to have somebody assess you, which I find disturbing enough…"

"He's a *cardiac* surgeon, not a psychiatrist, Matthew."

"There is also the question that he recognized my name."

"So…?"

"So, it could lead to my exposure and that of my family."

"No, I don't think so – he just assumed that you are quite a lot older – which, of course, is correct. There was no sign of him being suspicious or anything, I made quite sure of that. You did get my email, didn't you?"

"No, I didn't. But I never doubted I can trust you – even with something like this."

I burrowed closer, smiling. "And then I saw the newspaper

cutting from when you were in that athletics team. The chances of anyone connecting you to a photograph taken nearly a century ago are so remote as to be insignificant. It was all blurry anyway, and the photograph didn't do you justice.

"But *you* made the connection, Emma."

"Yes, but I *looked* for one."

"Nonetheless, it was there to be found." He fell into silence, the worry creasing his face once more. I waited for him to work through his thoughts, playing with the signet ring on his little finger. Now that I knew what it was, I felt surprise that I hadn't made the connection sooner between the worn crest and the inked image my grandfather had drawn so carefully. He finally drew a deep breath.

"Right… so what did you do then?"

"Then I went all guns blazing into tracing you. And you have that hair…"

He grimaced. "The bane of my life."

I looked at the glorious colour of his hair and waved a long strand of my own at him. "I hardly think so – I bet you were never called 'Ginger Pixie' when you were little." I pulled a face at the thought of the long list of names I had been called over the years. He took the strand from my hand and twisted it around his fingers, watching it glint in the light of the bedside lamp.

"I cannot think of anything more beautiful," he pondered. I made to reply with some tart rejoinder about flattery, but something in the way he contemplated the lock of hair made me stop. He saw me watching him.

"So, you noticed that my colouring is similar…"

"Exactly the same."

"Exactly the same then, as your grandfather, who came from this region with this specific colour, correct?"

"So you do remember that conversation?"

"I remember every word of every conversation we have ever had, Emma, but isn't hair colour – specific or not – far too tenuous a link to jump to any conclusion?"

"Yes it is," I said, "but I had to start somewhere, and I could only do that with what I knew or what I suspected."

"And that led you to Martinsthorpe," he said slowly.

"Martinsthorpe via the parish records, yes; and the church – or what remains of it. And the stories."

"What stories?"

"About you and your family; about your uncle."

Matthew paled; I put my hand to his face and stroked his cheek softly.

"It isn't so very long ago really, is it?"

He closed his eyes at the memory. "No, there are some things I cannot forget."

Faintly through the walls of the old house, time struck inevitable hours from the long-case clock in the hall. He opened his eyes. "You must be tired."

"I am, but sleep can wait. Let me finish telling you first." I paused, considering whether to tell him about the defaced monument, then decided it didn't need to be said. Having your name removed from a book might be one thing, but to have your image smashed beyond recognition amounted to a violation – a declaration that you no longer belonged – so I skipped that bit. "I went to Old Manor Farm – the church of St Martin's is now part of it; it's where the Seatons lived."

Matthew nodded slowly as he recognized the name.

"It wasn't known as that then, but I remember it well enough; we had relatives there."

"You still do."

He gave a gruff laugh.

"So, by the time I had been there, heard the stories and seen the window, I just about pieced together a cohesive picture. All I wanted in order for it to be conclusive, was a primary piece of documented evidence – a first-hand account."

Matthew looked at me swiftly. "And you found it? This journal you mentioned to your grandmother?"

"Yup, I not only found it; I've been in possession of it for the last six weeks or so. Not only that, but it was the precise document that I went to Maine to find in the first place, and that my grandfather had been preoccupied with all his life. Bizarre, isn't it!"

"Certainly serendipitous. So you are saying that this journal – this piece of evidence – was at the college? But that you have it now?"

I squirmed guiltily.

"Ah, well, yes… but there is a reason for that. I… er, borrowed it. I will take it back; I was going to."

I didn't know where to look; doing something wrong might be one thing and something I would deal with between myself and my conscience, but to have the person I loved know that, to all intents and purposes, I was a thief, was quite another.

"I take it from your reaction that the college doesn't know you have it?"

"I hope not."

"Good. And you have it with you?"

"Ye-es, it's over there," I indicated my desk and he rose from my bed. "But Matthew, wait." I crawled across my bed and went to my desk and found the journal in its leather bag. He put out his hand expectantly, but I held it against me, reluctant to let it go. Consternation crossed his face.

"Emma, may I see it?"

I looked at his face, which was frowning now, but more beloved to me than ever, and then at the journal, which had led me to him. Slowly, hesitantly, I held it out to him with both hands as if offering some great treasure – a sacred part of me. He took it without looking, his expression quizzical, before glancing down and removing the book from its bag. Turning it over, he swiftly unwrapped the leather lace that bound it.

"It's the diary kept by Nathaniel Richardson. Please, Matthew... don't be upset."

He looked at me briefly, already four centuries away. He took it over to Grandpa's chair and opened the first page.

For the time being I became redundant; I had served my purpose and brought the past and present together. But not only his past, but mine, and that of my grandfather before me. As I watched Matthew read, fully focused and intent on the task, I reflected on for whom I felt most scared: him – as he read the account of his betrayal and near death, of his rejection by his community, of his father's heartbreak – or me. I had found the journal and it no longer held any mystery for me, no allure. Now my *raison d'être* lay in the man sitting before me and, in transferring all my hopes to him, I wondered not only where he might lead, but whether I would want to go there.

12

Exit

My first thought on waking was: *He's gone.* The campaign chair sat empty and the thin light of early morning drifted through the window, across the floor, and lay on the barren bed beside me. My hand was partway in the arm of my dressing-gown when the door to my room opened.

"Good morning," he said, walking silently towards me. I blinked to clear my sleep-ridden eyes, expecting him to have vanished when they opened.

"You... here!" I managed to stutter.

He looked mildly surprised, and stopped short. "Yes, of course; where else would I be?"

Reaching out, I touched his hand and then curled my arms around his waist, reassured to find him real.

"Matthew, where is the journal; did you read it?" His expression clouded briefly. "I should never have let you see it."

In response, he touched my hair with an ephemeral lightness, and undid my arms.

"You must pack; we'll need to get to the airfield by ten; do you think you can do that?" I glanced at the clock and nodded. "Do you need help?" I shook my head. "All right, then," he said expectantly, and I climbed off my bed and went to shower, noting the impatience – no, *excitement* – in his voice, and how his eyes danced.

Mum fussed me into my quilted coat, making a stoic effort to be pleased for me. "Darling, take care of yourself; we'll be thinking of you at Christmas. Phone if you can and let us know how you're getting on, won't you? Oh, and phone when you get there so we know that you've arrived safely."

I kissed her soft cheek. "I will Mum, I'll be fine, and they don't hand out pilot's licences ad hoc, so don't worry. I'm more concerned that you look after yourself and… and spend lots of time with Nanna, won't you – for me? To make up for me not being here? And Beth – make sure she sees her too."

Mum looked mystified. "Of course we will, darling, but you'll see her when you come home. You will be home for Easter, won't you?"

That note of anxiety again, the one which had become more evident as she felt me slipping away from her.

"I don't know at this stage; I'm taking it one day at a time." I glanced at Matthew, but he had his back to us, looking out of the sash window by the front door. She gave a quick nod – her face still drawn tight – but she managed a smile, and we rubbed noses in our time-honoured fashion and she laughed. I took one last look around before I left for I didn't know how long.

Half an hour later Dad and I stood on the airfield waiting for Matthew to call me from the sleek aircraft that stood dormant on the airstrip. A generator had been wheeled away and a light mist that had risen in the night surrounded it, replacing the snow. Matthew vaulted into the plane from the ground without bothering to use the steps, his lithe body springing without hesitation. No one else was around to see him, and my father was still engrossed in working out how to use his new mobile phone, pushing random buttons long-sightedly.

"Use your glasses, Dad; it will make it a lot easier."

He stabbed at the cursor. "Give me a moment and I'll get used to the blessed thing. You could just call me on the landline, Emma; I really don't need a mobile, you know."

"I want you to be able to contact me at any time, just in case."

Defeated, he removed his gold-rimmed specs from the inside pocket of his thick tweed overcoat, perching them on the end of his nose.

"In case of what, Emma?"

"Make sure Mum spends time with Nanna; it's important."

He regarded me over his glasses, his heavy, straight eyebrows that always made him look as if he were scowling, slightly raised in a question.

"Do you know something I don't, Em?"

I looked at him directly. "I think that she needs to, Dad; Matthew…"

His eyebrows twitched higher. "Ah, is this a professional opinion?"

"Matthew says she hasn't much time left. She's quite comfortable and happy, but he thinks she has only a matter of a few months, and Mum…"

He patted my arm. "Yes, all right – I understand what you're saying. I take it you haven't told your mother, have you? No, of course not, she would have said."

"Nanna seems to know somehow and she doesn't want me to stay until… you know. I'm not trying to avoid being here."

I shuffled, pushing the toe of my shoe into the thawing

turf, letting the moisture darken the leather to chestnut before drawing it out.

"I didn't think you were. Will you come back for the funeral, do you think?" For once no layer of presumption of duty lay behind his question.

"I don't know; I haven't thought about it."

"Let's wait and see what happens first. And, Emma…"

"Yes, Dad?"

He placed his hands on my arms, gripping me lightly above my elbows as if he wanted to ensure I understood what he wanted to say.

"I hope all goes well with you – with you both. I'm just at the end of the phone if you need me and, for what's it's worth…" he paused, framing his thoughts carefully before continuing, "… you were right about me letting you go, about not trying to protect you – *smother* you, I think you said. I hope Matthew looks after you. He's not like Guy, is he? I can see that; but I'm still your father, so if you need me…"

His voice became gruff and he cleared his throat heavily, his embrace more than his customary brief affair, holding tangible affection, a warmth I wasn't used to, and I was able to return his hug with more genuine fondness than I had shown for a long time.

Perched by a window as the door of the aircraft shut conclusively, I watched the ghosting mist draw between us as Dad looked shrunken and forlorn standing by himself at the edge of the airfield. He raised a hand, briefly, before being lost to view altogether. Matthew crouched beside me and looked earnestly in my face.

"Do you want to stay?"

I shook my head vehemently. "No – no, it's not that; it's

just that it's the first time that I can ever remember being sorry to see him go." I gulped and gave a watery smile. "I didn't think it would ever happen."

A straggly end of mist-damp hair clung to my face, and he tucked it gently behind my ear.

"Miracles *do* happen," he said softly.

I looked at the quirky upturned corners of his mouth and the love reflected in the intensity of his eyes as he smiled at me. I remembered what we had both been through and what we had overcome, and I smiled back.

"Yes," I said, reaching out and touching the face that had turned my world upside down. "I believe they do."

13

Solo

"It looks very complicated."

The banks of controls were intimidating – the various lights, dials and switches meant absolutely nothing to me.

Matthew leaned over and checked that the straps holding me into the seat were secure.

"Like anything, you get used to them; you're my flight crew today, by the way."

I looked at him askance. "You do want us to get back to Maine in one piece, don't you? Or is this a suicide mission?" Grinning, he lowered himself into his own seat, but didn't rise to my challenge. "Anyway, if you need a second pair of hands, how did you fly here by yourself?"

He flicked a couple of switches and the whine of the engine coming to life filled the cockpit. I felt a familiar flutter of anticipation as I readied myself for the take-off, just as I did the last time I had flown to America – before I met him, before I knew what I did now and my whole world changed.

"Strictly, a jet like this should be crewed by at least two, but I can fly it by myself if I have to in the event of an emergency; it's one of the reasons I bought it. However," he went on before I could say anything, "the FAA would have me grounded and on charges if they caught me, so today – for the sake of appearances – you are my co-pilot."

Somehow I didn't think anyone would mistake me for a pilot; I knew as much about aircraft as my father did about history.

Matthew ran what I supposed must be pre-flight checks. He called the control tower for clearance to taxi to the runway, and the plane began to move slowly past the other aircraft slumbering around the apron of the airfield. He seemed completely at ease with the controls.

"How long have you been flying? You didn't tell Dad yesterday, I noticed, and don't say 'Quite a while', because that won't wash."

His eyebrows lifted in a show of surprise. "I wouldn't dream of it, although it has been a long time in aviation terms. Hang on, I need clearance for take-off."

He spoke into the headset and a distant voice answered him. The engines changed note, rising in pitch as the plane picked up speed.

"I started flying before the war – the First World War, that would be. I liked the speed and the freedom of it. I found it exhilarating – liberating – after all those years spent anchored to the ground. It was also a practical service I could offer at the outset – until they needed more doctors, that is."

The ground gave way beneath us, the buildings and aircraft becoming spectral shapes under the shrouding mist. He gave a low chuckle. "You can let go now."

I had been unconsciously gripping the sides of the leather seat, my fingers almost as white as the cream upholstery, as the plane soared into the sky. Mist blanketed the windshield in swathes of droplets. I could only just make out denser shapes on the ground that must have been the trees edging the fields we passed on the way to the airfield.

"How can you see?" I squeaked.

"That's what these instruments are for," he indicated in front of him. "We'll be above this in a minute; it's only low cloud."

Almost as he spoke, the mist thinned, brightened and then broke as we climbed into untroubled skies above the now obscured Lincolnshire landscape. The plane rose smoothly in a shallow turn, taking flight from the glare of the pursuing sun.

"I see what you mean," I murmured.

"About?"

"About the sense of freedom up here; it's beautiful." I resumed the previous topic. "So, if you flew at the outbreak of the war, who were you flying for if the States didn't join until 1917?"

"For the French initially; they didn't ask too many questions about who I was, or where I came from. Then when the US entered the war, I joined them, but by then I was of more use in the field hospitals. The gas didn't affect me, so I could get to the wounded more quickly than other medics."

"Surely people noticed?"

"No – in the conditions we were working in the men were either too far gone or too grateful for being helped to make anything of it. If anyone did say anything, they just put it down to my good luck, or shell shock, or a miracle, and left it at that."

In my mind's eye, Matthew's ever-young form bent over the broken bodies of the wounded and dying amid the mashed fields of the Western Front. Even through the mustard-yellow gas, his rich flaxen hair must have stood out like some vestige of hope. Then I recalled the whispered asides, the hushing looks, whenever war was mentioned at home.

"My grandfather was badly injured in the Second World

War; he didn't speak about it much, but it must have been terrible. If you can feel people's pain, how did you cope?"

"There was so much pain that I couldn't screen it all out and yes, it did hurt, but it didn't kill me or leave me with life-long injuries, as it did them. The suffering of those men was indescribable."

"As in all the wars you have witnessed?" I said softly, guessing – although he had not said and I did not ask – that he had seen many in his 400 years of life. A shadow passed across his face.

"Indeed," he said. "That is one aspect of war that never changes."

I studied him in the moments it took for him to check the instrument panel and make adjustments, and wondered what he had seen, what he had felt, because no evidence lay in the untroubled contours of his face; only in the telltale tension of his eyes and mouth did it show.

"When you say the gas didn't affect you, can anything harm you?"

"Physically? Nothing has yet – well, it can – but I heal almost instantaneously. You saw that when the bear attacked, or at least you didn't, which proves the point. I wouldn't like to test the theory as far as decapitation goes, however, although I've come close a couple of times." Without thinking, he had rubbed the back of his neck and now, conscious of the act, seemed to find the idea faintly amusing. "No indeed," he said philosophically; "I can't see a way back from *that*."

My sense of humour failed me at this point, his life no laughing matter.

"And emotionally, Matthew?"

Slowly, he lowered his hand, resting it on the flight controls.

"Ah, well, that's another matter – there doesn't seem to be a cure for the heart."

There wasn't much that could be said after that, and we fell silent as I tried to imagine what he must have witnessed over his lifetime, and as he tried to forget.

The plane gradually reached altitude above the sunlit cloud. He broke the silence a few minutes later.

"We're just leaving the mainland, Emma, if you want to say goodbye."

I shuddered. "Don't say that, it makes it sound so final."

Far below us through broken cloud, the coast formed a corrugated line between the blue-grey of the sea and the brown-patched land. Matthew took possession of my hand and held it beneath his with his strong fingers laced between mine.

"Why do you need your own plane? Or is it that you like the speed of it?"

"If I had a preference, I would fly a glider; it's not as fast but there is a greater sense of being closer to the elements – and to God." I looked at him swiftly, but he kept his eyes on the instrument panel in front of him. "I wanted something that could cope with transoceanic crossings, could manage on a short airstrip, was fast – and could take my family if need be."

"Why might that be necessary?" I asked quietly. He didn't reply, and at first I thought he hadn't heard me, except that his hand had tensed uncomfortably over mine.

"I have spent all my life – my existence – trying to avoid discovery, Emma. When I lived on my own, only my liberty was at stake, although what I might have been put through by whatever regime was in power at the time, I will leave to your imagination." I lacked neither imagination nor knowledge, and the combination of the two sent me into a cold sweat.

"But now I have a family to consider, and whatever happens to me will affect them. I can never, *ever* risk their welfare or their happiness – not for me, not for anyone."

Despite the frisson his words evoked, my interest prickled at the mention of his elusive family, about whom I knew virtually nothing. In the short time we had known each other, and before I discovered his true identity, he mentioned them rarely, and all I knew was the importance they held for him.

"Your family? Ellie, Harry and Joel aren't your niece and nephews, are they?"

The engines hummed in a soothing monotone, and the time it took for Matthew to reply confirmed my suspicions.

Finally, "No, they're not."

I nodded. "I thought they must be your children, but you couldn't tell me before because I would have known you are older than you appear. But that's what you are doing by telling me, isn't it? Risking them? Surely every additional person who knows about you puts you and – by association – your family at risk?"

His hand relaxed again and he squeezed mine lightly so that our intertwined fingers were one.

"I don't think so, and if I didn't tell you, would that have stopped you searching and discovering for yourself? If I had denied it, would you have believed me?"

"Probably not, no."

"The only way I could have prevented you from knowing, Emma, is to have avoided you from the start – not to have talked to you, not to have wanted you – and I'm too selfish to have done that. I had almost persuaded myself that I didn't need you, and that there was no connection between us. I told myself that you preferred Sam…" I tried to jerk my hand away, appalled, but he held on to it, "… yes, *Sam* – and that would have been a safer option for us all. But I would have had to let you die the night of the attack, and I couldn't let that happen. By that time it was too late anyway."

This sudden confession had my head spinning.

"I don't understand; what are you saying?"

"The night of the All Saints' dinner, I had a call from… somewhere, and I had to leave."

"I remember."

"If I stayed – if I had been there – I could have protected you from Staahl…"

"How? And anyway, you weren't to know."

"Yes, but that's just it, I *did* know, Emma, or at least I thought it possible. You remember the attack on the girl on campus, and the murder of the woman in town?" I nodded. "I suspected they were carried out by the same person but I had no proof. I was aware Staahl had been watching you for some time. We kept an eye on you – two when we could."

"We? You keep saying 'we'; who do you mean?"

"Members of my family: Joel, if he was on leave; sometimes Ellie; and Harry and Dan when they could."

That explained why Harry turned up at the diner, unexpected but oh, so welcome, the night Staahl followed me there. Then I had believed Harry to be Matthew's nephew. Now I tried to make sense of the relationships.

"Daniel's not your brother, is he? And Henry's not *your* father?"

"No – but that doesn't matter, Emma; what matters is that I knew and I was responsible for letting Staahl get to you when I should have prevented it. If I hadn't come back that night you would have died, and I and my family would be safe. But I couldn't leave you – I couldn't just let you die – and I had to make the choice. And once I made it…" He suddenly hit the control column in front of him and the plane banked sharply to the left. "I'm a fool if I thought I hadn't made it the first moment I met you!"

I clutched at the edge of my seat again, but already the plane had been smoothly brought back under his control. He switched to autopilot, pressed his palms to his forehead, and exhaled. After a moment in which I waited to hear him breathe, he took his hands from his head, and spoke again.

"Sorry. I'm sorry about everything. I hadn't meant to say anything until we were back in the States; it's all such a mess."

His fingers flexed open like a flick-knife then shut tight, and he stared out of the side of the cockpit into the empty sky. I was still struggling to get my head around what he had said.

"You knew about Staahl but you didn't tell me?"

"Yes."

"Why?"

"I thought that I could protect you until such time as I gathered enough evidence to get him arrested and charged. If I had told you, you would have been alarmed without being able to do anything about it, and you would have started asking questions about my involvement."

"Matthew, I already knew that Staahl was following me; I was already frightened."

"Yes, I'm sorry."

"And as for you, I tried not to be interested but I felt drawn to you. You are right, of course – the only way you could have stopped me from being *interested* in you would be to have let me die, then you wouldn't have had a problem."

"And I wouldn't have you."

"And you and your family wouldn't be in danger of discovery."

"And I wouldn't have you," he repeated.

I pressed the point. "Am I really worth it? All this nonsense when you could have had a more peaceful life?"

He fixed indigo eyes on mine. "I could ask the same thing."

I blinked as sharp sunlight reflected off a metal facia, breaking the bond.

"I think," I said slowly, "that if I couldn't be with you, you might as well have left me to die."

He smiled grimly. "You know I couldn't have done that, don't you? I couldn't have left you then – I can't leave you now. No matter what happens, I'm tied to you."

In any other circumstance or during another conversation, to hear him speak of such commitment would have had me whooping in paroxysms of delight. Now, however, I detected an undercurrent to those words that sent a tremor of apprehension through me.

"How much do your family know? Do they understand the danger they could be in?"

"We are too closely bound to one another to keep anything hidden, Emma. They know of the dangers facing the family – that's why we have this…" his eyes cast over the interior of the cockpit, "… in case we have to leave suddenly."

"And has that ever happened?"

"Only once; but we have to move on every so often anyway and start somewhere new where we're not known."

"Why?"

"As I don't appear to age physically, it would be a bit obvious after a bit. We stay together because of our ties of kinship, and that's something you know a little about from all your studies, don't you?"

I did indeed. "Yes, it's what people are prepared to die for – that and their faith."

"Precisely."

"And you would risk that for me?"

"As I said, I don't see you as a risk – do you?"

"No, I'm not; but Matthew, you couldn't have known that – not for sure."

"No."

A voice sounded out of nowhere, making me jump. Matthew answered, giving a rapid sequence of letters and numbers. The disembodied voice spoke again, asking a question. Matthew paused before answering, turning to me.

"We have to take on fuel at Shannon; would you like something to eat now or would you like to wait until we're airborne again?"

I opted for the latter.

The stopover took less time than I thought, but by the time we reached cruising altitude again, pangs of hunger told me it was past lunchtime.

"Help yourself to anything you'd like to eat or drink back there."

I nodded, unsurprised now if he anticipated my hunger, variable though it always seemed to be. He started speaking into the headset as the plane rose above the Atlantic and I unclipped the buckle around my waist and eased out of the seat.

Restless nights and emotionally fraught days were taking their toll. I yawned and stretched, locating the built-in refrigerator and a bottle of sparkling water. The fresh fruit next to it must have been left for me, since he didn't eat. I searched for a glass. The glossy range of bird's-eye maple cupboards were filled with an assortment of food in packets that lay ready in case a quick escape proved necessary. It brought home just how seriously he took the threat of exposure. The question then was, how long would this jet be no more than an idle luxury, and what would be the catalyst that would bring upon him and his family the eye of the world in that brief but catastrophic declaration of his existence? Because – if the one thing that had lain dormant but festering in the back of my mind became reality – at some point in the near future, there might be a trial and Matthew would be a key witness to Staahl's attack. If all the endless courtroom dramas I had watched over the years bore any relation to reality, key witnesses were flayed alive by the defence counsel.

I found a heavy and deeply cut glass, each facet reflecting diamond-bright in the cabin spotlights. Of course, there should be no reason for anyone to suspect that Matthew wasn't what he seemed to be – a highly respected surgeon with an impeccable record of service to his community, a widower and a family man. I poured the water into the glass, waiting for the bubbles to subside before filling it to the top. But Staahl had accused Matthew of trying to kill him when he tore him from me, and Sam – in talking to the police – had hinted at ulterior motives. Nothing much as accusations go, and they might be taken as no more than the desperate defence of the accused and the mumblings of a malcontent – but it didn't take much to set tongues wagging. I gulped a couple of mouthfuls of water nervously as I followed the train of thought.

History is spattered with the blood of men and women whose lives had been shattered by whispered deceits. Fiction and half-truth formed the nucleus of what I studied – the cause and effect of the events I found so fascinating. What had been an academic subject – devoid of impact upon me by time and dissociation – Matthew experienced first-hand in the accusations of those with whom he lived. In lives such as his lay the negligible difference between rumour and lies. And, by the time the difference had been distinguished, the damage was done: the rebellion started, the family hounded, the martyr burned.

I knew that nothing had really changed over the intervening centuries, for are we not taught – in that well-worn maxim – that it is in the nature of man to destroy that which he fails to comprehend?

"Did you find what you wanted?"

I started at the sound of Matthew's voice behind me, spilling my drink. I sank to my knees and automatically began to mop at it with my hankie while I composed both my thoughts and my features.

"Emma, leave it – it'll dry. Here…" he put his hand out to me and he pulled me to my feet, his tone buoyant, and his smile bordering on roguish.

"I've been waiting to do this for the last hour," he said, cupping my face between his hands, his eyes propositioning and his mouth real, inviting, alive on mine. So *alive*. My eyes widened.

"Who's flying the plane?"

Matthew laughed, "It's on auto – remember?" and he kissed me again, lightly this time. "Come on, I want to show you something."

He led me back to the cockpit and strapped me into my seat. I gave him a quizzical look.

"Well, I said that you're my co-pilot, so now's your chance to do some flying. Hands on the stick – like this."

Ignoring my protests, he waited until I placed my hands on the controls in imitation before disconnecting the autopilot.

The plane wobbled disturbingly.

"But…"

"You're more than capable. Right, now ease it forward and you push the nose down and the plane will start to descend. Easy now, or we'll go into a dive. Pull up just as gently – that's it – and you'll pull her nose up and we'll climb. Perfect. Keep her steady. It's difficult to stall a plane like this – not like the older aircraft I flew – but not impossible, so we have to match her speed as well. See this?" and he pointed to a series of dials. "These show you how fast we are travelling relative to the air. This one here, whether we are flying straight and level, and this – our altitude."

I tried to keep up. "Hang on a mo – you've had a few more years to learn all this than I have. Is that the altimeter or…"

"Yes, and the one next to it is the artificial horizon; keep the bar across the middle level – imagine they're the wings of the plane. If you want to bank port, ease on the stick, so." The aircraft moved smoothly to the left under his control. "And opposite for starboard. Go on, you try." The plane made a more radical lurch to the right and I winced, correcting the level of pressure I applied. "That's it, now level her up – easy. Fun, isn't it?"

"Great!" I said with more enthusiasm than I would have thought possible five minutes before.

"Are you happy to carry on for a bit? Just keep us on that compass heading – there."

I focused on the dials in front of me.

"Uh huh – but don't leave me alone, I don't want to jinx the plane."

"I hardly think you'll do that," he murmured, and I blushed as I felt him watch me intently with a look that had little to do with what currently occupied my attention.

The levels of concentration required to keep the aircraft flying straight, level and on course were far more taxing than I thought they would be, given the ease with which Matthew achieved far more complex manoeuvres; but I welcomed the distraction so that my mind could not wander down the paths of fear upon which it attempted to lead me.

After a while my eyes began to feel the strain of staring at the dials, and my shoulders ached from hunching forward.

"Had enough?" he asked.

I nodded and he flicked back on to autopilot. The aircraft noticeably adjusted into a more stable pattern of flight; Matthew saw me pull a face.

"We'll have you flying solo in no time," he said, with an alarming degree of confidence.

"Hey, hang on a minute, I didn't say anything about learning to fly!"

He chortled with that good-natured laugh I loved to hear because it meant he was happy.

There were hours ahead in which there were no interruptions, and we filled them with my curiosity and his answers as we wound our way through his life, and he questioned me about mine. Yet still I felt that he extracted more about me than I had about him. I barely scratched the surface, and there were questions he would not answer, deferring them until we were back in Maine; but it represented a start, and there was a sense that, for the first time, he began to reveal his true self to me.

At one point I became silent, and he asked me why, and I said that I had been gone so long without notifying the college that I didn't know how it might affect my position. He smiled and replied that there was nothing to worry about, and when I pressed him he admitted that – as my doctor – he had put me on long-term sick leave, hoping I wouldn't need it.

I took control of the plane several times more, each time a little easier than the last, until the pleasure of flying outweighed the apprehension, and I looked forward to the next attempt. I had just relinquished the controls to him again, when I saw that he examined the instrument panel closely, frowning slightly.

"What is it?"

"Nothing to be concerned about, I'm just plotting a course around that."

He nodded towards the vast head of a cumulonimbus that lay in our path, its ominous anvil lit brilliant white by the sun in contrast with the bulging grey flanks of the cloud.

"Is that part of the storm you told us about yesterday?"

"No – it's just an isolated thunderstorm, but we'll do a detour, I think." He didn't seem particularly fazed and my slight nervousness wasn't enough to prevent me from yawning; it had been a long day, made longer by the shift in time zones.

"Can't we go above it?" I asked, trying not to let my voice give away my unease.

"No, it's too high – about forty-five thousand feet or thereabouts."

"It's magnificent," I couldn't help but observe, the cloud almost boiling as it rose towering before us.

"Isn't it."

He spoke into the headset and I fell to watching the developing cloud and wondering what would happen if the aircraft came down in it. I would die, of course, but what about Matthew? Was he just long-lived or... and I almost laughed to think it... immortal, indestructible? I found it quite a comforting thought that he would live even though I died.

"Emma." He called through a fog of sleep.

"Mmm?"

"Welcome back to America. Strap in – we're coming in to land. We've just beaten the storm."

Runway lights lit a safe passage down which the plane's nose headed. Although the sun had shone strongly above the cloud, below it an obscurity lay upon the day, and the snow from the approaching storm hung above the encircling mountains, softening their outline. I watched him as he brought the aircraft in to land on an airfield barely bigger than the one we had left in England, his face eerily lit by the green lights on the instrument panel, his brow lightly furrowed in concentration, his mouth turned up at the corners even when he wasn't smiling, giving away his innate good nature. Swallowing my desire, I sighed audibly. He didn't take his eyes off the runway.

"Still tired?"

"Um, oh yes – a bit."

"It'll take an hour or so to get back – more if the snow doesn't hold off. We'd better get you something to eat; do you mind eating in the car as we drive?"

I shook my head. The plane came to a smooth full stop; I had hardly felt the undercarriage touch the tarmac.

The first flakes of snow began to fall as we left the airstrip – softly, lightly at first, testing the resistance of the air, catching in the cobweb strands of my hair lifted by the wind. The claret of Matthew's car was already muted as we drove out of the parking lot, a fine covering of frozen flakes whitening the road and verge. By the time we neared the campus, the distinguishing features of shrubs and rocks and road had been lost beneath the mantle of snow: anonymity its gift, given indiscriminately.

"Glad to be back?"

Matthew left my cases on my bed before coming back into the sitting room and opening the curtains to let more of the diffused light into my college apartment. The room had been rendered immaculate since I last saw it, and a new coffee table sat in front of the sofa where I had left the shattered remains of the old one in a state resembling my own. A world of difference lay between then and now: the difference between knowing and not knowing, between certainty and the mere apparition from his past that had kept us solidly apart. Now, back in this room once more, order had been restored to my life by the acquisition of knowledge. And knowledge was king.

I thought of being with him, and answered, "Yes." Then, thinking of the possibility of a trial, I added, "And no."

I joined him where he stood by the window. Together we watched the snow fall thickly, the cedar outside the barest shadow in the white. He put his arm around my waist and kissed my hair and I snuggled up to him.

"Will the snow mean we can't go into the mountains?"

"No, this is nothing; we'll get there. I have one or two things to do first; I expect you have too?"

Not really. I could certainly think of things I *must* do, such as contact my students, whom I felt I had neglected dreadfully; but not many things that I *wanted* to do, not without him. I shrugged under his arm in a gesture of non-committal.

"Yes, I have things to do."

"Give me twenty-four hours, then I'll come and collect you. Think you can wait that long? Emma?"

I studied my feet. "Yes."

He bent sideways and looked into my face so that I couldn't avoid his eyes, now cobalt in the snow-light.

"It's only twenty-four hours."

How could I tell him that his mere day was more than interminable for me, and that between us always hovered an uncertainty that a day might turn into forever. He read the anxiety in my face, soothing my frown with his lips.

"I know, my love, but it's not long. Now..." he took a step back, looking purposeful, "... make sure you have plenty of warm clothes; we have hot water up there but no electricity other than a small generator to pump water."

I made an effort to sound upbeat. "No electricity and no bears – what more could a girl want?"

He grinned. "I won't answer that. I'll see you tomorrow."

And with the suggestion hanging in tantalizing suspension, he left me wondering.

I sat disconsolately on the edge of my bed, swinging my feet, and considered unpacking, but I had more pressing things to do, so I set about getting them done. First, I contacted my students and arranged to meet those still on campus in my tutor room first thing in the morning.

Second, I phoned my father, as promised.

"Emma," he sounded relieved. "Did you have a good flight? What's the weather like over there?"

"I didn't manage to crash the plane, and winter looks like it should – lots of snow and very pretty. Look, Dad, I'm going to be away for a few days. If you can't get hold of me – if you need to, that is – leave a message on my mobile; it'll record automatically and I'll contact you when I get back."

"You're going away so soon? Anywhere nice?"

"Into the mountains somewhere."

I heard the sharp intake of breath at the other end of the line as he recalled the catastrophic aftermath of my last visit to the mountains.

"I hope Matthew knows what he's doing."

"He generally does, Dad."

"Well, I don't think that your mother need know. I'll tell her you called anyway."

"Dad, just one other thing... thanks for the marmalade – it looks like a vintage batch."

He gave his deep, throaty chuckle. "You found it in your bag, then. I double-bagged it so it wouldn't leak on your clothes. Hope you like it – I cut the Sevilles extra thick for you and there's a dash of whisky in it as well. Have a good time, Em, won't you." In those few words, he left nothing unsaid. I smiled at this new side to my father, and let the warmth of it carry in my voice.

"Thanks, Dad."

It wasn't a long conversation but, as conversations went with my father, it represented the most relaxed we had exchanged in a long while, and only time would tell if it heralded the beginning of a renaissance between us.

The third thing I felt compelled to do was source some food, since my fridge had been cleared – probably by Elena – of what would undoubtedly have been green and black and growing furry bits by now. Here, I had a choice: either I could go on an expedition across campus to the store – a decidedly unwelcome option, given the depth of the snow – or I could seek out Elena and scrounge something off her. I had missed her over the last month, but more than that, I owed her.

"Emma!"

Elena flung her arms around my shoulders, knocking the breath out of me in the process.

"I love your hair," I said, hugging her back.

She looked pleased but dismissive. "I do not care about

my hair. When did you get back? *How* did you get back? Wait until I tell Matias – he will be most surprised." Her accent sounded stronger because I hadn't heard it for a while. "Come in and have some tea and tell me what has happened. Come on." She almost dragged me across the threshold.

"I only came to scrounge – borrow – some food off you because my cupboards are bare. Don't think I'm going to tell you anything interesting!" I teased her.

She waggled a finger. "No, no – you will get *no*-thing from me until you tell me *every*thing."

She hauled me over to a chair and pushed me into it, sitting opposite, her long legs crossed under her as she leaned forward.

"Agh, it has been so boring without you; I have no one to… *gossip*, you say? Da, gossip with, and no excitement. Look, your arms are better, no?" I waved them in the air as evidence. "But Matias worried after we phoned you. Have you heard from Matthew? Is that why you have come back – to find him?"

My voice lit with suppressed excitement. "Nope, *I* didn't find him, Matthew found *me*! He flew all the way to England and brought me back – he flew me back, actually."

She regarded my animated face thoughtfully, suddenly serious.

"Does this mean you and he are together again?"

Her grave demeanour sobered me. "Yes, it does – very much so."

"Do you see your future with him now? You used to say you did not think about it, but I think this must have changed, no?"

"I think it must have, Elena, yes."

I looked at her from under my eyelashes, not sure what the

response would be, given her sombre expression of a moment ago, only to find her face spread in the widest beam. She clapped her hands in rapid succession, hardly containing herself.

"This is the best news; I cannot wait to tell Matias, he will be so pleased. Now you are with Matthew for the holiday, yes? You know what that means, don't you?"

I could think of a few possibilities.

"No, what?"

"It means it is *very* serious. Will you meet his family?"

"His chil... his nephews and niece, of course, and possibly... er, I'm not entirely sure; Matthew's been a bit vague about who's going to be there."

I made a mental note that I needed to be very careful in those unguarded moments where I might let something slip and, to be quite honest, I wasn't sure who would be there at Christmas; something else I would ask him, since I hadn't appreciated surprises ever since Guy's untimely disclosure at my expense – and his wife's.

Elena jumped to her feet, skipping about the floor in little steps akin to a complicated dance.

"I think we will have to go out and celebrate – a *big* celebration with much food and wine. Where shall we go? There is somewhere good in town and the men can pay. We go tomorrow or the next day, da? Before the holiday – I think it must be soon."

Already planning, she clasped her hands in front of her, occasionally gesticulating as she framed another idea. Food and alcohol were wasted on me and worse than pointless for Matthew.

"Hold your horses, Elena – we can't. Matthew and I are going away for a few days; let's wait until after Christmas and then at least I'll know how it's gone." She spun about on one foot, about to argue. I went on hastily, "Not to beat about the bush or anything, but I don't want to count my chickens before they've hatched, just in case it's all a storm in a teacup, so let's not make a mountain out of a molehill and jump the gun, shall we?" I grinned at her look of horror.

"What are you talking about you crazy, mad girl!"

It achieved precisely the diversion I needed.

"I'm just saying that I would rather wait until after Christmas to celebrate because I don't want to presume that everything will go well. Although I'm sure it will. I think. Maybe." I chewed my lip and then decided to put aside my natural caution and the niggling doubt that had accompanied me all the way back from the UK.

"Anyway, can I help you with that tea? I'm gasping."

"No, I do it. Stay there."

Elena made for the kitchen and I heard water flowing, then the kettle switch on.

"Where is Matias, by the way?" I called after her.

Elena reappeared, looking wistful and drying a mug on a linen tea-towel depicting garish Russian dolls.

"At the lab – he's been working on something. It keeps him awake at night too. Sometimes I think he doesn't sleep at all. But he is very excited, so I do not mind so much." I rather thought that she did because her mouth had turned down. She finished polishing the last drops from the mug with a final flick of the cloth. "What is all this 'chickens' and 'storms'? I do not understand you sometimes."

She went back in the kitchen and I raised my voice so that she could hear me over the rising note of the kettle as it came to the boil.

"It doesn't matter; it's just my ridiculous language. What are you and Matias doing for Christmas?"

The mugs chinked noisily. "We are going to fly to Finland first and then to St Petersburg." There was a muffled gasp from the kitchen. "Emma, did you say that Matthew *flew* you back?"

"Uh huh."

Her head popped around the edge of the doorframe, her dark, uptilted eyes betraying a smattering of Mongolian DNA tattooed into her family's Belarus origins.

"He has his own airplane?"

"Yup."

She leaned against the architrave, chewing a nail, looking at me.

"He must be very rich."

I hadn't thought about it; he certainly didn't flaunt it.

"I suppose so. It's not the sort of thing we've discussed. So when are you going to Finland?"

Elena roused herself from her trance and disappeared into the kitchen. A second later, I heard water being poured from the kettle and I went in to help her carry the mugs.

"We fly on Tuesday. So what do you talk about, Em? Or are you too busy making love to talk about anything?"

Narrowly missing the swipe I aimed at her, she held out a mug to me, her arched eyebrows framing playful eyes.

"I swear you are obsessed, Elena Smalova."

She swung her hips suggestively as she walked back into the sitting room, taking a bite out of a biscuit.

"Da, I have a *very* good imagination."

I took a biscuit from the packet and followed her. "Well, keep your imagination for Matias – he'll appreciate it more than I will."

I sat back down and dunked my biscuit into the hot tea just long enough for it to have enough crunch without it collapsing in a soggy mass at the bottom of my mug.

I couldn't fault my imagination on that score, either, but it was proving a tad frustrating keeping it reined in at the moment, more so than at any other time in the last ten years.

"Have you and Matthew, you know…?" She looked expectantly at me.

"And since when have we had the chance? I only saw him yesterday for the first time in ages – or was it the day before?" I shook my head, trying to get around the perplexing subject of time zones, and realized I must be much more tired than I first thought. "Anyway, we've had a lot to discuss."

She nodded sagely in an unspoken acknowledgment of the state of affairs, then brightened as her mind made the next logical step.

"Ah! Is that why you're going away – a romantic time *alone*. How delicious!" She pronounced the word "de-li-ci-ous", making it sound edible, wriggling on the chair.

"You have the underwear?"

"Er, yes. Elena – don't go there; I'm not an entire novice, you know."

"After ten years – you did say it was ten years since that man in England – what was his name…?"

I cringed. "Guy."

"Yes – *Guy* – that's it. Ten years is a *very* long time."

"But Elena, it's a bit like riding a bike – once learned, never forgotten."

She giggled. "But, Emma, it depends on the bicycle, doesn't it?"

I had to concede that one. "I'm sure it does. Anyway, as much as I would like to, we won't be sleeping together as in… well, you know what I mean. That's not why we're going."

We hadn't discussed it, but somehow we didn't need to, as there seemed to be a tacit understanding between us, although

I felt that it wasn't from a lack of desire on either side. On the contrary. Elena flicked her tongue over the chocolate-coated biscuit, all the while watching me.

"You love him, he loves you…" she waved the biscuit in the air, letting me fill in the rest of the sentence.

"Yes, but we're not married. We're not even engaged."

Her teeth dissected the biscuit and she chewed thoughtfully. "Matias and I – we are not married."

"That's your business, Elena; I won't judge you if you promise not to judge me." I thought of the journal tucked away in my bag, waiting accusingly to be returned. "You remember what I said about Sam and commitment?" She nodded. "Nothing's happened to change my view."

"So you won't have sex unless Matthew marries you?"

"Pretty much, yes."

"And will he ask you, do you think?"

"I hope that's what I'm going to find out in the next few days," I said quietly.

Elena proved far more domesticated than I would ever be. She sent me back to my room laden, and I slowly reheated the soup – as thick as a stew – standing over the saucepan, yawning intermittently and rubbing a hand over gritty eyes. I lingered under the shower, taking time to let the water run over my tired body, wondering, as I leaned against the warm wall, what this time tomorrow might bring.

Despite the lack of Matthew – or perhaps because he wasn't there to tempt me to fight sleep – I slept well.

There were some things about which I could be pedantic and one of them had been nagging away at me for weeks.

Usually by this time in December, I had bought and wrapped all my presents and written and sent all the cards that needed sending. This way, I avoided frantic last-minute shopping which would inevitably end in buying a present for somebody's birthday in July. This year, however, the routines and habits with which I protected my world had been turned inside out. Not all was lost. I had bought some fabulous knitting wool for my mother while at a conference in Edinburgh last April.

I should have been at a lunch laid on by the Société d'Histoire Internationale, but Guy had also been invited and, knowing my luck, I would have ended up sitting next to him. So instead I wandered around the side streets and found a tiny craft shop selling hand-dyed wool from remote Scottish islands. The balls of yarn filled the walls in all their delectable colours: squishy, soft bundles with cinched paper waists. Mum would adore the heathery greens and muted bronze – the colour of dried grass against a storm-grey sky. The wool must have been sold by the Troy ounce since it cost its weight in gold, and I spent so much time in there that I was late for the afternoon presentations. I slid in the side door clutching the bag, keeping as low a profile as possible. Even so, Guy had seen me, and I spent the rest of the conference doing my best to avoid him. I also managed to find a couple of small presents for the twins: scale models of knights on horses – accurate enough to satisfy the historian in me, and suitably robust for jousting around the legs of the dining table. But that was it where my family were concerned: no coins for Alex's collection, nothing else for Flora and not a thing for Archie. Dad was OK; he had chosen his present before I came to Maine and he should have it by now. I wondered whether he would have the patience to wait until Christmas before opening it. Beth, however, would both understand

and wait if the post didn't make it there on time, and Rob would be happy with a really good bottle of red wine. And Nanna? Nanna and I had come to an understanding with regard to presents some years back, and every year she chose which charity she wanted to support. Last Christmas it was a couple of goats; this year it would be a teacher. I had asked her how she wanted her present wrapped and she indulged me by laughing.

I spent a long and pleasurable time thinking about what to give Matthew, although getting it in time for Christmas would be another matter. What really bothered me to distraction was what on earth I would do about the Lynes. What *do* you give people you don't know and have barely met? And giving nothing was just not an option.

A random search on Google failed to inspire. I didn't know what they liked to eat or drink or whether they were teetotal or whether, come to think of it, like Matthew, they ate at all. In the end I went for the simplest option and ordered a Fortnum's hamper from the UK, and hoped it would arrive on time. I drew a complete blank on more personal gifts until I recalled Nanna's: bingo – simple and purposeful. I placed the orders and clicked "send", feeling pretty smug – no, not smug – *relieved*.

I saved Matthew's present until last. I knew what I wanted to buy him. I had known for some time when, in moments alone, I allowed myself to daydream about spending Christmas together.

Snow still fell when I left to meet my students, but there was the distinct possibility that it would cease altogether. I felt as pleased to see my tutor group as they were relieved to see me but, once I had asked after their studies and their general welfare, I gathered from their faces that what they really wanted to know – but were too reticent to ask – were the details of the attack. They had heard the rumours, of course – but why is it that people never hear the truth? And what alarmed me even more was that they needed to ask whether the rumours were true. Only Aydin, in his quiet, reserved way, made it clear that he considered the stories that circulated around campus days after the attack to be no more than malicious gossip.

"People try to understand what happens by making story to fit their ideas. It is not true and it is like fire in the forest that burns very quick and hot, and then it is gone and the wood, yes – it is black – but inside it is still *strong*."

I found the analogy as comforting as his faith in me, despite being likened to something charred and flaky. Josh – evidently going through a phase of exploring his inner Punk – fiddled with a chain of safety pins extending from his chest to his waist, his *über* cool only spoiled by the fact that the pins he sported were pink-tipped and usually used for old-fashioned nappies.

"Yeah, don't worry about it, Dr D. Nobody's talking about you *now* – are they, guys?"

Holly and Hannah shook their heads but didn't voice their assent. Leo had said very little since entering the room, but reclined in his chair with his hands behind his head. Every now and again, as we discussed their work, I found his eyes wandering over my body, calculating, invasive. I avoided his stare and, apart from the pervasive suspicion I felt sure some of them silently entertained, we managed to get down to some real work. By the end of the session I felt satisfied that my absence had done no lasting damage to their prospects. The question was, what would it do to mine?

14

Walls of Jericho

The snow held off, as Matthew predicted.

We reached the cabin just as the sun defeated the clouds, revealing an immense sky stretching from summit to summit in a great arc of blue above white. Heavily eaved and dwarfed by the mountain, the cabin hunkered down in deep snow behind a gentle slope that protected it from the worst of the winter weather.

The house was already warm. The log burner in the stone fireplace had been lit sometime earlier, and now the embers glowed sporadically through its glass face. I peeled off the layers Matthew had insisted I wore and wandered over to the full-height window that ran nearly the length of one wall. A long oak table and ladder-back chairs took in the view for which the house had undoubtedly been built, revealing a vast expanse of land as it dropped away from the cabin, matched in beauty only by the display of the sky. Matthew walked straight over to the far end of the room and checked the stove in the kitchen area before adding more wood from a neat stack in a purpose-built alcove next to it. He had not spoken since we arrived.

Balancing on one of the comfortable armchairs flanking the log burner, I looked around the honed simplicity of the interior, noting the white walls to reflect the cool light and the timber furnishings to warm it. Wool throws in chunky-knit fresh greens and fat, cream cushions embroidered in red snowflakes invited idle indulgence, but the rack of expensive skiing equipment in the front porch suggested the owners of the cabin also took an active interest in the world outside their door. I waited, expecting at any moment to hear the footsteps of whoever had lit the fires, but I heard no sound other than the *tik–tik* of the metal burner cooling after fierce heat. Matthew checked the room, added wood to the burner. There was a sense of urgency in his movements, and he was not at ease.

"Matthew, who lit the fires?"

He seemed distracted. "Come upstairs – I'll show you your room."

He took me by the hand and guided me to the stairs.

"Matthew…?"

He stopped at the bottom step as if he had only just heard me.

"It was lit for us earlier; there's no one else here now."

I hurried to keep up with him as he showed me upstairs to the main bedroom that shared a view of the landscape with the room below. The entire front wall up into the apex of the roof made a triangle of glass by which a bentwood rocking chair waited. The sun fell on the other side of the house now, the mountains and trees candescent with its sharp, pale light. An antique wood bedstead – cracked and gently coloured by considerable age – sat against the rear wall. From this vantage point, I imagined, the occupants would wake to find their day already blessed by such natural riches as they could see through the window. Matthew turned his back abruptly and went over to a door on one side of the room.

"The bathroom is through here," he said, standing aside so that I could see its understated opulence for myself, but it reminded me of being shown around a house by an estate agent: impersonal, businesslike, just doing his job. I hung back, trying to fathom what on earth was going on, and his eyes hardly skimmed the bed as he put my bag on the Scandinavian quilt in reds and whites that softened its outline.

"Would you like some tea?" he asked, solicitous despite his distraction. I wondered if – now that we were alone at last – he felt the same edge of nerves that had quivered in me as we left the car and embarked on the seductively slick snowmobile. I considered whether the prospect of discussing our future together made him nervous because of what had happened in his past. Whichever, whatever, clearly something played on his mind.

We went back downstairs and he made me tea, the cold, freshly drawn water taking an age to boil on the wood-fed stove, and then we sat on the veranda that wrapped around two sides of the cabin, and watched the sun cross the sky. The mountain slopes stretched out in a seemingly endless backcloth thickly interspersed with spires of snow-laden trees and the odd outcrop of rock – jarring and unsympathetic to the smooth undulations of the landscape. In the evening light, the glittering white desert bronzed as the sun moved towards the horizon. I put my empty mug down on the step, unable to bear the tension any longer.

"What's the matter? You've been pent up ever since we arrived."

The temperature began to drop rapidly with the sun, and I wriggled back into the shelter of his arms against the solid wall of his chest. His arms enfolded me, his chin rested on my shoulder, and his breath moved softly alongside my ear, yet he seemed further away from me now than he ever felt before. Minutes passed before he answered.

"You know that I love you, Emma, and I want you to be happy more than anything."

His eyes were troubled and he looked out across the snow-fields, avoiding me.

"Yes, I know that; what's bothering you?"

"Why do you think I've brought you here?"

His directness wrong-footed me; no way could I tell him what I hoped would happen, what I hoped he might ask, and I wondered if he had a different agenda from my own.

"I thought it was so that we can be alone together – so that we can discuss… things."

"Alone. Yes – so that we could be alone."

But his "alone" and my "alone" appeared to have two very different meanings. I slid right around so that I could see him clearly, and he confronted me now with an unswerving eye.

"Emma, when you look at me, what do you see?"

What sort of question was *that*?

"I see you, Matthew."

The creases deepened between his eyes, his face became unreadable and I shivered, but not because of the chill wind seeping under the steps.

"Can we go in now? It's getting cold," I asked, hoping that moving would shake him out of the dark mood that had taken him. He pressed his lips together but helped me stand where I had become stiff from sitting too long.

The fire still burned steadily in its stove. I hung my quilted coat on the back of one of the tall chairs as Matthew walked in silence to the window. Through it, the world lay untouched, glowing in the last light of the sun. Hands in pockets, he viewed it dispassionately, seeing without allowing its beauty to touch him because his thoughts lay elsewhere.

"But, Emma, *what* do you see?"

He turned, and his expression had darkened perceptibly. Behind the obvious question lay acres of subtlety I wasn't sure how to answer. Everything about him had become unnaturally edgy and I took a step towards him, then thought better of it; he was in no mood to be placated. When I didn't say anything, he turned around and stared at me until I felt obliged to answer.

"I see *you*, Matthew – the man I fell in love with."

"And who is *that*, exactly?" Unfamiliar acidity bled through his tone and, for the first time, my stomach fluttered nervously with fear. "Do you see a *doctor*, a *widower*, your *lover*? Or am I only a set of dates on a time line – some interesting facts bound up in a scientific anomaly?" He took his hands from his pockets and only then did I see the rigidity in his stance, as if he anticipated conflict. "You once said that the only consistent thing about me were the lies I told. What makes you think you know me at all? What makes you believe you can trust anything I say or do?"

I blanched at the sudden change in him. I took a step back, my hand feeling the edge of the table next to me. He waited for an answer and I stumbled to find one he would accept. Outside, the sun had set, the subtle sky fading into palest blue as the land melted into darkness. I found my throat had gone dry and I could hear the strain in my voice.

"I… I also said that you have total integrity, Matthew. I understand why you couldn't tell me who you are – how could you? And I know you haven't told me all that there is to know, but then that's why we're here, isn't it? To talk? That's what we agreed." He seemed to be listening intently, watching the nervous movements my hands made, so I continued. "It's irrelevant to me when you were born, and I don't love you because of what you are, whatever that might be, but because I love the man I *know*…"

I stopped as he ground his teeth, the muscles in his jaw contracting, and he looked as if he were only just managing to restrain his temper. Whatever I said seemed to enrage him further, and I felt suddenly exposed and very, very vulnerable. I resisted the urge to put the table between us and stood my ground.

"And you think you *know* me now?" He became quiet for a moment; then, when he spoke, his voice expressed anguish and I thought that the squall might be over. "Ah, Emma, what do you really know of me?"

I wanted desperately to go to him, to hold and comfort him, but I stayed put, not trusting this lull, knowing that whatever lay behind it had not yet shown its face.

"I know what you have told me, I know what I have learned… that you are a good man…"

"*Good?*" He spun round, glaring. "You think I'm a *good* man? Christ in Heaven, have I made a *fool* out of you as well as a…"

He shook his head violently, stifling the words, pent-up emotion on the brink of exploding. I backed around the table, feeling the solidity of the wood, but knowing that if it came to it, it wouldn't be enough against his strength and agility. He watched me with eyes that were mere slits and he laughed – a harsh sound, cruel and alien. He took a step closer.

"You're frightened of me; I wondered how long it would take you to realize what you're dealing with. And you know nothing – *nothing* of me. Frightened? You should be. I can kill you so easily; I can squeeze the life out of you as I would have done to Staahl, and no one would know. My *secret*…" he used the word disparagingly, "… would be safely buried up here."

He pulverized the air inside the crypt of his hand, and my heart thudded against my chest as I fought to breathe, keeping my voice steady although my legs were jelly and all I wanted to do was run.

"You're not a killer, Matthew. I don't know what's wrong and why you're behaving like this, but you won't kill me."

He curled his lips back over his even, white teeth and his eyes burned with a changing fire, although his words were now ice and he enunciated each with cold precision.

"But you are quite wrong – I *have* killed. I have wrested the life out of men for no other reason than their being my enemies – and what is that compared with what I have done to you?"

"What have you done?" I whispered, fear gluing me to the floor. "Why have you brought me here?"

Fists clenching and flexing convulsively, he moved until he stood over me, struggling with internal demons, his breathing harsh and ragged as he reached out a hand to the cross at my throat. I reacted instinctively, memories of Staahl and my impulse to survive making me lash out. He caught my wrist before I could hit him, holding it in a grip that could crush it like a cobnut in a vice.

"I could take you here and now." He pushed me back against the table – pinned and helpless between its sharp edge and his thighs – his eyes glass stones, blank and devoid of humanity. "I could make a whore out of you and then snap your spine…"

"No Matthew, stop it; this is not you…"

"… then I would be the monster men feared I had become."

I struggled, but the side of the table, no more yielding than his body, bit into my back. "You're not; I don't… please, let go of me. *Stop!* You're *hurting me*…"

Stunned, he released me as if burned, his eyes glazing in shock, seeing me for the first time. Hunching, then whipping round, he smashed his fist into the plate-glass wall. The window shivered and cracked in a radiating series of lines from the epicentre of impact, as a stone shatters the virgin ice on a pond.

I should have run – I should have taken the opportunity while his back was turned and fled into the snow. I should have ripped the door open and plunged into the known blackness to escape the unknown darkness that tore at his soul.

But I didn't.

Perhaps shock prevented me from moving, perhaps the knowledge that to flee into the wilderness was as good a way of ensuring my death from exposure as Matthew deliberately snuffing out the flame of my life. But neither was true. I stayed because I would gladly – willingly – have given him my life if it could have made his suffering any less. I stayed because he didn't expect me to, and because he needed me – and because I needed him.

I neither moved nor spoke. My mouth had turned to ash and every breath I drew through it was desiccation. My heart no longer thudded, but jumped – fitful and sporadic – like the convulsions of a decapitated frog. The table became a welcome friend, propping me up until my legs once more had a role to play in supporting me.

We continued to stand where we were and silence stood with us, its presence oppressive. Eventually Matthew straightened. I could see his reflection in the black mirror of the window, fractured with the pale cobwebs that shattered his image. He stared back at me, his eyes dark points glaring from the phantom of his face. His voice sounded flat and dead.

"Why are you still here?"

I remained silent, waiting for the re-emergence of the molten anger that had erupted from nowhere. He turned from the window. "*Why* are you still here, Emma?" he repeated, and this time, his question was one of genuine bewilderment.

I found my voice from somewhere. "Where else would I go?"

He knew I didn't refer to the frozen land beyond the cabin. I waited, and the minutes passed. Finally, I could stand it no longer.

"What was that all about, Matthew?"

It was his turn not to answer and he continued to stare without perceiving, his head averted.

"*Matthew!*"

He turned his face slowly towards me.

"Why are you still here? Why are you not running from me – after what I said to you? You were frightened – I saw it – I could taste it. But here you still stand."

He shook his head, confused.

"Yes, and here I'll stay. What you became just now – *that* frightened me – but I'm not scared of *you*, Matthew. I don't believe you would have hurt me, no matter what you said you would do." His shoulders slumped and he suddenly aged with the burden he carried. "Why are you trying to frighten me off? What have I done?"

The snarl resurfaced. "You? *You* haven't done anything."

I backed away again. He stepped forward, his hand out to me, pleading.

"No – Emma, please, you're right, I won't hurt you – not like that. But I am going to hurt you in other ways – I can see no other choice. I am going to hurt you and I don't know whether you will ever be able to forgive me."

CHAPTER
15

Secrets and Ties

My heart collapsed into the pit of my stomach.

"Is that why you brought me here, so that I couldn't run?" His lack of an answer verified my assumption. "What can be so bad that you think I would want to, anyway?"

His eyes slid to my face and then away again.

He banked the fire right up until the log burner was stacked full, his hand placing the timber in the middle of the flames leaving no more than a slight reddening of his skin that disappeared almost as soon as he withdrew it. The fire belted out heat but I felt cold. A steady stream of freezing air filtered from the broken window, now no more effective at insulating the room from the elements than a single sheet of glass. But had the triple-glazing been intact, I would still have shivered, both from the shock of what had happened and from the expectation of what might come.

He had hardly spoken since.

I sat stiffly, crammed against the arm of the taupe cord sofa, still fearful of his reactions and watching him warily. He made slow, deliberate movements and kept as far away from me as the confines of the seating area would allow. I strove to think of anything he could have done that might horrify me the way he believed it would.

A burning log fell against the glass of the door, breaking the taut silence.

"Is it because you have killed – is that it?"

"Yes, I have killed – a long, long time ago – and I would have killed again if you hadn't stopped me."

His eyes reflected the frantic dance of the flames.

"You said I was a whore, Matthew."

I couldn't keep the hurt from my voice; he had made all my longing for him seem cheap and dirty – no more than an overzealous slut in a hotel room.

His head snapped up. "No, Emma, I did not. I said that I would *make* a whore of you if I…" He swore quietly under his breath before he continued. "I asked you what you see when you look at me." He checked that I remembered, but it was something I would find hard to forget. "I'm going to rephrase that; what do you *know* of me?"

I licked my lips nervously, wondering where this would lead.

"I… I know what you have told me," I said, hesitant.

He pulled a face, indicating regret. "I won't get angry, no matter what you say."

"I know what I found out – you know that now, too. I know what others have said about you…"

"Ah." He nodded, a twist to his mouth. I stopped again, waiting for the reaction. "Go on," he said. "What *do* people say?"

"That you are one of the finest surgeons they know, a bit of a loner, a family man."

"Ah," he said again. My hand went up to my cross to jumpily fiddle with it. He followed every movement I made.

"What about my *family*?"

His tone had that quality that made me flinch, overly

calm, searing in its softness.

"That you are devoted to them," I said desperately. His eyes glinted and he leaned towards me, the firelight illuminating one side of his face, the shadow-side almost demonic in the dark contrast into which it was thrown.

"And?"

"And? And what? That you… you…" I began to stutter. I swallowed. "That you came to Maine after your wife's death…"

He startled me by leaping to his feet without warning, lithe as a cat, and began treading the small square in front of the fire.

"My wife, yes. I'm a widower – isn't that right, Emma?"

His head swivelled to look directly at me and he stopped pacing for a second,

"Y… yes."

A humourless smile carved across his face.

"Well, that isn't *quite* the case."

"What?"

A horrible, familiar sensation began to form where my stomach should have been. I wasn't following the script. He began his patrolling again – back and forth, back and forth.

"Emma, my wife isn't dead."

I felt as if he had just inserted his hand into my gut and was extracting it piece by piece.

"She's alive? You're still *married*?"

I waited for him to deny it, to say that it had all been a misunderstanding – even a sick joke – but he continued marking out my heartbeats with every step he took.

"You *lied* to me?"

He ceased pacing. "Isn't it what I do best?"

His words sank into place.

I was on my feet, yelling at him, blind fury taking over every sinew of my body, all fear and caution gone.

"You lied to me all this time? You could have told me – you utter and total *bastard*!… I would never, *ever* have looked at you, never let you touch me, if I'd known. I would have done anything for you, I would have died for you, I believed in you… And you do this to me… you've betrayed me, you've betrayed *her*."

And I flew at him as I had never done at Guy, because Guy had meant nothing to me in comparison to what this man had become. I wanted to hurt him in any way I could, I wanted him to suffer as I had, as I did, in the only way I could express it: beating him, hitting him, flailing against his chest, welcoming the pain it brought to my own arms as they made contact with his hard body, the frenzy of my attack made more passionate by the futility of it all. The pain became unbearable and he grabbed both of my arms and so I kicked at him instead, but he just stood back so that I abused nothing but the air. Overwhelmed with frustration, unable to find the words to tell him how his own had shredded my heart, I tried to break free from his grip, wrestling without result, ready to run, wanting to run, ready to find oblivion out in the frozen expanse. But he wouldn't let me go. I wrenched to free myself from him, my arm screaming in pain where the newly healed bone threatened to break again.

"No, Emma – stop!"

I tried to bite his hand, but he held it out of reach, so I tried to break his thumb instead, but it was useless; I was trapped.

"Emma – stop. Enough!"

He let go of one of my arms, then the other, swiftly encasing me in a ring of steel made of his own arms so that

I couldn't move any more. I attempted to twist out of them, duck beneath them, but there was no give in the cage he made around me.

"Enough, Emma; that's enough now." His voice poured balm on my wrath, but I would have none of it.

"*No!*"

"Emma, shh."

How dare he – how *dare* he try to calm me!

"NO! You lied, you lied! *Let… go… of… me.*"

"No."

"*Bastard!* Let me go – *now!*"

"No, Emma."

I pushed against his arms, dug my nails into his hands, but nothing I did made any impression on the confinement in which he held me.

"Let me go… *please…*"

Exhausted, what fight I had left in me evaporated, and my legs gave way. Matthew continued to hold me until he could feel my sobs coming harsh and freely, then he lowered me onto the sofa, where I buried my head in the deep upholstery, my body shuddering convulsively. He found a heavy blanket and wrapped it around me and then left me to cry.

I had been such a fool – hadn't he said as much only a short while ago? What ever made me think I could trust him any more than I could have trusted Guy? But I thought I could – my handsome, clever, good and trustworthy doctor – who had risked exposure to save me, who had crossed the Atlantic to bring me back, who undoubtedly loved me. But not enough. Not enough to tell me the truth and not enough to leave his wife for me. For all his extraordinary past, his present was as fallible, as imperfect, as *mortal* as my own. My anger burned from deep within – an all-consuming furnace that rendered void all other emotion – his betrayal complete.

"Emma, have this." I felt the touch of his hand on my shoulder, and shook him off roughly.

"Drink this, you need it, it'll help." His hand lay insistently on me.

"I don't want it," I barked at him.

"I know you don't, but drink it anyway."

I steadfastly refused to move and I heard him sigh and put something down on the floor. Placing his hands under my arms, he lifted me like a child, turning me around and putting me back on the sofa so that I faced him. I tried to cross my arms in denial of him but they hurt, and he winced. He crouched in front of me, lower than my line of sight so that I would have to turn my head to avoid looking at him, and I was blowed if I was going to do that. He held a red-and-white checked mug out to me, its cheerful gingham in direct contrast to everything I felt. Rage still purred through my veins: delightful hot fury, as vengeful as lust.

I lashed out. "I said I don't *want* it!"

Too quick, he removed the mug from the path of my arm before I hit it.

"I heard what you said," he said calmly – not the spooky calm of before, but the tranquillity gained from letting go of something that had haunted him for a very long time. "Emma, I want you to drink this and I want you to do so *now*."

I scowled at him and he held my gaze, but I couldn't not do what he told me, even though I resisted with every inch of my being. He raised the mug to me again and this time I took it.

"*Gheugh* – you've put sugar in it!"

"Drink it."

"Bastard."

"Yes, but drink it anyway."

"I didn't mean the bloody *tea*."

"Yes, I know you didn't."

"Stop agreeing with me."

He sighed again. I fully intended making his life hell and he knew it.

CHAPTER

16

Complications

There is that province that lies between sleeping and waking in which the tranquillity of the night still reigns before the harsh reality of day begins.

For those few brief moments before I became fully awake, I drifted comfortably in a half-world before the significance of the previous night imposed itself forcibly on my waking mind. My eyes cracked open and for a second I didn't know where I was. A chilly white ceiling climbed to an apex above my head with heavy wooden beams spanning the space below it. My resting pulse quickened as I remembered, and I jerked fully awake, leaning on one elbow as the fog cleared from my brain. He had put me to bed, still clothed. He had removed my shoes and loosened the waistband of my trousers, but that was all. My eyes and mouth were dry – tacky dry – and a taste clung to my tongue. A glass of water sat by the bed untouched. I lifted it and sniffed, but it smelled as it appeared, and I sipped it once before draining the glass. I strained to listen for any sounds that might tell me where Matthew might be, although what I would do if I saw him was anybody's guess.

An eddy of conflicting currents obscured my mind – a mass of information recorded in fleeting images and half-remembered words, confused by the chaos of emotion. The yo-yoing between his anger and the threat of violence, and the very real assault on my sensitized emotional state, left me crippled but seething with resentment.

I had been here before.

I hadn't believed my tutor at first because it was so much easier to pretend that it had all been a ghastly mistake. But she had presented me with the evidence of Guy's perfidy in the full knowledge that I would first examine the facts. And I did so, picking away at the mortar of our relationship so that, brick by brick, it disassembled before me; she knew it to be the only way I would accept what she told me.

I had crawled back to my room in the old stone college in a state of numbness, before making up my mind what to do with the information. I knew Guy well enough to know that he would have been content to allow things to continue in just the same way they had done before his little secret had been uncovered. I even thought that he would have rather enjoyed the additional titillation it would offer our relationship, especially since I then discovered that I had already met his wife.

She had been at a faculty party at the end of the Michlemas term – a tall, striking woman with dark-brown hair which she tied back from her face, elongating her already fine cheekbones and evening out the first telltale signs of age. She wore a tight-fitting black cocktail dress that showed off her toned legs and bum, and she told me that she ran by the River Cam every morning before taking the children to school. I found her self-assurance quite intimidating – gained, I supposed, from her success as a lawyer, and as wife to a leading academic. My sense of betrayal was as much for her as for me: we were both the unwitting victims of the same man's ego.

When I told Guy that our relationship was over, I listened to his excuses patiently before telling him exactly what I thought of him. Even then, he persisted – phoning, writing, waiting at the door of my room – until it all became too much and I told my father, because there was no one else in whom I could confide. It left me shattered – bruised enough to jeopardize my studies, but not damaged enough to destroy them.

Despite his protestations of love, there had always been a part of me that reserved judgment on Guy, never quite trusting him as fully as I needed to, but willing myself to believe that I did. That tiny part of me remained inviolate, cushioned from the full force of his deception by my passion for my subject. The journal had been the safety net into which I fell, and my new-found faith plucked me from the tangled mess in which I'd found myself, and put me back on my feet.

This was different. I had given Matthew every ounce of what made me whole; no part of me lay hidden from him and I felt fully exposed to whatever he chose to throw at me. What hurt all the more was that, unlike Guy, he never assumed I was his for the taking. I offered myself on a sacrificial plate, a willing immolation to his fire. Perhaps I had been wrong in supposing he felt the same way I did. Perhaps, because of his old-fashioned manners, I imagined we shared an old-fashioned attitude towards marriage. How *stupid*! I should have known better.

It snowed viciously now – hard flurries diving, rattling, hissing against the window-wall of the room. Drawing up my legs under the heavy quilt, I attempted to squeeze the gnawing discomfort from inside where all the nervous tension of the day before had taken up residence, and thought about where I would go from here. But there was no point staying in bed and I resented the fact that he had put me there. It had only ever been meant for the two of us and, without him, it made a mockery of my desire. I no longer wanted to be here. I had nothing left to stay for.

Hot water from the tank, heated by the log burner downstairs, flowed into the heavy bath, and I bathed quickly. Had circumstances been different, I would have enjoyed staying at the cabin; as it was, I couldn't wait to escape.

I couldn't care less what I wore. I angrily pulled on jeans, and brushed my teeth and hair in the same frame of mind, tying the hair into a rough plait; but that was it – that was all the effort I would make and it sure as anything wasn't for *him*.

The faint smell of cooking bacon interrupted my silent tirade. Despite my rancour, I felt hungry; I had missed a meal last night and fallen asleep soon after drinking the tea.

"*NO!*"

I realized now what the strange taste in my mouth had been when I woke. By the time I made it downstairs, I had worked myself into a fury and I knew who would get the brunt of it.

"You *drugged* me!" I accused him as soon as I stalked into the kitchen.

Matthew continued to break an egg into the griddle on the stove. It spat as the hot fat cooked the edges of the white, crisping them a friable gold. Strips of bacon kept warm on a plate next to the griddle.

"I sedated you; you were in a pretty bad state."

"I was angry – there was nothing wrong with me."

He spooned hot fat over the egg, the transparent white becoming opaque in an instant.

"You were distraught, you needed to rest."

"That was not *your* decision to make."

My fists clubbed as I readied myself for the fight. He looked at me for the first time, the blue of his irises intensified by the white of the snow outside and the cream sweater he wore.

"I rather think it was."

He remained infuriatingly calm, and returned to the task in front of him. I wanted to shake him, abuse him, reduce him to a writhing mass of black spite, as he had done to me – anything to get a reaction which would justify me hating him.

"What are you doing *that* for – you don't eat," I said rudely.

He refused to be goaded, placing the cooked egg precisely on the plate next to the bacon.

"No, but you do."

He held the plate out to me, but I stood there like a spoilt, stubborn child, my arms stiff by my sides, glaring at him.

"Emma, it's not much, eat it – you can argue with me as much as you like afterwards."

I snatched it from him, detesting my behaviour as much as I hated him. I slammed the plate on the table where already a knife and fork lay next to a slate place mat, hearing the satisfying *chink* of porcelain on stone. If I tried again a little harder, the fine china would disintegrate into as many pieces as he had broken me. Matthew watched as I picked up the knife and fork reluctantly – fighting my hunger – and then turned his back to allow me to swallow my pride and eat.

As I finished the last piece of bacon, he placed the mug in front of me, taking the empty plate away. I eyed it suspiciously.

"It's just tea, Emma."

He had the patient tone that adults adopt when dealing with a disgruntled child, but the food had taken the edge off my temper, despite myself. I was still up for a fight though, if he offered me one.

"That's what I *thought* it was last night." I took a sip anyway; he'd remembered not to sugar it, but then he wasn't trying to disguise the taste as he had yesterday. "Now what happens? Is this where you tell me that your wife doesn't understand you, or that you were going to leave her anyway?"

He had been in the process of cleaning the work surface, but now he turned slowly, leaned against the kitchen sink and folded his arms, regarding me sombrely.

"No, I won't leave her."

Now, why did that not surprise me? I gave a snort of a laugh.

"So, what do you want from me – do you expect me to be your mistress?"

I couldn't disguise the bitterness in my voice and he heard it, too.

"No."

I stared at him, wavering between hurt and rage. For all the protestations I made over Guy and his marriage, there had been the tiniest part of me that hoped – even if I wouldn't admit it to myself – that Matthew and I could still be together in some way. I felt another door slam in my face and my temper began to blaze from desperation.

"What, then? If you won't leave her and you don't want me to be your *whore*, I take it that you don't want me at all. You went to all that trouble to fetch me back from the UK and to bring me up here, to tell me *that*? You could have saved yourself the bother and told me a long time ago; then I wouldn't need to be here." Heat flooded my face. "Actually, you could have saved us all the time and trouble and not have spoken to me in the first place. Why did you do it? I was perfectly happy before I met you; why couldn't you just have left me *alone*, Matthew?"

A sudden gust of wind sucked at the chimney; inside the log burner, the flames stretched and flared, licking the glass.

"I told you once that I'm selfish. I didn't set out to fall in love with you; I tried not to…"

"You didn't try very hard," I snapped.

"I tried hard enough, believe me."

"After *this*? Why the hell should I?"

I found his quietude disturbing. "Because you love me as much as I love you."

"Don't bet on it," I hissed.

Matthew fixed me with his unwavering gaze, his head tilted slightly to one side. I felt as trapped by his eyes as a butterfly inside a jar. He spoke quietly.

"Are you telling me that you don't love me, Emma?"

I wanted to scream at him that I didn't love him, that I hated him, that I loathed the very sight of him, but why should he believe me if I couldn't even convince myself? So I didn't answer and looked sullenly at the grain of the table instead. With a slight movement of his hips, he pushed himself away from the sink and came around the side of the table, standing within a few feet of me. I felt his nearness like an open wound. I glared at him.

"There's no point in discussing any of this any more – it's all a farce, a total farce. Why couldn't you have just told me the truth to begin with? Why wait until now?"

"Would you have stayed if I did?"

I looked away, avoiding his eyes.

He answered for me. "You'd already made it perfectly clear that you wouldn't date a married man, and at what point would I draw the line and start telling you the truth?

How would you have reacted if I turned around one day and said, 'Hey, Emma, I'm married, oh, and by the way, I'm four hundred years old and should be dead.' Would you really have been able to cope with *that*?"

The wind gasped and moaned down the chimney. Outside the snow had thickened until the closest trees were entirely obscured by the sheer mass of it. Even if I told him to take me back to the college, we wouldn't be able to leave now, which made the situation all the more intolerable because I had no choice but to bear it. I looked back at him.

"So instead, you made sure I was well and truly hooked before I found out, is that it? Was that part of your game plan?"

"I had no plan. I didn't want to make things difficult for you, but I couldn't let you go. I won't live without you, Emma." He meant it as a declaration but it came out almost as a threat. I narrowed my eyes.

"So you said. Hah! You've not much choice, have you? You've certainly not given me any. Does your *wife* know you've been cheating on her?"

He flinched as if I'd struck him, taking a step back from me.

"It's more complicated than that and yes, she does know about us."

Incredulity followed scorn and I half stood up, shaking my head in disbelief, and leaning my hands on the table lest he conclude that my trembling limbs were anything other than unqualified rage.

"You stand there and tell me that she *knows*? You have the *audacity* to tell me that she knows, yet you won't leave her? And she's happy with this little arrangement? What, do you cuddle up at night and tell her all about it – all about *me*? Does she find it funny – do you both have a really good *laugh* at my expense? Or does the whole idea of it turn you both on?" Through my anger my voice began to break. He reached out to me, torment on his face.

I pulled back sharply. "Don't touch me – don't you *dare* touch me."

He kept his hand out, imploring. "Emma, let me explain, please; it's nothing like you think…"

Without the prop of the table I began to shake uncontrollably, as disappointment, rancour and despair combined with pungent humiliation.

"*Think?* I don't know what to *think*, Matthew, because you never told me."

He took another step towards me.

"I'm telling you now – I'm telling you *everything* now. Please, just listen."

17

Aftershock

As the wind rose to scream at us through the crazed window, Matthew ran his hands through his hair, preparing to begin.

"The car crash didn't kill her…"

"That's obvious," I sneered.

"But it left her – Ellen's – spine broken. She's been quadriplegic ever since."

Intent on my vendetta, there was nothing he could tell me now that would weaken my resolve to detest him.

"And that's your excuse – cheat on your disabled wife. Oh, this gets better and better; you are a *monster* after all."

That hurt; his mouth turned down and I could sense the tremor run through him, but he didn't stop.

"That's not all; the crash that paralysed her, killed our granddaughter."

I bit my lip; I could feel my resolve to hate everything about him weakening.

"Don't try the sympathy card on me, Matthew."

"I'm not telling you to gain your sympathy, Emma; I'm telling you so that you know all the circumstances. What you decide to do with the information will be up to you; but you need to listen – you owe me that much."

"I owe you *nothing*," I said sourly.

"Yes – you do. Did you hear what I said? I told you that our *granddaughter* died."

It finally registered.

"When?"

"Forty-six years ago."

"But that means…"

His voice dropped as he watched for my reaction. "Yes, what does it mean?"

He let me work it out for myself, just as my tutor did all those years ago in Cambridge.

"But… how old is she?"

"Ellen was born in 1914."

"She's…"

"Ninety-six, yes."

My pulse stammered into life as my curiosity gained the better of me.

"Is she the same as you? I mean, is she immortal – or whatever you are?"

"No, she's the same as you, Emma – she will die." Whether he meant to or not, he shuddered. "I cannot excuse what I have done to you, but I have not betrayed my wife. Whatever you might think of me now, that's one thing of which you cannot accuse me."

"So what do you call *this*?" I indicated the cabin with an angry glance around the room.

"Ellen knows we are here, and she knows *why* we are here. It was her idea in the first place; she insisted that I tell you."

"Matthew, this is *sick*."

He closed his eyes and his mouth drew into a thin line that hardened.

"I said that I would tell you everything; I didn't say it would be easy. Heaven knows I have sought every – *any* – way to make this easier, but the facts are what they are."

Shoving the chair away from me with my foot, I stood back from the table.

"I don't know what's worse: thinking you're cheating on your wife, or that she is complicit. Damn it, Matthew, she's *ninety-six* – she's older than my grandmother. Ugh!"

I went over to the broken window, ignoring the frigid air, and looked out as far as the blizzard would allow. I had already worked out that she must be older than he looked, but it never occurred to me that she would be *that* old. Yet – why not? After all, Matthew was four times her age and I hardly recoiled from him.

"What else is there – what else haven't you told me?"

Snow spat at the window; behind me, Matthew shifted position and took a deep breath.

"We have a son – Henry – and…"

"Henry is your *son*?"

"Yes, and Daniel is my grandson…"

"Not your brother."

"No. And Maggie is our granddaughter. Her sister was killed in the same crash that paralysed my wife."

I felt cold by the window and goosebumps crawled up my arms despite the thick jumper I wore. But I could hardly tell whether the ice that replaced the fire in my veins was the result of the air, or the leaching of hope that bled from me.

"Emma, please come away from there, come by the fire."

"Why?"

"Because you're getting cold. There's no point making yourself suffer."

"No, you've done enough of that for me."

"Yes, and it has to stop. No more lies, Emma; I don't want to keep anything from you any more."

I couldn't resist the temptation to resort to sarcasm.

"But I might *run*, Matthew – aren't you frightened that I might run? Doesn't it bother you that I might leave? It worried you before – what's changed?"

A note of resignation sounded in his voice.

"As you said last night, where would you go? I know that I have nowhere; we are as tied to each other as we are to this earth. And besides, I can't keep you without letting you go."

I turned around to face him squarely. "What's *that* supposed to mean?"

He shrugged his shoulders. "It means that I have to let you make the choice whether you stay or go, and you can't do that if you don't know what to base that decision on."

Echoes of the argument I'd had with my father filtered back to me, and then another conversation – one that Matthew and I held as he cared for me in his room at the college after Staahl's attack – when I felt equally confused but knew so much less about him than I did now.

"Complications, Matthew; this is what you meant, isn't it, when you said there were 'complications'?"

"Yes."

I came back to stand in front of the fire, but it made little difference to the cold inside me, and with a grudging degree of acquiescence I said, "You had better tell me the rest of it."

"It's complicated," he warned, frowning again.

"Everything about you always is," I told him, unsmiling, giving him nothing but the time to explain.

"I met Ellen in 1933. She was nineteen and the sister of Jack – one of the athletic team – and I stayed with her family on their ranch when we were in training one season."

I pictured him with a pretty young girl in the wheatfields of some prairie in the Midwest and felt instantly and insanely jealous. I pressed my hands together in my lap and said nothing.

"We grew to like one another and married the following spring. Henry came along several years after."

The thought of Matthew with anyone else galled me. I reminded my green-eyed self that I wasn't supposed to care, remonstrating with my alter ego for my inconsistency. But it was pointless. I pulled my cross from the confines of my jumper and rasped it angrily from side to side on its chain. Matthew had been observing me closely and, although I glared fixedly at the white-hot heart of the fire, from where I sat I saw the flash as his eyes lit at my poorly disguised envy. He pressed the advantage before I recovered, finding a crack in my defences.

"Emma, I was lonely – I'd had centuries of being alone – and Ellen allowed me to feel human for the first time in countless years. I could share some sort of normality with her, something of which I had been only able to dream."

I crossed my legs and leaned an elbow on my knee, swinging the cross back and forth tetchily, more angry with myself at this moment, than with him.

"Did she know about you – did you tell her?"

Matthew shook his head. "No, I didn't, not at first. She knew I was strong and fast, of course – she liked that – but not *how* strong, nor *how* fast. She always worried that I didn't eat enough – that was more difficult to hide – but not impossible." His voice became faraway and I felt the thrill of envy crawl through me again.

"Things were fine between us until after the war. I served as a medic again – wars are useful for creating enough confusion to lose oneself in all the paperwork; but when I came back, she noticed the difference in me."

"How?"

"Because I hadn't changed. I stayed on in Europe to help with the privations after the end of the war, so I'd been gone for some time. All the other husbands and sons returned scarred in one way or another – emotionally or physically and sometimes both – but I remained unchanged. And not only that, but I looked as young as I did when I went away."

Although I resisted, I could feel myself being drawn inexorably into the story of his life.

"How did you explain it to her?"

"Well…" He ran his hands through his hair again, making the gold strands stick up haphazardly before he repeated the action, smoothing them back. "I did and I didn't. Ellen didn't have the advantage of your education nor your perception, so I kept my background and my real age to myself."

I stopped sliding my cross and stared at him.

"She doesn't know where you come from? Still?"

He shook his head slowly. "No, I never told her; I didn't think she would cope with it, I thought she might…"

"Run," I said.

He raised his eyebrows. "Yes."

"But she must have noticed over – however many years you've been married…"

"Of course she *knows*," he interrupted. "She's not as educated as you are, but she's sharp, intelligent."

"I didn't mean to imply she wasn't," I said defensively; "just that she must have asked sooner or later."

"Sorry." He drew his hand across his eyes, a gesture he always made when confronted with something that made him uneasy. "Yes, she did. I told her that something had happened during the war – a nerve agent or some such nonsense – that had slowed the ageing process."

"And she accepted that?"

"Yes. Whether she believed me is another matter; but she accepted what I told her. I think that it was either that or face making a choice."

"Which was?"

"To stay or go."

"Oh, *that* one."

He threw an almost haunted look at me and I returned it stonily. He dropped his gaze and continued.

"We were happy enough together; Henry was growing up and we had a home – although we had to move every so often – and financially we were very comfortable. She stayed."

There was something in what he said or the way he said it that made me think there must be more to be said on that subject, but just for once I didn't press him, and let him carry on.

"The problems started when Henry met Monica. She was… feisty – also very bright – and a few years older than Henry. We hadn't been in the situation before of having an outsider join our small family; it was a bit of an unknown. Henry, of course, had grown up with me being the way I am; he accepted me because Ellen did and he had known no other life."

"Monica is no longer alive? You talk about her in the past tense."

He looked surprised. "Do I? I don't mean to." He slid forward from the armchair on which he sat and knelt on one knee in front of the stove. As he opened the glass door, a blast of heat scalded my face even where I sat, several feet away.

"*Matthew…!*" He looked back over his shoulder at me, a heavy piece of timber in one hand, ready to throw on the fire. The smell of scorching cloth reached me. "You'll set your clothes on fire!"

He looked down at his chest and brushed his hand over the wool of his sweater.

"Mmm, I'll have to be more careful."

"Yes, you will!" I wasn't supposed to care and, although I assumed him to be fireproof, I didn't want to test the theory, and the thought of him going up in flames was more than I could cope with at the moment. He threw the log on the fire and closed the door and settled back into his chair. He crossed his legs and placed the tips of his fingers together, looking like a learned professor about to lecture a student. He didn't say anything for a moment and I thought that he had forgotten what he was saying.

"Monica…?"

"Ah yes, *Monica*. Henry and Monica had two daughters: little Ellen and Margaret – Maggie. We all lived together in the same house; we had different parts of it, but we shared meals together, that sort of thing. Monica was observant – too observant. She began to ask questions – not only about me, but about Henry also."

"Why Henry?"

"Henry… how shall I put it?" Matthew paused while he formulated an answer, searching the pine-clad ceiling for words in which to describe his son. "He has some of my attributes, let's say. He looks like me, for a start, and he hasn't aged as you would expect."

"But he is ageing?"

"Yes, he is getting older." He sounded dejected and for a second looked away. "Anyway, Monica noticed. It was more obvious in me, of course, but then over the years with Henry also, and she started asking questions. When she didn't get the answers she expected, she searched elsewhere for them."

"What do you mean, 'searched'?"

"She consulted scientists, doctors – even clairvoyants. We had to talk to her, but she wouldn't listen, she wouldn't stop. Then there were the girls. They were showing the same signs of not ageing as quickly. Henry had reached his early thirties by that time, but looked at least ten years younger. Then little Ellen, especially, still looked only six or so, when she was ten."

I thought of Flora wanting to be very grown up at eight. "I bet she didn't like that."

"No, not much," he smiled sadly. "It wasn't as evident with Maggie – not then, at least. Monica started taking them to doctors to have tests. They hated it – they weren't guinea pigs, for goodness' sake, they were just children! Henry tried to stop her but she made life hell for him and she…" I heard a distinct crunch of teeth meeting as Matthew shut his mouth before he said something he might regret. "She became obsessed with the whole concept. Henry said that if she didn't stop he would take them and leave. But she wouldn't stop, Emma, she just wouldn't *listen*."

He looked at me and I saw a sliver of the desperation the family must have gone through reflected in his face.

"She must have been jealous," I said slowly, thinking about the woman.

"Jealous?"

"Well, there you were, looking the way you do, with Henry and her children not ageing much, and then there was she – what, mid to late thirties by then? – wrinkles beginning, stomach starting to sag around the edges, maybe hair beginning to go grey…"

"She was a very striking woman."

"Perhaps, but *she* was getting older – you weren't."

"Maybe so," he didn't sound convinced. "But it was when they were on the way to meet another specialist that the accident happened. Monica was driving, the children were in the back and Ellen had insisted on going with them. I think that she'd used the excuse that she wanted to take the children out for a treat afterwards – something like that. The girls loved ice-cream soda." His expression softened at the memory, then faded. "Maggie started to cry – needles frightened her, and she was only five. Monica told her to be quiet, Ellen defended her…" He tapered off and I waited until he caught up with himself. "It had been cold overnight; it was still early in the season and the road hadn't been treated – no snow chains on the wheels either. Monica drove fast – she always drove too fast – and they were late for the appointment. She and Ellen began to argue, the children started crying and… she lost control of the car." Muscles in his jaw worked, and he hung his head, and quietly, almost so that I couldn't hear him, said, "I have never spoken of this to anyone outside the family. I haven't spoken about it for a very long time."

"I'm so sorry, Matthew," I whispered, feeling the weight of his sorrow in my chest, and I would have reached out to him, but pride and hurt still bloomed too fulsomely to let me, and I locked my fingers together.

"Yes, well…"

I had nothing useful to say, so I didn't. Close to the fire, the room seemed warm, but down by the floor where my feet dangled, a layer of cold air hung in an invisible shroud. I kicked off my shoes, tucking my feet under me. If Matthew drank tea – or anything else, for that matter – this would be the point where I would get up and make him a cup. Whatever I thought of him at the moment – and I could feel my resolve waver even as he talked – it would be a small gesture of comfort and a sign that I recognized what he had been through. As it was, I could only sit there in silence without sniping or arguing, and be a token presence of common humanity. I watched him surreptitiously. Composed, grave – the only movement in his face where the light from the fire caught his eyes, imparting an orange flame to their intense blue. Absolutely still, his chest rose and fell imperceptibly, the soft sigh of his breathing neither fast nor slow. Only the incessant twisting of the ring on his little finger gave any indication of what he experienced in the recollection of that day. Careless of the moment, my tummy rumbled and his eyes refocused on me.

"It's your lunchtime; you must have something to eat."

"It hardly matters, Matthew; it can wait."

A slight smile lifted the corner of his mouth and vanished as quickly.

"I promised your mother that I would make sure you ate properly, so…"

"My mother isn't here," I interjected.

"I always *try* and keep my promises, Emma," he said pointedly. Reluctantly, I started to slip my shoes back on, but he rose and went through to the kitchen. He must have given some thought to how I would be fed while we were together; I had given it none.

"I can feed myself, you don't have to do anything," I said, following him, aggrieved. He glanced at me, then back at the shelves and the assortment of food in the cold store set in the outer wall that acted as a fridge in winter.

"It's not something I've been able to do for a long time. Let me at least make sure you eat, if nothing else."

Part of me still baulked at letting him do anything that might take away the sting of his confession – might make me almost beholden to him. But this wasn't manipulation or even a salve for his conscience, but exactly what it seemed, so I let him.

"Did you do this for your wi— for Ellen?"

He selected several items and brought them to the work-surface under the long kitchen window.

"Yes – sometimes, when work permitted or she let me; husbands weren't supposed to be self-sufficient then. But I'm quite domesticated, you know. Even if I have no need for food, I like to think that I can look after others."

Since he wasn't going to let me cook, I did the washing up from breakfast. Matthew showed me how to run hot water from the system heated by the wood stove. It ran erratically, and he hastily pulled me out of the way as scalding water hissed and spat into the deep sink.

"Thanks," I muttered.

"You're welcome," he said and again, the hint of a short-lived smile. I watched him curiously as he chopped various vegetables and trimmed meat. He seemed more at home with food than I did. I washed and dried the plate, knife, fork and various cooking implements from the morning, and he took them from me and put them away.

"Have you been here before?" I asked.

"The cabin belongs to Henry. We all use it from time to time."

The mention of his son reminded me of something I had meant to ask.

"Did you call him after your father?"

Matthew threw a handful of vegetables into hot fat and the moisture in them exploded furiously.

"Henry after my father, little Ellen after Ellen and Maggie after my mother."

"Yes, of course," I murmured, recalling his family tree. "Then the medical centre was named after your *granddaughter*; I thought it was after your... wife."

"Of course – that's what you were supposed to think –

you and everyone else. The lies go far beyond you, Emma. My existence is one big fabrication; it's the only way I know to keep us safe."

He stirred the sautéing vegetables rapidly before moving them to a plate he kept on one side. He replaced them with a piece of meat. I looked at it doubtfully.

"Don't worry, it's not liver."

I looked at him in surprise. "How do you know I don't like liver?"

"I asked your mother."

"Oh."

The smell of seared meat rose temptingly from the griddle, making me salivate.

I found it difficult to maintain a frosty distance with any dignity with my stomach intent on showing me up, so I tried to cover my growling hunger by cleaning the emptying sink noisily. Matthew obligingly ignored my embarrassment. Scrubbing at a tough spot, I returned to the original conversation.

"If Monica dug around for information, did she find anything incriminating?" Matthew moved the meat around on the griddle to stop it from catching.

"No, not that I'm aware. She left shortly after the accident – the marriage couldn't hold together after that. Henry was understandably devastated by the death of his daughter – we all were – and with his five-year-old daughter to care for and his mother in a critical state…" I had ceased cleaning, finding myself involuntarily drawn into the family's ordeal, watching it played out in the narration of his face. "I… I didn't know if Ellen would make it for some time after the accident, Emma. We were living on a knife edge for months. But what was worse – so much worse – was losing a child to the *certainty* of death." He flipped the meat over with more force than he needed.

Mopping up spattered fat, I said quietly, "But your wife did survive."

"If you can call it survival, then yes, I suppose she did. And so did Maggie – thankfully, with no more than minor injuries – physical, at least. The cruel irony of it is that only Monica remained unscathed. The car left the road over a shallow cliff and rolled. It was prevented from falling any further by a tree, but it hit it pretty hard on Ellen's side and little Ellie sat behind her. *Damn*, I've burned this." He took the griddle from the stove top, scowling at the steak which looked only singed along one edge; it wasn't what I would have called burned.

"It doesn't matter, Matthew; it's better than I would have cooked it."

I also wanted to say that I wasn't as hungry as I had been before he told me the details of the accident, and that eating after he had told me about what happened to his family seemed callous; but he placed the meat on the plate and spooned the vegetables next to it and set it on the table, standing expectantly with his arms folded. I resigned myself to eating and sat down.

I ate in the silence that followed as Matthew went to check the generator that pumped hot water to the bathrooms and to the kitchen tap, and I took in the essence of the crash. As much as I tried not to, the scene replayed over and over, and from the twisted remains of the car I saw the lifeless gaze not of the blonde-wreathed woman I had seen that first day in Maine, but of a little girl. In my mind's eye, her grandfather bent over her, covered her bare legs, and closed her eyes for the last time. Tenderly – because she mattered; because he cared.

Nothing could erase the memory of the crash scene I witnessed that September day when first I saw him, nor disassociate those events with what happened to his family forty years previously. It glued itself to my psyche as surely as it had left its mark on Matthew, and part of me resented the fact that – despite myself – I cared.

I cut a thin strip from the meat and added a tiny cube of potato to the end of the fork without thought. It required none. Routine offered respite: eating, drinking, breathing. Minute by minute, familiarization granted some relief from the devastating effects of his revelation. Like a tectonic shift in my life, the initial shock had been an earthquake that shook me to my very core, so violent that I found it hard to isolate any single emotion among the onslaught to my senses. Then, after the numbing first blow, the aftershocks had struck, rolling one emotion in after another: anger, grief, shame. Now I thought myself at the point where finally, after the turmoil, comes calm, and I might be able to stand back and take stock. Only then would I be in a position to determine what needed to be done and what I *wanted* to do about it. I remained acutely aware, however, that occasionally a tremor ran through me, reminding me that, although the main danger had receded, it left in its wake a bruised and battered spirit that would take time to heal.

I had always been jealous of Ellen, of the power of her status as wife and her pull on Matthew's memory. I understood it better now – my envy made flesh in the form of a frail and vulnerable old woman. Even if Matthew were willing to disavow her, I couldn't have lived with the guilt and it would condemn him further in my eyes, and there was no future for us in that.

Future.

A word made redundant by the facts. A false hope because, as Matthew said, he wasn't going to leave her, and the wedding ring he still wore declared as much.

But he had also said that he wouldn't let me go.

Left once again in a state of limbo – neither here nor there, neither one thing nor the other – I floundered. He said that he would give me all the information I needed to make an informed choice, but all the information in the world wouldn't alter the fact that he remained married. So my choice seemed to be limited to accepting the status of friend – I cringed at the thought – or leaving. The latter would mean cutting all ties, severing the knot that bound us, *never* seeing him again because – if I knew one thing about myself – once a decision like that had been made, I would not go back on it.

When I left Guy, I did so completely. Except when he turned up outside my door, or telephoned in the middle of the night, I had nothing more to do with my former lover. I refused to speak to him, I didn't answer his letters and, when he loitered at the back of the lecture hall, I left by another exit. The only time I voluntarily spoke to him since making the decision was when I visited him in hospital. No half measures.

So what terrified me now was not so much what I would decide to do, but the thoroughness with which I would do it, leaving me no way back. It made the choice that much harder, and so, with this in mind, I had to keep talking, keep delaying the decision, put it off for as long as possible until my way became clear, or a decision was made for me.

I had fallen into a reverie, lost so deep in my own thoughts that I failed to notice Matthew had not returned. I went upstairs, but felt his absence. The blizzard still swarmed outside and, even given the vantage point of the bedroom window, I could see no further than ten feet into the storm through the distorting anarchy of snow. Then I heard the door shut downstairs.

I slowed when I reached the head of the stairs and descended at a measured pace as if I hadn't detected him gone. I allowed myself to look at him when I reached the bottom step; caked in snow, he stood in the porch brushing himself down, his cream sweater now white, his hair rigid ice.

"Where have you been?!" I exclaimed without thinking.

He looked faintly amused. "I wouldn't have thought you would mind; I went out to the woodpile."

Evidence lay in a load of logs on the floor behind him. Caught caring and thrown off guard, I bent to pick up the timber, but he moved to take it from me, and snow fell in slushy lumps on the polished floor.

"Wait – you'll get snow everywhere," I fussed, pushing him back into the porch.

He grunted a laugh.

"What's so funny?" I demanded.

He cast a quick glance at me. "You sounded just like my wife."

It was the wrong thing to say and at the wrong time. "Well, I'm *not*," I said sharply, then drew a breath when I saw the hurt flash in his eyes and moderated my tone. "You're soaking, you'd better get changed."

When I said "changed", I expected him to go upstairs; instead, he pulled his sweater over his head in one go, capturing the snow within the folds of the fabric. I wasn't prepared for the effect that simple, unconscious act had on me, but it must have registered in my face because Matthew looked at me curiously. He wore a T-shirt which revealed the breadth of his shoulders and the well-developed musculature of his upper body to which the material clung. I blushed immediately and turned away, furious with myself. Blast it, he was making this harder and harder. I had almost succeeded in persuading myself that the physical attraction he exuded – and to which I responded all too readily – was safely under control. When I sneaked a look at him again, he shook melting ice out of his hair, his muscles flexing with each movement. I retreated rapidly to the kitchen to put the kettle on the range, standing by it as the water heated and I cooled. It maddened me that I couldn't be sure if he knew the effect he had on me. What I found even more galling in the current situation, was that I *did*.

By the time the kettle boiled, he had changed into another sweater – V-necked in a soft wool, blue-grey and paler than his T-shirt. It disguised his chest to a certain degree, but accentuated his neck, and even that amount of skin proved difficult to ignore.

"Do you want to hear the rest?" he offered, following me into the living area once I'd made a cup of tea and he'd supplied a bar of chocolate without me needing to ask.

"I think you'd better."

He raised an eyebrow in query but I busied myself fidgeting about on the sofa until I made myself comfortable. It was quieter in the room, and only then did I realize that the blizzard had dropped. Through the broken window I could just make out the snow still falling steadily, no longer driven by the tireless wind.

Matthew stood to one side of the fireplace, leaning an elbow on the tall shelf that served as a mantle.

"After the accident, you can imagine how difficult we found life for a time. It took several months to stabilize Ellen, and Henry had to bury one daughter while looking after the other. Maggie and her sister had been very close. Maggie didn't speak for a time afterwards and I'm sure she's never truly come to terms with what happened. That sort of thing leaves scars."

"It must do," I said softly.

"But then Henry met Pat – Patricia – a theatre nurse at the hospital where he worked as a surgeon at the time. They married – he and Monica had divorced by then, of course – and they went on to have Daniel."

"Who did they name him after?" I asked, although it wasn't particularly relevant to the story.

"No one. By the time he was born, we were being more cautious about such things."

"Why?"

Matthew twisted his ring before replying.

"As Henry aged, the physical similarities between us became more apparent. Monica had noticed but she wasn't the only one. Then when he met Pat, we had to make the decision whether to tell her something… anything. We took more precautions. Henry chose to grow a beard…" I pulled a face unintentionally; he smiled at that.

"It suits him well enough, and it disguises the shape of his face – you'll see when you meet him…" He halted abruptly when he saw my eyes first widen, then narrow. He held up his hands in recognition of his slip. "I apologize – *if* you decide to meet him. He also made sure that his son's name from his second marriage bore no relation to any of those in my family – just in case. Then we also started to alter our relationships."

I forgot to be cross. "Meaning?"

"Meaning up until then we had always skirted around the subject of who was related to whom. It had been less of an issue in Henry's youth, but by the time he reached his late twenties or so, we had to come up with something that outsiders would believe. So, he became my brother. Before I married, of course, life had been simpler – I just moved on after five or ten years, depending on circumstances but, as soon as other people became involved…" He rubbed his chin. "Well, as soon as I had a family, it added layers of complication."

"But Ellen must already have been – no, *looked* – older

than you. How did you manage? Didn't people notice?"

By my rough reckoning, Ellen must have been in her forties and, with a husband looking so much younger, comments would surely have been made. Ah, *rumour*, my old friend – never very far away, always just around the corner waiting for an opportunity to inject a little poison.

"Yes, well – that had been a potential issue. Henry became my brother; his son, my nephew; and Ellen, first my older sister, then my mother, then, well… you probably get the idea."

"That must have been so difficult for you all – and upsetting."

"Indeed, especially for Ellen – yes, particularly for her." He became quiet. I filled the space in the silence.

"So now, she's what… your grandmother? And Daniel and Maggie are your brother and sister. So Henry's your…"

"My father, yes."

"And Ellie, Joel and Harry? They can't be your children, can they?"

"No, they're Daniel's – they are my *great*-grandchildren."

Matthew followed my movements as I leaned forwards and put the empty mug on the floor; I had a feeling he waited for some big reaction again.

"It makes sense – if you're trying to protect the family," I said, thoughtfully. "But wouldn't it have been easier for Henry to have lived separately? Wouldn't it have been less noticeable?"

"Probably, but we are a very close family. I did suggest it once… but when you've been through a lifetime of being different and sticking together, it's difficult to live apart. We are… interdependent, I suppose you could say."

"And when you move, you *all* move?"

"Yes."

"But haven't the younger members of your family asked why? It must have meant taking them away from school, their friends?" I remembered Beth resenting being taken from one Army posting to another, never settled for more than a few years at a time until she went to boarding school, which caused its own issues. Matthew moved away from the fire and sat down in the generous armchair next to the sofa, closer now than he had been all day.

"When the children were little they accepted the situation they were used to – as children do; but when they started to ask questions, then we told them."

"*What* did you tell them?"

He rested his elbows on his knees, his head silhouetted against the fire as the light outside faded rapidly, darkening the corners of the room.

"Henry and I told them I am different – that *we* are different – and that we look after each other as a family. It wasn't easy; it was important to get the timing right. Pre-puberty seemed more effective than leaving it to when they were straining at the leash and getting rebellious."

"But even so, it must have been dicey. What would have happened if they didn't accept the need for secrecy; what then?"

"We've been lucky so far; I think moving from place to place has helped make us closer, be more reliant on one another. But we have to be guarded all the time, and that can be difficult, especially for the younger children."

"You do it very well, though."

"Obviously not well enough in your case."

"Perhaps with us the circumstances were different?" I suggested.

He looked at me swiftly. "In what way?"

I stretched out along the length of the sofa in the warmth

of the fire. I caught Matthew examining my movements, his lips slightly parted, and I self-consciously drew up my legs and wrapped my arms around my knees.

"I might be wrong, but you seemed to be less guarded with me. I mean, with you… I saw… oh, it doesn't matter." I gave up trying to explain, but he wasn't going to let it go.

"Go on, Emma; what did you see?" His eyes glinted.

I shifted my feet up a little more so that my legs took on the shape of an acute angle, and rested my chin in the cradle made by the gap between my knees.

"I *think* you weren't trying quite as hard to hide things from me as you normally would do from others."

"Mmm." He considered, his eyes now narrowed.

"Matthew…?" I paused, not sure how to continue.

"Yes?"

"Do you always live in fear of being discovered? Can you ever feel really safe, especially as more and more people know about you? And what about Pat and any other newcomers to the family? They must know about you; do you have an initiation rite, or something?"

To my surprise, he laughed. A laugh with real humour, not the mirthless laughter accompanying scorn, or a bark threatening violence. It came as a welcome sound and, with a wrench, I recognized that I had missed it.

"An 'initiation rite' – excellent – I hadn't thought of that," he chortled to himself again, then sobered. "No, nothing like that. We learned a lot through our dealings with Monica. Any potential 'newcomers' – I like that, it's much better than 'outsiders' – we have to treat very carefully; we have to *vet* – I think you might call it."

"And the fear?"

The smile dropped. "Ah yes, there is always the fear."

I regarded his even profile, trying to see beyond his physical appearance, beyond our present state, and into the future – if there could be any future for the two of us. If I chose a life of friendship and unfulfilled desire with him until such time as he became free, I would also have to accept an existence built on deception, half-truths and fear.

Matthew continued, "Daniel married Jeanette – Jeannie – although she doesn't like to be called that. They had Ellie, Joel and Harry…"

"And they're your *great-grandchildren*…"

He didn't reply but remained watchful, waiting.

"Great-grandchildren," I mused. "Wow. *Wow!* There are compensations, then, for living the life you do."

It was his turn to look astounded. "That doesn't bother you?"

I thought about it. "No, not really; the age thing with you – the age difference – doesn't worry me that much."

He shook his head from side to side. "Hmm, I don't understand you sometimes, Emma. I remember you saying something like that before, but I didn't think it would apply in reality."

"The other new members seem to accept it, though, don't they?"

"They only know part of it – what they need to know. You know it all. In fact, you are the *only* person who knows it all."

I felt a thrill course through me before I could stop it, the feeling you get when you know something nobody else does. I knew more even than his *wife*.

"Ouch!" Cramp tightened my left calf and I jumped up quickly to straighten my leg before it set in, in earnest. I flexed my foot back and forth rapidly.

"I've been sitting around too long," I said, trying to stretch my leg by putting my foot on the arm of the sofa and pushing down, but succeeded in nearly falling over instead.

"Here…" Matthew knelt on the rug and patted the floor next to him. I hopped on the spot and put my foot down, arched in spasm. He took my foot in one hand and my calf in the other, kneading deep into the muscle until my leg began to relax and the pain faded. He continued to massage my calf longer than he needed to, but not as long as I wanted. My pulse rushed ahead of itself, and I pulled my leg away, not sure if I could cope with his closeness.

"Better?"

"Yup. Thanks."

I couldn't look at him and he rose to his feet, inches from me, inches too close. *Blow it*, he knew *exactly* what he did. He must have been able to see the pulse in my neck at that distance.

"Matthew, I don't think…"

"What?" He wasn't touching me, he didn't need to.

"This isn't fair."

"What isn't fair, Emma?" His voice had taken on the velvet tones of a lover. I gave him a speedy look to see if he mocked me, but he seemed deadly serious. His head bent towards me, so as I lifted mine, I unwittingly brought my lips closer to his. My limbs started to melt. Then I remembered. I jerked back.

"You can't tell me you are still married and then… then… do this; it's adulterous."

I hadn't meant to upset him – not this time. He stepped swiftly away without another word, turning his back so that I couldn't see the expression on his face. Passing seconds dragged regret from me.

"Tell me," he said finally, "if I wasn't still married, would that make any difference to how you feel about me?"

"Of course, Matthew – you know that."

"Then it's not who I am, or what I am, or the lies?"

"It's never been about who you are, and I can't say about what you are, but I understand why you didn't tell me the truth – sort of, anyway. That's not the problem." And as I said it, I realized I meant it. What had been an insurmountable difficulty this morning no longer seemed the dilemma it appeared.

But he remained married.

How could we maintain friendship when desire ran so close to the surface that it threatened to break through? If, despite all we had been through over the last twenty-four hours, we felt the pull of intimacy as strongly as before, could we succeed in resisting? True, Ellen could not stop us; Ellen would not know.

But we would.

Echoing my thoughts, his voice strained thin and tight as if reining himself in, he said, "Adultery is something I feel very strongly about… as strongly as you do." His sweater snagged against his watch and he eased the cuff over the worn case, his fingers on the dial in a brief caress. "Emma, when we first met I told Ellen about you, about how I felt about you."

My hand shot up to my mouth, my eyes wide. "You told her about me *then*?"

"Emma, I know that it might seem hard to believe, and goodness only knows why you would believe anything I say now, but I have never betrayed my wife in *any* way since we first met. I wouldn't – I haven't – looked at another woman until I met you. I knew as soon as we met that I was in danger of *falling* for you, shall we say. I only came to your reception party out of curiosity because of your name. I had no idea – *no idea* – what the consequences of our meeting might be. I had to make a choice then – we all have to make choices, don't we?" He gave a bitter-edged smile. "I could have ignored you – but that proved impossible for a number of reasons; or I could have deceived my wife – which I wouldn't do. Alternatively, I could tell her at the outset, and that seemed the only *right* thing to do." He turned around and faced me fully and I chewed my lip, regarding him doubtfully.

"Look, Emma, it might be a strange set-up – yes, all right, it *is* a strange set-up – but I have always been honest with Ellen…"

"Apart from the lies."

"I never lied to her."

Vitriol was still too close to the surface to contain. "Not like you did to me, then."

He sounded exasperated. "You know why I lied to you; don't confuse the issue. Many years ago, when we realized she was going to survive but would not be able to live any sort of normal life, she said that if I ever met anyone else – anyone I wanted to be with – she would understand. She wanted me to be happy, Emma; she *wants* me to have some sort of normality. This is difficult – I'm sorry, I'm not explaining it very well."

"I get the drift," I muttered sourly.

"The thing is, I want her to be as happy as she can be for however long she has left – and I *know* you understand that."

I thought of my grandmother – wholly dependent on others. I thought of the thin line that separated her from those who found themselves loveless and alone.

"So who's looking after her now, if you're here?"

He looked surprised. "I don't…?"

I thought it self-explanatory. "Well, if you're here, she can't be by herself, unless the other members of the family are looking after her."

"No, Emma. Ellen doesn't live with us; she's been in

a residential nursing home since the accident. She needs complete nursing care – more than I can give her. I thought you realized," he said, almost to himself.

I slumped onto the sofa arm. I hadn't understood. The thought of that poor woman paralysed at such a young age and no longer able to live with her family – with Matthew – knowing that one day, in all likelihood, he would meet someone else and knowing that she would have to give him up. Permission or not, it still felt like adultery.

A match struck in the darkness as Matthew lit the first of the oil lamps and the yellow glow sprang up when the wick caught and flared. He adjusted the flame and it burned steadily as he put it back on the table by the stairs. He walked over to the next one on the kitchen table. As the second flame settled, he ventured tentatively, "I realize this sounds odd, but Ellen would like to meet you."

"OK, OK." I stood up abruptly. "That's enough for one day, I can't take any more; I'm going to bed."

"You haven't eaten," he protested in alarm.

I took the lamp from the table by the stairs and climbed them in a pool of light.

"I'll survive."

CHAPTER 18

Taking Stock

Now you have freely given me leave to love,
What will you do?
Shall I your mirth, or passion move,
When I begin to woo;
Will you torment, or scorn, or love me too?
THOMAS CAREW (1594/5–1639/40)

I didn't sleep as much as I had hoped. The wind dropped, the sky cleared and the moon – one day short of being full – shone brighter than the sun had all day. I didn't need the lamp's yellow light, made dull in comparison. Instead, I wrapped myself in the quilt from the end of the bed, and sat in the rocking chair by the window, watching the surreal shadow play on the landscape below.

The anger and hurt of the past few days, fuelled by deep wounds from my past, had filled me until their clamour drowned out love, leaving no space for hope. I struggled then to find my faith. So intent was I on searching that I had forgotten that I didn't need to look, because it was already there. There were no easy answers – just as there hadn't been with Guy – but nor was I alone.

Eventually, having spent several hours grappling with an unquiet mind and finding no rest, by about three in the morning, I gave up. I ran a bath. The moon had shifted so that its brilliance glazed the rooms, and I bathed without the need of any more light than it gave. The hot water came up to my chin, and my face floated above the mercury surface where the moon struck the water at an angle. I lay as still as death so as not to disturb the tranquil plane. I had moved beyond anger; even the hurt of the deception had lost some of its potency in the wake of his disclosure. Amid all the lies, what struck me most at this point was Matthew's honesty. When I thought about it, I couldn't remember him lying to me outright. He hadn't told me the truth, but his dishonesty lay in obfuscation; and even with Ellen, it seemed, it was not so much a case of lying, as not giving her the whole picture.

I let my body sink a little further into the water and pressed my lips together as if preparing to whistle, and blew steadily across its surface, creating regular ripples that broke up the superficial appearance of calm. Matthew had been correct in that his fraud went far beyond deceiving me. Guy sought an affair at the expense of both his wife and me, fulfilling his own pleasure, careless of whom it hurt – until it nearly destroyed him. He had been cavalier in the truest sense of the word and his lies were self-serving. But Matthew created an illusion meant to protect those to whom it belonged, and not harm those beyond it. I felt the sting because I had been drawn to the perimeter of the circle that the artifice was intended to protect. Now that I stood at its edge, my choice lay in stepping within the circle, or staying outside it.

And if I decided on the latter?

I would then be in a similar position as Monica found herself, except I knew far more than she ever did – I knew *everything.* My knowledge would make me a permanent threat to the security of the family for as long as I existed, and how far were they willing to go to protect that? "I could snap your spine," Matthew had said in the depths of anger. "I could crush the life out of you and no one would know."

The shifting shape of my body beneath the mirrored surface of the water became deception, the cooling water no longer comforting. I slid quickly out of the bath, hurriedly winding the moss-soft towel around me. If I truly believed Matthew capable of killing me, would I still be in the cabin with him? Would I let him near me; would I be contemplating a life with him? The trouble with obsession, I concluded, is that perception is warped, and nothing is what it appears.

Sleep seemed pointless. I brushed my teeth and dressed as if ready for the day, creeping downstairs, using the moon to light my way. Padding softly in thick socks across the cold floor, I went to feed the stove more fuel, dropping the pieces of chopped wood into the mouth and, one by one, watching them ignite and burn. I placed the kettle quietly on the metal surface – it would have been a crime to disturb the peace of the moon – and turned around to wait for it to boil.

He sat on one of the ladder-back chairs by the broken window. Through dark orbs he watched me as I started and froze. He neither moved nor spoke, and it was only in the reflected light in his eyes as he followed my hand to my throat that he showed any sign of life.

"I… I didn't see you there," I stammered when my heart settled into a trot rather than a gallop. His mouth twitched in amusement and his eyes widened, losing their predatory look.

"I didn't expect to see *you*," he replied, his smile broadening as he rose to join me. Adjusting the kettle on the stove,

I avoided the invitation to look at him, fixing my gaze on his throat instead, which I thought a safer area of focus.

"I couldn't sleep."

The moon bled through the fractured glass, casting his hair pale gold in its broken light and shining upon his neck – smooth, supple, strong.

"What are you doing down here?" My question sounded blunter than I meant it to. The sardonic lift to his mouth mildly mocked me.

"Even 'monsters' need some downtime. I was writing when you disturbed me."

A gentle *sssss* as drops of water evaporated on hot metal.

"I didn't mean it – calling you a monster – I was angry. I'm sorry I said it."

I checked to see if he looked annoyed, then rapidly down again as he moved closer, blocking out the light. Even in the dusk that his silhouette cast, his eyes glittered.

"We both said things we didn't mean, but we said many more we did," he said.

I lifted my face to look at him. "Matthew, what did you mean when you said you wouldn't let me go?"

"What do you think I meant?"

Used to his prevarication, I countered, "*I'm* asking the questions here."

He lightly touched my cheek with his fingers, setting off a shimmer of warmth in my blood. I backed away.

"Matthew…" I warned.

"I only meant that I would use every device in my power to persuade you to stay." He moved forward a step, raising his hand and tracing along the length of my jaw with his thumb, making it difficult to concentrate. I stayed still this time.

"Such as?"

He stroked down the side of my neck with the back of his hand, setting the fine hairs on edge. Lips slightly parted, he bent cautiously towards me as my pulse quickened, waiting to see if I would reject him and push him away. Reaching the base of my neck where my spine joined my skull, he curled his fingers around the back of it, using a slight pressure to pull me towards him. I didn't resist, smelling the fresh-air scent that closeness to him always brought, the skin of his throat only a faint gleam in the shadow-light.

"This is taking unfair advantage," I breathed into the hollow at the base of his neck.

"Do you want me stop?" His lips brushed my cheekbone, the late-night stubble softly grazing my skin.

"I'll have to think about it."

His hand moved up the nape of my neck into my hair, wrapping his fingers through it and pulling gently so that my face tipped willingly towards his.

"Do you need persuading?"

I was losing myself in his touch, no longer able to fight him on any level. I closed my eyes and concentrated on my breathing.

"Yes, please."

He hesitated and I opened my eyes to see him searching my face, before his smile intensified.

A breathless whistle rose to a high-pitched scream as the kettle came to the boil.

"*God's teeth!*" he exclaimed, killing the kettle with a look that would have had me squirming.

"Matthew!" I reprimanded his blasphemy, made no better by the antiquity of the oath.

"Sorry." He smiled down at me apologetically. "It's

probably just as well." He twisted off the sofa and went to remove the protesting kettle from the stove. I sat up, feeling a little dazed. His voice came from the denser form his body made in the unlit kitchen.

"Emma…"

"I know."

I could hear him pouring water into a mug.

"We don't possess a teapot – not here, anyway."

The significance lay in what he didn't say. I rearranged my clothing to cover the gap my jumper made as he had lifted me, and flopped back against the cushions, putting an arm over my eyes as if the darkness were too intrusive.

His voice sounded suddenly closer. "It's not that I don't want to – goodness only knows I do."

I lifted my arm away from my face and stared at the ceiling. "I know, Matthew; you don't have to explain."

Placing the mug on the floor next to me, he raised my legs like a barrier and, putting them across his thighs, sat down.

"I know what Ellen said, but I still made a promise to her when we married."

"I understand."

He rubbed my legs for a moment, rapidly at first, then slowing to the rhythm of his thoughts.

"Does this mean that you'll stay with me?"

He continued to rub up and down the length of my shin but the movement was just a vehicle for the tension he felt.

"Oh, I think you've managed to persuade me," I said lightly.

He frowned. "I'm being serious."

I pushed myself up on my elbows and regarded him.

"I didn't need you to persuade me, Matthew, I just needed to work things through. I'm not sure how this is going to work between us, and heaven only knows it's complicated enough without all the additional stuff thrown in; but as you said, we *are* tied to each other. There are still things I'm not sure about…" He raised his eyebrows, but I carried on. "… But I'm not going to let them prevent me from being with you – not now, not any more. So, you're stuck with me, whether you like it or not."

His hand stopped moving and became still and he hung his head, his eyes closed. Light from the log burner, orange and low, glowed in fits and starts on his face and only a fine line that developed between his eyes acknowledged that he had heard what I said. I tried to sit up further and my legs shifted against his. He sighed a long, slow exhalation of breath held for an eternity. Deliberately, and with words articulated with great care, he asked, "Are you saying that despite everything, despite what you know and how I have behaved, you are willing to join with me?"

I thought "join" an odd choice of word.

"Through thick and thin, hell or high water, yes – I think so."

He seemed pensive still. "It may yet come to that," he muttered.

"Matthew, this *is* what you want, isn't it?"

Hearing the anxiety in my voice, he lifted my legs from him and, taking my face between his hands, cradled it, piercing the veil of apprehension that lay between us.

"I have waited for this… for you… all my lifetime, and there is nothing – *nothing* – I want more than for us to be together." He did not smile and the words came not from his mouth but from a place deep inside that I had only glimpsed in the past. "I cannot say when that will be and I can offer you nothing more than hope, Emma, and I have no right to ask you to wait. But I do. I need to know with certainty – will you wait with me?"

This unforeseen path had led to a door that stood open and waiting. Beyond lay a road I could not divine. To step through it and tie my life to this man would commit me to an uncertain future. But I had spent the last ten years hiding from life, and felt compelled to cross the threshold. So – without hesitation, without a backward glimpse at what I left behind – I took a deep breath, uttered a silent word of prayer and strode forward.

"Yes, Matthew, I will wait."

Dangerous Liaisons

"Tell me one thing," he murmured into my hair as I curled up to him, my head against his chest, sleepy at last.

"Mmm?"

"Tell me that I didn't bruise you this time."

I pulled at the neck of my shirt and squinted down as far as I could.

"Don't think so, no – do you want to check?" I offered innocently, opening the shirt a little more than I needed to.

He rolled his eyes. "I'll have to take your word for it. I think it had better be time for your breakfast."

I laid my head back against him. "It's too early," I protested, feeling the muscles of his chest move delightfully beneath my cheek as he raised his arm to look at his watch.

He chuckled ruefully. "Lead me not into temptation…" And easing me away from him, he stood up.

"Ow-h," I grumbled, and over the back of the sofa, I watched longingly the supple ease with which he moved to the kitchen area. The moon had set and he travelled from the light of the fire into darkness. A sudden flare lit his face as he opened the lid of the stove and threw in more wood; it blazed greedily.

I rose, and followed to where I could watch him from a chair, my feet resting on the stretcher to keep them off the chilly floor.

"Can you see, Matthew? It's awfully dark."

"Better than you can, but I'll light the lamp anyway."

"S'okay, I'll do that." I lit it, trimming the wick inexpertly so that it nearly went out. By the time I conquered the flame, Matthew was preparing something and I peered curiously to see what it might be. It looked liquidy, gooey and unfamiliar, so I let him get on with it.

"Did Ellen like cooking?"

He whisked the liquid in a large bowl, bubbles rising and popping in the mixture. He added salt, the grains making little dimples on the surface.

"Yes, she was renowned for it. Henry used to bring hordes of friends home from school; I think we used to feed half the town's children sometimes. There wasn't enough room around the kitchen table and they used to sprawl all over the porch." He smiled as he remembered.

"Uh huh." *Oh, happy families* and *she could cook. How could I ever compete with a Domestic Goddess?*

He set the bowl to one side and removed a piece of delicate pink gammon from its wrapper, laying it in the griddle, where it began to hiss hot.

"And then there were the birthday and celebration cakes she used to make. Some of them veritable works of art; she won prizes. She even made cakes for the fourth of July and Thanksgiving; have you ever seen a cake in the shape of a turkey?"

I shook my head doubtfully, and then saw him laughing.

"Don't tease; I don't know what weird customs the Americans have. So, Ellen was a good cook, was she?"

"Undoubtedly." He turned the slice of gammon over so that where its edges had crisped and curled a little, it now stood proud of the pan until it sighed and settled back onto the hot surface. "Yes, she was a good cook…" I could see him trying not to smile at my envy. "It's a shame that it was wasted on me."

I giggled. "Well, you won't have that problem where I'm concerned."

He grinned back. "Indeed not."

It turned out that he had been cooking waffles which were to accompany the smoked gammon, and he trickled them with maple syrup before I could stop him.

"Try it first before you object."

I pulled a face but did as he asked. It tasted fabulous – the balance between sweet and savoury intensely satisfying.

"Not as bad as you thought?" he asked as I finished.

"Ghastly, thanks," I said, sliding my finger across the plate as he took it from me, licking the aromatic juice from my finger.

"Glad to hear it."

"Matthew," I said as I started to clear up, "do you remember things such as what you ate for breakfast when you were, er – young?"

"Ah hah!" he exclaimed, slipping my plate into the sink of hot water.

I looked at him in surprise "*Ah hah*, what?"

"I wondered how long it would take you to get around to asking me to fill in the gaps in your historical knowledge." He sank his hands into the soapy water, and cleaned the plate with the sort of old-fashioned string mop my grandmother used to favour. I pretended to huff as I wiped the kitchen surfaces, deliberately reaching in front of him to rinse my cloth in the hot, sudsy water.

"I think I have been very restrained, and it's really no different from asking what music you liked in the eighties."

"That would depend on whether it was the *sixteen* eighties or *nineteen* eighties."

I sidled up to him and put my arms around his waist, looking coyly at him.

"You don't *really* mind, do you?" I nuzzled against him and he groaned. "Only it would be a little bit like keeping a dog and..."

"Wagging my own tail. How very daintily put; most apposite, thank you – how could I possibly resist such a request?"

I danced away, laughing at the mock chagrin on his face. He caught me before I moved more than a few feet, one arm encircling my waist. I had forgotten how fast he could move.

"Everything comes at a price, Emma." His mouth caressed my ear but his hands were not where they were supposed to be.

"What's the currency?" I breathed.

"Payment in kind."

I arched my back as he kissed down my throat but he let go of me suddenly.

"No, no, *no* – you'll be the undoing of me, wench; get thee gone." He drew a hand across his forehead, his eyes tight shut until he felt more in control. I leaned against the kitchen table, reviewing the results of my wanton behaviour.

"Aw, I'm sorry..."

"No you're not," he said adamantly, looking at me again.

"No, I'm not," I agreed, smirking.

He glanced out of the window where the sky began to lighten subtly.

"Come on, get your gear on and I'll show you what's out there; I think it's time you went out to play, young lady."

"That's what I thought I was doing," I said soulfully, allowing myself to be ushered towards the stairs nonetheless.

By the time I had struggled into the heavy winter boots that gripped my calves like cramp, donned several more layers of clothing topped by my winter coat, and found my gloves from where I had left them to dry when we arrived, the sun had breached the horizon. Matthew waited with barely restrained impatience by the door to the porch, checking the progress of the sun every few seconds. He didn't make any pretence of needing outdoor clothes, and he wore the same T-shirt I had happily investigated earlier in the morning.

He had cleared the porch. Remaining ice-dust lay strewn like sand across the wooden boards and he held on to me as I gingerly stepped out into the dawn air. Across the horizon where the snow-smoothed ridges of the mountains touched the sky, the remnants of cloud were no longer a threat to the oncoming brilliance of the day. The beauty of the landscape was as yet unmarked. It was both compelling and intimidating, and I longed to step into it, but the thought of disturbing its tranquillity held me back. Matthew didn't seem in a hurry to move either.

"I never grow tired of the mountains, although I have seen countless ranges over the centuries. I can lose myself in them; there's nothing here to measure the minutes of my existence."

"Are you happiest here, Matthew?"

He looked down at me and took my hand in his. "Sometimes."

The lack of wind made the air beguiling. He pulled the zip of my jacket right up over my chin and mouth, encasing me in the softly quilted material.

"Ready?" he asked.

Like a sheet on an unmade bed, the swell of snow rose and fell in gentle undulations. I tottered tentatively on the icy platform and took a wide step out on to the snow. It held my weight for all of about five seconds before the crust of wind-compacted ice gave way and I sank to my hips. I stood stock still like a toddler in new boots, and twisted around. Matthew grinned at me from his vantage point of the porch.

"You knew that was going to happen, didn't you?" I accused.

His eyes shone wickedly but he didn't offer to help.

"It was always a possibility."

I tried to pull first my right leg, then my left out of the confines of the snow but didn't have enough clearance to get myself free. I struggled to widen the tubes in which my legs were stuck, and heaved. Matthew chuckled.

"Instead of amusing yourself, I would *really* appreciate some help here."

"You remind me of a newborn moose calf trying to get to its feet," he leapt gracefully next to me, sinking only to his knees, "and not succeeding."

The handful of dry snow I launched at him disintegrated in a harmless scatter of crystals. "However…" he continued, emphasizing the depth of my predicament by lifting his long, strong legs easily out of the snow, and stepping around to the other side of me and inspecting me from another angle, "… it'll certainly take your mind off things."

The sun caught his hair, setting it on fire.

"It'll take more than that," I grunted. Since he evidently enjoyed the spectacle of me wallowing like a hippo far too much to be of any practical use, I resorted to throwing myself inelegantly onto my stomach to spread my weight, and commando-crawled inch by inch until more of me was out of the snow than in it. I lay puffing, my head on my arms, until

I had recovered enough for one last effort. I didn't need to; Matthew put his hands underneath my arms and plucked me from the icy prison, holding me above the surface with my legs dangling like a vastly overgrown Archie.

"Now, we have a choice: either we use snowshoes – unless you can ski, that is? No? All right then, snowshoes or snowmobile it is or, I can carry you if you promise to behave yourself. What is it to be?"

His eyes were just about level with mine, the dark lashes emphasizing blue as clear as the sky above us. I couldn't make a promise I knew I might not keep.

"I think it'll have to be the snowshoes – I've never tried them and we'll go back on the snowmobile, won't we?" Matthew gave a quick nod. "OK, snowshoes it is."

He took several long strides and put me down on the unyielding surface of the porch.

"Snowshoes," he said, "take some getting used to, but these will take you anywhere when you do."

They were not the simple traditional racket-shaped snowshoes I expected, but platforms of lightweight metal and plastic that looked seriously high tech. He showed me how to strap them on and I flapped my legs up and down with my new appendages, feeling the unfamiliar weight of them. They reminded me of wearing swimming flippers for the first time, without the benefit of looking more fluid in water as recompense for looking ungainly on land.

He was right – they did take some getting used to; but once I did, having fallen over enough times to no longer be embarrassed about it, they allowed us to travel quite a lot faster with relative ease.

He led me through the wooded slopes, climbing steadily until the trees thinned, and we looked out across the vast landscape. I bent over, my hands on my knees until the stitch in my side eased and I could breathe without raking cold air into my lungs. Matthew waited patiently. Even had I been proficient in the use of snowshoes (and, frankly, they were an art form, and I was useless at art), he would have left me behind long ago, had he the will to do so. As it was, he stood perfectly still, his breathing as even and measured as if reading a book by the fire, while mine rasped noisily beside him.

Finally I straightened and joined him in surveying the land, feeling the perspiration start to cool beneath my layers of clothing. The trees were sparser up here where the land lay exposed. Below us, a veil of smoke rose and flattened in the cold layer of air, marking where the cabin hunkered down behind the ridge that protected it.

"This is so beautiful; I love the way it goes on forever. We don't have this in England now – not to the extent where it looks like eternity." At home I would always be aware of the finite – that just over the next hill there would be a town or city; and night came inevitably accompanied by an orange glow from light pollution, so I could hardly make out the stars. "No wonder…" Matthew looked quizzically at me and I realized I had spoken out loud without meaning to. I finished the thought so that he could hear it. "No wonder you like it up here – you can be yourself – no pretence, nothing to hide. You don't need me slowing you up, though, do you? You could have done what you liked then."

"I've had more than enough of being by myself, Emma. This is the first time I've had company for a very long time."

"But I thought you come up here with the family?"

"I do, but that's not what I mean. They accept my differences – of course they do – but they don't know *all* of me."

"What about Henry – haven't you told him?"

I shifted from one leg to another as my calf muscles tightened uncomfortably.

"Would you like to sit down?"

I cast about for somewhere to sit, but there was nothing but snow in every direction.

"No, it doesn't matter; I'll stand, thanks."

"Wait a minute," and he was off to the nearest conifer, snapping branches from the inside near the trunk like dry spaghetti. He came back with an armful, placing them on the snow one by one and building an insulating layer for me to sit on. I sat awkwardly, then took off my snowshoes.

"Thanks, that's better. You're always doing things for me, Matthew; I never seem to be able to do anything for you. I can't even make you a cup of tea."

He sat next to me and put his arm around my shoulders so that I could lean against him.

"You have no idea what you have done for me, Emma D'Eresby, nor what being with me – being part of *my* life – might ask of you."

A whiffle of wind lifted the edge of my hood and found its way down my neck. I pulled it closer about my ears.

"You didn't say about Henry," I sidetracked.

Matthew allowed himself to be. "Henry only knows I'm long-lived; he thinks I'm probably just over a century old. He knows my attributes but he doesn't know who I am or where I come from."

He scanned the horizon with restless eyes.

"Who does he think you are, then?"

"He thinks I came from the eastern seaboard around the turn of the twentieth century. The family believe I'm only a little older than Ellen, and I've never disabused them of the idea."

"So when *did* you arrive in the States?"

"I came here towards the end of the century – the seventeenth century, to be precise."

"And have you been here ever since?"

"I've come and gone – Europe mostly, but also Cathay, India, parts of the African continent, Java and its environs. I spent quite a bit of time in the old Arab seats of learning. But not home. Never home."

As I moved slightly, a branchlet spiked my leg. I broke it off and scratched the spot through my sock where it had left a tickle.

"What were you doing when you travelled?"

"Trying to discover what happened to me and, in doing so, acquiring the knowledge to do what I do now. And various other things."

"And did you get any closer to discovering your true nature and what made you like this? What you are?"

"No, not really."

"And are you still looking?"

He lifted his face to the sun and breathed out, "All the time."

I turned my head to where his hand draped over my shoulder and kissed his palm. His hand – his bare arm – felt no more warm or cold than it ever was.

"I love you, whatever you are – whatever you might be," I whispered.

"Even if I turn out to be a monster after all?"

"I think that being a monster is more a reflection of someone's behaviour and their spiritual relationships than their physical state."

He looked glum. "Then I failed on that score the other night."

He had, we both knew it, but we had moved on since then.

"You're not a monster, Matthew."

His palm caressed the side of my face and he kissed my head through my hood in acknowledgment.

"No, physically I'm not – I know that much. I'm as human as you are – just more so. But why – *how* – that is something I haven't yet found an answer to."

"And reading Richardson's account in his journal didn't bring you any closer to finding out?"

"No."

"Warm enough?"

We had worked our way along the crest of the slope accompanied by the soft soughing of wind and the song of small birds. He had pointed out the shallow tracks of a bobcat as it hunted rabbits, described the predatory antics of blue jays and, when I exclaimed at what I thought to be the trilling call of a coal tit, identified the chickadee perched on a branch flexing in the breeze. Now, sitting huddled on a tumbled boulder, although getting chilly around the fringes, I didn't want to disrupt what we were doing or go back – not yet. Matthew used his body to shield me from the wind as we looked out over the mountain range where it touched the sky, a slight haze smoking the highest peaks in the distance.

"Why haven't you told your family the whole story; don't you trust them? And if you don't trust them, how on earth can you trust me?"

I bent my knees so that I could tuck my booted feet on the rock and he adjusted his posture accordingly.

"It's not that I don't trust them, but knowledge makes them more vulnerable."

"What they don't know can't hurt them?"

"Something like that. Sooner or later, somebody would

let slip some insignificant scrap of information in front of someone like Monica, and then there would be an investigation: the press, government agencies… have you ever seen the inside of an animal testing facility? We would be hounded, experimented on… without a doubt, this life we have built for ourselves would be destroyed. Any of my blood relatives would be exposed to the same testing. I've seen it in different guises all over the world, through the centuries – using a vast panoply of excuses: in the name of democracy, autocracy, religion, national security, science, medicine…"

"Witchcraft."

"Quite. So you see, the less they know, the more we can protect ourselves and I can protect them."

That brought me back to the uncomfortable questions I had been asking myself during the night.

"Would you do anything to protect your family?"

"Yes, just about."

"And what if someone says something, or goes AWOL, or gets drunk or… or has a grudge and threatens to tell what they know – what then? How do you stop them?"

"That's where having a close-knit family comes in."

That wasn't enough to satisfy me. "But Monica left, and then there's me…" I stopped as Matthew's expression became glacial at the mention of her name.

"Monica. Monica is no longer a problem; she won't say anything; and you? Well, mmm, there's a thought. You, who know everything. You, who could expose every inch of us to the cold scrutiny of this world… I wonder, what would it take for you to betray me? Money, envy, passion, hate… fear? Money doesn't do anything for you, does it? No. Hate, then? Could you hate me enough to betray me? Hate can be such a close companion to love. Or fear – I saw fear in you the other night."

I could feel the muscles in his chest constrict against my back as he spoke.

"Yes, but not because you threatened me, but because it wasn't *you*. I didn't know who you were, and that frightened me."

"Perhaps that was the monster within me; perhaps that's what I truly am."

I put my head against his heart and listened to its steady beat to show him I didn't believe it.

"Emma, would it help if I told you that the other night I was testing myself?"

I lifted my head and looked at him in disbelief.

"Next time you want to *test* yourself, would you mind telling me first? If you had been anybody else, I would have taken a knife to you if I'd had one; you scared me enough."

His mouth flickered with humour. "Emma, if I had been anybody else, that might have worked. As it is, I was angry with myself for lying to you, deceiving you. And I felt frightened – scared that I would lose you – and I was pushing us both to the limits… No, that sounds too calculating. I didn't do it consciously; I didn't set out to frighten you."

He struggled to explain something he didn't fully understand himself.

"I hope you don't make a habit of it, that's all."

He shook his head apologetically. "I haven't done anything like that for quite a few hundred years."

"Then why do it now?"

"I thought that might be obvious?"

"Not from where I'm sitting, no."

He removed a stub of twig caught in the wool of my socks and used it to score the snow next to him in regular lines.

"That's the effect you have on me."

I shook my head, irritated. "Oh, that's an old one. 'I didn't mean to rape her, m'lud, but she was just asking for it.' I don't think so."

"That's not what I meant and you know it."

"I'm not sure if I do."

"Emma, I've spent tens of decades coming to terms with who I am and what happened to me, living in a world in which I don't rightly belong, never able to reveal what I am to any other being. I build a life for myself, I find a way of making that life worthwhile through my work in order to find some sort of peace, and then you come along, and it's as if I'm back at square one again. All those emotions, all that fear, hope, *desire* – all stirred up – all because of one frail package of *you*." He stabbed at the snow, leaving pockmarks.

"But you had Ellen…"

"Yes, and I loved – love – her, but not in the same way. She knows only part of me, she loved only that which she knew, but I could never let her know the rest. But you do. Have you any idea what it means to me that you accept me as I am – *despite* what I am? When I married Ellen, she thought she was marrying a 'regular guy', as she would say. She found it difficult to come to terms with me not being… normal."

"I can't say I blame her."

"No, and I didn't either, but you can see why I have to conceal my true self from her as well as from the rest of my family, can't you?" He bent his head so that he could search my face around the edge of my hood. I thought of the laboratory animals I had seen on emotive Animal Rights videos as an impressionable undergrad. I recalled the scenes of inquisition and torture from my countless books and manuscripts, from the documents I had scoured over the years: graphic, mind-numbing, horrific – and entirely true – and I understood completely. I understood to my core, and

I would do *anything* to prevent it from happening to him. I looked at him.

"Yes, I do understand, Matthew, better than you might think."

Closing his eyes briefly, he rested his forehead on mine.

"And that is why it is safe for you to know who I am and why I do trust you with my life, because even when you feared me or when you were angry – and rightly so…" he said before I could interrupt, "there was never a moment when I doubted I could trust you, no matter what we said to each other at the time." He paused, then added, "You realize, don't you, that you know as much about me as I do myself – fundamentally, that is."

"Do I?"

He found my ear beneath my hood. "You do." He kissed the tip of it, and then ran his nose down to the edge of my jaw, making me shiver with pleasure.

"That makes me a potential lab rat as well then, doesn't it?"

He stopped and drew away so that he could see my face. I regarded him steadily.

"Yes, it does, but I wouldn't let that happen to you."

"But you couldn't stop it, Matthew, not once it starts and they – whoever *they* are – get their teeth into us. It would be beyond your control."

His tone became stony. "I said I wouldn't let it happen to you, Emma."

What on earth did *that* mean? I stared at him, wondering whether to press the issue.

"It's getting cold," he stated. "Time to get back and get you some lunch."

He handed the snowshoes to me.

I yawned. "Bath and bed, as well. To sleep – bed and *sleep*," I said quickly, but not before I heard him laugh quietly as he led the way down the slope.

Although the fire burned low, the cabin felt baking after the sub-zero temperatures outside. My skin glowed with cold but I withstood the temptation to roast my hands in front of the fire in fear of chilblains, and wandered instead towards the kitchen with vague thoughts of hunger.

"I'll get lunch, you go and do… whatever you want to." Matthew steered me towards the stairs.

"But I can get my own lunch," I resisted, although the lure of the bath was mightily compelling.

"We've been through this once today already – upstairs, now. Go."

I needed the second bath more than I had needed the first. Every muscle made itself known, shouting abuse loud and clear. And although in want of sleep, my body wouldn't hear of it; so, having changed, I went back downstairs.

"What happened to the sleep part?" Matthew asked as I mooched into the kitchen, feeling fuzzy around the edges.

"Not sleepy," I lied. He eyed me sceptically, taking in the stiff limbs and yawns that accompanied me downstairs.

"You'd better go sit by the fire. This won't be long."

I smiled to myself, noting the Americanism as I willingly did as bidden, sinking into the upholstery and yawning again. Matthew had stoked the fire, and it blazed contentedly behind the glass front of the stove. Curling up, I rested my head on the arm of the sofa and watched the play of the flames.

That was another meal I managed to sleep through.

I woke because Staahl pursued my dreams – the ones I never had. Next to me in an armchair, his hands clasped on his chest, Matthew sat. I stiffly raised myself onto an elbow and rubbed sleep from my eyes; it was not yet dark.

"Bad dream?"

I shrugged, not wanting to make it real by acknowledging it.

"Sorry, I keep falling asleep, don't I?"

He smiled in response as he pushed himself from the chair.

"You were tired; I thought you might sleep, so I put your lunch to one side; it's just about ready now."

I must have been particularly quiet as I ate because he kept giving me quick glances as if checking on me. Finally, as I dried my plate and put it away, and hung the tea-towel in front of the range to dry, he broke the silence.

"What is it, Emma?"

I picked up a cloth and wiped down the already spotless kitchen surface by the sink. Matthew took it from me, put it down and turned me around so that he could see me.

"Well…?"

I suppose one or two things *had* been niggling away at the back of my mind.

"I'm still confused about where we stand – where *I* stand."

"In relation to…?"

"You. Before I knew about your wife I could at least have a role as your sort-of girlfriend – no, I know, I don't like the term either. But now? I don't really have a designation, as such, do I? I'm neither one thing nor the other – not a mistress, not a girlfriend – nothing; it's confusing. *I'm* confused."

He studied me for a moment, then took my hands and drew them around his waist so that my fingers clasped each other against the small of his back, and not even a hair's breadth was left between us.

"Yes, it must be confusing. I don't have an answer, not an easy one. I shouldn't ask you to accept the situation as it is, yet

I do. Were I not married, we wouldn't have this dilemma. But the fact is, I am, and only time, inevitably, will change that."

Time.

Yes, in time Ellen would die, but how long did I have to wait until he was free? How many years would it leave me to spend with him? I tried not to resent this woman who, after all, had more claim to him than I ever could. I played the role of interloper, the gatecrasher on their marriage. It was no good; I had to say what dogged my mind.

"I'm jealous, Matthew; she had all those years with you, and was so much younger than I am now when you met. I won't have that, even if, even when…"

I felt my face screw up as I tackled the desire to give free rein to my resentment.

"Perhaps not, sweetheart, but, if it pleases God, we will have some."

I turned my head away. "*Some* is not enough. How old was she when you married? Twenty?"

"Nineteen."

"Cradle-snatcher. She had you for ten whole years more than I ever will." I sniffed begrudgingly. "What was she like before the accident?"

"Would you like to see a photograph of her?"

"You have one?"

He disappeared into the porch and a moment later came back with a leather wallet and drew out a photograph. It was small – perhaps three by two inches – an odd size, and not an original, but a copy of a much older one.

"This was taken on our wedding day. The original had been damaged during the war and this is the best copy we could make at the time."

An unremarkable face – pretty, but not outstanding –

smiled up at her new husband, who stood a foot taller than she did. Matthew looked exactly the same as he did now, only his clothes came from another era. Ellen looked young – little more than a girl – and her fair hair, paler than his, was pinned in unnatural wedding curls, 1930s style, around her oval face. My mother would have called her "well covered", but attractively so, in a wholesome, comely way. Her eyes were set well apart, but quite narrow because she smiled – and they pointed down at the corners. Her small mouth was used to smiling and she had rounded cheeks. I found it hard to tell, but I thought she had dimples – one more pronounced than the other. Steady, dependable – she looked good-natured but determined – someone you would like as a friend, someone you would be happy your son brought home to Sunday lunch.

"She was lovely," I found myself saying.

"She *is* lovely; it's only her body that's changed, Emma; she's still the same person beneath."

"It's easy for you to say, but it's not how she – or I – would look at it."

His voice betrayed his annoyance. "*Easy* for me? You think so? Watching those you love wither and die around you…"

I put my hand on his chest, as if that would still his rising temper; I didn't want to argue, not now.

"I'm sorry, I didn't mean to upset you. I know I haven't lived through what you've experienced, and I can only imagine what it's been like; but as someone who *is* ageing, I do know what it must be like getting older – becoming decrepit while the person you love remains unchanged, feeling that you are losing them, time eating away at you like maggots. I don't know who has the worse deal – you, or those of us who love you."

It was his turn to apologize. "Sorry, I'm a bit touchy on that subject. It's bad enough knowing that at some point she will die, but meeting you and loving you the way I do… *wanting* you…" He didn't finish, but briefly caressed my face.

"Makes you feel guilty?"

He dropped his hand. "As guilty as hell."

I laid my head against his shoulder. "Me too," I whispered.

We sat for some time and watched the sky redden, making the room turn gold, then pink, before it took on the grey cast of dusk and the sun sank below the mountains as night began its reign. As the room chilled, Matthew built up the fire so that the new fierce flames vied with the cold. He put his arm around me once again, but he wavered, which meant he wanted to say something he wasn't sure I would like.

"There's something I would like to ask you. Who's Guy?"

Bother! I thought that he had forgotten about him since our brief conversation in Stamford, and I really didn't want to talk about him now, his memory a polluting pall of smoke on a spring day. But Matthew wouldn't let it rest this time.

"He was your boyfriend, yes? First, second, last – what?"

My face glowed hot even though, on the scale of what Matthew had confessed, Guy didn't rate.

"Why are you embarrassed about me knowing?"

I shifted obstinately in my seat, bumping his arm out of the way.

"He was nothing."

"Yes, OK – then tell me. You *are* embarrassed, aren't you?"

"Not so much embarrassed…"

"Ashamed? Surely not!"

"It's something I would rather forget, Matthew. And he was my first and *last* boyfriend, by the way. I don't make a habit of sleeping around."

He could see he had found a sensitive subject.

"Emma, I didn't think you did," he said gently. "But he obviously did some damage along the way and I want to understand what."

"It's not very interesting."

"No, it might not be, but this isn't for my entertainment. Tell me, please; I have a vested interest in what's happened to you, after all." The photograph of his wife – fresh-faced, innocent, married – rested in his hand. I scowled at a bit of fluff stuck on the toe of my sock, nipped it off, crushed it into a tiny ball and flicked it dismissively at the log burner.

"Sweetheart…"

"I met him," I all but spat, "he *screwed* me – in several ways. End of story."

He didn't react to my coarse use of the word.

"And that's not very enlightening. Where did you meet him – at Cambridge, wasn't it? And he was a student, lecturer…?"

"*Lech*, more like," I muttered, begrudging the way he extracted information out of me as deftly as winkling a crustacean from its shell.

"A lecturer then; so, you were a student?"

Now only a shade off surly, I retorted, "Yes."

"So, he was a lecturer, you a student, and he abused his position of trust." He waited for confirmation as I removed a pine needle from the loose weave of my wool trousers and used it to jab at the soft skin of my hand, leaving tiny pockmarks on the back of it.

"Yes, he did, in more ways than one. I was naïve; I thought there must be more to it than there was. But there wasn't."

"And…?"

"And he wasn't entirely honest with me."

"Oh?"

I stabbed ferociously and broke the pine needle's back, releasing its sharp, resinous scent. I didn't want to say anything else; I didn't want him to know. Suddenly, tea and chocolate became very appealing; more than that, they were indispensable.

"I'm going to make a cup of tea," I declared.

I almost managed to get up when his hand flashed out and caught me by my wrist. "Oh no you don't; finish what you were going to say first."

He pulled me onto his knees and put both arms around me so I couldn't go anywhere.

"Emma…"

"He was married, Matthew, all right? That's what the real betrayal was about – his being married and me having to find out about it from a tutor. His being married and thinking he could get away with it and having no intention of leaving his wife – even if I wanted him to, which I *didn't*." I shoved at his arms and he released me. I stood up, my back half-turned to him, but still wanting to know how he would react. "Well, you wanted to know and now you do; I didn't want to tell you."

He surveyed me gravely. "Ah."

"Yes."

"I see." He considered me for a moment. "I understand now."

"Yes."

"And you thought that I might come into the same category of 'utter bastard', I think you called me?"

"Yes. No – NO! I don't think you're like him…"

"But you still thought that I had betrayed you."

"Well, yes… oh, *don't*," I squirmed. "It makes me feel guilty and that's not fair."

"I wasn't trying to make you feel guilty, I'm just trying to see it from your perspective. So, you discovered, in a totally degrading way, that your boyfriend – what a foul word – had abused your trust. And then, what?"

"I dumped him."

"Just like that?"

"Oh, *yes*." I glared ferociously at the burning logs, gnawing at my lip, remembering all too vividly the one, the only, the final confrontation we'd had.

"So," he said softly, "I had it relatively easy in comparison."

I flumped down on the sofa next to him. "There *is* no comparison."

"And he survived your wrath?"

I bent my knees and wrapped my arms tightly about them. "Sort of. Well, no, not really; he tried to commit suicide – which was pretty ripe, since he'd played his Catholic conscience card with the 'no divorce' thing, the two-timing…" I took a deep breath. "Anyway, his wife stuck by him, poor woman. It was embarrassing for me, not humiliating like it was for her; I've felt bad about that ever since."

"Ah," he said again. "Hence Ellen."

"Yes, well, I wouldn't like to be at the receiving end; it's very much a case of 'do as you would be done by'."

"Very laudable."

"I don't muck about with my conscience, not if I can help it; it's too closely bound up with my soul."

"Quite right, too." He heard me, he responded, but he had drifted to another place. "He deserved it," he said, coming back to me. "But I would have to say that you are lethal at thirty paces. I count myself fortunate indeed, to have survived your spleen."

I glowered at my toes. "As you say, he deserved it."

Out of the Frying Pan...

I woke with a start; somewhere a phone rang and my heart thumped at the unexpected interruption. I listened, trying to place it. No, more like a chirruping – *chirrup, chirrup... chirrup, chirrup* – a mobile phone, answered almost immediately. Not far away, Matthew's voice – low, soft, urgent – replied, using the same hushed tones I had heard him use before: it must be a member of his family. He said nothing, and then a barely audible reply. I rubbed my eyes and sat up; it was still dark.

"I'm sorry, did I wake you?" He stood right behind me, the mobile still in his hand, the face lit. I jerked around, now fully awake. "Sorry," he said again. "Do you feel better?"

At some point he had put a rug over me, its warmth enveloping.

"Yes I do, thanks. Is everything all right?"

"How quickly can you pack?"

Alert to the change in his voice, I said, "Now – minutes. Why, what's wrong?"

He looked at his watch, calculating. "Eat first, then pack; we have time." Agitation broke through his usual composure. "That was Henry; I need to get back." He looked over his shoulder, as twitchy as if being hunted. I swung my legs on to the floor.

"I can see that, but why?"

"It's Ellen, she's had a seizure of some kind; I won't know for sure until I get there. Emma, I'm really sorry…"

Already heading for the stairs, I said, "Don't be daft. I'll go and pack."

I packed in under seven minutes. I ate what he cooked for me because he wanted me to, not because I had any appetite. I watched him nervously as he stalked the room, checking for forgotten items, and then upstairs, taking the steps three at a time before coming back down and scouring the room once more. I washed my things and put them away as the sun rose. He held out my coat but I wasn't fast enough and he was putting my arms in the sleeves before I had a chance to do it myself. Taking his scarf, he bound my face, leaving only my eyes, which he covered with goggles. I felt ridiculous but he stood back and checked me out, nodding to himself.

"Let's go," he said grimly. I took a last, quick glance around, missing it already, and then we left.

He had the snowmobile ready and waiting. If I thought he had driven fast on the way there, it was the leisurely pace of a sightseeing tourist in comparison to the speed at which he now took the most direct route back. Even through the layers of winter clothing, the wind bit and nipped. I clung to his waist as the trees sped past, snow thrown in rainbow drifts by the rapid changes of direction, ice crystals catching the new sun as Matthew anticipated every hidden rock, every dip, every bump. The skin of my face burned and I hid behind his sheltering back, conscious of letting my body move with the machine so that I wouldn't get thrown off and waste valuable time.

We drew to a standstill in a controlled skid as Harry let down the tail of the trailer attached to the big off-roader parked at the rendezvous point. Matthew leapt off the snowmobile, helping the boy almost before the engine died, speaking swiftly as they worked, and quietly – like a mime. I climbed into the car, removing the goggles with clumsy, frozen fingers and shedding the hood and scarf, rimed with ice where my breath had solidified in the folds. By the time I had shaken them out of the door, Matthew was in the driving seat next to me, the engine turning over. Harry climbed in behind and the wheels skidded slightly before Matthew slowed enough for them to find their grip, and the heavy snow tyres did the rest. Matthew glanced in the rear-view mirror.

"Any news, Harry?"

"None since Gramps spoke to you."

I twisted in my seat to see him. "Hi, Harry," I greeted him. The last time we spoke he had just collected my parents from the airport. That seemed an age ago – before I knew what I knew now, before he *knew* that I knew. Was he any more at ease with the situation than I?

"Dr D'Eresby, ma'am."

Matthew shot him a look. "Harry..."

"Yeah, sorry." He whipped the knitted ski hat off his head and removed his sunglasses. I had forgotten how similar to Matthew he looked, except at this proximity, he wasn't just similar but *exactly* the same – just a younger, more fashionable version and without Matthew's other-worldly quality. His *great*-grandson. Matthew watched me from the corner of his eye while maintaining a steady speed on the road. He caught my glance and the swiftest smile passed his lips.

"Harry, I want you to escort Dr D'Eresby to her apartment and then take the car back home. I'll go directly to Valmont."

"Sure, no problem. Do you want me to tell Gramps you're on your way?"

"Has he already left?"

Behind him, Harry checked his watch. "He must've by now."

Matthew gave a short nod. "If you would. Let me know once you've accompanied Dr D'Eresby safely, please."

"Sure…" Harry was going to add something but decided against it and sat back in his seat, staring out of the window. We were passing through a section of forest. The road was clearer here where the densely growing trees had broken the voracious appetite of the storm, and Matthew sped up.

What a weird life it must have been, growing up with a great-grandfather who never aged, who – when you reached an age of cognition yourself – was just about old enough to be your father and whom you called "uncle", but your grandfather called "dad". More to the point, what did they call Matthew when they were at home? And – for that matter – what were they going to call me?

The sun had risen as high as it was going to by the time we reached the college. Reflected light dotted the windows of the façade as we swung around the side towards the medical centre. Only a scattering of cars remained in the car park, and the campus seemed almost devoid of life.

Matthew drew up by his own car, barely recognizable but for the distinctive shape under the covering of snow. He helped me out of the off-roader, holding both my hands in his.

"Emma…" his tone sounded strained, urgent.

"It's all right, Matthew, just go; you need to get there."

He lifted my hands to his lips, then bent down and kissed me on my brow, a lingering touch that said everything he wanted to say, but couldn't. Behind him, I saw Harry stiffen and look away.

"I hope Ellen's OK," I said softly.

"I'll be back when I can, I promise."

"I know you will. Don't worry about me – I'll be here when you need me."

I watched the red tail-lights of his car until they disappeared around the corner, where he would join the main drive and pick up speed – too fast, always too fast.

"Right then," I said with more resolve than I felt, and turned around to find Harry watching me gravely. "It's OK if you want to go, Harry; it's not far to my apartment. I'm sure you'll want to get home."

He swapped my bag to his other hand. "Thanks, Dr D'Eresby, but I'll see you back, if it's all right with you."

We started to walk to the steps that led to my wing, my breath making little clouds of vapour in front of me.

"Yes, of course that's fine, but Harry…" I considered the wisdom of what I wanted to say, then decided I would ask anyway. "Do you always do what your… what Matthew asks you to do?"

He grinned unexpectedly. "Yes, *ma'am!*"

"And does that include calling me by my title, or can you call me by my name?"

His face straightened. "If you don't mind, Dr D'Eresby, I'd prefer not to be so familiar. I'll use your title for now."

He had distanced himself since we last met, and I felt taken aback by the degree of formality he now adopted, making me feel as if I had somehow transgressed a social nicety, and should have known better. Despite the easy grin, Harry appeared to be reserving judgment. This hardly surprised me, given what I had put Matthew through over the past months, and I wondered what the family now thought of me, and whether we could make this work.

We entered the covered pass which led to the quad, the gritty ice giving way to the dry herringbone brick path that linked the two areas. Seeing the campus eerily silent, I welcomed his company, and took the opportunity to attempt to build bridges.

"Are you at college, Harry?"

"I'm reckoning on starting college next fall; I've started applying for places."

"To study what?" Dissected in places, the snow of the quad had been broken into shoe-shaped dishes, freezing now so that they crunched underfoot.

"I'm not sure, Philosophy of Science probably – but it'll depend on the courses I'm offered, and where."

"Do you think you'll go into medicine as well, or get a more generalized degree in science first?" We reached the door to my building; Harry held it open for me.

"No, ma'am."

I led the way towards the stairs to the first floor, unzipping my coat in the immediate warmth of the corridor.

"I'm sorry, Harry, I don't follow; 'No' to what?"

"I mean 'No', ma'am – I'm not going into medicine, and I already have a general degree in science, so I won't be doing that either."

I stopped with my hand on the newel post of the stairs, my mouth open. He grinned, and took off his hat, riffling his spiked hair and looking like Bart Simpson.

"But you're nineteen!"

"Yeah, but I took it early."

I'd had a similar conversation with his sister, Ellie, about qualifying as a doctor. That must have been less than two months ago, if I recalled correctly.

"It doesn't by any chance have anything to do with your…" I lowered my voice, just in case, "great-grandfather… Matthew… Oh, this is ridiculous, Harry – what *do* you call him in public?"

"'Matthew' is just fine, though I call him 'uncle' if I have to."

I pulled a face unconsciously, masking it as soon as I realized what I'd done; but Harry's eyes had already narrowed.

"Sometimes it's necessary, Dr D'Eresby."

I smiled apologetically. "Yes, of course, I'm sorry; I'll just have to get used to… to the…"

"Lies. Yes, ma'am – we all have to get used to the lies."

We reached my door and I fished the key out of my pocket, but it slipped from my hand and fell with a clatter on the hard floor.

"Bother," I muttered and started to bend to pick it up, but Harry beat me to it and held it out to me. "Thanks. So, did Matthew help you with your degree?" I asked, resuming the conversation and tucking my cross back into the neck of my shirt where it sat momentarily chill against my skin. Harry's eyes moved slowly from my neck to my face.

"He did; I couldn't have done it without him. He knows so much, you know? And not just the basic stuff, but the history, the philosophy, the ethics of science. He made it interesting, sure, but what I really liked was that he made it relevant to people as human beings, and not just machines."

I heard real warmth in his voice born out of a deep regard. I smiled at him, understanding entirely how he felt, and he returned it, a little less reserved than before. "Anyway, I'll be off then, ma'am, if you don't mind."

I stepped over the threshold. "Thanks for the company; can I ask just one thing of you?"

He put his head on one side, just like Matthew. "Ma'am?"

"If you could possibly not call me 'ma'am' quite so much; it makes me feel dreadfully old and awfully... starchy, and I don't think I'm ready for the boneyard just yet."

His broadening smile was totally infectious – open and engaging – before time and care might erode its innocence.

"Sure thing," he said.

My cupboards were devoid of food, bar a dented tin of soup left behind from my first few days at the college in September. It looked as appetizing now as it had done then, and I fingered the crease, tossing up the chances of acquiring botulism if I ventured to eat it. I flipped the lid of the bin and chucked it in.

Elena must have left for the holiday with Matias. She had pushed a note under my door – an elongated bright yellow envelope lying on the floor. It was my first – and possibly last – Christmas card of the year. She had signed it from them both, finished with a little heart beneath their names. Alongside my name, she had also written "Matthew" in a slightly different style, as if she had asked Matias if she should include his name before adding it to mine a moment later. *Emma* and *Matthew*. Matthew *and* Emma. Names that belonged together; names that should never have been apart. Somewhere, in a place called Valmont, Matthew looked after his wife. The frantic rush to get back had made me all but forget the reason for it. Now, all alone with nothing but thoughts to occupy me, in my heart I was by his side as he tried to save her. Was this the end for her, but the beginning of something else for us? And could he even contemplate a new life when the old was just a heartbeat away? I felt callous even thinking about it.

Just a few days ago, I had stood at this same window with him looking beyond the cedar tree at the snow-covered landscape. Then, I had hoped that he would put his old life behind him and propose a new life with me, justifying our love for each other in the perpetual bonds in which we both believed. But those ties were with another woman and, no matter how old or frail, the vows he took with her were as sacrosanct now as when he made them decades ago.

As if on cue, my mobile buzzed furiously from the pocket of my coat, draped where I'd left it over the armchair.

"What's happening?" I asked, as soon as I heard his voice. "How's Ellen? Are you OK?"

He sounded drained, his voice flat and without expression.

"She'll be all right. We managed to stabilize her. It's not the first time it's happened and the doctors here do a good job… but it's specialized work and we'd rather be on hand…"

I heard a siren somewhere in the distance. "Are you in the car?"

"No. I'm still at Valmont – outside." As if to confirm it, a nearby door clanged open, then closed. He waited, then said, "Emma, I'll stay on until I'm certain Ellen's stable."

"Yes, of course."

"I'll be back as soon as I can."

"I understand."

"Make sure you eat, won't you? The staff dining hall will be shut but the store should be open. Go while it's still light and stick to the paths – they'll have gritted them."

"Matthew, I'll be fine."

This conversation had nothing to do with food and everything to do with our current situation.

"You could order something from town…"

"I doubt they'd come this far with a pizza. Don't worry, I can take care of myself."

I visualized the can of soup and tried to sound upbeat. "I have something in the er… cupboard."

"Mmm," he sounded dubious.

Neither of us spoke of love, or of missing each other; it wasn't necessary and didn't seem decent, somehow.

As I terminated the call, I noticed the tubby little cactus sitting on the shelf above my desk. After weeks without water, the determined plant lived on, seemingly unscathed. Mr Fluffy, I'd called it, because the light-brown prickles covering the bulging green body reminded me of my father's lowered eyebrows when in one of his moods, and he was anything but fluffy. Elena had said, "You are a survivor, Emma" when she had handed me the bright-orange pot in the days following Staahl's attack. "Like this cactus, you will survive." And I had – despite Staahl, despite Guy, and now this.

I reached out and delicately pressed my finger against ginger spines. The bristles gave an illusion of softness, but the spikes pierced my skin like tiny swords, leaving fine beads of blood on the surface, and spines embedded in my skin. Yes, I had survived – I would survive. I pressed my thumb against my forefinger and wiped the blood away. None sprang to the surface in its place, but I felt the remnants of the attack in the bruising that lay invisibly beneath my skin. Like those tremors, I thought, that had shaken me so conclusively days before, I would feel the effects until time and altered circumstances rendered the memory impotent. And the change in circumstances would be wholly dependent on the life of the frail old woman whose claim on her husband was absolute and just. Every moment Matthew and I spent together lay heavily on our consciences.

I remembered Guy's wife. I remembered imagining myself in her shoes and how I would feel if I discovered that the person with whom I had spent so many years had betrayed the trust placed implicitly in our marriage. Matthew said that

Ellen knew of me. He implied she had given her consent to our relationship, but neither of us believed that made it right.

I switched my mobile onto silent and left it charging on my desk, and went to put the kettle on, retrieve the soup, and change my thoughts.

Later, I phoned Dad to let him know when I would be leaving to stay with Matthew and to catch up on family news.

"There you are." My father sounded particularly cheerful. "It's good to hear from you. Pen's in bed sewing seams on Archie's jersey – whatever that means; I can take the phone to her, if you want a chat?"

"Sorry." I squinted at my watch, counting on in my head. "I forgot; it must be very late. Don't bother her now. How's Nanna?"

"That's all right, I couldn't sleep; I wanted to check the heater's working – can't risk the seedlings getting chilled – make sure everything's all right, you know. Marvellous present, Em. Couldn't wait until Christmas." I smiled to myself. "Isn't Matthew with you? I thought you were going away."

"Yes, we've been away, but Matthew's had to rush off. So Nanna's OK? And Mum?" I could hear something rattle in the background; it sounded like hail on the brittle glass of the potting shed. "Are you *outside*, Dad?"

"Yes, I'm getting used to this heater. Doing a splendid job of bringing these cineraria on. Thought I might get the tomatoes going early, too. Perhaps even try peppers this year. Should be able to avoid damping off altogether with this thing – has a built-in fan, you know. Wonderful." And he laughed. I didn't join in because gardening represented a foreign language to me and "damping off" sounded like something you did with a bonfire.

He continued, "But you want a situation report on Nanna? It's all fine, situation normal. Quite chirpy when I saw her last, and she asked after you, of course. Always asks after you – and that young man of yours. Quite taken with him, by all accounts. I rather think she hopes to be around to hear some good news in that direction, Em. Formalize the arrangement. Make his intentions clear." Subtlety didn't figure in my father's vocabulary. When I didn't answer because I had no answer to give, he made a rumbling noise as he cleared his throat. "When are you going to Matthew's family for Christmas; have you a date in mind?"

As it was just a week to Christmas, it would be soon.

"Er, not sure. Soon – I'll let you know."

I could almost imagine the level frown emerging across his forehead at the lack of precision in my forward planning, but his voice didn't betray him if it did.

"That's fine, let us know when you do."

"Will do, Dad. Love to the family."

"And returned."

That counted as the second conversation with my father in under a week that hadn't resulted in an argument; it must be a record. My family would be preparing for Christmas now. The twins would have drawn up their lists in ever-burgeoning hope, and my sister and father would have planned Christmas lunch down to the last sprout. I wrinkled my nose. Sprouts. And suddenly I remembered I was out of food.

When with Matthew, I didn't have to think about food – he did that for me. When alone, however, I had to fend for myself. In Cambridge, provisions were within easy reach, and I didn't have to use my imagination to devise a menu and cook it. Food arrived on a plate and, more often than not, I would eat it. I ate in Hall when obliged to do so, but I preferred the relative anonymity of the riverside cafes where I could secrete myself in a corner with a book for hours on winter nights, when the water beyond the window became no more than a series of shifting reflections. Or I might take myself to the deli across the park which stayed open late and sold the sorts of things you only have a yearning for in the middle of the night, like olives, and stuffed vine leaves, and fine chocolate. I had taken to going there after my break-up with Guy. The place used to be almost empty late at night, which suited me very well – fewer people I knew to ask me how I fared. Now, however, as I stared at the white carcases of the kitchen cupboards, I had nowhere to go. The problem with being fed on a regular basis is that your stomach gets spoilt and starts to expect food at the most inconvenient times – such as now – when there isn't any. By my watch, the college store would shut in about fifteen minutes. I slammed the cupboard door in resignation, grabbed my coat and bag, and set off for the dismal trudge to the store across the abandoned campus.

The conversation with Matthew left me feeling hollow and achingly alone, and Dad's assumption that an engagement was imminent prickled. Hunger didn't help. Trees pressed in on the poorly lit path, ghostly in the subtle darkness, and even the moon and stars, so vivid and alive the night before, were veiled by the cloud that stealthily covered the sky. Wheezing a little with the cold, by the time I reached the store I felt all over the place and on edge.

The shop window represented the only real brightness spilling onto the snow. The girl perching on a tall stool by the till gave a phlegmy cough in my direction and continued reading her magazine as I entered the stale warmth of the store. The stock must have been run down before the holiday because reject Christmas cards loitered on a wire rack near the door and most of the shelves stood empty. I inspected the last, squashed bag of sliced bread and decided that I must be a beggar tonight, since I had no choice. As no fresh food remained on the shelves to make me feel guilty about not choosing it, I selected dried pasta and sauces that would take little time and no imagination to cook, which suited me just fine. I had to squint at the minute writing on the labels that waved and flowed under the inadequate lighting, so I wasn't paying much attention when the door of the shop opened and then closed, quietly, bringing with it a slip of cold air.

Plonking the heavy basket down beside the till, I groaned inwardly as the girl slowly scanned and packed my purchases in two large, brown paper sacks. Although I deemed the common use of paper sacks commendable, they were a blessed nuisance when only a good old-fashioned, non-biodegradable, politically incorrect and frankly downright useful plastic carrier bag would do. I paid, thanked her and, managing to balance both bags, began to turn around, promptly colliding with an immovable object.

"*Heck* – Sam!"

I didn't mean to say it out loud and I almost dropped one of the bags in my harried confusion. I put it back on the counter before the contents spilled all over the floor.

"That's one way of greeting an old friend, I suppose, Em; nice to see you too. What a coincidence."

His dark hair grew too long and he hadn't shaved for a couple of days, but it gave a rakish air to his good looks that the shop assistant found irresistible; I silently wished her luck. Sam leaned around me – closer than comfortable – and handed over a twenty-dollar bill without looking at her. He tucked a small bottle in his side pocket.

"Want some help?" he asked, eyeing up the bag as I tried to pick it up again, but he took it from me anyway, languid brown eyes taking in every inch of my face. Hugging the other bag, I avoided looking at him.

"You gave me a surprise, Sam; I didn't expect to see you here."

"Yeagh we-el," he drawled, "I reckon I've got nowhere else to go." I tried to regain possession of the bag. "Nah, I'll get that," he said, holding it beyond my reach. "Didn't expect to see *you* again, Freckles; thought you'd gone for good."

I looked towards the door, thinking I could make an excuse and leave without him.

He interpreted my glance correctly. "Going back to your place? I'll carry this for you – and the other one."

He took it from me before I could object, and began walking towards the door, ensuring I followed him. We pushed into the cold air.

"Sam, have you been drinking?"

"Nope, not yet, honey, not yet." He patted his pocket with his elbow. "*Pl*-enty of time for that."

He walked quickly out of the pool of light and into the dark along the path down which I had come. I trotted to keep up with him.

"Sam, slow down and give me those bags," I panted, the cold air making me breathless.

"Sure thing." He slowed but didn't hand them over. "So, you came back," he stated.

"Yes, of course," I puffed. "Why wouldn't I?"

He looked at me sharply. "No need to get defensive, Em. You left suddenly; it made me wonder… you know… if everything was all fine and dandy in the boyfriend department. I'm just asking as a friend."

Blast! I heard the hope in his voice. I didn't want to get drawn into some protracted argument involving Matthew, but he wasn't going anywhere other than in my direction, so I was stuck with him for the time being if I wanted my food back.

We were passing the most densely planted trees now, where the dim lights couldn't penetrate the shadows.

"I shouldn't talk to you, Sam."

"How d'you reckon that?"

"After our last conversation – if you could call it that – remember? And I heard you've been talking to the police and stirring things up. *Friends* don't do that."

He didn't deny it.

"Lynes isn't my friend." Sam had the collar of his dark jacket turned up so I couldn't see his face, but I could hear the resentment in his voice.

"But he is mine, Sam, and whatever you do to him, hurts me."

"Huh." Sam shifted the bags to balance them better. His mood darkened. *Now,* I thought, *is a good time to change the subject.*

"How's work going?"

"Sure, *work.* Yeah, fine – students, projects, reports, work – y'know – work's what it always is. You?"

I tried to sound enthusiastic, but found it as hard as he did.

"I'm working on… things. My students are getting on well, so they didn't miss me much."

"Yeah, right."

"I think one of them has a pretty good idea of what he's doing and the rest are more or less there – they need a bit of direction, but that's all. They haven't needed as much supervision as I thought they would."

Sam remained silent and we traipsed around the corner of the main block towards the side door of my wing.

He cleared his throat. "So, you think you'll stay the rest of the year – see it out?"

I wrapped my fingers securely around the key to my room.

"I don't see why not. I want to get this bunch through safely; it's what I'm here for, after all." *And all the rest*, I thought, *and ALL the rest.* "Then there's the research I want to get finished."

"Yeah, that diary thing."

I was surprised he remembered. We climbed the stairs, and Sam quickened his stride and stood there as I unlocked the door. I turned, blocking the doorway, and held out my arms for the sacks. He paused before reluctantly handing them over.

"Thanks..." I said, "and have a good Christmas." I shut the door before he could say anything, listening for the sound of his footsteps on the wooden boards before taking the bags through to the kitchen.

Shunting out of my coat and returning to the sitting room to check my mobile, I flicked the phone back onto the menu and saw I had three missed messages. My heart skipped a beat and I fumbled to locate the button to retrieve them, but a soft set of rapid knocks on the door interrupted me.

Sam stood outside, leaning against the opposite wall. He screwed the lid back on the small bottle and tucked it in his pocket.

"Say, Em, but you bought the last loaf of bread; mind if I have some? I'm clean out."

He wasn't making any move to shift, and he regarded me with half-closed eyes, as if standing straight would have been too much effort. He might have been standing there since

I closed the door on him, for all I knew. I left the door open so as not to be totally rude by not asking him in, and that was a mistake. He followed me.

"Just a couple of slices'll do."

I made for the kitchen where I had left the bags untouched, banging my hip on the edge of the door frame in my hurry to find the bread and get rid of him. Sam stood outside the narrow kitchen, leaning again, his head slightly hunched forward as he watched me search through the first bag, taking each item out as quickly as I could, in no order and with little care. The stupid bread should have been on top of everything else so it wouldn't get any more squashed than it already was. Sam seemed in no hurry – even his speech had slowed to a drawl, and a faint aroma of alcohol moved with him. Only his fingers twitched on the wooden frame.

"You've made this pretty homey in here, Ginge," he said, indicating the rest of the apartment with a nod.

"Thanks."

I started on the second bag and found the bread halfway down; it would have trouble getting in the toaster in the shape it was in.

"Found it!" I said, with evident relief.

"Good for you," Sam burred. I started to shuffle through the unfamiliar bag drawer, looking for a roll of plastic food bags. "Any chance of a coffee?"

I turned around slowly and looked at him.

"Sam, I don't think that's a great idea, not tonight; I'm hungry and I'm tired. I just want to eat and go to bed."

I swear there was nothing in my voice or in my look that could have encouraged him.

"Sure you're *tired*." His lips parted slightly and his eyes became hooded. I pushed past him, thrusting the bread into his hands as I went to the front door.

"Hey, Freckles, I'll give you a hand – make something to eat." I turned around to see him in the kitchen. "This looks good."

He had found the pasta and sauces and now searched a cupboard for a saucepan. With a lurch I had a flashback to Matthew cooking for me and I missed him – *blow*, how I missed him! Sam filled the kettle and switched it on and then looked through a drawer.

"Hey, Ginger, got scissors?"

I shook my head curtly and he shrugged and tore the packet with his teeth, pouring the dried pasta in a rattling flow into the pan.

"So-oo, you just got back, then?" he asked as I folded my arms and looked away. "Huh, shame you skipped Thanksgiving. Great party – I missed you – lots of dancing, music, you know – *slow* dancing. But then, you weren't back, were you?"

He turned back to the hob and poured the boiling water into the pasta pan, drowning the contents. I watched him as I tried to decide how to handle the situation.

"You don't have to do this, Sam; I'm capable of cooking for myself."

"Sure you are; you do a great line in toast."

He tested the pasta, then drained it, before pouring it back in the dry pan and emptying the sauce on top and letting it heat through, my intense irritation almost overcome by hunger as the aroma of spices and herbs rose on the head of steam. He thrust a bowl of hot pasta into my hands with a fork balancing precariously on top of it, and followed me through to the sitting room. Accepting *anything* from him wasn't one of my best decisions, and it was only then that I noticed he also had a bowl of food. I would let him eat and then tell him to go. But he wasn't eating. He charted the movement of my fork to my mouth, and back again.

"Hungry, huh? Yeah. Looking good, though – *look*-ing *go-od*." He smiled and sat back in the chair opposite me, looking as if he meant to stay. "Fixed anything for the holiday yet, Em? Going anywhere?"

Fishing, by the sound of it, I thought. I continued to eat, but warily, something badgering away in the back of my mind.

"You know," he said, staring around the room, "I swear you had a different table here." He pointed to where the coffee table once stood. I didn't remember him ever seeing it.

"It broke."

"Oh." He didn't seem very interested. "So, Christmas…" He forked some pasta into his mouth, chewing slowly, monitoring me all the time. I put my bowl down on the arm of the chair.

"What about you, Sam – what will you do? Will you be with family?"

My thoughts drifted to being with the Lynes at Christmas: what it would be like as a stranger among them, whether – in the circumstances – they could accept me. Then I wondered how Matthew fared with Ellen, how serious a crisis it might be, and when he would be back. Sam had been talking.

"… That sort of thing. You know, got a lot of work on, might visit the kids, nothing fixed in stone. Could do with some company, though; gets pretty lonely here when there's no one about. I've missed you, Freckles, missed you loads. How about we give it another go? Reckon we could make it work if we try; we get on OK."

I hadn't been listening until that point. My head shot up and I stared directly at him.

"Sam, that's not possible; please don't ask me."

He stopped eating. "Why not?"

I stood abruptly and took my bowl through to the kitchen and turned around to find him behind me.

"Why not, Em?" he repeated, but this time with a tainted smile. I edged around him and into the open space of the sitting room.

"Time to go, Sam – *now*, please," I said firmly and walked briskly to the door, opening it wide for him. He drifted over.

"Elena said you were back. Left in a hurry, didn't you? Came to see you after that misunderstanding that day – at lunch, with your Mom and Dad, remember? Yeah, sure you do. But you weren't here. Matias Lidström was, though. Place in a bit of a mess – said you'd had an accident, or something. Not very forthcoming. Looked like a bust-up to me."

He waited for me to fill in the gaps, but he would have to wait for an eternity, because that was what it would take before I would be prepared to tell him anything that happened between Matthew and me that day. He ran an idle finger over the surface of the lamp table by the door, and inspected the faint film of dust left in a tide-mark on its tip.

"You never did say what'd happened to Lynes. Haven't seen much of him recently; moved on to pastures new, has he? Told you he would, though, didn't I?" He stood too close, his hand now on the door as if he were about to leave. "You know," he hummed, "you are so beautiful…" I hadn't seen his other hand until he put it palm down and hot against my collarbone, his fingers playing with the chain around my neck. I could smell the booze on his breath. This I didn't need.

"Get off," I said, curtly, knocking his hand out of the way; "I'm not interested."

His face went blank; only his sour brown orbs spoke.

"Sure, sure."

He turned to leave but as I started to close the door on him, I suddenly remembered what had been plucking at my mind.

"Did you follow me to the store?" I accused. He turned, shrugged, and fingered the stubble on his chin, his gaze averted, shifting. He didn't say he had, but he didn't deny it either. I felt more disgusted than frightened. "That's sick – you're sick, Sam. I didn't think you'd resort to *that*. Get out!"

I screwed my hands into balls and flexed my fingers out behind my back, stiffening them into weapons. He didn't say anything but held up a finger, as if something had been bothering him and he was searching for an answer.

"Just one thing, Ginger." He smiled with a frown. "You didn't say why not." He made no move towards me and I hesitated, not sure what he meant. "Well?"

I viewed him suspiciously.

"I… I don't know what you're talking about."

Fleetingly, he looked more doleful than anything else.

"You and me – us – why not?"

I stammered the only reply I could give him.

"I… I don't love you, Sam."

"Why not?"

I thought wildly. "I don't know – it's hard to explain. You're… you're like a black hole, and sometimes it feels as if you're dragging me into it. You're suffocating, Sam. I can't see anything beyond you – beyond what *you* want." He blinked. "I really liked you when we met – there's lots to like about you, but you overwhelm me…" I ran out of words to explain how I felt and still he stood there, and I could see that he didn't understand. His mouth was pulled down, curdling his smile.

"Are you're still hooked on Lynes? Is that it? Or is it because I'm older than he is… what?"

An involuntary laugh – half alarm, half disbelief – broke from my lips.

"Yes, I'm in love with Matthew, but age has nothing to do with it."

Evidently, he hadn't registered what I'd said.

"Is it because he's better looking than me? Or because I've been married? I'm struggling to understand here, Em. Help me out, and don't tell me it's the size of his *intellect*."

He had been standing side-on, so I hadn't felt as threatened, but now he faced me again with the gap closed between us. Cold sweat itched my neck and the chain rubbed uncomfortably. Sam's breathing increased; he licked his dry lips and I swallowed nervously, wondering where he thought this was going. I managed to back away from him, but it only drew him further into the room.

"Looks have nothing to do with it. I didn't like that you've been married before, it's true, but it's not that either. You can't help who you are, or who I am…"

"Or who Lynes is," he sneered.

"No – nor who he is. It's just something you can't make happen. Even if I hadn't met Matthew, I don't think I could have gone out with you…"

"Yeah," he snorted, "but it would've helped, babe. You and me could have had *something*." He lowered over me and I hadn't realized before just how big he was, his frame heavier than Matthew's, thickset, built-up, worked on.

"Sam, I'm sorry. It's like when you tell me I'm beautiful, but I don't believe you – it's what you think I want to hear. I'm all 'Freckles' and 'Ginger' to you, but I'm not – I'm *Emma*. Matthew makes me feel like *me*; he doesn't have to tell me I'm beautiful."

"But you *are* beautiful, Em; didn't he ever tell you that?"

I started to reply, then decided that I didn't want to get into a dissection of what Matthew had or hadn't said: it was none of Sam's business. His mouth twisted, distorting his face into an ugly, triumphant mask.

"He hasn't, has he? Been holding out on you? I said you weren't the only one – *Lynes' Kittens* – always on the make for a new little *pussy*."

I fixed him with a look of iron. "That's not the point; you're missing the *point*, Sam. Listen, will you? What I wanted to say is that he doesn't need to *tell* me I'm beautiful, because that's how he always makes me *feel*. But you keep telling me as if… as if you are trying to convince me – or yourself."

Anger and frustration replaced the victory in his face.

"You *bitch*!"

I didn't see his hand until he hit me. He used the whole of his palm across the side of my face and I tasted the blood from my mouth almost immediately. I put my hand to my lip and looked at the bright-red stain on my fingers and then up at him, in shock. Sam's shoulders hung forward belligerently, fascinated by the sight of my blood. My face stung from the force of the blow and anger ripped through me, making me reckless. Sam reached out and I didn't know if he was trying to touch me or hit me or what, but I lashed out with the only weapons I had against his beefed-up body – my nails tearing his hand. He yelped in pain, bloodshot eyes darkening, and he drew his torn fist to his mouth, then raised it higher. This time I did not doubt his intent. I shied away.

"*Don't touch her!*"

It was a voice used to being obeyed. Sam swung round, his fist suspended, ready to strike, and his face warped in a malevolent sneer.

"Aw – look, honey, it's the cavalry."

"Matthew!" I gasped, his name blurred by my lip as it rapidly swelled. He stood by the open door, his hands already tightly compressed, unblinking and poised. The satisfied look on Sam's face made it clear that he welcomed this unforeseen development. Matthew didn't take his eyes off him as he held out his hand to me.

"Come here, Emma. He won't stop you."

I edged away from Sam but, the focus of his derision now wholly fixed on Matthew, he made no move to prevent me from reaching the protective arc of his arm. Matthew scanned the damage to my face, his eyes hardening as he took in my bee-stung lip and scarlet skin, and looked back at Sam, whose shoulders were squared and ready for a fight. Matthew's voice was quiet – too quiet, too calm.

"You shouldn't have done that, Sam; you shouldn't have hurt her."

A darker, more deadly quality emanated from him, as unfamiliar to me as it should have been to Sam. This was something else entirely, but Sam missed the warning signs.

"And what the hell are *you* going to do about it?"

I felt the shiver of tension run through Matthew's body, but outwardly he remained unnaturally tranquil.

I looked up at him urgently. "Mafhew, pleasthe – don't fight."

"That's right," Sam sneered. "You don't want your *boyfriend* getting hurt by the big, bad man."

I felt a gush of warmth on my upper lip and an iron tang, strong and salty, making me feel sick. I wiped my hand across my mouth and it came away red. I fumbled for a tissue from my sleeve and held it against my face, all the while silently pleading with Matthew to stop. His eyes became veiled and the line between them deepened as he looked at me, and then he pushed me gently towards the open door.

"Wait outside, I won't be long," he said, and then turned to face Sam, who evidently enjoyed the spectacle of my distress. I didn't move. Matthew changed his stance, his body taut.

"It would be better if you left now, Sam; I don't want to fight you."

"Matt'hew... *pblease!*"

Sam's head thrust forward in a show of belligerence. "Sure you don't, might spoil your delicate surgeon's hands." He held up his hands and waved his fingers foppishly, mockingly, as if there were nothing he would have liked better at that moment than to break them. "Didn't tell you how she invited me in tonight – missed me, she did – she just had to *show* me how much."

He made an obscene gesture. Matthew closed his eyes and the muscle in his cheek contracted as he tried to control his temper.

"Samb, stopd it. Matthew, he'th wbinding you up!"

Blood dripped from my nose, making me want to choke. I spat it in my hand. Matthew's eyes flicked open, narrowed, hardened. Sam paced the floor in front of him, keeping just out of reach.

"She has some moves on her, I'll give her that," he leered. "Said you didn't do it for her. Said you're not *up* to it. Came to where she could get some, and man, didn't we just." He tapped his lip and held up his torn hand. "All good, clean *fun*."

Making a supreme effort to hold himself in check, Matthew looked as if he were on the point of combustion.

"Sam..." There was a tremor beneath the calm. "I don't want to hurt you..."

But Sam was too far gone into the game to give up now and he misinterpreted Matthew's control as fear and, like a bully, continued to goad. I clung on to Matthew's arm, making one last attempt, my words mush.

"Mafhew, it doesnb't matter – he's not worfth it – *I'm* not worfth it…"

Matthew touched his fingers briefly to my face and I knew it was too late. Sam laughed coarsely.

"Yeah, sure, honey, you tell him," he jeered. "Run away, Lynes, 'cos the *bitch* ain't worth it…"

He didn't stand a chance. Matthew took a quick step forward. With the heel of his hand in a movement almost casual in appearance, he engaged Sam's jaw with an audible *snap*. Sam careered backwards into the side of an armchair, shunting it across the wooden planks, lying crookedly for a moment before sliding crumpled onto the floor, holding his face. There was a momentary silence.

"Oh, Samb," I groaned.

Matthew appeared unrepentant.

"He deserved it."

"That'ths not whath's worrying me," I whispered as best I could.

He looked down at me, his face softening. "There are some things I can't – won't – let pass."

Sam moaned from where he slumped, clutching his jaw. Matthew went up and stood over him, considering, then he bent swiftly and hauled him to his feet with one hand, none too carefully.

"You've sustained a broken jaw; you need to get it seen to. Can you walk?" Sam nodded and winced, and winced again, holding his face with both hands. "Get yourself over to the med centre; they'll fix you up."

He propelled Sam, stumbling, towards the door and shut it on him as soon as he was through it.

"He'llb make trouble…" I said, beginning to fret.

Now by my side, Matthew tilted my head towards the central ceiling light so he could get a better look.

"No he won't."

"He willb," I insisted. "They'll ask himb whadt habppened and he'll tell themb anbd then the pbolice…"

Matthew secured my face between his hands so that I couldn't move.

"Keep still. No, he won't. He won't say anything because he has his pride. He won't admit to having his jaw broken in a scrum over a girl, and besides, the college authorities take a very dim view of staff getting involved in fights – doesn't look good in the papers." He pressed gently against the bridge of my nose.

"Ow," I said, more in anticipation of pain than in actual discomfort.

"Mm, this'll be sore for a few days but nothing's broken – which makes a change. Let's get you cleaned up."

He steered me into the same armchair Sam had fallen against and went into the kitchen, where I could hear him opening and shutting cupboards, followed by a suppressed oath. He came back with a clean tea-towel, cold with water, and wrung out so it didn't drip.

"You must be the only person in college not to have ice, peas – *anything* – in their freezer."

I continued to hold the blood-soaked tissue to my face as I looked at him in surprise. He took it from me, replacing it gently with the tea-towel.

"Whabt freezer?"

He rolled his eyes. "I'll be back in a minute," he said, taking a plastic bag from the kitchen and disappearing out of the apartment. He must have run, because he returned in what seemed like less than a minute, the bag stuffed full of snow. I heard him in the kitchen again, then he came back with half the snow in a plastic bag wrapped with a dry, fresh tea-towel, creating a makeshift ice pack. He knelt on one knee beside me.

"Here, try this; it'll take the swelling down."

I found it difficult to breathe out of my left nostril, but the ice pack felt cool on my burning skin. "Ankoo." I swallowed some blood. I lifted the pack away.

"Whabt he said's nobt true."

He frowned and took the ice pack from me and put it back on my face.

"Don't talk. I know it isn't; give me some credit for knowing you – and him."

I pushed his hand away. "I dibn't invite hibm in."

"Stop talking."

I needed him to understand. "He sorbt of febd me..." I mumbled into the tea-towel. Matthew's eyebrows rose. "*Sort of* fed you?"

I pushed the tea-towel away again – it hurt too much to move my lips against it; this time Matthew let me. "Well, I dibdn't wanbt him to, he just sobrt of took ovber and then..."

"So you've eaten?"

Matthew put the pack back so that it covered as much of my swollen mouth and nose as possible. The bleeding had trickled to a stop.

"Mmm – 'es."

"In that case, he did you one good turn, I suppose; you'll find it difficult to eat for the next twenty-four hours."

Situation normal, I thought.

He took my hand and placed it over the ice pack. "Hold that in place and don't move. And don't talk," he added, rising and going back into the kitchen, coming back with a small cooking bowl of water and a roll of kitchen paper.

"Mafew – wbhy are you here? Wbhat about Ellen – how

is she? Shouldn't you be wiv her?"

He hunkered down next to me again, placing the bowl in front of him, the water shiny and sloppy as it settled. He tore off a couple of sheets of paper, folded them into a wad and dipped it in the water. He started to work on the rapidly drying blood on my chin, wiping down my neck, changing the side of the wad to a clean area as he went.

"Ellen's going to be fine – she's in better shape than you are right now." He tipped my chin up to get at the blood underneath it. "She sometimes has a problem with her heart which needs careful intervention, but she'll be all right for now. She asked after you, by the way."

I regretted pulling a face, as my lip split again, seeping fresh blood.

He took the ice pack away and used fresh, wet paper to soak the blood streaked up the side of my face where I had smeared it with my hand.

"I couldn't get hold of you. Harry confirmed he brought you here, but you weren't answering your cell or picking up your messages so, when you didn't answer, I came back. Didn't you have it switched on?"

"Es, I dibd." I tried to look over my shoulder to where it lay on my desk, but he brought my face back with his fingers to continue working on it.

"There, that's most of it off, except around your mouth and nose, but that's too swollen at the moment. I'll change the ice pack."

While he was in the kitchen I took the opportunity to scoot into the bathroom to survey the damage and wash the blood off my hand. I looked a mess. The gash in my top lip bulged, and dried blood still caked the area between it and my nose, already discolouring with a bruise. Now only faintly pink, my cheek looked as if I had spent an hour too long in the sun. Other than that, the ice pack had started to reduce the swelling and the rest would heal a great deal quicker than Sam's jaw. The blood-soaked collar of my shirt did my face gruesome justice so I took it off and ran a basin of cold water and left it to soak. Taking a last look at my face, I became conscious of missing one little pearl of the pair of earrings Nanna had given me ages ago, the tiny gold base plate where it had been naked and glinting dully in the light. Throwing a towel around my shoulders, I went straight through to the sitting room and started frantically searching the floor where Sam had struck me, my face throbbing as I bent over.

"Are you looking for this?" Matthew held the pearl between his fingers. I almost snatched it from him, mumbling a relieved "Fank you." I explained, "My granbmother gave themb to me."

"Then that makes them doubly precious," he said. "Here, let me take it and I'll get it mended for you." He took in my semi-naked state and the goose pimples roughening my bare arms. "I'd better get the fire made; it's going to be a cold night and the college heating's not up to the job."

The first flames were licking the dry kindling hungrily as I pulled my pyjama jacket over my arms. Matthew had his back to me as he fed the fire more wood.

"Emma, I don't think Sam will bother you again." He put another stick on. "But how about I take you home anyway? It'll only be a few days earlier than we planned."

He swivelled on one knee to gauge my reaction. For a moment I thought he meant back home to Stamford and, when I realized he didn't, the relief was immediately replaced by horror.

"Nobt like this – I won't see *anyone* likbe this. I'll stay here, thanks; it's going to be difficult enoubgh to meet your family withoubt being all mashed up. It shoubld only take a few days to heal, shoubldn't it? It looks worse than it is." I drew breath through my right nostril. "Anbd besides, where are you goinbg to be?"

Matthew joined me by my chest of drawers as I did my top button.

"Mashed or not, I'll be happier if you're not on your own. I've some work I need to get done so I won't be around much and anyway, it'll give Pat someone to mother."

"I donb't need mothering, thankbyou very mubch, especially not by your *daughter-in-law*. I can look abfter myselbf. And when I *do* meet thebm, I want to have the advabntage of not looking like I've jubst been dug up. I don't wabnt to see anyone for a *week*."

He grinned down at me. "Indeed; well, you'll have to see me, even though it might not be as much as I would wish." He kissed the tip of my nose very, very gently.

"I'll mabke an excebption for you," I conceded.

He laughed. "Oh, wilth youb. Howb veby kind ob you," he teased. "Are you going to put on a bathrobe, because you are looking very tempting like this."

I looked down at myself but I wasn't exposing anything I shouldn't. "I'bm perfectly decent," I protested.

He sighed. "Perfect – yes; decent – no, not the way I'm feeling. Right then, bathrobe and ice pack – in that order."

I managed a giggle. "Is the ice pack fbor you or fbor mbe?"

I curled up next to him on the sofa, as he insisted on holding the ice-pack on my face for me.

"So what did you do to make Sam lose it?"

I looked as maligned as I could, given the bulky cloth being held to my face. At least my lip was less puffy, making talking easier; Matthew had given up trying to keep me quiet. He pulled me closer to him and I rested my head on his chest. "Emma, you know what I mean – what was the catalyst?"

I had been thinking about that. "I tolbd him that I love you and why."

"That was it?"

"Basic'lly, yes – stubpid idiot. I've been trying to tell him for ages that I'm nobt interested in him, but he woulbdn't listen."

Matthew was quiet for a minute, then he said softly, "He can't help being in love with you, Emma."

I twisted around in his arms to look at him, ignoring the discomfort as the bag momentarily scraped my lip before he lifted it away.

"Whabt sort of love is it that he habd to hit me?!"

He smiled sadly. "A desperate love, and I know how *that* feels."

I didn't want him likening himself to Sam in any way, shape or form.

"But you didn't hibt me."

"No, I threatened worse."

"But you dibdn't *mean* it and you dibn't *do* anything."

"That may be so, but I've had centuries more than Sam in which to practise self-control; and, besides, stop making excuses for me, Emma, I don't deserve them, and neither does Sam, for that matter."

I settled back down against him and thought about what he had said. An ocean of difference lay between the two men in my mind, not least the way in which they seemed to love me.

"Sabm will be alrighbt though, won't he?"

"Physically, he'll be fine; he has a simple fracture and it

won't take long to heal. It'll put him out of action for a bit, which might give him time to reflect on what he's done."

I didn't think that Sam would risk crossing Matthew again in a hurry – unless his broken jaw only served as a vehicle for his revenge.

Matthew considered our previous conversation. "So you're determined to stay here?"

"Yub. I'll be fine; I've lots to do, so no sneaky visits frobm your relatives checking ub on me, or… or brin-ging Red Cross food parcels, or anything."

He looked decidedly shifty. "Oh…"

"And you'll be back in the evebnings, won't you?"

"I'll have to work through the night, but I'll be back as much as I can when you're awake." My pout was made much more effective by the swelling of my lips. "I won't totally abandon you, I promise, but what I have to do won't wait. We'll go home on the twenty-third, if that suits you?"

"OK." I already had several things I wanted to get done that he didn't need to know about. "Will you stay wbith me tonight?"

"I think I'd better."

It was the first time I had drifted to sleep in his arms for what seemed like ages, lulled by the regular rhythm of his chest and the security of his closeness. The fire ticked as it burned in the grate, and outside the frozen campus cracked as the frost deepened. My face ached and, despite Sam and Ellen and the possibility of an impending trial, I felt more secure than I had done for a lifetime.

Defining Boundaries

I knew that what I had to do had to be done quickly.

Despite what Matthew said, I couldn't allow matters to rest. For one thing, if Sam did love me, there was no knowing what he might be prepared to do, and his fractured jaw and injured pride might only serve to increase his rancour, not lessen it. Judging from his performance last night, Sam was beyond reason and I couldn't put Matthew at risk of any gossip, no matter how insignificant it might seem.

I waited until Matthew left in the morning, then rapidly showered and dressed in clothes I knew made me look pallid and emphasized the damage to my face. I pulled the hood of my coat around it, hiding as much as possible, in case I met anyone on the way. The fewer questions asked, the better.

It took Sam some time before he opened the door to his apartment in the new accommodation block. He turned away abruptly when he saw me and went back into his room without a word. I followed him into the main living area, which was flooded with light as the sun streamed beneath the half-lowered blind. He wore an old T-shirt and striped boxer shorts, his jaw distended and bruised, his eyes black from lack of sleep. His dishevelled appearance was at odds with the expensive, indulgent Italian furnishings. If I had thought about it at all, I would have imagined him living in chaos, waiting for the next woman to come along to pick him up and brush him down and put some order back into his life. Sam looked as if I had woken him from a broken sleep.

"What d'you want?" he mumbled, barely glancing at me. I waited until he turned towards me before I lowered my hood and let the strong light shine on my face.

It took a full minute for him to react as he took in the injuries he had inflicted. Although less swollen, what my lip lacked in size was more than made up for in red and purple discolouration. Enough dried and caked blood remained between my upper lip and my nose to look as if I had been in a prizefight and lost, and the bruising across my cheek and the bridge of my nose completed the picture of violence. When certain he understood what he had done, and I saw it in his eyes, I prepared to make my thoughts on the matter clear. If he entertained any misapprehension that I came to apologize or sympathize for his broken jaw, I would leave him in no doubt about the real purpose of my visit. The muscles in my throat constricted in anticipation of my attack.

"Sam, I am not going to report this to the police or to the college authorities," I began, indicating my face. He looked guardedly relieved. "However…" I continued, "if you ever give me – or Matthew – cause to do so, not only will I report this, but I will add a charge of intimidation and attempted rape as well. In the time it would take to clear your name, enough damage would be done to your reputation to ensure that no female will trust you again, and you will find securing a post in any other reputable institution very difficult indeed."

I paused to let the significance of what I had been rehearsing since last night sink in. I didn't want Sam to think that Matthew had something to hide, and I wouldn't let Sam see my fear that he might report Matthew to any authority that would be obliged to investigate his own injury.

"Last night before you hit me, you called me a *bitch*. Well, Sam, I wasn't one, but that's what you've just made me. Don't make me into a *liar* as well; stay away and leave me alone."

I didn't wait for a response. I left him looking as if a bow-wave had hit him and he was wallowing in the aftermath of the ocean swell.

Rumours and lies – they can work both ways.

I made it downstairs and out to the far corner of the building before my nose started bleeding afresh, and the bright scarlet drops stained the blank face of the snow. It had taken everything in me to face him and to make clear the steps I would be prepared to take in order to protect myself. And, had it been merely for myself, I might never have screwed up the courage to do it, because a part of me felt sorry for Sam and mourned the friendship that could have been. But I didn't do it for me, and for that I was prepared to perjure myself.

The next few days passed more quickly than I thought possible and, by the time the morning of the twenty-third came, I put the confrontation behind me in anticipation of a greater horror. Awash with nerves, I sat in front of the mirror examining my image. My face had healed just in time, and the last of the bruising lay disguised under a thin veil of make-up. Not used to wearing it, my skin felt horribly fake, as if I were trying to hide my true identity beneath it. I wondered what Matthew's family would see, and what they would think of me. Equally worried about what to wear, in the few short hours I saw Matthew when he wasn't working, I managed to glean that his family were pretty informal. And that was it. He couldn't say much about what I should wear for Christmas – except that whatever I might choose would be "fine". Although always loving, he appeared distracted when we were together. Once, I asked him how his work went and he said that it was "going well". But the less he said, the more intensely he said it and, whatever it was that occupied him, had possession of his mind.

On the Thursday before we left, he stood by the doorway to my bedroom, his strong, supple body clothed in the pale-blue sweater I liked and looking so good I could have cried. He held up a bunch of keys and offered me his car so that I might go to town to buy something.

"I can't drive your car – it's far too beautiful and, besides, I'll bet it's not even legal for me to drive it. And anyway, I've not driven for ages so, for the sake of other road users, I'd rather not."

He pursed his lips briefly. "You'd better get used to it; you're going to need to drive if you stay here and want any independence."

I found myself speechless as what he implied sank in. It must have been the first time he mentioned my staying on in the States beyond the generalized comments about me not leaving him. This sounded more like a life plan and his eyes had danced, giving him away, and my little stomach sprites performed a delightful jig to accompany them.

Now, however, the sprites took refuge, to be replaced by an army of ants that scurried around my tummy. I reapplied the lipstick already chewed off twice before, and gazed glumly at myself in the mirror, only then seeing his reflected image. Caught fretting, I swivelled around on my chair, sheepishly.

"You look beautiful and you'll be fine," Matthew reassured me, holding out his hand. "Ready?"

"I suppose…" I mumbled, but took his hand anyway, feeling the strength flowing from him to me.

A dull day, grey with a threat of yet more snow. I huddled into the seat, wishing he would drive somewhere we could be alone again. The car tyres crackled over the frozen ruts in the college car park, leaving only two cars under their blankets of snow. One of them – I realized – was probably Sam's.

"I don't even know where you live," I said.

"You'll find out soon enough," he promised.

We picked up speed once we were on the main road, juggling between vehicles on the busy highway until we found near solitude on the minor roads. Here, only a few late deliveries were being made by corporate vans – gaudy in the monochrome landscape. Everything jarred when normally I would have found beauty in all that I saw. My pulse hammered away and I felt sick with nerves.

"I just don't know how they'll feel with me in the house. It doesn't seem right somehow – I'm a… a usurper, an interloper, a cuckoo… *and* it's a sensitive, family-ish time of the year, to boot. It was bad enough when I thought I was going to meet your parents, but your *son*, Matthew…"

He looked at me sideways and smiled his half-smile. He had heard this anxiety a number of times over the last week; he had been very patient.

"I know you don't find this easy, but Henry and the family are looking forward to meeting you. Even if one or two of them might find it awkward at first, they'll get used to the idea."

I had a feeling from the way he said it, that it would be a case of their having to like it or lump it, because he was as immovable as the boulders we passed by the roadside.

I hadn't been taking much notice of where we were going. We headed west, away from college and the town, where the land rose in a series of low hills – rising until they became mountains as part of the chain that flanked the low-lying area on which the college stood.

Matthew swung the car ninety degrees down a slender road, barely more than a track, running through thickly wooded slopes. At times a river flowed so close I could almost lean out of the window and touch it, the waters bouncing around the iced rocks lining its bank. We came out of the trees and there, on a gentle slope overlooking the river valley, stood a house. Or rather, it wasn't a single house but a range – like an abbey grange – made up of buildings that appeared to form a square.

"Here we are," he announced cheerfully. He glanced at me, measuring my initial reaction, but my petrified face remained as frozen as the surrounding landscape. I craned to look at the fine weatherboarded house sitting securely on a rise set back from the river in gardens of snow. Trees – unadorned except for their temporary mantle of white – kept a reverential distance beyond the river. A long, two-storey wing that must once have been a barn, ran back from the front face of the main house at right angles.

"That is Pat and Henry's home." Matthew indicated the barn. "On the other side is Dan and Jeannie's house. They converted it from the stables."

"And yours?" I asked, already guessing the answer when we drew up in front of the classical façade and came to a standstill. "Ah, I see…"

"Do you like it?" he asked a little anxiously as emphatic silence replaced the sound of the engine.

"Couldn't you find anything bigger?"

He grinned, and then came around the side of the car, opening the door for me before I could think up any more excuses. Leaning forward, I swung my legs onto the snow and took his proffered hand. On looking up, an unexpected movement caught my eye as a face appeared at a first-floor window. Ghost-pale and with silver-white hair, hollow eyes punctuated its skull. The disembodied face hovered momentarily before retreating into the darkness. I stared. I blinked.

Matthew's face came into view as he peered into mine.

"Sweetheart, what is it?"

With a shiver, I shook my head free of the uneasy image.

"Matthew, is your house haunted?"

His gaze followed where mine was drawn like a magnet, but the windows gleamed darkly wholesome, and all I could see of their benign surface was the mirror of the snow.

"Not that I'm aware," he answered, turning back to me with a questioning look. "If it were, it soon wouldn't be. I'd give any spirits short shift; they have no business in my home."

I pulled myself out of the car, hearing the snow compact solidly beneath my boots and welcoming its reality.

"Yes, silly of me to have suggested it; I expect it's just a figment of my overactive nerves. Talking of which…" I regarded the broad steps leading up to double doors painted the same soft white as the rest of the house and framed by delicate webs of wood in the fanlight and the sidelights. Altogether corporeal movement shifted behind the glass and I suspected a welcoming committee. The spectral face forgotten, I moaned, "Matthew, do I *have* to do this?"

He smiled broadly. "Come on – it won't be nearly as bad as you think, and remember, you've already met Ellie and Harry – that's nearly a quarter of us, for a start; what can possibly go wrong?"

I was about to tell him in some detail when he grasped my hand firmly, half-tugging me towards the steps. Still I hung back, and his grin softened as he took in my scared face. Featherlight, he touched his fingers to the lines chasing my brow, imbuing in me some semblance of his peace.

"Emma, whatever happens, wherever this may lead, remember that you are with me now, and we are together." And he slipped his arm around my waist as we mounted the final step so that when the front door opened a second later, and with his words echoing in my heart, there was nowhere else to go except forward.

Author Notes

Tucked away in the aisle of a medieval English church in a once-prosperous village lies a broken tomb. Traces of paint decorate the armorial shields and countless hands have polished the folds of marble over the years. The dog lying at his master's armoured feet still guards his rest, and around the slab-sided tomb on which he and his wife lie, his sons and daughters kneel in stony supplication. One of these figures, alone of all the rest, has been defaced – a deliberate act conveying malice, and it was this that caught my interest on a cold spring day. What had driven someone to perform this act of hate in a place of sanctity? Who was the victim, and what story could they tell?

The story of the *Secret of the Journal* series mainly takes place in Maine, USA, and in and around the towns of Stamford and Oakham in the United Kingdom. Although these settings are real, some of the places mentioned – such as Howard's Lake College and Old Manor Farm – are figments of my imagination for the purpose of storytelling, as are all the characters who appear in the series.

The tale, however, has its roots in elements of human nature that preoccupy us as much now as they did in the past: the tendency to mistrust that which is different; the desire for love and acceptance and a community to which to belong; the hollow treachery of some, and the boundless loyalty of others; the need for forgiveness; the hope of all. Persecution is a subject that consumes Emma almost as much as the journal. She is both fascinated and appalled by it and can cite countless examples from her research into the English Civil

War. She never imagined that it would be something that she would experience at first hand.

The genesis of the story revolves around an extinct village a few miles to the south of Oakham, and the house that once stood there. Marooned in the centre of England is the tiny green county of Rutland. A swathe of land now lies under the reservoir near Empingham into which the River Guash (or Gwash) flows. Between the Guash and the River Chater a lone building stands on the crest of a rise beside a few sparse trees and grazing sheep. Once part of the fine seventeenth-century manor house, this is all that remains of Martinsthorpe. The rubble of the house and the original medieval fortified manor crumpling the ground all around beg to tell a story. It is from this scene that I grew Old Manor Farm, where Emma goes in search of answers.

Researching the history of the area involved digging through archival material, including original documents and historical sources dating from the late medieval period and English Civil War. I spent time surveying the archaeological reports and walking the site, taking in the aspect of the land and talking to people who remembered this small rural county before its heart was flooded to make Rutland Water. I visited the surrounding farms and villages that would have existed in the early seventeenth century, and spoke to the very helpful and informative museum staff in Oakham and Stamford.

Unlike Martinsthorpe, Emma's birthplace is very much alive and kicking. Lying on the Old North Road almost at the intersection of four counties, the town of Stamford, Lincolnshire, is riven with the past. Despite the many elegant Georgian façades, much of the town has kept its original medieval street plan, including slender Cheyne Lane, and secretive St Mary's Passage, squeezed under a Norman arch and leading to the Meadows by the River Welland. Although the museum in Stamford has, sadly, now shut, the Rutland County Museum in Oakham provides an invaluable insight into the region, and the history of both towns is evident wherever you walk.

The region has seen its fair share of intrigue and rebellion. A few miles away is the site of the Battle of Empingham, otherwise known as Losecoat Field (and locally as Bloody Oaks), fought in 1470. Here, Sir Robert Welles, 8th Baron Willoughby de Eresby clashed with Edward IV, and forfeited his head for his treachery.

I took artistic licence and the opportunity to mix fact with fiction. While some of the family names such as Fielding, Harrington, and Seaton are common to the area, "Lynes" is one I have introduced for the sake of the story. The D'Eresbys, on the other hand, I descended from a fictional cadet line of the Willoughby de Eresbys, a family that played a major role in the region for hundreds of years. Like many old families, the D'Eresbys are dwindling. Emma and her sister are the last of her line to bear the name and, with their deaths, the family will pass back into the soil from which it came, and be forgotten like so many before them.

The need to belong and to have a sense of understanding of where you came from weaves throughout the story. Emma has discovered Matthew's origins, but that is only the beginning; in order to prepare for the future, she must also discover his past.

The Secret of the Journal continues with *Rope of Sand*.